Dottie bustled in, her cheeks rosy from t

'Well!' she exclaimed, closing the door behind her. 'You do look cosy in here.' She set her bag on the table and looked at them. There was an odd air of repressed excitement about her, but she said nothing and after a moment Stella glanced at Felix, then said, 'Has something happened, Dottie?'

'Well, something has, since you ask.' The little woman turned away slightly so that it was difficult to see her face. She opened her bag and peered inside, as if searching for something, then turned back towards them.

'You'll never guess who the wind blew in to Burracombe this afternoon. Joe Tozer, that's who – Ted Tozer's brother, that went to live in America – and his boy Russell. The image of his dad at the same age.' She paused, then added quietly, 'And if he's anything like his dad in other ways, I reckon he's going to set a few hearts fluttering around here!'

Lilian Harry's grandfather hailed from Devon and Lilian always longed to return to her roots, so moving from Hampshire to a small Dartmoor town in her early twenties was a dream come true. She quickly absorbed herself in local life, learning the fascinating folklore and history of the moors, joining the church bell-ringers and a country dance club, and meeting people who are still her friends today. Although she later moved north, living first in Herefordshire and then in the Lake District, she returned in the 1990s and now lives on the edge of the moor with her ginger cat and black miniature schnauzer. She is still an active bell-ringer and member of the local drama group, and loves to walk on the moors. Her daughter and two grandchildren live nearby. Visit her website at www.lilianharry.co.uk or you can follow her on Twitter @LilianHarry

BY LILIAN HARRY

April Grove quartet
Goodbye Sweetheart
The Girls They Left Behind
Keep Smiling Through
Moonlight & Lovesongs

Other April Grove novels
Under the Apple Tree
Dance Little Lady

'Sammy' novels
Tuppence to Spend
A Farthing Will Do
A Penny a Day
(*also a Burracombe series novel*)

Corner House trilogy
Corner House Girls
Kiss the Girls Goodbye
PS I Love You

'Thursday' novels
A Girl Called Thursday
A Promise to Keep

Other wartime novels
Love & Laughter
Three Little Ships
A Song at Twilight

Burracombe novels
The Bells of Burracombe
A Stranger in Burracombe
Storm Over Burracombe
Springtime in Burracombe
An Heir for Burracombe
Secrets in Burracombe
Snowfall in Burracombe

Other Devon novels
Wives & Sweethearts

Secrets in Burracombe

LILIAN HARRY

An Orion paperback

First published in Great Britain in 2011
by Orion
This paperback edition published in 2012
by Orion Books Ltd,
Orion House, 5 Upper St Martin's Lane,
London WC2H 9EA

An Hachette UK company

3

Typeset by Deltatype Ltd, Birkenhead, Merseyside

Printed and bound in Great Britain by Clays Ltd, St Ives plc

The Orion Publishing Group's policy is to use papers that
are natural, renewable and recyclable products and
made from wood grown in sustainable forests. The logging
and manufacturing processes are expected to conform to
the environmental regulations of the country of origin.

www.orionbooks.co.uk

To the memory of my dear brother Alan Banks (1930 – 2011) and to his wonderful wife Lesley, who has been a 'second sister' to me.

BURRACOMBE
BARTON
– The Napiers

TOZERS' FARM
–Ted, Alice & family

VICARAG

THE CHURCH

Pettifer family

THE BELL INN
– Bernie & Rose
Nethercott

Norman
Tozer

Great Oak

VILLAGE GREEN

Dottie's
Cottage

Miss
Purd

CHARCOAL BURNER'S
COTTAGE

Miss Kemp's Ho

STONE CIRCLE

Chapter One

Bridge End, Hampshire, October 1953

'A baby?' Maddy Forsyth sat bolt upright. 'You're having a *baby*?'
'Yes,' Ruth Hodges said softly, 'we are. Apart from the family, you're the first to know.'

Maddy glanced away, then looked back, shaking her head in disbelief. 'But – it's so soon after Sammy ...' Her eyes filled with tears and she took a shaky breath, then said in a low, taut voice, 'How *could* you? Don't – don't you *care*?'

Dan Hodges opened his mouth to make a hasty retort, but Ruth laid her hand on his arm and replied, in the same quiet tone, 'Of course we care, Maddy. You shouldn't even have to ask that. We didn't really mean this to happen, but now it has, we're glad.' She hesitated, then added, 'It's like a miracle.'

'A *miracle*?'

'I thought I was too old. I was surprised when I had Linnet, and she's seven years old now. I never expected to have another child.'

'But you're going to, all the same,' Maddy said in the same bewildered tone. 'And I expect you're hoping it will be a boy.' She turned away and whispered, 'A replacement for Sammy.'

'*No!*' This time there was no stopping Dan's outburst. 'You got no right to say that, no right at all. There'll never be a replacement for my Sam, never. Nor for his brother, Gordon, who you might remember I lost in the war. They were themselves, and this baby will be himself too. Or *herself*,' he added as Maddy turned back. 'And whatever it is, we'll love it. But that don't mean we'll ever forget Sam.' He stopped, breathing heavily.

Maddy stared at him in shock. She had always known that Dan had a temper but had never seen it unleashed before, and certainly not directed at herself. She felt her distress and bewilderment turn to an anger of her own, and the grief that was never far away welled up inside her.

'All right, Dan,' Ruth said, tightening her hand on his arm, 'that's enough. Don't upset yourself, Maddy. We knew it would be a shock for you. It has been for us too, to tell you the truth. Look – let's all calm down and I'll make a fresh pot of tea and we'll talk about it together.' She held out a handkerchief. 'Wipe your eyes, my dear,' she said gently. 'Dan, why don't you go and get some more wood for the fire?'

Dan got up, but Maddy pushed Ruth's hand away. 'Tea? What good will tea do? It won't bring Sammy back, will it? Nothing will ever bring Sammy back. And whatever you say, you're going to be happy again – you've got each other and Linnet and your new baby – and you *will* forget him.' She saw Dan's face flush again and his mouth open. 'Oh, not entirely, I know that. You'll always be a bit sad, when you think of him or visit his grave in the churchyard. But your lives will go on – you'll still have a family. What will *I* have? Nothing! Nobody! Just when I thought I'd have Sammy for the rest of my life. Sammy, and the family *we* would have had. Your life has hardly changed at all; mine's been turned upside down like a jigsaw puzzle, and the pieces have fallen all over the place. I can't get them all together again – I never will.' She jumped to her feet, her voice rising to a plaintive wail. 'Never, never, *never*!'

Ruth leaped up too, and they faced each other, tears streaming down their cheeks. Ruth held out both hands but Maddy turned away and felt blindly for her coat, hanging on the back of the door.

'I don't want any tea. I'm going back to West Lyme.'

'But you were going to stay the whole weekend. Maddy, please—'

'How can I stay here now?' she demanded in a thick, choking voice. 'Knowing this – seeing you both so happy. Don't try to say you're not – I can see you are. And Linnet – she must be so excited, knowing she's going to have a baby brother or sister. How can I pretend to be pleased, when all I can think about is Sammy?'

'Linnet don't know about the baby,' Dan said stiffly. 'It's too early to tell her yet, and anyway we haven't told anyone else apart from Ruth's sister and her family.'

'We wanted you to be one of the first.'

Maddy shook her head, half blinded by her tears. 'Well, I wish you hadn't. I wish I could have had this weekend – just one last weekend – with only Sammy to think about.' She picked up the overnight bag she had brought with her and turned towards the door. 'I'm sorry, Ruth, but I have to go. You must see that.'

'Maddy!' Ruth started forward and caught at her arm. 'Not like this! Please! I can't bear it!'

'But *I* have to bear it, don't I?' Maddy said through her tears. 'Just as I had to bear seeing my fiancé run down before my very eyes; just as I've got to bear spending the rest of my life alone. There'll never be a baby for me.'

She jerked the door open and stepped out into the autumn afternoon. She had only been in the cottage an hour, yet it seemed as if in that short time her life had once more come crashing down about her ears. She was shaking all over with a mixture of emotions: shock, distress, a resurgence of the grief she'd been suffering for the past six months, and an obscure sense of betrayal. The cottage where she had enjoyed so many happy times, both as an evacuee from the war and more recently as Sammy's sweetheart, had become a trap, and she had to get out of it, and away from the two people who had dealt her such an unexpected blow. She couldn't look at their faces any more, and as Ruth tried once again to stop her, she pushed the older woman away and almost ran down the path to the wooden gate.

'Maddy!' Ruth cried as Maddy slammed the gate between them. 'You can't go all the way back to West Lyme now? Please, come indoors and let's talk about it.'

'Where else can I go? There's a bus to Southampton in five minutes, and I can catch the train. The Archdeacon will send someone to fetch me, or I'll take a taxi.' Maddy paused and turned her ravaged face towards Ruth. 'What is there to talk about? It's happened. There's nothing anyone can do about it. There's never been *anything* anyone could do about what happened to Sammy and me!'

She turned away and set off down the lane, walking with fast, jerky steps. Ruth stood with both hands on the gate, hardly able to see the younger woman through the tears that flooded her eyes. Then she felt Dan come behind her, his big body warm as he took her in his arms.

'Let her go, love. She's in no state to listen to reason, and we knew it might upset her. She'll come round in her own time.'

'I don't know if she will,' Ruth said, allowing him to guide her gently back into the cottage. 'She's still grieving and we were the only people she could really grieve properly with. She feels we've let her down. She feels we've let *Sammy* down.'

'Well, we haven't,' he said, ducking his head through the low doorway. 'We haven't let anyone down, Ruthie. And that young madam got no right to blow up at us like that. Look, we didn't mean this to happen, but we got to go on with our lives. We can't just let everything stop. And there's Linnet to think about, too. It's a good job we sent her up to your Jane for the afternoon. I wouldn't have wanted her hearing all that.'

'Nor would I, but we've got to try to understand Maddy's point of view, Dan.'

'Why?' he asked indignantly, pausing by the range. 'Is she trying to understand ours? Did she give a single thought to how we might be feeling? If you ask me, that young lady's been spoiled all her life and it's made her selfish. Oh, she's as pretty and sweet as they come, and I'm not saying I'm not fond of her – I am, just as much as you are. But see what happens when things don't go her way? Everyone else is wrong. And she's always been the same. Look at that time she made Sam take your Silver out on a picnic in the woods, even when you'd told him not to. You could have lost that parrot then, and as it was it got us off on the wrong foot, first time I come here to see him. When I saw my boy, sitting at this table crying into a bowl of bread and milk, I didn't know what to think.'

'They were just children, Dan.'

'So they might have been, but it was her led him on, and I wouldn't be surprised if it was her led him on back last winter. A boy of his age, getting engaged!' He scowled.

'They really did seem fond of each other.'

'I'm not saying they weren't. All I'm saying is, they should have waited a bit, and it's for the girl to hold back. They usually got a bit more sense than a boy only just twenty-one.' He took a breath, then shrugged impatiently. 'Anyway, that's all over and done with, more's the pity, and we all got to make the best of it. Now then, you sit down and I'll make us that cup of tea.' He lifted the steaming kettle and poured water into the fat brown teapot, while Ruth sank down on the small settee and began to wipe her eyes.

Dan went outside to the wire gauze meatsafe and brought back a jug of milk. He poured two cups of tea, added a spoonful of sugar for Ruth and two for himself, and came to sit beside her, setting the cups on a low table. He put his arm around his wife's shoulders and drew her against him.

'I don't like to say this,' he began, his voice a little more moderate, 'and I got to admit I didn't know the girl when she lived back in Pompey, but Jess Budd told me her sister Stella was like a little mother to her, and their dad used to treat her like a princess. And then, after their mum and dad were both killed and the two little girls got separated, young Maddy – or Muriel, as she was then – fell right on her feet, getting adopted by that actress, Fenella Forshaw or whatever her name was, and—'

'Forsyth,' Ruth murmured. 'Fenella Forsyth.'

'Fenella Forsyth, then – and being looked after down in Devon until the war was over and Fenella Forshort started to take her—'

'For*syth*,' Ruth murmured, with a faint twitch of her lips. 'You're doing it on purpose, Dan.'

'Well, maybe I am, but I got to get a smile back on your face somehow. Anyway, what I'm saying is that life's been pretty easy for her since then, what with living in luxury and being taken all over the Continent. And you know as well as I do, we were both a bit worried about our Sam taking up with her. He'd never known that sort of life, and he'd never have been able to give it to her, neither. I know he was a bright boy and he had his ambitions, but when all's said and done, we're just ordinary working people and we don't look for that kind of thing.'

'I don't think Maddy did, either,' Ruth said thoughtfully. 'Stella told me when we saw her at Rose Budd's wedding back in January, when it all started, that the woman Maddy lived with in Burracombe – Dottie something, wasn't it? – is a real homebody, always baking cakes and living in a cottage not very different from this one. Maddy didn't live a life of luxury there.'

'No, but she's always been treated with kid gloves. And now she's got something to grieve over—'

'Dan, you can't begrudge her that! She had a terrible experience and she's lost the man she wanted to marry. Of course she's grieving. *We're* still grieving.'

'Yes,' he said gravely, 'but we also know we got to go on living. We can't stand still for the next thirty or forty years, Ruthie. And neither can she.'

'It's only six months since it happened. And she's right – her life was turned upside down. It's only natural that she can't believe it will ever be better.'

'I know that. But *we* know she's wrong, don't we? We've both lost people, Ruth – you lost your Jack before the war; I lost my Nora, and then Gordon, and now Sam – and we'll never forget any of them. But we found each other and now we've got Linnet and a new baby to give us joy. And Maddy'll find someone else too, eventually. It might be natural that she can't seem to move forward just yet, but she wants us to stand still with her.'

'She came to share her grief,' Ruth said quietly. 'We shouldn't have told her so soon, Dan.'

'We had no choice,' he answered. 'Whenever we did it, she'd have been just as upset, and I reckon it would have been even worse if we'd left it. It's not the sort of news you can keep to yourself for long.'

Ruth reached out at last for her cup of tea. 'Well, all we can do now is hope she'll come round, and keep the door open for when she does. However long it takes, we must always keep the door open for Maddy.'

To Maddy, sitting alone in the corner of a compartment of the train back to Dorset, it didn't seem to matter if she ever went through Ruth's door again.

Ruth had put her finger on exactly the right spot when she'd said that Maddy had come to share her grief. There was nobody else in the world who had loved Sammy as much as the three of them, nobody who had been so bereft by his death. They had been united by their sorrow, and on Maddy's previous visits she had felt the comfort of not having to pretend that she was recovering. But the news they had given her today – almost, it seemed, as soon as she had walked through the door – had struck at her heart. It was as if they had told her, in plain and brutal words, that their sadness had ended and they were ready to live their lives again; as if Sammy no longer mattered.

Leaving Maddy with no one to turn to.

That wasn't true, of course. Even in her misery, she had to admit that. She still had her sister, Stella, to turn to, and Dottie Friend, the warm-hearted Devonshire woman who had brought her up since the age of nine, as well as Felix, Stella's fiancé, who had been the curate in Burracombe and was now vicar of the next village. And there were all the other villagers she had known as a child: the Tozer family at the farm; Hilary and Stephen Napier, at the Barton; dear old Jacob Prout and – oh, so many others. Their love and sympathy had wrapped about her like warm, open arms every time she went back. And there was just as much comfort to be had at West Lyme, where she lived in a tiny flat in the Archdeacon's house and worked as his secretary. Yes, in truth she had plenty of people to turn to.

But none of them were quite the same as Dan and Ruth Hodges – Sammy's father and stepmother. None of them had lost Sammy in the way that she and the Hodges had done. None of them could share her sorrow and grieve with her.

The train was drawing near to the station where Maddy must change for the little branch line that would take her to West Lyme. She got up and reached to take her overnight bag down from the luggage rack above her head. Then she hesitated.

If she stayed on the train, it would take her straight to Tavistock, the nearest station to Burracombe. She would be there by early afternoon and she could pay the extra on her ticket and spend the rest of that day and the next with her sister and Dottie. The Copleys weren't expecting her back at West Lyme until Sunday evening, and she was sure Felix would run her back to the station in his sports car. And he, Stella and Dottie would all understand why she couldn't possibly stay at Bridge End with Ruth and Dan. They would give her the comfort she so badly needed. She might even see Stephen Napier, if he happened to be at home on a weekend pass from his RAF station.

She pushed her bag back on to the rack and sat down again, watching the Dorset hills roll by as the train steamed along on its journey into Devon.

Chapter Two

Burracombe

In Burracombe, folk were celebrating happier news.

'Hullo,' Alice Tozer said, pouring tea as her son Tom walked through the farmhouse door, a pile of envelopes in his hand. 'Be that the post you've got there?'

'Well, 'tisn't a loaf of bread,' he said, and caught his wife Joanna's look. 'All right, Jo, I'm not being rude. Here you are, Mum. Hey – what's this one? It's airmail – got an American stamp on it.'

'American? That'll be from your Uncle Joe.' Alice wiped her hands down her apron and took the envelope, scrutinising the address on the back. She went to the door to the staircase and called out, 'Ted! There's a letter here from your brother Joe.'

'Our Joe?' Ted clattered down the stairs and came into the kitchen, tucking his shirt into his trousers. 'What's he writing for? Bit early for Christmas, isn't it?'

'He do write other times as well. Why don't you open it and find out?'

Ted thrust a big thumb into the flap and tore the envelope open. He drew out three sheets of flimsy airmail paper and read them, while Alice waited impatiently. The rest of the family gazed at him with expectation.

'Bless my soul,' Ted said after a minute or two. 'He's coming over to see us. Bringing young Russell and all. Well, if that don't beat the band!'

'Coming over?' Alice's face flushed with delight. 'That's good news. When? Bringing the girls as well?'

'No, just Russell. He don't say exactly when. But they must be on their way now – he says they'm coming on one of they *Queens*. Don't say if it's the *Mary* or the *Elizabeth*, but I dare say us could find out. They dock in Southampton, don't they? Or is it Liverpool?'

Nobody was quite sure. Folk in Burracombe didn't follow the doings of the great transatlantic liners much. They looked at each other doubtfully.

'I seem to remember young Maddy Forsyth telling me she'd seen the *Queen Mary* going through the Solent when her lived that way as a kiddy, before the war,' Alice said at last. 'But there, her could only have been tiny then, I wouldn't go by that. And it don't mean to say they still go that way. You can find out, Tom, can't you? See when they're due in next, then us'll have some idea when Joe and Russell might be arriving. I'd want to have summat special on the table to welcome them.'

'Best thing would be for you to get their beds ready and just wait till they shows up,' Ted said, passing the letter over to her. 'They won't want no special preparations. 'T isn't like Joe didn't grow up here, he knows what the place is like.'

'Mother's going to be some pleased,' Alice said, skimming quickly through the pages before laying a breakfast tray ready for Minnie Tozer. Since her bout of pneumonia during the winter, Ted's ninety-year-old mother had been persuaded to get up later in the morning, although she still insisted on doing her share of the cooking and even a little housework if Alice didn't keep a sharp eye on her. She also took a nap in the afternoons, though she strenuously denied it, claiming that she was 'just resting her eyes'. Apart from that, she was as busy and energetic as ever, planting seeds in the vegetable patch, preparing vegetables, paring apples, baking cakes, mending the men's socks and working out new harmonies for the hand bells that hung from the beams above the kitchen table. She also wrote to Joe every week in the beautiful copperplate she had learned as a child, which would have been the envy of Miss Kemp had she seen it.

'Take her the letter,' Ted said, putting it on the tray. 'And there's a note specially for her, too – put it on top, so she sees it first.'

'I wonder how long they'll stay,' Tom speculated, sitting down to the plate of eggs, bacon, mushrooms and fried mashed potato that Joanna set before him. 'You've never met Uncle Joe, Jo. Here, that's going to be a bit confusing, having two "Joes" in the house!' He laughed. 'What does Russell do? I'm surprised he can afford the time to come over here for his holidays. Or the money, come to that,' he added with a mouth full of potato.

'Can't recall if Joe's ever said,' Ted answered. 'If he has, I dare say your mother will remember. Ask her now.'

'Ask me what?' Alice bustled into the kitchen, beaming. 'I told you her'd be pleased. Over the moon, she is, and all for getting up straight away and going into Tavistock to buy wallpaper.'

'Wallpaper?' Ted stared at her, his fork halfway to his mouth. 'What on earth do she want wallpaper for?'

'To put on the walls, of course. The spare bedroom,' Alice added impatiently. 'She says it's not fit to be seen, and she's right, it isn't. Not been decorated since before the war, to my knowledge. I wouldn't be surprised if your Joe don't remember the pattern from last time he were here, and that were back in nineteen twenty-three.'

'He'll have a better memory than me, then,' Ted grunted. 'I'm not sure I can remember it now, and I was in there only last Wednesday, looking for that old screwdriver we lost.'

'Anyway, Mother says it got to be done before they come, and since us don't know when that is, us better get on with it sharpish. Me and Joanna will go in on the bus on Monday, soon as Robin's gone to school.'

'But they could be here next week!' Ted expostulated. 'How are we going to get it done in that time? You don't want them to come and find us all stuck up with paste and wallpaper.'

Tom grinned and began to sing the old music-hall song, '*When Father papered the parlour, you couldn't see him for paste. Sticking it here, sticking it there, paste and paper everywhere. The kids were stuck to the ceiling, and Ma was stuck to the floor. I never saw a blooming family so stuck up before . . .*'

Alice gave him a look and turned back to her husband. 'By getting on with it, like I said. You will come with me, won't you, Joanna? You can bring Heather in that sling you and Val made. I'm no good at choosing that sort of thing on my own.'

Ted cast a glance of resignation at his son. 'No use fighting these women once they gets ideas about decorating,' he said gloomily. 'And just as if us haven't got enough to do, what with all the ringing competitions coming up, not to mention Deanery Day, and that's not even taking farm work into account. Just you make sure you choose one that's easy to match,' he added to his wife. 'I don't want to be trying to figure out all those trailing ivy and roses like the paper we got in our room. I still haven't made out what's wrong with that bit over the door.'

'It's upside down, that's what's wrong with it,' Alice retorted, refilling his big teacup. 'Irritates me every time I look at it, that do. And now you've brought the subject up, you might as well strip that bit off while you're doing the spare room, and do it again – there's a couple of yards of that paper left in the cupboard, you're bound to find a match.'

Ted rolled his eyes and opened his mouth to protest, but Tom roared with laughter and said, 'You might as well admit she's got you there, Dad! You shouldn't have mentioned it.'

'I shouldn't,' Ted agreed with a sigh. 'I never learn, do I? Take a tip from me, Tom – only open your mouth to put food in it. That's the only way to stay out of trouble round this place!'

Stella Simmons, with no idea of what was happening to her sister Maddy, had just finished her breakfast in Dottie Friend's cottage when Felix arrived in his sports car, Mirabelle. She looked up in surprise as he came in through the back door.

'We're having a day out,' he announced. 'Get your coat and we'll drive down to Cornwall. The autumn colours are just beginning to look really good and it's a shame to miss them.'

'But it's Saturday. You're usually so busy.'

'I know. But I've got my sermon written for Matins, and with Uncle John preaching at Evensong there was only that one to write. And everything else is ready for tomorrow's services, and as there are no weddings – not that we get many at Little Burracombe – I thought I could take a few hours off to be with you. As you say, it's not often we get the chance.'

'We will once we're married,' Stella said, following him outside and settling into the passenger seat. 'I shan't be teaching then, so we can have your midweek day off together.'

He started the engine and they set off through the narrow lanes out of the village. The high Devon banks rose on either side of them, topped with hedges that were turning brown and gold with the shades of autumn. Now and then, as the lane led down through a steep little valley, they dipped below arching branches that would soon turn to a tunnel of fiery bronze.

'Will you miss teaching very much?' he asked, pulling close against the high bank to let a horse and cart trundle by.

'I suppose I'm bound to. All the children – it's been so good to watch them progress, from tiny infants to big, confident seven-year-olds. And, of course, in such a small village I see a lot of them even after that, until they go to school in Tavistock. It will seem very strange to be cut off from all that. Burracombe School has been a big part of my life – it's the reason I came here in the first place.'

'And very glad I am that you did,' he said, smiling sideways at her. 'We might never have met if you hadn't.'

'And I might never have found Maddy, either. Why do you think the authorities ever thought it was a good idea to separate little children like that? Sending us to different orphanages when we'd already lost our parents and little brother – it was cruel.'

'I know, and it still goes on,' Felix said soberly. 'I know a boy who was separated from his sister when their parents died only five years ago, and they completely lost touch. He's about fourteen now and determined to find her once he's an adult, but even if he does, they'll have lost so much of their childhood together.'

'That's how I felt about Maddy. And I think it's partly why she's finding it so hard to get over Sammy's death. We knew him when we were children – he was her special friend even then – so as well as losing her sweetheart, she's lost yet another link with the time when we were together. She tries so hard to be independent, you know, with her job at West Lyme and everything, but inside she's still a little girl who needs someone to look after her.'

Felix was silent for a moment or two. Then he said, 'It's still only six months. That's no time at all to recover from the sort of experience she had.'

'I know. I just wish she'd let me help a bit more.' Stella stirred restlessly. 'She ought to have stayed in Burracombe a bit longer at the start. Dottie and I could have looked after her.'

Again, Felix was quiet. He glanced sideways again at Stella and then said, 'I'm not sure that would be such a good thing, you know.

Maddy has to grow up and maybe too much mothering is bad for her.'

'What do you mean?' Stella demanded indignantly. 'Are you saying we shouldn't look after her when she's so unhappy? We should just turn her away?'

'No, of course not. But maybe you shouldn't look after her quite so *much*. The sort of grief Maddy is suffering now is something that can't be shared. It's her own special grief, and although I believe we should give her as much support as we can, we shouldn't try to stop her feeling it. To my mind, she's *entitled* to feel it – she's entitled to be sad. It doesn't help her to try to pretend that life is still good, when she clearly can't believe that yet, or to make her feel guilty for being unhappy—'

'I don't make her feel guilty!'

'No, of course you don't,' he said gently. 'Not deliberately, anyway. But I think sometimes that just trying to cheer someone up makes them feel guilty for not being able to be cheerful. Grieving can be a very lonely thing. The best we can do for someone in that situation is grieve with them. Or, at least, allow them the freedom to grieve.'

Stella was silent as they emerged from the lanes on to the main road and Felix stopped the car. At last she said, 'Well, Maddy will be able to share her grief this weekend. She's gone to stay at Bridge End with Ruth and Dan Hodges. But I'm not sure you're right, Felix – it seems to me that that's just wallowing in it, and I really don't believe that's a good thing at all.'

He sighed. 'I'm afraid it's two steps forward and one back when you're trying to get over a loss. But as long as you end up having taken one step, it's a little bit nearer to recovery. Anyway, there's nothing we can do about it today, so let's enjoy the few hours we've got together.'

'Perhaps it's just the way we are,' she said thoughtfully. 'I'm a teacher and I'll soon be a vicar's wife – looking after you and helping you to look after your parishioners. It comes naturally to me to look after people. And Maddy is the sort of person everyone wants to look after – as if it's a part of her nature to draw people to her.'

'You may be right,' he said, smiling. 'Lookers-after do need people to take care of. Maybe we shouldn't try to fight it.'

'But you're right, too,' Stella went on. 'Maddy needs to share her grief with Ruth and Dan, who must feel it just as much. They can help each other in a way that I never can,' she ended rather wistfully.

'In which case,' Felix said as he stopped the car at the head of the steep combe running down to Polperro Harbour, 'she's in the right place this weekend, and let's hope she'll manage to take two huge steps forward and *no* steps back.'

Chapter Three

Maddy took a taxi from Tavistock station to Burracombe. It was an extravagance, but there was nobody there to meet her – how could there be, when no one knew she was coming? – and no bus until late in the afternoon. She felt too miserable to spend time wandering around the little market town, lovely as it was, or even treating herself to tea in one of the tea shops. She just wanted to be with people she knew and loved, who would give her the comfort she longed for.

At first, she hesitated between going to Burracombe itself or to Little Burracombe. Stella might be over there, with Felix in his vicarage. But if she wasn't, Maddy would have to walk through the fields and across the little wooden bridge to the bigger village, whereas if she arrived at Dottie's cottage to find Stella absent, Dottie herself would welcome her and give her tea and listen while Maddy unburdened herself. And Stella and Felix would not be long – Felix always went to Dottie's for tea on a Saturday.

The taxi dropped her outside the cottage and she paid the driver and opened the gate. The front door was shut and she went around to the back, expecting to find that door open but it, too, was closed. Albert, the fat black cat, was sunning himself on the wooden bench and Maddy, puzzled to find the cottage closed up on such a fine afternoon, opened the door.

'Dottie?'

There was no reply. She hesitated for a moment, then went in and put her bag on a chair. The room had a deserted feel about it, with no teacups laid out on the table, even though it was nearly four o'clock, and no smell of baking coming from the range. Maddy couldn't ever remember coming in here without finding signs of some activity – sewing or knitting set aside on the small table, the local newspaper lying on the settee or, at the very least, a note under the glass paperweight on the sideboard to say when either Dottie or Stella would be home. She felt a sudden twinge of anxiety, almost fright. Where could they be?

There were no clues upstairs. Maddy looked into Stella's room, which appeared just as usual, with no clothes left lying on the bed or piled on the chair, only her woollen dressing gown hanging on the back of the door and a neat pile of school books on the small table she used as a desk. The soap on her washstand was dry, as if it hadn't been used for several hours.

Maddy paused before going into Dottie's room. As a little girl, she would run in and out as a matter of course, treating Dottie as the mother she had always tried to be to the orphaned evacuee, but since she had grown up Maddy had respected the older woman's privacy. Now, though, her anxiety growing, she lifted the old wooden latch and peeped in.

Dottie's room was as tidy as Stella's and there was nothing to tell Maddy where she was now – until she turned to go, and saw that the back of Dottie's door was bare.

Maddy stopped abruptly. Surely the old wrapper that Dottie used as a dressing gown ought to be there? She turned back to the bed and looked under the pillow, where Dottie always put her nightdress – cotton in summer, flannel in winter. There was nothing there.

Thoroughly frightened by now, Maddy hurried down the stairs. Where could her sister and Dottie be? Dottie never went away. She always said she had spent enough time in London and travelling the country as Fenella Forsyth's dresser, before the war, to want to go jaunting off. And Stella wouldn't have gone away now, in the middle of the school term. And surely, if she had, she would have let Maddy know.

In the living room, Maddy hesitated again, feeling suddenly very alone. The cottage felt all wrong without anyone else in it and her emotions, which she had so desperately wanted to share, seemed to be bumping about inside her, hitting painfully at her rib cage and bringing tears to her eyes. She felt totally deserted and now, added to her own misery, was the fresh worry about Dottie and Stella. There must be something seriously wrong for Dottie to have taken her night things away, and the only thing that Maddy could think of was that she had been taken to hospital and Stella had gone with her.

With a sob of fear, Maddy turned and ran out of the door.

'But where are they?'

Maddy had been across the road to Aggie Madge's cottage, where Felix had lodged when he was curate in Burracombe, and where Dottie sometimes slept if Maddy was staying for a few days. But Aggie too was out, and the village seemed deserted. Disconsolate and frightened, Maddy wandered back to Dottie's gate and stood looking up and down the street. Her feeling of abandonment returned and she thought that she had never felt so alone in her life. Even when Sammy had died, there had been people around to comfort and look after her and, in all the months since, she had never been without someone to turn to. But now everyone seemed to have left her. She felt cold, isolated and forgotten, and this time the tears that pricked her eyes brimmed over and trickled down her cheeks.

A sound made her turn quickly and she saw Jacob Prout coming along the road, whistling cheerfully, his dog at his heels. He looked surprised when he saw Maddy, and even more so when she ran towards him, holding out her hands. He stopped as she came nearer, his kindly face creased with concern.

'Why, whatever be the matter, maid? There ain't nothing amiss with Dottie, I hope?'

'I don't know!' Maddy cried. 'I don't know where she is – or Stella. There's nobody in the cottage and I can't find Mrs Madge either. I was beginning to think the whole village was deserted. Where are they, Jacob? What's happened to them?'

Jacob took off his cap and scratched his bare head. 'I dunno, maid, I'm sure. There weren't nothing wrong this morning, as far as I know, but I been up the Top Wood all day, doing a bit of clearing ready for the pheasants. You say Dottie and your sister are both out?'

'Yes, of course,' Maddy said impatiently. 'Otherwise I wouldn't be worrying, would I? I'm sorry,' she added at once, penitently. 'It's just that I'm so worried. Dottie's taken her night things as well, and all I can think of is that she's been taken to hospital and Stella's gone with her.'

'Took her night things?' He stared at her. 'Well, that do put a different light on things. I must say, her seemed bright enough when I passed the time of day with her early on. But I didn't have time to stop and chat, and her seemed in a bit of a hurry herself, now I come to think of it. You don't think her's been doing too much and had a heart attack or summat, do you?'

'Oh, *Jacob*!' Maddy's eyes filled again as she gazed at him. 'Oh, I hope not. I couldn't bear to think of losing Dottie as well. How can we find out? Would Dr Latimer know?'

'He'd be as likely to as anyone would, I suppose. But if her was took off in an ambulance, someone would have seed it. Have you tried Mabel Purdy, next door?'

Maddy admitted that she hadn't, and they went together to knock on Mrs Purdy's door. But once again, there was no reply. It seemed as if all Burracombe, except for Jacob, had been spirited away. Maddy looked at him in despair.

'Now, don't you go fretting before we knows there's summat to fret about,' he said, laying a big, calloused hand on her shoulder. 'Us'll go up to the doctor's house together and find out if anything's happened, and I wouldn't be surprised if us don't run into someone along the way who can tell us, too. And then you'm coming back to my cottage and I'll make you a cup of tea, because it strikes me you need one.'

Maddy shook her head. 'I just need to know what's happened to Dottie and Stella,' she said dolefully. 'I wanted to see them so much.'

'And so you will,' he said comfortingly. 'There's a simple explanation for all this, you mark my words. They've probably all gone into Tavistock to do a bit of shopping, and that's all there is to it.'

'Taking Dottie's nightdress and dressing gown?' Maddy asked. 'I don't think so, Jacob.'

'I'd forgotten they,' Jacob admitted. 'But couldn't they be in the wash? Have you looked in Dottie's basket or wherever she keeps her dirty washing?'

'Of course I haven't,' Maddy said impatiently. 'Why would I do that? Anyway, she wouldn't have put them in on a Saturday – Monday's washing day.' All the same, she had to admit that Jacob could be right. I'm probably making a fuss about nothing, she thought, but I was so upset when I found no one at home. I wanted to be with someone who

I could talk to about Ruth and Dan, someone who would understand how I feel about it. I wanted them to be *there*.

They walked on towards the village green. Rose Nethercott was outside the Bell Inn, watering the big barrels that Dottie had planted up for the Coronation in June. The red, white and blue themes had been replaced by small trees with dark red leaves that glowed in the October sunshine. The innkeeper's wife turned as the two approached and Jacob said, 'Rose'll know, for certain.'

'Know what?' Rose asked, straightening her back. 'Hello, Maddy. I didn't know you were coming this weekend.'

'Nobody did. I just ... came. But I can't find Dottie or Stella, and I'm worried that something's happened to them. Dottie's taken her night things with her. She's not ill, is she? Has she been taken to hospital?'

'Bless you, maid, no. Gone over to Buckland Monachorum, her has, to her cousin's girl's wedding, and stopping the night seeing as there's no buses back of a Saturday evening. You mean to say she never told you?'

'Well, no,' Maddy said, realising that she seldom took any interest in Dottie's doings, since they were usually much the same. 'And I suppose Stella didn't see any reason to say anything, either. But Stella didn't go too, did she?'

'No, her was off early this morning with the young Reverend – come over to fetch her, he did, in that sports car of his. Looked as if they were going for the day, but I dare say they'll be back before long. I should go back to Dottie's and wait for them if I were you.'

'But they might be gone ages,' Maddy said. 'Felix might take Stella back to Little Burracombe and not bring her home until late this evening. And if I walk over there, and they come here instead, I'll miss them that way too. What am I going to do?'

Rose and Jacob looked at her woebegone face. Rose, evidently thinking that an evening waiting in a comfortable cottage wouldn't be the end of the world, picked up her watering-can and turned away, but Jacob's soft heart was touched.

'You come along with me, like I said, maid. You can pop back and leave a note first and then I'll make you a cup of tea. And then you can come in next door and see Val and Luke and their new little babby. Just over a fortnight old, he is now, and a sturdier little chap you never saw. I reckon he knows me already and I'm sure he smiled at me yesterday, though Val says 'twas only wind, and – why, Maddy, whatever be the matter now?'

'No!' Maddy said, walking swiftly away. Her voice was tight and she sounded close to tears again. 'No, thank you, Jacob, I won't do that. I'll just go to Dottie's and wait there. I don't really want to see anyone else just now. I just want to see Stella.'

She was almost running as she spoke the last few words, and Rose and Jacob stared after her, and then turned to each other, bemused.

'Well, what do you make of that?' Jacob asked, spreading his hands.

Rose Nethercott shrugged. 'Goodness only knows. I suppose we just got to remember the poor maid's still grieving, but if you ask me that were more like a spoiled kiddy having a tantrum because things haven't gone all her own way. She were always a bit like that as a little tacker, if you remember, Jacob. Seems to me her's still got a bit of growing up to do.' She turned away again. 'Well, I dare say her sister will sort her out. I got me own work to do, and without Dottie behind the bar of a Saturday night there's twice as much. I'll be seeing you later, I suppose, for your usual pint?'

Jacob nodded. 'I expect I'll be along. But I'm still a bit worried about that young maid. Say what you like, her's had a bad time, and if her needs a shoulder to cry on it's a bit hard if there ain't one available. I hope Felix brings his young lady home soon, but if not 'tis a pity her wouldn't come along with me and spend an hour or two with Val and Luke.' He went on his way, shaking his head and pondering.

It was almost as if it was the mention of Val's baby that had upset the girl and sent her running.

Dottie Friend had gone out soon after Stella and Felix had departed. She had been invited to the wedding of the daughter of a cousin who lived near the village of Buckland Monachorum, and Bernie Nethercott, who ran the Bell Inn where Dottie worked as a barmaid, had agreed to her having the day off. George Sweet, the baker, had given her a lift along the mile or so to the main road in his bread van, so that she didn't have to spoil her best costume walking if it happened to rain, and she'd caught the bus to Yelverton and then to Buckland. Fortunately, it was a fine morning and she walked through the maze of lanes to her cousin's cottage, arriving in good time, to find the usual pre-wedding chaos going on, with one of the small bridesmaids in hysterics and her mother nearly as bad.

'My stars, Betty, whatever's going on?' she asked her cousin as she walked through the back door. 'It's not been called off, has it?'

'No, of course not. It's little Susie's frock – she caught it in the door and pulled some of the stitches out of the hem. Our Jean's worse than useless with a needle and I'm trying to get Meg into her dress. I'm sure she've put on weight since the last fitting.'

Dottie, who had made the bride's dress, pursed her lips, having a very good idea – and feeling sure that Betty had an equally good idea – why Meg might have put on weight. The wedding had been arranged rather too quickly for comfort and that wedding dress, in Dottie's opinion, never ought to have been white. But there you were, it had happened to many a foolish young woman in the past and would no doubt happen to many more, and the important thing now was to calm down little Susie and her tearful mother.

'Pass me that needle and thread,' she commanded. 'And you slip that frock off over your head, Susie, and give it to me. I'll have that hem done in two shakes of a duck's tail and no one will ever know what happened. What time are we supposed to be at the church?'

'In half an hour,' Betty said, fastening buttons up the back of her daughter's dress. 'You and the others are going in Dave Button's big cart with his Shire horse, Tamar, all in his best brasses, and then me and the bridesmaids are going in Miss Frobisher's little pony and trap, all done up with ribbons and such. Meg and her dad will go last, so as to give us time to get everyone settled.'

Dottie nodded and concentrated on her work. No matter how little time there was, she was determined that her hem stitches should be as tiny and neat as if she had spent all afternoon on them. The little bridesmaid was hopping with impatience by the time she finished, but her tears had dried and she gave Dottie a tremulous smile and a grateful kiss when the primrose-coloured dress was once more safely over her head and the wide blue sash tied around her waist.

There was still time for a quick cup of tea and a sandwich before they all clambered up into the big cart and rumbled away through the narrow lanes. St Andrew's church stood in the middle of the village street, surrounded by a cluster of stone cottages, its tall grey tower

I ought to have stayed behind, Dottie thought, but the minute she does arrive, I'll pop out and make sure everything's all right.

The bells stopped again and everyone gave a little sigh of relief. But as the minutes passed, it became apparent that the bride and her father had still not arrived, and the anxiety grew. As the bells started again, the best man hurried down the aisle, his face taut, and Dottie saw the groom staring after him with what looked very like despair. The poor boy, she thought, and almost without thinking about it, got up and walked quickly out through the porch and into the churchyard.

Betty was trying frantically to keep the bridesmaids and pageboys in order, but her manner was distracted and she looked at Dottie almost without recognition.

'I don't know what's keeping them,' she wailed. 'They were ready when I left. D'you suppose they've had an accident? I knew we shouldn't have borrowed that little trap, it's as flimsy as a kiddie's toy, I thought me and the little ones were going to be shook out any minute, but Miss Frobisher would insist, and her's been so kind ... I keep thinking of it, turned upside down in a ditch with our Meg and my Bill squashed underneath – and her in that lovely frock you made her and all!'

'Of course they've not had an accident,' Dottie said firmly. 'They've probably got stuck behind a herd of cows.' She knew that this wasn't very likely, in the middle of the day, but it was the first thing that came into her head. 'Where's Terry gone?'

'I don't know. He went off up the street. They won't be coming that way, I told him, but he didn't take no notice ... Here he comes now. Terry! Where have you been, for goodness sake?'

'I saw Miss Frobisher's trap parked in the road up past the pub,' he panted. 'So I went up to see why he hadn't fetched Meg and her dad, and do you know what he said? He said he thought Dave Button was getting her!'

'But Dave took Tamar down the other way, into the old chapel meadow,' Betty exclaimed in dismay. 'You mean they'm both still here in the village, each one thinking the other's gone to get my Meg, and she's at home wondering why nobody's been back to fetch her? Well, I don't know what to say! You'd better get one of them on the road, Terry, and smartish–like, too.'

'I have. Miss Frobisher's groom's on his way now. Gave him the rough side of my tongue to be going on with as well.' He looked help-lessly at Betty. 'It'll take 'em a good half-hour, though, time he's got there and loaded 'em up and come back again, and *that's* if they don't meet nothing on the way.'

'Well, at least we can tell everyone there's nothing really wrong,' Dottie said bracingly, but Betty wasn't ready to be comforted yet.

'*Nothing really wrong?* Our Meg must be half out of her mind, won-dering what's happened, and you know my Bill's temper, he've got a short fuse at the best of times. Oh, what a way to start a wedding!' She looked round the churchyard as if seeking divine intervention, and gave a shriek of horror. 'Oh, *what* are those boys doing? Stop it, you little terrors! Stop it at once! And you girls – get up off that damp grass!'

The children, bored and irritated, had begun to race around the churchyard, the two boys playing leapfrog over each other and the tombstones, while the girls had settled on the grass to make daisy-chains. As the three adults stared at them, the bigger boy misjudged his leap and fell against the two girls, knocking them flying, and Susie and her sister, who were no shrinking violets, immediately jumped up and began to pummel the boys with their fists. In no time at all, they were in the middle of a free-for-all and Dottie, Betty and Terry had a hard job pulling them apart.

'Look at you!' Betty cried, close to tears. 'Just look at you! Your lovely frocks all covered in grass stains and look, Susie, there's a tear in yours. And after Auntie Dottie took all that trouble to make it for you. You're naughty, naughty girls, both of you. And as for you boys – well, what your Uncle Bill is going to say when he sees you I just do not know. He never wanted Meg to have pageboys in the first place.'

'He won't have to worry,' Terry said grimly. 'They can stay in the porch all the way through, and if I hear a peep out of either of 'em, they'll be sorry afterwards. And they won't get no wedding cake at the reception, neither.'

Between them, Dottie and Betty got the children into some sort of order. The bridesmaids' frocks were wiped down with as many hankies as could be mustered from the congregation, and one of the sightseers outside the churchyard, who were thoroughly enjoying the unexpected entertainment, ran into her cottage and brought out an enamel bowl full of warm water. Sullen faces were washed and hair brushed, and by the time the bridal pony trap finally arrived, with the bride looking tearful and her father thunderous, the little entourage looked more or less presentable. The vicar was outside by now and came forward to calm things down, asking Meg in a quiet voice if she was all right.

'There's no need to hurry,' he said, taking her hand. 'Another few minutes won't make any difference now, and the ringers need to call the bells round before they can stand. Just take a few deep breaths and give me a big smile. You're getting married, and nothing else is going to go wrong now.'

Dottie saw him close his eyes for a moment, as if praying that this was true and that the best man wouldn't lose the ring or – worse still – that someone wouldn't stand up and say that there was 'just cause or impediment'. Meg obviously had her doubts as well, but she gave him a tremulous smile and he nodded and patted her hand before letting it go and turning to enter the church and make his way up the aisle.

Betty had already gone in to take her place in the front pew and Dottie, giving a last twitch to Meg's gown, indicated that she would slip in last. The little procession formed up and the bride's father, his daughter on his arm, turned to make sure that everything was as it should be. His face darkened again and he scowled.

'If you don't take your finger out of your nose,' he snarled at the red-headed pageboy, 'I'll chop it right off!'

Chapter Four

Maddy let herself into Dottie's cottage again, thankful that nobody in Burracombe seemed to consider it necessary to lock their doors. She stood for a moment in the room that was used both as kitchen and as living room, staring despondently around at the old armchairs, re-upholstered by Dottie a year or so ago, and the scrubbed table where she did her cooking and spread her embroidered cloth for tea. The range was out, but kindling had been laid in the firebox and Maddy decided to put a match to it. At least she would be able to make a cup of tea, although it would be a while before the fire was hot enough to boil a kettle.

Once the flames were leaping up, the cottage seemed a more cheerful place. Maddy drew up a chair and sat close to the range, pulling her cardigan around her. While she had been busy, her tears had stopped, although she was still shaken by the occasional sob, but now they began again. She thought over all that had happened that day – her journey to Bridge End, walking through the village that she and Sammy had known so well, arriving at the Hodges' cottage and feeling herself welcomed with a warmth that never failed to comfort her, even though she invariably broke down in tears as she first saw Ruth and Dan. And then, as they sat over their tea and scones, the shock of the news they had broken to her. A baby. A *baby*.

How could they have let it happen? Whatever Ruth might say, it couldn't be an accident. They must have wanted it. They *must* have done. And so soon after Sammy had died. How could they?

They can replace him, she thought sadly. They can forget him – oh, not entirely, I know that, but with a new baby to look after as well as Linnet, how will they even have *time* to remember? And they've already got each other – and Linnet. It seems almost, well, greedy, somehow.

And what have I got? I've lost Sammy, and all the children we might have had together, and I've got nothing left. My life is never going to be the same again.

The tears were falling once more and she forgot the tea she'd meant to make. She sat curled in her chair, watching the flames as they settled into a glow, adding some more wood from time to time but otherwise almost unaware of her surroundings. As the sun went down, shadows began to creep around the corners of the room and Maddy's tears slowly stopped. She had cried herself almost to sleep, and as darkness fell she had no energy left to stoke the dying fire, but curled more tightly in her chair, her arms wrapped around her body, and tucked her head down as if she wanted nothing more to do with the world.

It was like this that Stella found her when she and Felix came in an hour or so later. They had gone back to the vicarage for supper, and Felix had reluctantly agreed that Stella should leave while it was still early enough for his parishioners to notice her departure. Some of them would also be looking out for his return, so he was already observing that he couldn't stay long but would just see Stella safely indoors, when she stopped with an exclamation in the doorway.

'What's the matter? Is something wrong? It's not Dottie, is it?'

'I don't know.' Stella went forward cautiously into the darkened room. 'But there's someone here – and the fire's been lit. She should have been out from early this morning. Dottie?'

'No, it's me,' said a muffled voice, and Maddy's head rose above the back of the armchair. 'Oh, Stella, I thought you were never coming home!' And she burst into tears again.

'Maddy!' Stella took three quick steps across the room and, as Felix turned on the lamp, she gathered her sister into her arms. 'Why are you here? I thought you were going to Bridge End for the weekend.'

'I was,' Maddy sniffed, clinging to her. 'I did. But Ruth—' Her tears overwhelmed her. She tried again. 'Ruth … Oh, *Stella*!'

'What's the matter with Ruth?' Thoroughly alarmed by now, Stella turned to Felix. 'Make up the fire, would you, and put the kettle on? Maddy, come and sit on the settee and tell me what's happened. Is Ruth ill? Has she had an accident?'

'No.' Maddy allowed herself to be led to the small settee and sat down, still clinging to her sister. 'No, she's not ill, she's—' The tears burst out again and she gave way to noisy weeping. Stella and Felix stared at each other in real apprehension.

It took almost five minutes to calm Maddy down enough for her to be able to speak coherently. By then, the kettle was coming to the boil and Felix made the tea. He brought two cups over to the girls and sat down in the armchair, cradling his own cup in both hands and watching anxiously.

'Take a sip of tea, Maddy,' Stella ordered. 'Now, a deep breath and tell us what's happened to Ruth. And what about Dan? Is he all right?' Privately, she wondered why Maddy had come here if the Hodges were in such trouble. Shouldn't she have stayed, to give what comfort and help she could?

'Nothing's happened to Ruth,' Maddy said drearily. 'At least, nothing like that. And Dan's all right – they're both all right. It's ... it's ...'

'It's what?' Stella asked quietly. A new thought struck her. 'It's not Linnet, is it?'

'No. I didn't even see Linnet, but she's all right. Oh, *Stella*!' She lifted a tear-stained and woebegone face to her sister. 'Stella, they're having a baby!'

There was a stunned silence. Stella threw a quick glance at Felix, then looked back at Maddy. She was aware that she needed to tread very carefully.

'Are they upset about it?'

'No, they're not – they're pleased. Ruth said it's like a miracle. A *miracle*! With Sammy gone only six months! It's as if they've turned their backs on him – as if they don't care!'

There was a brief silence. Stella met Felix's eyes again, then took both Maddy's hands in hers.

'Darling, of course they care. Ruth was devastated over Sammy, and so was Dan. They both loved him as much as any parents could possibly love their child—'

'Sammy wasn't Ruth's child.'

'She loved him just as much. I'm sure she did. She'd had him since he was eight years old, before she even knew Dan. You know they loved him.'

'Well, it doesn't seem like it, not when they go and have another baby before he's even cold in his grave.'

'Maddy, that's a horrible expression.'

'So you're on their side!' Maddy burst out. 'You think it's all right. They've already got Linnet but now they want another Sammy. What about me? *I* can't have another Sammy – I can't *ever* have another Sammy.' She wept again and added brokenly, 'I don't even *want* another Sammy. I just want the real one back.'

'Of course you do,' Felix said, leaning forward. 'That's what we'd all like, but you know that can never happen. And Ruth and Dan know it too. I'm sure they're not trying to replace Sammy. And I'm sure they're telling you the truth when they say they hadn't intended it. These things aren't for us to decide,' he added quietly.

'Oh, so you think it's a miracle too! I don't know why I came,' she cried out bitterly. 'I thought you'd be as shocked and upset as I am. Can't you see? It isn't *right*. It's an insult to his memory!'

'Maddy, that's enough,' Felix said sharply. 'This is a new life we're talking about – it can never be an insult. And if it brings joy and hope to a couple who have suffered such sadness and loss—'

'But that's just it! Joy and hope for *them*. What's it bringing to me? Just a reminder, that's all – a reminder that I'll never have a baby of my own.'

'Maddy, that's nonsense!' Stella exclaimed before she could stop herself. 'Of course you will!'

'It's not nonsense. I'll never have *Sammy's* baby. I'll never have a little boy who looks like Sammy. But *they* may have. By this time next year, they could have a baby boy who looks just like Sammy. And how can I ever go and visit them again? How could I bear it? They were the only people who I thought really understood – and now they do this!'

Felix and Stella were silent, gazing at each other in dismay. Then Felix handed Stella her cup. She took the tea and drank mechanically, without tasting it, and he said, slowly and quietly: 'Maddy, you're very upset and you're not really thinking clearly. For one thing, any baby Ruth and Dan have is *not* going to look like Sammy. He looked like his real mother – remember that photograph we saw once?' He paused, to make sure that she had heard and taken in his words. 'For another, if they say they didn't intend it to happen, we have to believe them. And not begrudge them their love for each other and the comfort it can give them.' Another pause, watching Maddy's face. 'They haven't done it to spite you, you know. They're still grieving over Sammy, just as much; this must have come as a shock to them, too, and perhaps not a very welcome one to begin with.'

'I still won't be able to go and see them again,' she said miserably. 'It's all different now.'

'Tell me, Maddy,' Felix said, 'just why have you been going to see them?'

'I told you why! Because they're the only ones who really understand – at least, I thought they were. They used to let me share whatever I was feeling with them. They'd let me cry, and they'd cry too – well, Ruth did and Dan nearly did, sometimes. They knew how awful it was for me.'

Felix hesitated. He glanced at Stella, then said, 'And did you ever try to comfort them?'

Maddy raised her wet face and stared at him. 'What do you mean? Of course I did.' But her voice wavered a little.

'Are you sure?' he asked gently. 'Or did you just go to them expecting comfort for yourself?'

'Felix ...' Stella said, but he put out a hand towards her and went on.

'Everything you've said since the moment we came in, Maddy, has been about how *you* feel – how miserable you are, how let down you feel about this, how you went to Ruth and Dan for comfort, how they let you cry and cried with you. Did you ever wonder if they really wanted to cry? Or if they would have liked to smile for a change? To feel that there was still hope in the world?'

'I thought *you* understood, at least,' Maddy said after a long silence. 'You're a vicar – you're *supposed* to understand.' She stood up, and said stiffly, 'I suppose it'll be all right for me to sleep in Dottie's bed, since she's not here? I don't want to be a trouble to anyone. I'll go up, then. No, I don't want anything else, Stella – I couldn't eat or drink a thing. I'll see you in the morning, and then I'll go back to West Lyme.'

She left the room and they heard her footsteps on the stairs and in the room above. Stella turned to Felix in distress.

'Oh, Felix! Poor Maddy. She came here expecting to find someone to console her, and we were all out. She must have felt so alone. And now you've made it even worse.'

'I know,' he said soberly, 'but those things had to be said, darling. I'm as sorry as you are about what Maddy's going through, and I wouldn't dream of telling her she's got to get over it, but she does need to remember that she's not the only one grieving. And how must Ruth and Dan be feeling tonight? They really are entitled to their joy, you know.'

'Yes, I do. And Maddy will realise it too, when she's had a bit more time. She's not a selfish person, Felix. And she really has lost a lot, during her life.'

'I know. And so have you, my darling.' He moved to the settee and took her in his arms and they looked seriously into each other's faces. 'Maddy's lost more, but she's also *had* more, in a way – being adopted by Fenella Forsyth, living here with Dottie, while you grew up in an orphanage. I'm not saying she's spoiled, but she's never really had to consider anyone but herself, has she? Perhaps if she had, this wouldn't be so difficult for her now.'

'She needs our help,' Stella said, and he nodded.

'She does. More now, perhaps, than ever before. But most of all, she needs to mend her bridge with Ruth and Dan, because until that's done she'll never begin to heal.'

Chapter Five

By the time Dottie came home next afternoon, Maddy was back in West Lyme. Felix had come over after morning service to drive her to Tavistock to catch the train and she had gone, her face white and set. She had refused to speak of Ruth's baby again.

'I don't want to talk about it,' she told Stella when her sister brought her a cup of tea and a jug of hot water next morning. 'Obviously neither of you understands, and I don't want to hear any more about how awful it is for Ruth and Dan. Somehow, I thought you'd think about how awful it is for *me*.'

'We do,' Stella said, sitting on Maddy's bed. 'Really, we do. But you have to realise—'

'No, I don't,' Maddy said, humping herself over in the bed and nearly sending the tea flying. 'I don't have to realise anything. I've already said I don't want to talk about it, and anyway I'm going back to West Lyme as soon as I can get a train. There's one at ten o'clock.'

'Well, you'll never catch that one,' Stella said, glancing at her watch. 'It's nearly nine now.'

'It can't be! Why didn't you wake me sooner?' Maddy sat up abruptly and this time the tea did go flying, all over Stella's dressing gown.

'Because you didn't ask me to,' Stella snapped, dabbing impatiently at the tea. 'Honestly, Maddy, you can't expect everyone to run about in circles for you all the time. If you wanted to get up early, you should have done something about it yourself. There does happen to be an alarm clock on the chest of drawers.'

Maddy stared at her, shocked by her gentle sister's outburst. Then she said in a truculent voice, 'I suppose you agree with Felix, that I'm just a spoiled brat. Well, perhaps you're right, but if I am, it's not my fault.'

Stella sighed. 'Nobody's called you a spoiled brat, Maddy. All Felix was trying to do was get you to see Ruth and Dan's point of view as well as your own. There are always several ways of looking at a situation, you know.'

'And I can only ever see my own, of course,' Maddy said petulantly. 'Well, as I've said, I'm going back to West Lyme today so you won't have to worry about me any more. There's another train this afternoon, so I'll catch that. I won't bother Felix about running me to the station – I'll ring up for a taxi.'

'Don't be silly,' Stella said shortly. 'Of course he'll take you. I'll walk over to the morning service and ask him, and he'll come round straight afterwards.' She stood up, holding out the half-empty cup. 'You may as well finish this now. I'm going to have my wash and get dressed, and then I'll get breakfast ready. And don't say you don't want any – you had nothing last night and you must be hungry. Maybe when you've got some food inside you, you'll feel a bit less sorry for yourself.'

Maddy opened her mouth to make an indignant retort, but Stella was gone. For a minute or two she stared at the cup of tea in her hand, wondering if she dared throw it at the door. Then she realised that she actually was very thirsty, and decided to drink it instead.

Sorry for myself! she thought indignantly. So that's what they think about me, is it? A spoiled, self-pitying brat. And all this time, I thought they understood – that they were really trying to comfort and help me. Well, now I know the truth, I won't bother them again. I'll manage by myself.

After a little while, she heard Stella moving about downstairs and smelled bacon frying. She got out of bed and padded across to the washbasin where Stella had set the jug of hot water. She washed her face and hands, got dressed and went down the narrow staircase.

Stella looked up, a smile on her face, but Maddy ignored it. She slid into a chair and waited to be served her breakfast. They ate in a stiff, dejected silence, and then Stella left to walk across the river to Little Burracombe, while Maddy sat outside the back door in the morning sunshine and waited to be fetched.

*

Dottie listened to Stella's account of what had happened with a deep furrow of concern across her brow.

'The poor little maid. To come all this way, thinking us would be all ready to take her in our arms and let her cry her heart out, and then to find nobody here. And not even knowing where us had gone! She didn't really think I'd been took to hospital, did she?'

'I think she did, at first. She must have felt so alone. And I'm afraid we didn't help her much.' Stella told Dottie what Felix had said. 'And then I made it even worse this morning. She looked as if we'd really let her down.'

'I dare say she did,' Dottie nodded. 'Mind you, he was right, and so were you.'

'Were we? I've been feeling guilty ever since. When we said goodbye – well, she kissed me, but it was like being kissed by a statue. And Felix said she hardly spoke on the way to Tavistock.'

'She've got a lot to think about,' Dottie said. 'But her *will* think about it. Not straight away, perhaps, but over time, when her starts to get over the hurt. Maddy's a dear little soul, but her does have a way of thinking everything's got to happen to suit her.'

'I don't know why she should,' Stella said gloomily. 'Nobody could say things have happened to suit her in the past few months.'

'No, but they did before that, and her had a happy time here as a little girl – I did my best to make sure of that. Not that I ever spoiled her, mind,' Dottie added quickly. 'But even then, her could throw a tantrum if her felt like it.'

'Yes, she could,' Stella said with a smile, recalling the days when Maddy, as a toddler, would stamp her feet and scream until she was given what she wanted. Their mother would ignore these demonstrations, but Stella and her father were more inclined to give in – just as Stella's immediate response now was to give Maddy the comfort she demanded. 'But this is a bit different from losing a favourite doll.'

'Yes, 'tis,' Dottie agreed. 'And nobody would say the maid don't need a tidy bit of looking after. But she's still got to realise that other people are grieving too, and those poor folk at Bridge End most of all.'

'I don't think she begrudges them their grief,' Stella argued. 'It's the new baby that's upset her – she feels they've *stopped* grieving. She feels they've let Sammy down.'

'And that's what she's got to get to grips with,' Dottie said. 'One of these days, her'll find a way to live with it and go on with her own life. She's too young to lock her heart away – she'll find another man. And then she'll realise that you *can* be happy again, and us all got to be allowed to come to it in our own time and our own way.'

'But how long is that going to take? And how are Ruth and Dan going to feel in the meantime?'

'If they got any sense,' Dottie said, 'they'll know all this just the same as we do, and they'll let her come round in *her* own time.'

'And what about us? Maddy's so hurt and angry – I'm afraid she'll let this spoil things between us. And there's our wedding coming up, too. I couldn't bear it if she refused to be my bridesmaid. We've never quarrelled before, Dottie. I don't know what to do.'

Stella was nearly in tears and Dottie put her arm around the young woman's shoulders.

'Don't you worry about it, maid. 'Tis a shame it's happened and a shame Maddy took your words the way she did, but she's not going to let it come between you, not once she gets over the first aggravation. She'll think it all over, you mark my words, and turn up on the doorstep one day with a smile, just like always. And all you can do is the same as the Hodges. Keep the door open for her. 'Tis all anyone can do.'

Chapter Six

The Tozers had spent the weekend in a flurry of preparations for their visitors. Ted and Tom, seeing little need for all the fuss and commotion, took themselves out of doors, where there was plenty of farm work to be done, but the women were completely taken up with plans. Where were they both to sleep? Joe would have the spare room, of course, but he was hardly likely to want to share the double bed with his son, so the small room where Robin slept was to be cleared of his belongings for Russell, and Robin would go in with his parents and baby Heather, where he would sleep on the old camp bed Tom had brought home after he'd left the Army. What with the cot already in there, squeezed beside Tom and Joanna's bed, it would be a bit crowded, but nobody minded that. They were all too excited about the visit.

Alice and Joanna caught the mid-morning bus to Tavistock, along with the usual little knot of people wanting to go to town for one thing or another. Amongst them was Jennifer Kellaway, whom they greeted with smiles of pleasure.

'It's going to take a while to get used to you being Mrs Kellaway instead of Miss Tucker,' Alice told her as they climbed aboard the little bus. 'How be you liking married life, then? Us haven't seen you since the wedding.'

Jennifer blushed and smiled. 'I like it very much. Mind you, I'm having a bit of a problem getting used to it myself – I keep wanting to sign my name as "Tucker", and when someone called me "Mrs Kellaway" the other day I couldn't think who he was talking to!'

'Did you have a nice honeymoon?' Joanna asked, settling herself and baby Heather in a seat and twisting round to talk to the other woman.

'And are you settling down well in the estate manager's house?'

'Yes, to both questions. We're calling it Wood Cottage, by the way – it's never had a name of its own and we want a proper address. And guess what Travis gave me as a wedding present – a puppy! The dearest little Jack Russell you ever saw. I'm calling her Tavy.'

'Tavy! Like the river! That's a nice name,' Alice said. 'She'll be good company for you when Travis is out catching poachers of a night.'

Jennifer made a face. 'That's the only thing I don't like the idea of – him going out at night. Some of those poachers are really rough types.'

'And some of them are like Arthur Culliford, and just out for a pheasant or two for the pot or maybe to sell to one of their mates,' Alice remarked. 'Not that I approve of it, but you always get one or two like him in a village – part of local life, they are. It's those gangs who come out from Plymouth that cause the real trouble.'

'I know,' Jennifer said. 'They're the ones I mean. It was that sort of poacher Travis was after when Betty Culliford got hurt that time, so he's told me.'

Alice nodded, remembering the anger in the village at the time. Arthur swore that he had only been bringing Betty home from a visit to her grandmother that night, and it could well have been true, but there were still those who thought it a strange coincidence that he should be in the woods just at the time when the poachers' gang had been there. Whatever the truth, the upshot was that a little girl had been injured and Colonel Napier and Hilary had been furious about it.

'Well, 'tis water under the bridge now,' Alice said. 'Best forgotten. Us is all glad to have you living in the village permanent. You'll be joining the WI, I take it?'

'I expect so, when I've settled in. There's still a lot to do. The Colonel's been very kind and had the house decorated for us, and a new bathroom put in, but I've still got curtains to make for some of the rooms. That's why I'm going to Tavistock now, to look for some fabric.'

'We're going for wallpaper,' Joanna told her. 'Father's brother's coming over from America and Mother wants to decorate the spare room.'

'From America?' Jennifer exclaimed. 'How exciting! I didn't know Mr Tozer had a brother in America.'

'He's been over there for years,' Alice said. 'Went in 1919, just after the Great War. He did come back a few years after that with his wife, Eleanor, but then they started their family and he's never been back since. It'll be strange to see him after all these years.'

'And is his wife coming with him?'

'No, she died a few years ago. He's bringing his son, Russell – he's twenty-four or twenty-five now – but the two daughters have got their own families, so they can't come.'

'Just as well, really,' Joanna remarked. 'I don't think we'd have had time to redecorate enough bedrooms for all that lot.'

Alice shook her head at her, and Jennifer turned her attention to Heather, sleeping peacefully in the sling Joanna had made her.

'She's a lovely baby. And this sling is such a good idea, but you won't be able to carry her in it for much longer – she's getting so big. How old is she now?'

'Seven months, and she's trying to crawl already. We're going to get a pushchair for her soon, it'll be easier to take her about then.'

Jennifer didn't ask why Joanna never used a pram to push Heather about in. It was in the big, double-ended twin pram, loaned to her by old Constance Bellamy, that Heather's twin sister Suzanne had died without any warning or apparent cause, as the babies lay sleeping on Easter Sunday afternoon a few months ago. After that, the pram had been returned to its owner and put back in the shed where it had been for so many years. Joanna had not been able to face putting Heather into it again, nor buying another. In any case, she had hardly left the farm until just recently, when she'd begun to be seen around the village again and even in Tavistock, with her remaining baby kept close to her in the sling she and Val had made.

The bus arrived in Tavistock and decanted its passengers in Bedford Square. Jennifer set off for the fabric shop while Alice and Joanna made for Baker's, the hardware store on the corner of King Street. They pored over a few of the big, heavy books for a while and Joanna sighed.

'There ought to be a law against all these different patterns. How is anyone ever supposed to choose?'

'Well, I want a nice, fresh, pretty floral,' Alice declared. 'Or something with leaves on – autumn shades would be nice.'

Joanna smiled, remembering Ted's words about the paper being easy to match. 'What about these abstract patterns? This one's quite nice.'

Alice stared at it. 'No, I don't like that sort of thing at all. It doesn't seem to be *about* anything. Here, I like this one – look, it's got little pictures on it. Mountains and lakes. That would be lovely to lay in bed looking at.'

'I'm not sure Dad will agree,' Joanna said doubtfully.

'Well, he's not going to be laying in bed looking at it, is he? Not unless I can't put up with his snoring no longer.'

'No, I meant he might not find it easy to match.' But Joanna could see that this argument was going to carry no weight with Alice, and when they finally left the shop, after searching through every book until Joanna was dizzy, Alice was carrying enough rolls of paper to make Joe think he was sleeping in the Himalayas.

By this time, Heather was becoming restless and Joanna suggested going into Perraton's for a cup of tea. They crossed the road, pushed open the door of the café and went inside. Joanna led the way to a table in the window and they sat down, looking out over the square.

'There's plenty of time before the bus comes, and she can have some milk. It's much easier now she's having a bottle some of the time. What are you having, Mother? Anything to eat? I'm a bit peckish myself.'

'Tea, please, and we'll share a toasted tea-cake. Mustn't spoil our dinner. I put a casserole in the oven before we came out.' Alice glanced around. As usual, there was a good crowd of customers at the tables and she knew some of them. She smiled and nodded, and was soon deep in conversation with a couple of women from Horrabridge at the next table. They admired little Heather and, while Joanna asked for some milk to be warmed so she could give the baby her bottle, they told Alice the latest news about a family who lived at Grenofen and were well known for having trouble with their family of unruly boys.

'Well, did you ever!' Alice said to Joanna when the two women had paid and left the café. 'Their eldest is coming up in court next week for stealing from shops in Plymouth, and it looks as if he might end up in prison. And the younger two are no better. Vandalising telephone boxes, if you ever heard of such a thing! I don't know what young folk are coming to, I really don't. It makes me worry about the whole world, when I hear things like that. I mean to say, is this what we fought a war for? Young louts like that, going around smashing up telephone boxes?'

Joanna shook her head. 'It's not all of them, Mother. There are still plenty of decent youngsters about. I don't reckon we'll ever have that sort of trouble in Burracombe, not with Miss Kemp to teach them their manners if they don't learn them at home. Look at how well she and Stella have brought on the Culliford kiddies.'

Alice pursed her lips. 'So they might have done. But the Cullifords are little girls and say what you like, girls are easier to bring up right. Just you wait until those Crocker twins are a bit older – we'll see a few sparks fly then, you mark my words.'

Joanna smiled. 'You may be right. But in the meantime, if you really want something to worry about, you might start wondering what Father's going to say when he sees that wallpaper!'

Stella was still despondent when she got up that morning to go to the village school, but she had discovered before that you couldn't stay miserable for long when surrounded by bright, inquisitive five- to seven-year-olds, and today was no exception.

'Miss!' It was Shirley Culliford, Betty's little sister, waving a sheet of paper. 'Miss, Mum got me some crayons in Tavi on Saturday and I've drawed a picture of your wedding. Look!'

Stella took the sheet of paper. She was shown as a triangular figure with a long white dress and yellow curls, while Felix, another triangular figure, was apparently wearing his plain black cassock. Behind them was a fair representation of the village church, and around them a crowd of smaller triangles, dressed in the gaudiest colours Shirley's crayons could achieve, while a hailstorm of coloured dots – presumably confetti – rained down around them.

'That's very good,' Stella said. 'And I see the sun's going to shine as well. Thank you, Shirley. We'll pin it on the wall, shall we?'

This caused an instant outcry from the rest of the children. 'Miss! Miss! Can us draw wedding pictures, too? Can us?'

'Yes, you can all draw wedding pictures this afternoon,' Stella said, pinning up Shirley's creation. 'No, not this morning, Edward. We're going to do some other lessons first. Now, get out your copybooks, please.'

There was a universal groan as the children opened their desks and took out the hated copybooks. Nobody liked trying to fit neat, sloping letters between the narrow lines already marked out, and Stella privately wondered if it really achieved anything anyway. People of her parents' generation all seemed to have beautiful copperplate handwriting, so it had clearly worked for them, but today's children seemed to forget all their writing lessons as soon as they were released from school. Miss Kemp deplored this, but Stella thought that as long as their writing was legible, it didn't really matter. Sadly, it often wasn't.

'Perhaps they're all going to be doctors,' she'd suggested once, and Miss Kemp had given her a look and remarked that Felix Copley was having a bad influence on her. 'That's just the sort of thing he would say.'

Stella had smiled and agreed. However, watching the children with their heads bent over their copybooks, their tongues sticking out of the corners of their mouths as they scratched away at the pages, she promised herself that she would reward them with a really good drawing session after dinner. Not that the boys would want to draw weddings – she decided on a football match for them.

Her thoughts went back to the day before. Maddy's distress had gone to her heart, yet there had been a disquieting element in it too. She knew that Felix had put his finger on it when he'd pointed out that all Maddy's concern had been for herself. Her visits to Bridge End had been to share her own grief with the two people she'd thought – quite rightly – would understand it most. But what if they didn't want it to be poured out on them? Perhaps it only increased their own sadness.

Stella sighed. How could anyone ever know what was best for other people? She thought of Maddy's white, set face as Felix had driven her away in his car yesterday. It was the first rift that had occurred between the sisters since they had rediscovered each other after all those years apart. We can't let this happen, she thought miserably. Yet Maddy had rejected her attempts at conversation, her efforts at mending the quarrel, and she had turned her face away from Stella's goodbye kiss, her cheek as cold as marble to Stella's lips. And Felix had said she was no better on the drive to the station, nor as they'd waited for the train. 'She's not going to forgive us easily,' he'd told Stella when he returned. 'I'm so sorry, darling.'

reaching up to the blue sky and surrounded by the gold and bronze autumn colours of trees edging the fields beyond the churchyard. As the big horse, his ebony coat shining as if it had been burnished with Kiwi boot polish, came to a halt outside the church wall, Dottie saw a crowd of people waiting to see the wedding party, and heard the bells ring out in welcome.

The church was almost full of family and friends. Dottie slipped into a pew at the back so as to be handy if any more repairs were needed, and knelt to say a brief prayer for the bride and groom before sitting back and looking around her.

She had always loved this church with its high vaulted roof and the carved wooden angels gazing serenely down on the congregation. The ringing captain called the changes at the back of the church, just as Ted Tozer did at Burracombe, and the organ played softly as the wedding guests gathered in the old wooden pews. At the front sat Mike, the groom, shifting nervously in his seat next to his best man, Terry. After a little while Dottie heard a bustle in the porch that denoted the arrival of Betty, the bridesmaids and the two small pageboys.

Dottie didn't approve of pageboys. It was, she believed, out of place at a village wedding between ordinary farming families to have little boys dolled up in smarter suits than most of the men present. She felt sure the boys themselves didn't like it either, and were likely to show their annoyance by behaving badly. Not that boys needed any excuse to behave badly in Dottie's opinion, and these two were well known for their pranks, especially the red-headed one.

The bells stopped ringing and everyone got ready to stand up and greet the bride. She was already ten minutes late, but that was her privilege and Dottie was sure she must be at the gate now, in that smart little trap Miss Frobisher had lent for the occasion. She felt a cool draught and, without actually looking round, knew that Betty was ushering the children outside, so that they could come in behind the bride. But nothing happened, and after a minute or so, to her surprise, the bells started to ring again.

The congregation began to shift in their seats and whisper to each other. Dottie hesitated, wondering whether to slip out and see what was happening, but finally decided to stay where she was. There was nothing she could do, after all, unless Meg's dress needed some attention. Perhaps she had had an accident with it, like the little bridesmaid.

There was nothing to do, Stella, thought, but keep the door open, as he'd advised the night before, and hope that soon Maddy would decide to walk back through it.

Chapter Seven

Gilbert Napier was spending the morning with his estate manager, Travis Kellaway, visiting some of the more outlying farms.

'I don't know about you,' Gilbert remarked as they climbed back into the Land Rover, 'but if I'd stayed in that cider-house much longer I'd have been staggering. The smell's rich enough to bottle, never mind the liquid.'

'Looks like old Jem Prior's having a bumper year,' Travis agreed. 'And the apple juice itself tastes pretty good. I'll have to make a note to come back when it's fermented.'

'You could do a lot worse,' Gilbert said. 'It's not all his own apples, mark you. Once he's finished his crop, he'll be getting farmers from miles around bringing theirs for him to crush. There's a good three months' work there for Jem.'

'Not once we get the electricity laid on. He'll be wanting an electric press then. It's hard labour, working that hand-press.'

Gilbert snorted. 'I doubt it! You know how difficult it is to get these old chaps to move with the times. I doubt if he'll even want electricity. Some of them still seem to think it's the work of the devil.'

'Still, we should be getting it to some of these remote farms,' Travis said. 'The old wood-fired cooking ranges and paraffin lamps are all very well, but there are a lot of advantages to being able to press a switch. We should be looking into the cost of generators for them. And if he didn't have to do all the crushing by hand, he'd be able to feed more of the pomace to the cows – at the present rate it takes three days, and by then most of it's fermented and useless. Can't have the milk tainted.'

Gilbert shrugged. 'True, but he gives it to old Josiah's pigs then. I've often seen them sleeping it off afterwards, like a lot of village drunks. There's not much goes to waste hereabouts.'

They drove back to the Barton, and Travis dropped his employer off before returning to Wood Cottage. Gilbert made his way into the house, shucking off his boots in the gun-room, and washed his hands before going through to the dining room where Hilary was just setting a jug of water on the table.

'Oh, you're here. I'll let Mrs Ellis know. She was wondering whether to keep lunch back for a while.'

'Not late, am I? It's barely five to one.'

'No, you're not late, but she just thought you might be, I suppose.' Hilary went out to let the housekeeper know they were ready, and came back to find her father looking through that day's edition of the *Western Morning News*. 'Anything interesting? I haven't had time to look at it yet.'

'Nothing much. You'd think that sugar coming off the ration was more important than Khrushchev becoming head of the Soviet Union.' He laid the paper down as Mrs Ellis brought in a tray bearing a dish of shepherd's pie and a bowl of vegetables. 'That looks good, Mrs Ellis. Thank you.'

He laid his newspaper aside and Hilary began to serve the food. Gilbert watched thoughtfully for a moment or two, then said, 'Haven't heard from Robert this week.' As usual, he gave his grandson's name its French pronunciation. 'Shouldn't we have had a letter by now?'

'I expect it will come soon. He's only been there a couple of weeks – he's still settling in. It must seem very strange, suddenly finding himself at an English public school instead of at home in France.' She helped herself to cabbage and carrots. 'I'm still not at all sure it was wise, you know.'

'Not wise? For Baden's son to receive a proper English education? What on earth are you talking about? How else is he going to be fit to inherit the estate when the time comes?"

'I'm not disputing that he shouldn't be educated,' Hilary said patiently. 'And if you're determined that he should inherit, then of course he must be ready for it. All I'm saying is—'

'What do you mean, *if I'm determined*? I thought we'd been through all that. If Baden had lived—'

Hilary set the serving spoon back in the dish of cabbage and took a deep breath. She spoke very quietly, aware that her voice was tense and that if she allowed it, it would grow loud and probably shrill. 'Father, let's come to an agreement over this, shall we? I'll stop saying things like "if you're determined" if you'll stop saying "if Baden had lived". Baden *didn't* live. He was killed in the retreat to Dunkirk. That's a fact. It's no use trying to change everything that's happened since, to make it the same as if that hadn't happened. It *did* happen and we've got to go on from there.' She stopped and looked at her father, grateful that she'd been able to maintain her composure.

Gilbert's face was reddening. He made no attempt to control his own voice, and it thundered through the room. 'I'll thank you not to tell me what and what not to say in my own house, Hilary! And try to remember, if you will, that everything I do regarding young Robert and the estate stems *directly* from what would have been done *if Baden had lived*. There's no other way of looking at it.'

Hilary looked down at her plate. A moment ago the rich meat mixture, the golden, crispy mash and the dark green cabbage and sunset orange of the carrots had looked appetising. Now, she wondered how she would get through it, but she would not give her father the satisfaction of seeing her struggle to finish it or, worse still, leave it uneaten.

'It's just that you never stop saying it, Father,' she said in a low voice. 'You object when Stephen or I point out that Baden's dead, but you never stop saying it to us. We were hurt by it too, you know. You lost your son, but we lost our brother. We were children together. We looked up to him. I used to lie awake for hours wondering how it had been for him, those last few hours, those last moments, and knowing I would never find out. I still do sometimes – especially after Marianne came here and brought Robert with her.' Her voice cracked a little, and she bit her lip.

There was a moment of silence. She looked up at last to find her father staring at her. There was an unaccustomed softness in the lines of his heavy face.

'I'm sorry, Hilary,' he said gruffly. 'I suppose you must have been upset by it, in your own way, children though you were. But your mother and I – you must understand ...'

'I always understood. I had to, didn't I? But don't fool yourself into believing that children don't feel these things, Father. We did. We felt them very much. And I wasn't exactly a child, anyway. I was eighteen, and doing war service myself not so very long afterwards, and Stephen was thirteen and just starting at Baden's old school. There were other boys and masters there who remembered him well.'

She thought back to the nights during that summer after Dunkirk, when she had lain, staring wide-eyed into the darkness as Stephen, on holiday from school, crept in from the other room, whispering that he couldn't sleep. She'd held him close as he asked, over and over again, each word a stab to her own heart, why their brother had died. And, worse still, *how* he had died.

But that was something none of them would never know. All Baden's unit had been killed with him, and there was no one left to tell the family about his last moments. Nor even to tell them of his marriage to a young French girl, just two days earlier.

It was only now, in the past few months, that Marianne had brought Baden's son to be introduced to his English family. Until then, they hadn't even known of either her or his existence but his arrival had turned all their lives upside down.

'All right,' her father said. 'You've made your point. But I can't see how I can stop referring to Baden. The fact remains that Robert is here, and must be treated as he would have been if –' he caught Hilary's eye, 'if his father had lived. If he had grown up here.'

And if Marianne had lived here too, as mistress of the house, Hilary thought.

'Very well, Father,' she said, beginning to eat her shepherd's pie. 'Let's think about how life would have been then. For instance, what would have happened to me? Would I have been allowed to live my own life?'

The momentary softness left Gilbert's face. 'What do you mean? You've always lived your own life.'

'No, I haven't. I stayed here to look after Mother when she was ill, and then to look after you.'

'And do your damnedest to take over the estate,' he retorted.

'Because *you* were ill then. You had your heart attack and Charles Latimer said you shouldn't have any strain. I *had* to take over.' She had been just about to leave home for London, she thought, to start work as an air hostess, but her father's illness had put paid to that.

And, to her surprise, she'd found that she liked managing the estate, and was good at it.

'You don't have to do it now I've brought in Kellaway.'

Hilary sighed and pressed her fingers to her forehead. 'We're going over all the same ground, Father. When will you understand that I *like* working on the estate? Burracombe means as much to me as it does to you. Once you'd agreed – or I thought you'd agreed – to my taking over, I felt my life was at last going the way I wanted it to. But then you started to say I ought to be getting married, and brought in Travis, and I felt as if I'd been brushed aside.'

'You get on all right with Kellaway.'

'I do now, yes. Once we'd got a working relationship agreed, and he knew that I had the final say—'

'*I* have the final say.'

'All right, *we* have the final say.' She held his eyes for a moment. 'Once he understood that I was a working partner and not the lady of the house, arranging flowers and supervising the dusting – well, everything's been all right. But now that Rob's here—'

'Robert needs you here,' her father interrupted. 'It'll be years before he's ready to take over.'

'If he ever does,' Hilary said.

Gilbert stopped abruptly. 'What's that supposed to mean?'

'How do you know he'll want to take over?' Hilary asked. 'Inheriting, yes – he'd be a fool to turn down an estate with several farms and thousands of acres of land, not to mention this house. But taking over the running of the place – learning how it works, how to manage the whole thing, talk to the tenant farmers, run the shoot and fishing – all the million and one things involved – are you really sure he wants to do all that? Have you actually asked him?'

Gilbert was pushing food into his mouth. He chewed vigorously, scowling, then swallowed and said, 'Of course he wants to! You've heard him – asking questions about his father, asking about the moors and their history. You've seen him tramping off with that geological hammer of his, exploring the old stones. Not to mention that ridiculous exploit in the mine! Of course he wants to run the estate.'

'I'm not so sure,' Hilary said. 'Being interested in the history of the area isn't the same as wanting to devote his life to it. And Stephen says he wants to be an engineer.'

'An engineer? Robert? Nonsense! Just one of those ideas boys get at his age.'

'Exactly,' she said, leaning forward. 'Boys of his age *do* get a lot of different ideas. So how can we be sure that Rob really will ever want to take over? And what happens to me in the meantime – and when he finally makes up his mind? If he does go on with his plan to be an engineer, or maybe a geologist? Or something none of us has thought of yet?'

'Well, then you'll get your way, won't you?' Gilbert said. 'You can stay on and look after things. Don't see the problem, myself.'

'No,' Hilary said with another sigh, 'you don't, do you? And you never will, because you don't even try. The idea that I might want some certainty in my life – that I might want to know where I shall be in ten years' time – that just doesn't ever occur to you.'

'It wouldn't occur to you, either,' he said curtly, 'if you'd done what I wanted in the first place, and found yourself a husband.'

Hilary stared at him. Then, no longer caring about her meal, she stood up and pushed her chair back.

'Just as if all I had to do was turn over a leaf and find one waiting,' she said, her voice shaking. 'Just as if I'd not lost my own fiancé in the war, and never been able to leave this place since. Just as if I wasn't well past the age of doing the Season, where society girls usually find their husbands. I'm thirty years old, Father, in case you hadn't noticed, and times have changed. Women like me want something more out of life than a wealthy husband and a big house to look after. And what you *still* don't understand is that I love Burracombe and love looking after it. But I *don't* love playing second fiddle or not knowing if I'll even have a fiddle to play in ten years' time.' She turned and walked out.

Gilbert sat quite still for a minute or two. Then he ate the last forkful of shepherd's pie and pushed his plate away. He went to the door and opened it.

Hilary was halfway up the stairs. They glowered at each other for a moment, then he said harshly, 'All this was just because I happened to remark that we hadn't heard from the boy this week. I think you ought to go and see Charles Latimer, my girl. Get something to calm those nerves of yours.'

Hilary's forehead creased and her mouth half opened. Then, without a word, she turned and ran the rest of the way up the stairs.

Chapter Eight

'Well, Russ, here we are,' Joe Tozer said, getting out of the car and stretching his arms wide. 'Burracombe. The place where I was born.'

His son got out of the other side and gazed around. There was nobody about. The thatched cottages seemed to be dreaming in the October sunshine and the great oak, its leaves turning to a mass of burnished auburn, stood like a majestic guardian in the middle of the village green. The doors of the Bell Inn were closed and the tubs outside, which had been filled with red, white and blue flowers all summer, were now filled with dark-leaved shrubs. Above and behind the pub, the grey stone tower of the church stood square and solid against the tender blue of the afternoon sky, surrounded by the shimmering golden leaves of soaring beech and elm trees. As the two men watched, a flock of cawing rooks appeared from nowhere, momentarily darkening the sky before settling in the high branches and bickering amongst themselves.

'Pretty quiet,' the younger man observed. 'I thought you said there'd be folk around on a Saturday afternoon.' His accent was, like his father's, distinctly American.

'I guess there will be in a while. Ted's probably milking. And something's going on, for sure – look at the green.'

Russ looked at the bales of straw set out on the grass. They seemed to be in formation, two long parallel rows with a wall at one end. 'Nine-pin bowling?' he hazarded, and his father chuckled.

'Skittles they call it hereabouts, or maybe bowling for a pig, I reckon! Look, someone's coming now.'

Dottie Friend had emerged from her cottage and was hurrying

towards them, her thoughts absorbed with her worries about Maddy. She was wearing a short cherry-red jacket and grey skirt, and she carried a basket over one arm. She slowed her step as she drew closer and stared at the two men, first with curiosity, then with dawning recognition. Her heart seemed to jump in her breast and she came to a sudden halt.

'My stars!' she exclaimed. ''Tis never Joe Tozer!'

'Dottie?' Joe said. 'Is it really you?'

'It is.' Her gaze took in the younger man, taller than his father, but with the same bright blue eyes, and hair the colour of the conkers that littered the ground beneath a clump of horse chestnut trees on the other side of the green. 'And I can see who this is – why, he'm the spitten image of you as a young chap. Whatever be you doing here, Joe?'

'What do you think, Dottie? Come to see the family, of course. But I never reckoned on you being the first person I'd lay eyes on.' He stepped forward and put out his hand. Dottie took it and he looked at her for a moment, then swiftly drew her closer. 'What am I thinking of, shaking hands? Let me give you a hug!'

'Joe!' She struggled free, her colour rising. 'We'm in the middle of the village street!'

'So we are. And where's everyone else? The place is deserted. I thought there'd be a few people about.'

'A lot of 'em are in the church. There's a ringing competition on and they'm just having the service. I'm helping with the teas – and you'd better come along too, because your Ted and Alice will be there. Didn't you let them know you were coming? And you still haven't told me this young man's name,' she added with a touch of asperity.

Joe laughed. 'Still the same Dottie. This is my son, as you've already guessed. Russell's his name, but he answers to Russ. He's my youngest – the two girls are married with their own families, so they couldn't come. Russ, this is Dottie Friend. Dottie and me grew up together. And sure I told the folks here we were coming, but we didn't really know when we'd arrive.'

Dottie looked at the long, sleek car. 'You didn't drive all the way from America in that!'

He grinned. 'Hired it in Southampton. We came over on the *Queen Elizabeth*. Docked in Southampton the day before yesterday and stayed a couple of nights to get our breath back. Anyways, here we are now, large as life and twice as ugly.'

They were interrupted by a sudden peal of bells from the church tower and at the same moment the doors opened and men began to pour down the path towards the lych-gate. Dottie, who had been shaking hands with Russell, released him and gave Joe a little push.

'I'd better go. They'll be wondering where I've got to, and I've a basket of scones here that want buttering. You go on into the church, you'll find Ted and the others ringing. Home team rings the service peal, if you remember, and in Burracombe they always likes to ring the others in to tea as well.'

She set off again towards the village hall, still feeling flustered. Of all the people she might have expected to meet in the village street on a Saturday afternoon, Joe Tozer was the last. Why, it was thirty years since they'd last met – she was surprised they'd even recognised each other.

There would be a lot more folk just as surprised, she thought, going into the village hall where the bell ringers' wives were busy laying out the tea. Alice Tozer was amongst them, cutting a Victoria sponge into slices, and Dottie went straight up to her.

'Well, you kept that quiet, I must say,' she accused her. 'I just bumped into your Joe out by the green. You never said a word about him coming to Burracombe.'

Alice stared at her. 'You mean he's here already? Us only knew ourselves a few days ago. Where is he now?' She began to unfasten her apron.

'I told him to go into the church. I dare say your Ted'll bring him to the hall for his tea. They'll be here any minute – no point in you going up there now.'

'No, I suppose not.' Alice hesitated, her face pink with excitement. 'But fancy him coming this afternoon, just when us is in the middle of all this. Oh well, I expect you're right – Ted'll bring him along d'reckly. Did he have his boy with him?'

'He did, and the spitten image of his father he be, too. You'll have to keep your eye on him, Alice, while he's here. A real heartbreaker, that one – just like his father was.'

She turned away and began to take the scones out of her basket and lay them out on large plates, while Alice went back to her sponge.

Joe Tozer, back in Burracombe, and his son with him! They'll liven us up, she thought, and no mistake.

Joe watched Dottie bustle away, then grinned at his son. 'Pretty little thing, Dottie was, and as bright as a button. The man who married her was a lucky guy.' He turned towards the church gate, where the ringers were already emerging on to the green. They took little notice of the newcomers, and strode past towards the village hall where tea awaited them, while the two Americans made their way through and into the little church.

'Gee,' Russell said, stopping in the doorway. 'This is amazing. Why, it must be hundreds of years old.'

His father came beside him and nodded. 'Pretty special, isn't it. But there's churches as old as this everywhere you look in this country. Stood here for a thousand years or more, some of them. Look at those old pillars, as thick and round as tree-trunks. That shows they were built by the Normans. You'll have to get your Uncle Ted to tell you all about it, sometime.' He turned to the west end of the church, where the ringers, behind their wrought-iron screen, were pulling away at the six ropes. 'And there he is, see? Ringing the treble. And that's your cousin, Tom, a coupla years older than you. We had a photo of his wedding a few years back. And that big guy ringing the tenor, I think he's Alf Coker. I guess he's blacksmith now, like his father was. He sure looks like his old dad.'

There were two boys of about twelve standing near the screen. They turned and stared at the newcomers and the bigger boy said in an awed voice, 'You'm Americans!' and the other one cut in eagerly, 'Are you film stars?'

Joe and Russ laughed. 'No, kids, we're just plain Yanks.' Joe told them. 'But I grew up here. My name's Joe Tozer. That's my brother Ted there.' He stuck out his hand. 'And I'd make a guess your name's Coker.'

'Mine is,' the bigger boy said. 'Micky Coker, and that's my dad. He's the blacksmith now and I'm going to be, when I leave school. Henry and me are ringers too. We were in the novice competition.'

'Can you ring as well?' Henry asked. 'I bet they have huge bells in America.'

Joe shook his head. 'No bigger than yours, and none where I live

– not for ringing, anyway. There ain't many in the US at all. I used to ring here before I went away, though. Might try a pull, sometime.'

The bells were being lowered now, their voices quicker and softer as they were controlled into the mouth downwards position. The ringers tied up their ropes, shrugged into their jackets and began to come out. Ted Tozer was first and stopped in astonishment at the sight of his brother.

'Our Joe! Well, I be danged. Where did you spring from?'

'You knew I was coming,' Joe said, grinning as they shook hands. 'I wrote to Mother weeks ago.'

'So you might have done, but the letter only just come and us didn't know when you'd be here, zackly. Not that 'tisn't good to see you,' he added quickly. 'Welcome as the flowers in May, you be. And this is young Russell, I take it.'

'That's right, Uncle Ted,' the younger man said, shaking hands in his turn. 'It's good to meet you.'

'Well, now.' Ted stood for a moment, beaming at them, while the other ringers crowded round. 'Let's see who you might remember. Norman, your second cousin, and Alf Coker, of course. And this is our Tom, and this ugly-looking brute is Ernie Crocker, you oughter remember him. And this chap's Travis Kellaway – manages the Burracombe estate for the squire.'

'Don't let Hilary Napier hear you say that,' Travis warned, holding out his hand. 'She'd tell you we manage it together, and so we do.'

'Hilary Napier?' Joe repeated. 'Is that the squire's daughter? She was just a baby when I was last here. Didn't she ever get married?'

Ted shook his head. 'Her chap died in the war, same as our Val's first sweetheart, and she don't ever seemed to have fancied no one else. Pity – a fine figure of a woman – but that's the way it goes for some folk. Anyway, us mustn't stand here gossiping, us ought to be down the village hall now, having our tea. You'd better come along too, the pair of you. Alice'll be there and she'll be real pleased to see you.'

They set off down the church path and Joe stopped again. 'How did you get here, anyway? Where's your luggage?'

'In the car,' Joe said, nodding towards the lych-gate. 'We drove down from Southampton.' He grinned as Micky and Henry dashed forward and came to a halt by the car, staring at it in awe. 'Have to admit, I'd forgotten how narrow your Devon lanes are.'

'A bit grand for hereabouts,' Ted said. 'I suppose you Americans think it's just a little runabout.'

Joe laughed. 'It'll do us very well while we're here. Burracombe doesn't seem to have changed much,' he went on, looking around as they strolled along the little street. 'Still the same old cottages and still the same people living in them. Though I guess quite a few must have passed on now. How many of the boys and girls we grew up with are still here, Ted?'

'Let's see – Jacob Prout's still here, took over as village roadsweeper and hedger and ditcher from his dad and still keeps the place looking fresh and tidy. Jed Fisher, what lived next door, he's gone, died a year or two back – quite a story there, Alice'll tell you – and our Val lives there now with her Luke. I dare say Mother told you they've just had a kiddy. Born second Saturday in September.'

Joe shook his head. 'I expect the letter would have arrived after we left home. She's kept me up pretty well with family news, but I don't know so much about the rest of the village. Oh, we ran into Dottie Friend just now, too – I was telling Russ about her, wasn't I, Russ?'

Russell nodded. 'You said the man who married her was a lucky guy.'

'Dottie's never been married,' Ted said. 'Don't ask me why. Would have made a good little wife, Dottie would.' He glanced sideways at his brother. 'Seem to remember you were sweet on her yourself.'

'I was,' Joe admitted. 'But she gave me short shrift. Still, I guess most of us boys were sweet on all the girls at one time or another. We didn't have that much choice, did we! You settled down with your Alice, but I had to go halfway across the world to find my Eleanor. This is the village hall, Russ,' he added to his son. 'Built as a memorial for the First World War – the one I was in. Everything happens here – flower shows, whist drives, wedding parties – you name it.'

Ted led the way through the door and Alice, pouring tea at the long tables, looked up and said, 'Here you be at last! Us thought you'd got lost. And look who you got with you!' She stopped, lowering the big teapot to the table. 'Joe! By all that's wonderful!' She set down the teapot and came hurrying around the table to give him a hug. They held each other at arm's length, studying each other and laughing.

'I swear you don't look a day older than when I last saw you!' Joe exclaimed, and she shook her head at him.

'You always were a charmer! I were just a slip of a thing then,' she told Russell. 'Come to be maid to your gran, I had, during the Great War, and fell in love with my Ted the minute I laid eyes on him. I had a nineteen-inch waist in those days – you'd be hard put to get a tape measure round it at all now!'

'I can see that's not true,' Russell smiled, taking her hand and kissing her on the cheek. 'I reckon if Dad hadn't been in France then, he'd have fallen in love with you himself and carried you off to America, and you'd have been my mother instead of my aunt.'

'And 'tis easy to see who *you* take after,' she told him. 'Now, I got to get on with serving tea, some of these poor chaps haven't had a drink since Bernie shut the pub doors at two o'clock. You'd better sit yourselves down.'

They did as they were told, taking the seats that had been left at the end of one of the long tables. One of the men already there leaned across and said, 'There's no mistaking whose brother you be. More like twins than ever, I reckon. Don't you think so, George?'

The man next to him surveyed the Tozers, taking in their crinkled grey hair, cut closer and smarter in Joe's case, and their square, corrugated faces, both equally tanned, and bright blue eyes. If anything, Ted, although the younger, looked slightly older; his hard, outdoor life had left him toughened and weather-beaten. But as Dottie had remarked, the family resemblance had transmitted itself to Joe's son as well, and both brothers had once had the same chestnut-brown hair and craggily attractive features that Russ had now.

George Sweet, the village baker, nodded. 'Used to lead the maids a merry dance, if I remember right. The rest of us didn't have a chance when they two were about. A relief all round, 'twas, when Joe Tozer upped sticks and went to America to be a Yank.'

'I can't have been too much of a problem to you,' Joe observed, accepting a cup of tea from Alice and helping himself to a sandwich from one of the heaped plates on the table. 'I was away for most of the war years and then got that darned flu pretty soon after I got home.'

'Ah, that were a bad time, all right,' someone else agreed. 'Lost a mort of young chaps in the war, and half of them that did come back died of the flu, Didn't seem fair, after all they'd been through.'

'Still, our Joe didn't die,' Ted said through a mouthful of egg sandwich. 'Takes more than that to kill off us Tozers.'

There was a brief silence as his words reminded them that a very young Tozer had died unexpectedly in her pram only a few months earlier, and then the conversation resumed, a little awkwardly to begin with but soon flowing as smoothly as ever. The two Americans listened quietly, trying to tune into dialect, but after a few minutes Russell whispered to his father, 'What are they talking about, Dad?'

Joe grinned. 'The ringing competition. There are still two or three bands to ring after tea, but they reckon Little Burracombe have got a good chance, if Meavy don't put up a better show. The judges are sitting up in a room at the pub and don't know which one's ringing, so there can't be any favouritism. They note down every fault that's made, then tot 'em all up and announce the winners at the end. It always annoys Burracombe if Little Burracombe win, especially when it's held here, because the home team can't compete, y'see.'

'Little Burracombe's the village across the river, ain't it?'

'That's right. The two villages have been at daggers drawn as long as they've been there, I reckon. It's not a bad little place, mind you, and got a pretty good pub – or at least, it used to be when we were youngsters and used to go across the Clam to court the girls there.'

'The Clam?'

'An old footbridge over the river. It was a tree-trunk once upon a time but I guess it's been brought up to date a bit since then. Probably got at least two planks of wood now!' He laughed at Russ's expression. 'I told you before we came, you've got to be ready to step back about fifty years!'

Alice came to their end of the table and refilled their cups. 'You two don't want to hang about down here. You'd better go up to the farm when you've had enough to eat. Your mother's there, and our Joanna and her little ones, Robin and the baby.' She lowered her voice a little. 'You remember I wrote to you about Heather's twin, Suzanne.'

Joe nodded. 'Sad business. How's Joanna coping with it?'

'Oh, pretty well, considering. Has her ups and downs, of course. But it takes time, and I don't reckon you ever gets over losing a child, especially a baby that seemed healthy and thriving. Anyway, you go on – they'll be some pleased to see you. Mother's been like a cat on hot bricks, wondering when you were going to arrive. Had me and Joanna traipsing off to Tavi to buy wallpaper for the spare bedroom. And that were a wasted journey, too, since Ted's not had time to put it up yet.

Anyway, I'll be back as soon as we've cleared up here, but goodness knows when Ted'll be home – once the results have been announced, they'll all be going into the pub, I don't doubt, to drown their sorrows. You could walk down and join them later on if you wanted to.'

'I might,' Joe said and stood up, pushing back his chair. 'Come on, Russ, it's time we made ourselves known to the rest of the family. Your grandmother's waited long enough – we'll be in trouble the minute we walk in, when she finds out we've been down here eating and drinking when we could have been up there with her.' He glanced at his sister-in-law. 'How's she been keeping, Alice? I know you were worried about her last winter when she had that turn. I was on the point of coming over then.'

'And we were on the point of sending for you,' she admitted. 'But she'm a tough little body and made up her mind she was going to pull through. You'll find her pretty hale, but she gets tired these days and us have managed to get her to rest in the afternoons.'

'That's good to hear,' Joe said. He paused, then added, 'To tell you the truth, that's really why I came over now, before the next winter takes hold. Didn't reckon I ought to leave it any longer, not at her age.'

Alice nodded. They all knew that Minnie might not have many years left to her. 'You can tell her I said there weren't no sense in you going up to the farm straightaway, since us knowed she'd be in bed! But you'd better go now, all the same. I'll be up dreckly, and I'll call in at our Val's as well and bring her along, and Luke, too, if he's not busy painting one of his pictures. Pity our Jackie won't be there, but she's in Plymouth now, working at the hotel.'

'Almost the whole family,' Joe said, and smiled. 'I shall feel as if I've never been away.'

Alice regarded him thoughtfully. 'I don't know about that, Joe. There's too many you don't know – all our youngsters, and the next generation coming along as well, not to mention the incomers. Burracombe might look the same on the outside, but I reckon you'll find a lot of changes.'

'I guess so,' he said soberly. 'The world's moved on and I suppose even Burracombe has had to move with it. But I hope it isn't too different. I want to find the village I've been remembering all these years. I don't want too many changes in Burracombe!'

Chapter Nine

Minnie scarcely knew where to put herself when her son walked in through the farmhouse door. She had come downstairs an hour ago and was sitting in her rocking-chair by the kitchen range, looking at a book with Robin. She glanced up as the door opened and almost leaped from the chair, dropping the book to the floor.

'Joe! Here you be at last! Why didn't you let us know? Us got a telephone, you know.'

'I wanted to surprise you.' He was across the kitchen in two strides, taking the tiny body in his arms for an enormous hug. 'Look at you, bright as a button and not a day over seventy, I'd swear. I thought you were supposed to be getting old – must be the Burracombe air.'

'Go on with you! You always were a flatterer. Not that you'm looking so bad yourself,' she allowed as they took stock of each other. 'And so this is my other grandson, is it? Come you here, Russell, and give your granny a kiss.'

The young man stepped forward and took her in his arms, rather more gently than his father had done. He kissed her cheek and she studied him in much the same way as she had done his father.

'You'm the image of your father when he was your age,' she said. 'Mind, he'd already gone off to America by then, but there's not much difference between twenty-two and twenty-five. You'm like my Ted, too, but then you would be, those two were always as like as peas in a pod. Folk used to take 'em for twins sometimes, even though there were a few years between them.' The door to the stairs opened and Joanna came through, carrying the baby Heather in her arms. 'Look who's here, Joanna – our Joe, and his boy Russell. And this is Joanna and little Heather, and this little chap here – take your thumb out of your mouth, Robin, you'm a big boy now, at school and all – this is Robin.'

Joanna freed her right hand and held it out to the two men. They stood awkwardly for a second or two, then Minnie said briskly, 'Well, sit you down and Joanna'll put the kettle on for some tea. You must be parched. How far have you come?'

'Well, as a matter of fact we've only come from the village hall!' Joe admitted. 'We met Dottie Friend and she told us there was a ringing competition on, so we went up to the church and Ted said we might as well go along to the hall. I'd forgotten what ringers' teas were like!'

'So you've seen Ted and Alice already, then.'

'Yes. I'm sorry, Ma. We ought to have come straight to the farm, but—'

'Bless you, it don't matter a jot,' she declared. 'What's half an hour when you'm stopping with us for a few weeks? You are stopping, aren't you? Us got your rooms all ready for you, though it's not been done up nice like I wanted. You might as well put that kettle on anyway, Joanna,' she added. 'I want my tea, if nobody else does!'

'We're planning to stay over here until after Christmas, but we won't be here all the time. I want to show Russ a bit of the rest of England – maybe even the Continent. But you'll see plenty of us, don't worry.'

Minnie nodded. 'There's lots to see – not that I've seen much of it myself. Your father and me were always too busy to leave the farm for holidays and such, though us did go up to London once for a wedding, and there was that time us went on the train to see my old Uncle Jack, who lived in Newcastle. That was enough travelling for me! Been happy to stay here in Burracombe all my life. Now, tell me how the rest of the family are. I hope you've brought some photographs of the girls and their children. I know you've been good about sending cards but you got to admit you're not much of a letter-writer. It was your Eleanor who had a gift with a pen in her hand.'

Joe nodded soberly. 'I know, Ma. But we're here now and we can have plenty of chinwags about it all. I've got a lot of catching-up to do myself. What's all this about young Jackie working in Plymouth?'

'Been there for quite a while now.' Minnie accepted a cup of tea from Joanna. 'Seems to like living in the city. She's in the Duke of

Cornwall Hotel – remember it? Up near the Hoe. Started off as a chambermaid and waitress and now she's moved up to reception.'

'I suppose she comes home every evening,' Joe observed, and nodded as Joanna raised the teapot enquiringly. 'Thanks, Joanna – it's thirsty work, all this talking! We'll see her later, I guess.'

'No, her lives in. Used to stop in Devonport, along with Jennifer Tucker, that married Travis Kellaway a few weeks back, but now Jennifer's given up her place Jackie's got a room at the hotel.'

'Which is what she wanted all along,' Joanna remarked, handing both men cups of tea. 'Not that she'll stay there long, if I'm any judge – I'll be surprised if she doesn't find herself a job in one of the big London hotels before she's finished.'

'Ted and Alice won't like that,' Minnie said. 'She had enough of a fight to get them to agree to her going to Plymouth. Anyway, I'm not so sure you'm right, Joanna, not now that Roy Pettifer's back from Korea. Seems to me that's all going strong again now. Jackie might find she's not so ambitious after all.'

Joe looked at his son with a wry smile. 'Alice was right about changes,' he said. 'Half these names I've never heard of. Well, I guess we'll just have to pick it all up as we go along. The main thing is that you're all right, Mother, you and the rest of the folks. I was real sorry to hear about your baby,' he added, turning to Joanna. 'That's the sort of thing nobody ought to have to go through. This little lady looks a charmer, though. And I haven't said a proper hello to young Robin, either.'

By the time Alice came in, with her basket now half full of sandwiches, cakes and scones left over from the ringers' tea, they were gathered round the range, chatting as if Joe had never left the farm. The bells were ringing again and they could hear the cows lowing as they ambled through the yard after afternoon milking. Joe leaned forward and put some more wood on the fire in the range, and blue and yellow flames leaped up the chimney.

'You know,' Russell, said, looking round the circle of faces, 'I feel somehow as if I've been here all my life. As if this is where I belong. Even though I've never been here before, I reckon there's always been a part of me in Burracombe.'

Alice stood for a moment with her hand resting on his shoulder.

'Tozers always did belong to be in Burracombe,' she said. 'Always did and always will – no matter how far away they go. And us is proper glad to have you here – both of you. Stay just as long as you like.'

Dottie Friend had no time to think about the new arrivals that evening, for as soon as she finished helping clear up after the ringers' tea she went on to the Bell Inn to work behind the bar. There was plenty of custom this evening, for the teams who had already rung came in to buy a pint and take it outside while listening to the last few competitors. At nine o'clock, they all returned to the church to hear the judges' results and once those had been declared back they all came to discuss the whole event.

'Whitchurch come first,' Ted Tozer told Dottie. 'Turned in a fine peal, they did – Harry Mudge got every right to be pleased with his team, and his cousin Charlie's a good steady ringer too. It won't be long before he can bring along that little tacker of his – young George – to see what 'tis all about.'

'Go on,' Dottie said, serving him his pint. 'The poor little chap can't be more than five years old. There's a few years to go before he's big enough. He might not even want to learn to ring.'

'Oh, he will,' Ted said with a grin. 'If Charlie's got anything to do with it! Anyway, I can't stop too long, with our Joe and his boy up at the farm. Mother will want to see the whole family together before she goes up to her bed. I dare say you and Joe'll have plenty to talk about too, Dottie.'

Dottie's rosy face coloured more deeply. 'I don't know what you mean by that, Ted. It's nice enough to see him, I don't say it's not, but we don't have anything special to talk about.'

'Well, I never said you did,' Ted said, surprised. 'Only that us was all young together and got a lot to catch up on. There's a lot of water gone under the bridge since those days.'

'And some of it best left there,' she retorted. 'I'm not sure I hold with all this harking back. Still, you can tell him he's welcome to drop in for a cup of tea one afternoon if he feels like it, and bring that young man with him. Don't know where he got *his* good looks from!'

Ted laughed. 'And there was me thinking he was just like me and Joe at that age! I'll tell him, Dottie, so you'd best get some cakes baked special. Now, I wants to have a word with Harry Mudge before he gets back off to Whitchurch with that trophy, and then I got to be going meself ...' He moved away, his tankard in his hand, and was swallowed up in the crowd of ringers.

Dottie turned to serve the next customer. She was annoyed with herself for reacting so sharply, but she was also annoyed with Ted for being tactless. He'd probably forgotten what happened – it was a long time ago, after all – and if Ted had, the chances were the rest of the village had, too. And that would be just as well, she thought, taking a shilling and a sixpence from Norman Tozer for his pint and giving him his change. Probably everyone had forgotten, but her.

Perhaps even Joe himself had forgotten.

While Dottie was serving behind the bar, Stella was sitting in the living room of the cottage with Felix planning their wedding.

'You know,' she said thoughtfully, 'now I've had time to think about it a bit, I'm coming round to Maddy's idea of a rainbow wedding. After all, if I've *got* to have six bridesmaids – although I still think that's far too many – to have them all in one colour would be a bit overwhelming. And it would certainly cheer up the January weather!'

'What are the rainbow colours?' Felix asked. 'I can never remember.' He held up his hand and they began to count them off on his fingers. 'Red – orange – yellow – green – blue – indigo – violet ... Is that right? I make it seven.'

'It does sound awfully bright,' she said doubtfully. 'And I'm not keen on orange, so perhaps we could leave that out.'

'Yes, but you're right about six bridesmaids all in one colour,' he urged. 'I mean, imagine six girls in pillar-box red—'

'I wouldn't *have* pillar-box red! It would be blue ... or pink ... or—'

'Not pink,' he said firmly. 'And remember, they'll want to be able to wear their dresses afterwards for parties and things. Honestly, darling, I do think the rainbow idea is a good one. And they needn't be too bright. The red could be a bit darker. Val could wear that.'

'Yes, it would suit her. And Maddy could be in blue. A nice strong blue – delphinium's her colour, and wouldn't be overshadowed by Val's red, don't you think?'

'I expect so,' Felix said, trying to think what a delphinium looked like. 'So that's the two big bridesmaids settled. Who's next?'

'Maureen Budd. Jess says she's thrilled to be asked and they're all looking forward to coming. I just hope the weather doesn't hold up the trains. I think yellow would be nice for Maureen. Have you decided which of your nieces to ask?'

'There are so many of them,' he said despondently. 'That's the trouble with coming from a large family. But if we want someone Maureen Budd's size – how old is she?'

'Fourteen.'

'Well, I've only got one about that age,' he said in relief. 'That's Button, Dominic's eldest. But there are any amount of little ones, and you want at least one child from school.'

'*Button*?' Stella repeated in disbelief. 'Felix, I don't believe even a brother of yours would call a child Button!'

'Well, it's Pearl really, but we've always called her Button,' he said apologetically. 'Anyway, about these little ones ...'

'How many are there?' she asked in a resigned tone.

'Let's see ...' He held up his hand again. 'Dom's youngest, but she's only nine months old ... then there's Vivienne, my sister's little girl, she's six ... and Julie, she's nearly five ... and the twins, Carole and Holly – they were born on Christmas Eve – let's see, they must be coming up to three now. I think that's all.'

'They'd look very sweet,' Stella said wistfully. 'But I really think three is a bit too young. Vivienne and Julie would look nice together. But that's the six and I really should have someone from school.'

'There *are* seven colours in the rainbow,' he said coaxingly. 'And if you had one from school, walking behind the others, she could wear orange, which you were going to leave out. And it wouldn't matter what size she is.'

Stella sighed. '*Seven* bridesmaids! I wanted it to be a quiet wedding, Felix. And think about the cost. We're supposed to pay for their dresses, you know.'

'I've told you, you're not to worry about that. My parents are very happy to foot the bill – can't wait to get me married off to a nice, sensible girl. They didn't think anyone would be crazy enough to take me on, you know.'

'Well, I can't be both sensible *and* crazy. But if you're sure it would be all right ... All I have to do now, then, is think which child to choose from school, and I haven't the faintest idea how to do that.'

'Have a lottery,' he suggested. 'Put all the names in a hat and get

Miss Kemp to draw one out. That way, nobody can accuse you of favouritism. You'll probably end up with the ugliest girl in the school,' he added thoughtfully, 'but nobody can look really pretty in orange, so that doesn't matter.'

'I'm not worried about her being ugly,' Stella said. 'But I would like it to be someone I actually *like*. Suppose I got landed with someone like – oh, that spiteful little Wendy Cole.'

'Is Wendy Cole spiteful? She always looks as if butter wouldn't melt in her mouth.'

'I know she does, and they're always the worst. Oh well, we shall just have to hope for the best. At least she'd look nice in the photographs, and orange will look better on her than on Susan Price with that bright ginger hair of hers.' She scribbled a few more words on her pad of paper and leaned back. 'Don't let's think about it any more tonight, Felix. My head's going round and round with names and colours, and you'll have to be going soon.'

'Dottie should be in at any minute,' he said, and at that moment they heard footsteps on the path and the door opened. Dottie bustled in, her cheeks rosy from the cool October air.

'Well!' she exclaimed, closing the door behind her. 'You do look cosy in here.' She set her bag on the table and looked at them. There was an odd air of repressed excitement about her, but she said nothing and after a moment Stella glanced at Felix, then said, 'Has something happened, Dottie?'

'Well, something has, since you ask.' The little woman turned away slightly so that it was difficult to see her face. She opened her bag and peered inside, as if searching for something, then turned back towards them.

'You'll never guess who the wind blew in to Burracombe this afternoon. Joe Tozer, that's who – Ted Tozer's brother, that went to live in America – and his boy Russell. The image of his dad at the same age.' She paused, then added quietly, 'And if he's anything like his dad in other ways, I reckon he's going to set a few hearts fluttering around here!'

Chapter Ten

'You look smashing,' Roy Pettifer exclaimed, as Jackie came swirling out of the staff door of The Duke of Cornwall Hotel, wearing her new coat over a red taffeta circular skirt and black top. 'I ought to be taking you somewhere really special, instead of a church hall.'

'There just isn't anywhere else to go dancing,' Jackie said grumpily. 'Not until they get the Guildhall rebuilt, anyway. You'd think they'd have done something about that by now – the war's been over for years and Plymouth's still only half done. People need somewhere to go for a bit of fun.'

'Well, we'll have fun anyway,' he said, tucking her arm into his. 'And Plymouth looks pretty good to me, after all that time in Korea.'

'I suppose anywhere would,' she agreed, and they walked in silence for a few minutes.

'I've been meaning to say this ever since I got back,' Roy said. 'Thanks for writing to me all the time I was away. I really liked reading your letters.'

Jackie gave a small shrug. 'That's all right. It didn't seem right to let you be on the other side of the world and never get any letters. I mean, you didn't have any other girls to write to you, did you?'

'No, I didn't. There was only you, Jackie. You know that.'

'Even though we broke up before you went away? You could have got another girlfriend then. A lot of chaps would.'

'I didn't, though.' He squeezed her arm against his side and said, 'I kept hoping we'd be all right again. I never wanted us to break up.'

'You shouldn't have kept on at me, then. Not after that scare I had. I really thought I was going to have a baby, you know. I was so relieved when I found I wasn't. I never want to go through that again.'

'I wouldn't have let you. I'd have been careful. That first time—'

'The *only* time.'

'Yes, well, that first time I wasn't expecting it. It just sort of happened – we got carried away and—'

'And it's never going to happen again,' Jackie said. She stopped and turned to him so that she could look him in the eye. 'I told you, Roy, I'm not taking any more chances like that. Never.'

'Come on, Jackie, that was two years ago now – we're both older. You've had other boyfriends since then.'

'Only one. And Vic and me never ... well, we didn't, that's all,' she finished, glad that it was too dark for Roy to see her colour rise.

'You really have finished with him, haven't you?' he asked, and she nodded.

'Yes.'

'So there isn't anyone else?'

'Not at the moment, no.'

Roy sighed. 'You see, Jackie, I don't know where I stand with you. You seemed so pleased to see me when I came back. It was like I'd never been away, like we'd never split up. But since then – well, you've sort of cooled off, and I don't know why.'

'I don't know why you're saying that. I've been out with you twice since you came back. I'm out with you now, aren't I?'

'Yes, but it's not like it was before. You won't even let me kiss you. Why were you so pleased to see me, if you didn't really care?'

'Of course I was pleased,' Jackie said, with a slight wobble in her voice. 'You'd been fighting in Korea – you could have been killed. I didn't want that. And I'd been writing to you because you were my friend. We've always known each other. It stands to reason I'd be pleased to see you back, safe and sound.'

'So you don't really want to go out with me, then,' he said, sounding depressed.

'Depends what you mean by "going out",' she said. 'I don't mind going to the pictures or the church hall hop. But that's all it is, Roy. I'm not going to be your girlfriend again.'

'I see.' He was beginning to sound aggrieved now. 'So if someone better comes along, you'll drop me like a hot potato.'

'I've never even picked you up,' Jackie said. 'Not that way. Look, you've been away a long time and you want a bit of life again. I don't mind going about with you for a while, as friends, but if you want anything more than that you'd better look for someone else. And then *you* can drop *me* like a hot potato!' She studied his face for a moment, then laughed. 'And you can stop looking like a little boy whose best conker's been smashed! Come on – let's go and enjoy ourselves. You never know, you might meet some gorgeous girl there who'll be your dream come true.'

'I won't,' he said sullenly, but Jackie was already twirling away and he followed her along the city street, with its bombed sites interspersed with new buildings. 'I don't know why you want to live in this dump,' he added disparagingly. 'It's a lot better in Burracombe. This place is a mess.'

Jackie tossed her head. 'It's not always going to be a mess, though, is it? It's going to be a really good city, when all the rebuilding's finished. And anyway, who says I want to live here for the rest of my life? I've got other plans.'

'What sort of plans? Where d'you *want* to live?'

'Oh, I don't know yet,' she said, shrugging. 'London, probably. Or even abroad. Paris – New York – Rome. Anywhere. There are big hotels being built all over the world, Roy, and I could work in any one of them. Or I could be an air hostess and fly everywhere. *Now* d'you see why I don't want to be tied down? The world's my oyster, Roy Pettifer, and *no* man's going to stop me doing what I want!'

The truth was, Jackie thought later, when she was back in her room on the top floor of the hotel, that she didn't really know how she felt about Roy Pettifer – or any other man. She'd believed herself truly in love with him a few years ago, and had been terrified when she'd thought herself pregnant. Only her sister Val had known about that, and about her relief when she found it had been a false alarm, and Jackie had been determined never to take such a risk again. That hadn't stopped her falling for Vic Netherton, but it had certainly stopped her from letting him have his way. And the shock when he'd got tired of taking no for an answer had put a complete stop to their relationship.

Since then, she'd begun to wonder if she'd ever be able to let herself fall in love again. The letters she'd written to Roy, begun as no more than friendly village gossip, had grown warmer after her break-up with

Vic, and she knew she'd reacted impulsively when he'd suddenly appeared at Jennifer Tucker's wedding. But afterwards, she'd wondered why she'd run down the hall like that to greet him – just like a girl welcoming her sweetheart home again – and although she had agreed to go to the cinema with him and now to this dance, she didn't believe it could ever be serious between them any more.

Roy didn't seem to feel that way, though. He'd been even more persistent when he'd brought her home this evening, and although she'd let him kiss her goodnight, he'd made it clear a kiss wasn't enough.

'Come on, Jackie. You know what it was like before. We really got on well, didn't we?'

'We were just kids then, Roy. A lot's happened since then. You've been away in the army, and I've been living away from home.'

'And just what does that mean?' he demanded. 'Able to do what you like, that's what, with no one to keep an eye on you.'

'That's not what it means! And I was living with Jennifer Tucker until a couple of months ago. That was the only way Mum and Dad would let me come to Plymouth at all.'

'Don't tell me you don't meet a lot of men, working in that hotel,' he muttered, glancing up at the big building. 'I bet you could be out every night of the week.'

'Maybe, but I'm not. Not that it's any of your business if I was. Look, Roy, I told you, I don't mind going out with you now and then, but there's not going to be any more than that. If you don't like it, we'd better call a halt here and now because I'm tired of all this arguing.'

There was a short silence. Then he said in a grumbling tone, 'You've changed, Jackie, you know that? You're not a bit like the girl you used to be.'

'And isn't that just what I've been telling you?' she asked. 'We've both changed. You just seem to want to go back to Burracombe and settle down like you were before, being a garage mechanic. But I don't want that sort of life. I'm sorry, Roy, but it's never going to work for us now and that's all there is to it. If you can't believe that, like I said, we stop seeing each other at all. I'd be sorry if we did, though,' she added. 'I'd like us to be friends.'

'Friends!' he exclaimed in disgust. 'That's what all girls say, isn't it?' He put on a mincing, falsetto tone. '*I don't love you, but we can still be friends.* Well, I don't think I do want that, thanks very much. I dare say we'll see each other around the village, when you deign to come home, but like you said, that's all. I'm just glad I found out before it was too late!'

He swung away from her, and Jackie sighed and called after him, '*Roy* ...' But he was walking away fast, his head down and his hands thrust deep into his pockets, and he didn't turn. She watched him until he was out of sight and then turned to go in through the staff door.

I did try to tell him, she thought sadly, climbing the stairs to her room. If he'd just been willing to go out together as friends, who knows what might happen after a while? But that's men all over – they want everything all at once; they're just not prepared to give it time. And anyway, what I said was true – Roy and me, we want different things. He's right, it's just as well we both found out, before it was too late.

With a sigh, she undressed and hung her taffeta skirt and smart top in her narrow wardrobe. Goodness knows when I'll wear them again, she thought, now I haven't got a boy to take me out.

'So when are we going to meet Jackie?' Russell enquired at breakfast on Sunday morning. 'Does she come home much or is she a city gal now?'

'Oh, she comes back most weeks.' Alice set a plate of fried potato, eggs, bacon, tomatoes and mushrooms in front of him. 'She don't work regular hours, though, so once in a blue moon she'll pop home for an afternoon in the middle of the week and sometimes it'll be Saturday or Sunday. But she don't manage it *every* week, now she's making her own life in Plymouth.'

'She ought to make an effort to come back and meet her uncle and cousin, though,' Ted said, tackling his own breakfast. He had been up early as usual to milk the cows and was ready for a substantial meal. 'Maybe us ought to ring up the hotel and let her know they're here.'

'Don't do that,' Russell said. 'We'll go to Plymouth and surprise her. Take her out to lunch, maybe. Give her a bit of a treat. D'you know what hours she'll be working this week, Aunt Alice?'

'I'll have a look at the paper she gave me,' Alice said, and ferreted about in one of the dresser drawers. 'Here it is. She'll be working mornings Sunday to Wednesday, then she changes over to afternoons and evenings. Her shifts change at two o'clock, so I'm not sure which would be best if you want to take her out for her dinner. Most places would stop serving by then, and if you took her earlier she'd have to be sure to be back in time.'

'I'm confused already!' Russell said with a grin. 'I guess we'll just wander in one day and see what she has to suggest. She works on the reception desk, didn't you say? Should be easy enough.'

Ted finished his breakfast and stood up. 'I'm off to ring for morning service. I'd say come along for a pull too, Joe, but I reckon it'd be better for you to wait till practice night, being as you haven't touched a rope in thirty years. You coming to service, Alice?'

'Don't I always? And you'm welcome to come too, of course,' she said to Joe and Russell. 'There'll be plenty of folk wanting to have a chat afterwards.'

'Sure we're coming. Never miss church at home.' Joe laid down his knife and fork with a sigh of satisfaction. 'That was a real good breakfast, Alice. Thanks.'

'You're not saying you've finished!' she exclaimed, turning back to the range and lifting a wire toaster off the hotplate. She opened up the two halves to take out four slices of golden toast, and set them into a china toast-rack on the table. 'There's some of our own butter and a pot of Mother's best marmalade to go on it, and there's a jar of honey from Mrs Harvey's bees.'

'And you'll be expected to eat a full Sunday dinner after church,' Joe said to his son. 'Not to mention tea later on, with scones and cream, and probably a sherry trifle.'

Russell stared at him and then at Alice. 'But you didn't even know we'd be here! How did you have this feast ready so quickly?'

'Bless you, 'tis just our normal Sunday,' Alice told him. 'Sunday roast, with our own vegetables, and an apple pie with apples from our own tree, and our own baking at teatime. You'm wrong about the trifle, though,' she added. 'The jelly won't set in time, but we've got a cider cake Mother made a day or two ago and Joanna says she'll make a lemon sponge. With a ham salad and some fresh scones and maybe a dish of junket and our own cream—'

'Stop!' Russell begged. 'I won't be able to move. I'll have to go for a long walk, if there's time between all these banquets.'

'Go on, you'm as daft as the rest of the Tozers,' Alice said, giving him a nudge. ''Tis no more than good country cooking, and don't forget there's eight of us to feed, not to mention our Val and Luke if they comes up for their dinner.'

'And bringing the newest member of the family with them,' Ted added. 'It'll be young Christopher's first outing – three weeks old, he is, and a real little Tozer.'

'I don't know about that,' Alice said. 'I think he's got a look of his father about him. Anyway, Val said they'd only come if the weather was all right to bring him out. It's her first day out too, so her don't want to take no chances. Now, if you've all had enough, I'll get on with the clearing up, and Ted, you might slip upstairs and see if your mother's finished with her tray. We make her stay in bed for her breakfast since she had that turn back in the winter,' she told Joe. 'Once her's up and about, there's no holding her down, if you see what I mean – got to be busy all the time. Don't seem to realise she'm ninety.'

The family got up from the table, Russell and Joe insisting on doing the washing-up while Alice swiftly tidied the big kitchen and put the vegetables out ready for preparation. Sunday dinner was always later than during the rest of the week, she explained, to give her time for church, but Joanna would probably make a start when she came down from feeding Heather. Tom had already had his breakfast and taken Robin out to help take the cows back to their field and wash down the milking-parlour, and Robin had also been entrusted recently with the job of seeing to the hens, letting them out of their shed and collecting the eggs. He came in while Joe and Russell were working, proudly carrying a full basket.

'I can see what you meant about it being a good life,' Russell observed to his father. 'What I'm not so sure about is why you ever left it.'

Joe shrugged. 'It's a good life, all right, but back then it didn't seem there was room for two of us to work the farm, and Ted was always keener than me. I went to America in the first place to see what it had to offer, and it suited me, so I stayed. I guess I had itchy feet.'

'And that's what I reckon our Jackie's got,' Alice said, dumping a large cabbage on the wooden draining-board. 'Itchy feet. But it's to be hoped they won't take her overseas, like they did you. If you ask me, Plymouth's quite far enough away.'

Chapter Eleven

'I wanted to ask you about the christening,' Hilary Napier said. 'Have you decided on a date yet?'

'We thought just before Christmas. Maybe the second Sunday.' Val had just finished giving Christopher his six o'clock feed and propped him on her knee, rubbing his back gently. He let out a loud burp and they all laughed. 'D'you want to hold him for a bit, before I put him to bed?'

'Yes, please.' Hilary held out her arms and Val placed the baby in them. Hilary cuddled him against her, looking down into the tiny face. 'Oh, he's so gorgeous. And you can see a likeness to Luke already, can't you?'

'I think that's the first time anyone's called me gorgeous,' Luke commented from the tiny kitchen, where he was washing up the tea things. 'Even at second-hand.'

'It *is* weird, that a baby can look like Luke and yet still be gorgeous,' Hilary said solemnly. 'But Christopher's managed it. He's obviously a very special baby.'

'He's certainly that,' Val said, and Hilary gave her a quick look of understanding. She was one of the few people who knew about little Johnny, the baby Val had miscarried on the way home from Egypt, and she'd shared her friend's terror when her life, and her baby's, had been threatened during her pregnancy. Motherhood had not come easily to Val, and Hilary wondered if she and Luke would ever dare have a second child.

'Anyway, about this christening,' she said. 'Don't you think it'll be rather cold in December?'

'We can wrap him up well. If we wait for warmer weather, it won't be until spring. And then there's Stella and Felix's wedding just after Christmas, so it's going to be very busy for those last few weeks.'

Hilary nodded. 'And the other godparents are Tom and Felix? You're sure Jackie doesn't mind not being asked? She is your sister, after all.'

'I know, but we had a talk and she's quite happy about it. She knows we've been friends for a long time. And she is Heather's godmother.'

Hilary nodded. Jackie had stood godmother for both Joanna's twins at the service performed not long before Suzanne had died so unexpectedly in her pram. That, as Basil Harvey had pointed out, hadn't been the actual baptism, which had been held in Joanna's bedroom at the farm almost immediately after the twins were born, but had been an opportunity for the godparents to make their promises. She wondered if Val's desire to have her own baby christened so soon had anything to do with what had happened to Suzanne.

'So long as she's not upset. I wouldn't like her to feel I'd pushed her aside. So you're going to be my little godson,' she said to Christopher. 'That means you're going to be very special to me.'

Nobody spoke for a moment, then Val said, 'And how is Rob getting on at Kelly College?'

Hilary rolled her eyes. 'Don't ask. He seems determined not to like it. Not that he's writing much in his letters. We didn't get one at all last week, and then this week he said he doesn't like it and he wants to go home.'

'Back to France?'

'Yes. Mind you, I can understand it – he doesn't seem to have had any choice in what happens to him; but then children don't, do they? They just have to do what adults think is best for them. I suppose it might be different in France.'

'It's a bit different for Rob, too,' Luke said, coming back and sitting on one of the upright chairs by the table. There was only space for two armchairs in the little cottage room. 'He didn't have any real idea why his mother brought him here a few months ago, apart from the fact that his father had been English, and suddenly he found he had a family who owned a big house and a large estate and a grandfather who was looking for an heir. It must have been a shock for a boy of thirteen. And then your father simply took him over and started to try to mould him into a second Baden. I'm not surprised he's in a bit of a panic.'

Hilary stared at him. 'That's rather blunt, Luke.'

'Well, isn't it true? He's got a family at home, hasn't he? A grandmother, an aunt, a brother and sister. Apart from one short visit, he hasn't seen them since June, and he doesn't know when he'll see them again. He's not even going home for Christmas.'

'Well, it hasn't actually been decided yet ...'

'But your father doesn't want him to go, does he?'

'He'd like Rob to have Christmas with us,' Hilary admitted. 'But that means Marianne coming over too, and if she comes she wants to bring the rest of the family.'

'And you don't want that?'

Hilary sighed and looked down at the baby in her arms. 'I know, Luke. It sounds very mean and inhospitable, but – well, Marianne's not an easy person. And we don't really know what she wants.'

'You mean you think she's a gold-digger.'

'Perhaps.' Hilary thought of the French woman's behaviour during the summer. 'Yes, as a matter of fact, I do. Not that she needs to worry, since Father's completely determined to leave the whole estate to Rob anyway.'

'And does anyone know what Rob thinks about that?'

'Luke,' Val said, 'this really isn't any of our business.'

'It's all right, Val,' Hilary said. 'I know anything I say to you two won't go any further, and maybe it's a good thing to talk to someone outside the family about it.' She sighed. 'No, I don't think anyone really knows what goes on inside Rob's head. I've never been able to get close to him. Stephen talked to him a bit in the summer, but he hasn't been home much for the past few weeks. All I do know is that he seems to have made up his mind to be miserable. Father just shrugs and says it's normal for a boy to take a while to settle down, especially if he hasn't any experience of English public schools, and he'll be all right by the end of the term. But I don't know.'

Val stood up and lifted Christopher from Hilary's lap. 'Time for you to go to bed, my boy. You're practically asleep.'

She carried the baby out of the room and up the stairs. Luke and Hilary looked at each other.

'Sorry,' Luke said after a moment. 'I didn't mean to go on like that. I know it's nothing to do with me.'

'It's all right. It's good to hear someone else's point of view.'

'Even Rob's?'

Hilary gave a wry smile. 'You mean we haven't been thinking of him? But Father does nothing else but think about him. Although you're right, he does see Rob as a copy of Baden.'

'He's not, though, is he? And he never can be. He's a French boy, he has no knowledge of English ways, and to be honest, Hilary, I don't think sending him to a public school now is going to be much help. Do you know if he gets bullied?'

Hilary looked at him, startled. 'Oh, I'm sure he doesn't!'

'I'd be willing to bet he does,' Luke said grimly. 'Look, I went to a minor public school myself and I know what goes on. Anyone who's a bit different, who doesn't know the ropes, whose parents aren't part of the network, is going to be an easy target. And bullies like easy targets.'

Hilary rubbed her forehead. 'But Father knows the headmaster well – he explained about Baden and Marianne being married.'

'And you think the head called the whole school together and explained to *them*? Come on, Hilary! They won't know the truth but they'll have sniffed out something odd in Rob's background, and that's enough. I should think the poor lad's got every reason to be miserable. And thinking *about* him – in the way your father does, as a second Baden, an heir, almost as a possession – isn't the same as thinking *of* him and seeing things from his point of view.'

Hilary stared into the fire. 'What do you think we should do?'

Luke shrugged. 'It isn't up to me, is it?'

'No, but I'd value your opinion. You saw quite a bit of Rob during the summer – he was interested in your paintings, he used to go and see you at the charcoal-burner's hut. You probably know him as well as any of us.'

'I don't know if anyone really got to know Rob,' Luke said thoughtfully. 'He's a quiet, enigmatic boy – doesn't give much away. And he seemed rather bewildered by what was going on. But I do think he's more attached to his family – his French family – than anyone's considered. It's natural that he should be. As for what you should do ... Well, that rather depends on how much influence you have over your father.'

'Not much,' she said ruefully. 'As you well know. Father's a law unto himself. But I don't like to think of Rob being unhappy. Maybe you're right, and we haven't given him enough consideration.' She gazed at the flames again and then said, 'I'll give it some more thought, Luke – and thank you.'

'Think nothing of it,' he said with a grin. 'Always happy to give advice where it hasn't been asked for! Anyway, you haven't heard our news yet. Tell her about your rich American relatives, Val,' he added as Val came back into the room.

'Rich American relatives?' Hilary said. 'What's all this about?'

'Oh, Luke thinks all Americans are rich.' Val sat down in the armchair and Luke moved to sit at her feet, leaning back against her knees. She ruffled his thick, dark hair. 'It's Dad's brother – my Uncle Joe – and his son, Russell. They've come over for a visit – arrived yesterday. We met them when we went up to the farm for our Sunday dinner.'

'I don't remember your Uncle Joe,' Hilary said. 'Did he ever come back before this?'

'Years ago – about five years after the Great War, I think. He brought Aunt Eleanor with him that time – it was before they had any family. Before I was born. I suppose they would have come again, but they had their family and then the second war started and everything changed. Aunt Eleanor died about two years ago.

'You should see Granny,' she went on with a smile. 'She's over the moon to see him again. And Russ as well, of course. It's just a shame the two girls couldn't come too, but they've both got families.'

'Russell's not married, then?'

'No, but I bet he's got swathes of girls after him back home – and he'll turn a few heads here, too, I expect. A real heart-throb, he is, with wavy chestnut-coloured hair and blue eyes that look right through you. I'm surprised he's not been snapped up for films. And he's only twenty-five,' she added. 'Too young for you, Hil!'

'Well, thanks for pointing out that I'm old and past it,' Hilary said with dignity. 'Are you sure you want me to be Christopher's godmother? You don't think I'll peg out before he's grown up?'

Val laughed. 'I think you'll stay the course. Anyway, you'll meet Russ soon, and you can make up your own mind. Uncle Joe would be a good catch too,' she added thoughtfully. 'Only just over sixty … He could be your sugar-daddy – *ow*! You shouldn't throw cushions at people who've not long given birth.'

'I don't know why I came here,' Hilary said. 'I can stay at home if I want to be insulted ... Have you seen Travis and Jennifer yet, by the way? They're more like two lovebirds than ever – quite sickening.'

'I wouldn't ever call Travis Kellaway a lovebird,' Val said. 'But Jennifer looks as if she's walking on air. She called in soon after they got back from their honeymoon and we almost didn't need the light on, her eyes were so bright.'

'Yes, it's nice to see her so happy,' Hilary said, determined that no one should pity her because Travis hadn't chosen her for his bride. She knew that the village had expected it, and for a while she'd half hoped for it herself. 'Jennifer's just the right wife for him. I'm just sorry you couldn't have the estate manager's house. I still feel guilty about not being able to let you have it, after I'd promised it to you.'

'Don't worry about that. We like being in the middle of the village. And as long as Jennifer lives in Wood Cottage – nice name, don't you think? – we can stay here. So don't give Travis the sack, will you, or they may decide to turn us out and live here themselves!'

Luke got up. 'I'm going to make some coffee. All right for you two? And then I thought we might ask Jacob in and have a game of cards. Or you can just sit and natter, if you'd rather.'

'A game of cards sounds fine,' Hilary said, smiling at the thought of her father's reaction when she went home and told him she'd been playing cards with the village roadman. Colonel Napier was very conscious of his position as squire, but for Hilary and her friends things had changed considerably since the war, and class played little part in her relationships with local people. She knew Jacob Prout for the fine man he really was, and some of her father's friends – Arnold Cherriman, for one – for the snobs and bullies they were, and she would rather spend an evening with Jacob any day.

The evening passed in several cut-throat rounds of Solo, and Hilary walked home smiling. But as she drew nearer the Barton, she remembered Luke's remarks about her dead brother Baden's son Robert, and her smile faded.

We've never given that child enough thought, she told herself. He's so quiet, we just assumed he'd go along with everything, but look what we've done to him – torn him away from his real family as if they don't matter any more, arranged his whole life over his head, without any kind of consultation, used him as an object rather than a human being. We've been thoughtless and unkind. We may even have been cruel.

Had her father been fair to the boy, or had he ridden roughshod over him in his desire to have an heir for the estate?

And if so, was he doomed to disappointment?

Chapter Twelve

Stella was spending Sunday evening at the vicarage in Little Burracombe, with Felix. It had become a habit for her to attend morning service in Burracombe itself, then walk across the old footbridge to the smaller village, where Felix would be just finishing his own service. One of the village women, who looked after the house for him while he was still a bachelor, would prepare the vegetables for a roast dinner and put the joint into the oven before going to church herself, leaving Stella to finish the cooking when she arrived. They would then enjoy a peaceful afternoon before Evensong at six thirty, and Felix would bring Stella back to Dottie's at about ten.

Dottie had cold meat and pickles for her supper and sat in her armchair, knitting a new cardigan for Val's baby while she listened to *Grand Hotel* and *Sunday Half-Hour* on the wireless. Her cat, Albert, lay stretched to his full length on the rag rug in front of the fire, which Dottie had lit for the first time this evening. Jacob had brought in some logs from an old apple tree he had cut down the previous year, and the sweet aroma filled the little living room. The dark red curtains were drawn against the sharp cool of the evening and the room felt very snug.

After a while, Dottie laid her knitting in her lap and stared into the fire. There seemed to be almost too much to think about these days. Baby Christopher bringing new life and joy to the Tozer family after their sadness; Stella's wedding, only two months away now, and all the dresses yet to be made; poor little Maddy, still grieving for her lost fiancé Sammy; and now the return of Joe Tozer with his boy Russell, all bringing new ideas and old memories to jostle together in her mind.

A knock on the door jerked her out of her thoughts and she put her knitting on the little table beside her chair and hurried to answer it. For a moment, blinking into the darkness, she didn't recognise the bulky figure standing there. Or maybe it was because she was still half lost in the past.

'Aren't you going to ask me in, Dottie?' Joe asked, his American accent still faintly tinged with a Devon burr, and she stepped back hurriedly.

'Joe? You caught me by surprise. I don't get visitors on a Sunday evening as a rule.'

'That's why I came,' he said, bending his head to come through the doorway. 'Alice said your young lady lodger – Miss Simmons, is it? – was likely to be over the water with the young vicar for the evening, and I thought it'd be good to have an hour or two together on our own. Catch up with old times, and all that.' He stood looking around the little room. 'Hasn't changed much. I remember that old corner cupboard from when your ma and pa lived here – when you were just a slip of a girl.' His eyes met hers, and Dottie blushed and looked away.

'That's a long time ago now, Joe.'

'It sure is. Mind if I sit down?' He glanced at her knitting and took the chair opposite, on the other side of the fireplace, his eyes taking in the beams on the ceiling and the big stones of the fireplace. 'Just as cosy as ever.'

'I suppose it looks very small and poor to you,' she said a little tartly, taking her own seat and heaving Albert on to her lap. 'But it's been my home all my life, and I like it.'

'Sure you do. Why not? And it doesn't look small and poor at all. Don't forget I grew up in Burracombe – I was in and out of this cottage all the time. Like I said, it's cosy. But didn't you go away for a while? To London?'

'Yes, for a while. I was a dresser in the theatre. I came back when the war started.'

Joe nodded. 'I was sorry I wasn't here. Felt I ought to be helping the old country.'

'You did your bit in the first lot,' Dottie said soberly. 'And you wouldn't have wanted to be here, Joe, not really. I remember the night Plymouth was blitzed. It was just terrible. Knowing all those poor

souls were being bombed and burned to death in the buildings …'
She shuddered.

'It was a bad time,' he said quietly. 'A bad time all round.'

They sat for a few moments, gazing into the fire, each busy with their own thoughts. Then Dottie said, 'And how about you, Joe? Have you had a good life?'

'I have, Dottie. America suited me from the start, and I was lucky to find a woman like Eleanor. Not that there weren't quite a few things I missed about Burracombe,' he added, glancing at Dottie again. 'Specially to begin with. I was pretty homesick for quite a while.'

'You never thought to come back, though? Except for that one visit?'

'No, I didn't – never seriously, anyway. There just didn't seem to be much going for me here. Dad and Ted had the farm pretty well under control, and Ted was married to Alice – it was obvious they were making the place their home. Not that I begrudged 'em, mind. I'd been away in the Great War and then got that damned flu. Stood to reason Ted was going to make the best of his chance, and why not? I'd have done the same. But farming was never in my blood the way it's in his, and when I got my chance – to make something of myself in the building trade in America – I took it. And I never regretted it.'

'Even though you were there right through the Depression?' she said. 'You did well for yourself, Joe.'

'I was lucky. Right place at the right time. And I found a good woman to be my wife, too – that was the luckiest thing of all.'

'I'm glad you did, though I'm sorry you've lost your wife now. But you've got a good family. Two daughters married with their own children, and a fine son.'

'Yes, I've been very blessed.'

There was a short silence; then he said, 'I was surprised to find you'd never married, Dottie. You must have had plenty of chances.'

'Oh, I don't know – maybe I never looked for them. Theatre people weren't my sort, and when I came back to Burracombe after the war started I was past the age to be looking for a man. And then the actress that I used to dress – Fenella Forsyth – brought little Maddy for me to look after, and I made my own life here. Never really looked for nothing else.'

'Alice mentioned a little girl. Your lodger's sister, isn't she?'

'That's right. Maddy – well, her first name was Muriel but Miss Forsyth didn't care for that. She changed it to Madeleine, but us couldn't get our tongues round that so Maddy her became. Pretty little dear, and she's grown up into a lovely young woman, but had a sad time of it this past year.' She gave him a brief account of Maddy's ill-fated romance with Sammy Hodges. 'Knocked down and killed in front of her very eyes, he was, the day they got engaged. She haven't got over it yet, not by a long way.'

'That's terrible. Does she still live hereabouts?'

'No, she works as a secretary for the Archdeacon of West Lyme, up the coast. He's Felix Copley's uncle. They look after her well there, but at a time like this a young woman needs her mother, and that's just what poor little Maddy don't have.'

'She has you, though. You must have been a mother to her.'

'Never quite enough,' Dottie said sadly. 'It's somebody who's been through the same thing that she needs. Somebody who knows what 'tis like to have loved and lost.'

They were silent again, and presently she reached out and put another log on the fire. 'Joe, I don't know what I'm thinking of! I haven't even offered you a cup of tea. Or are you so American now you only drink coffee?'

'No thanks, Dottie. I guess I'll have to be going. They go to bed early at the farm and I don't want to disturb them, coming home at all hours.'

'All hours!' she said with a laugh. 'Why, 'tis only a quarter to ten. You'm right, mind – us keeps early hours here in Burracombe. But don't go just yet – Stella will be home any minute and you can say hello to her and young Felix. In fact, I reckon that'll be them now.'

A moment later the two came in, smiling and bright-eyed after their moonlit walk across from the other village. Dottie introduced them, and they shook hands all round before Joe said his goodbyes and left, promising to come again soon.

'Come to tea one afternoon, when Stella's home from school,' Dottie invited him. 'And bring that handsome son of yours. It's time Felix here had a bit of competition to keep him up to the mark!'

Maddy herself was going to bed at much the same time as her friends in Burracombe. She had spent the week going quietly about her work, with little to say to anyone, although each time the Archdeacon or his wife had asked if anything were troubling her, she had shaken her head and turned their questions aside. Wisely, they had left the matter there, but she had caught them looking at her once or twice with concern and been tempted to pour out everything – the news of Ruth's baby, the unkind things Stella and Felix had said to her, even the way nobody had been around in Burracombe when she'd arrived there in such need. But whenever she found herself on the brink, she had drawn back, aware of that tiny, whispering voice that suggested that perhaps she was wrong to mind so much about the baby; that perhaps Stella and Felix were right to imply that she was spoiled and selfish.

And what if I am? she asked herself indignantly. Would that be my fault? Children don't ask to be spoiled. It's the people around them, giving in to them all the time, who spoil them. Stella's right – Daddy did call me his little princess and make a fuss of me. And Fenella did give me everything I wanted, and take me to London and France with her when she was acting. But was that my fault? In any case, I don't think I am spoiled. I can remember lots of times when I didn't get what I wanted. And Dottie certainly never spoiled me.

Gradually, however, she began to feel that, although a child might not be able to help being indulged and spoiled, an adult had a choice. You could learn to be unselfish. You could decide to think about other people. You didn't have to spend your entire life screaming and stamping your feet when things didn't go exactly as you wanted.

Had she really been doing that? Surely this was different. She was mourning the man she'd loved best in all the world, angry because he'd lost his life. And she was hurt for *him*, that other people didn't seem to feel the same.

Especially those people who *ought* to feel the same. Especially Ruth and Dan.

Chapter Thirteen

'We're really going to have to do something about Maddy,' Stella said to Felix a few days later. 'I've heard nothing from her since she went back to West Lyme. Whatever we may think about the Hodges and their new baby, she's really upset about it, and I don't like to think of her being so unhappy.'

'I know. I'd suggest going to see her, but it's not easy when you only have weekends off and Sunday's my busy day.'

'Next weekend's half-term,' Stella said thoughtfully. 'We get Friday and Monday off. But then Maddy will be working too.'

'Oh, I'll speak to my uncle about that,' Felix declared. 'He'll understand. They must realise she's miserable, even if she hasn't told them why. They probably think she's going through a bad patch over Sammy, but in any case they'll be pleased if we can cheer her up.'

'I feel sorry for Ruth and Dan, too,' Stella said. 'They must be upset about the way she's reacted. It's such a shame.'

'Why don't we go and scoop her up and bring her home for the weekend? It'll do her good to be back here. If I know Maddy, she's just desperate to see you again but frightened of making the first move. We were a bit harsh with her, you know – at least, I think I was.'

'Yes, I think that would be good,' Stella agreed with relief. 'I'll ask Dottie if she can stay with us. I might mention it to Hilary as well – she could ask Stephen to come too, if he can get a weekend pass.'

'Are you sure that's wise? I got the impression that Stephen's keeping his distance a bit. Maddy's never really given him much encouragement.'

'She needed time to come to terms with losing Sammy, and she probably needs a lot more yet, but Stephen's been a good friend to her and he usually manages to put a smile on her face. I'm sure he'll come if he can.'

Stephen Napier, however, declined to come home for the weekend to distract Maddy from her woes. 'I've wangled a lot of weekend passes over the past few months,' he told his sister when Hilary telephoned the RAF airfield where he was stationed. 'I can't get any more for a while. And Maddy's made it pretty clear that there's not much chance for me, anyway. A chap has to know when to give up.'

'But not yet, Stephen, surely,' Hilary pleaded. She had known Maddy since she was a child and the actress Fenella Forsyth, who had been a friend of her mother's, had brought her to stay with the Napiers before taking her to live with Dottie Friend. The thought of Maddy as a sister-in-law was much more attractive to her than the French woman, Marianne Aucoin. 'It's still only a few months since Sammy died. She needs more time.'

'She needs more than that,' Stephen said crisply. 'She needs to feel something more for me than just friendship. There was a time when I thought … But it didn't happen and now I don't think it ever will. It's best if I keep away.'

'It isn't just that, though, is it?' Hilary said quietly. 'It's Marianne as well. But, Steve, you don't need to keep away from her – she's not even here. She's back in France.'

Stephen was silent for a moment. Then he said, 'It doesn't make any difference whether she's there or not, Hil. What happened with Marianne still comes between me and Maddy, even though Maddy knows nothing about it. It's a secret I can't get rid of, and I don't think it's ever going to go away.'

Hilary opened her mouth to reply, but he had already put down the phone. With a sigh, she replaced her own receiver and turned away.

Marianne Aucoin had a lot to answer for, with her hasty early marriage to Baden, and her decision to bring their son Robert to Burracombe so many years later. And, more than that, with her attempt to seduce Stephen, which, if it had been successful, would have brought chaos to the family; and had already resulted in his deliberate absence.

And she's coming here for Christmas, Hilary thought despondently, with her other children as well as Robert. Will Stephen come home then? Or have we lost him completely?

'I didn't think you'd ever want to see me again,' Maddy said tearfully when Stella and Felix arrived at the Archdeacon's house on Friday. 'I've been such a pig.'

'No, you haven't,' Stella declared, hugging her tightly. 'You were just shocked and upset. Anyone would have been.'

'I don't know,' Maddy said. 'I don't think they would. *You* wouldn't.'

'You don't know that. I don't know myself how I'd have been. Anyway, don't let's talk about it any more. You're coming home with us for the weekend. It's all right –' as Maddy opened her mouth to object, 'Felix has already arranged it with his uncle. You can spend the weekend in Burracombe with us, seeing all your old friends and just relaxing, and we'll bring you back again on Monday. All you have to do is pack your case.'

'And there's no hurry,' Felix added, kissing Maddy's cheek. 'We're staying to lunch. I arranged that with my aunt!'

'It's true, though,' Maddy insisted later as they drove back along the undulating hills of Dorset. 'I'm behaving as if I want everyone to be unhappy because I'm unhappy. That's what it amounts to, isn't it? Just a nasty, spoiled little brat who doesn't care about anyone but her—'

'Now, just stop that, this minute', Felix said sternly. 'You're not at all selfish, Maddy. You may be unhappy, but that doesn't make you selfish. It makes you see things differently, that's all, but that won't last.'

'How do you know that? I might be like this for the rest of my life. You were right the other day, when you said I'd never had to think about anyone but myself. Everyone's done my thinking for me – my mother and father, Fenella, Dottie – I've always been looked after. I haven't *had* to think about anyone else. So why should I change now?'

'Because,' he said steadily, his eyes on the road ahead, 'you're a very nice young woman, who *does* care about other people. That's why so many people have loved you and looked after you. People don't generally love spoiled brats or selfish pigs – they avoid them like the plague. How many of your friends avoid you, Maddy?'

'Well – none, that I can think of. But I just happen to have some very good friends. I don't know why. I don't deserve to be so lucky.'

'It's not luck! It's because of who you are. Look, we can't talk while I'm driving.' They were passing through the village of Charmouth as he spoke, and he turned left, down the winding lane that led to the sea. Nobody spoke again until they arrived at the end of the road, and Felix stopped the car.

The sea lay spread before them, a glittering expanse of blue waves topped by the foamy manes of white horses. The beach was covered in large, round pebbles leading to silver sands, and on either side rose the steep, green downs of the Dorset cliffs. Although it was October, the fine weather and half-term holiday had brought a good many families to picnic for perhaps the last time that year, and the air was filled with laughter.

They sat gazing at the scene for a few moments, then Felix turned in his seat and spoke to Maddy again.

'Maddy, it's not surprising you feel as you do. It takes a long time to get over what you've been through, and of course you feel that nobody else can understand. But we do try, you know. And we all love you and want the best for you.'

Maddy's eyes filled with tears. 'I feel in such a muddle,' she whispered. 'I don't want to be like this, but I can't seem to help it. I want to be happy again, but every time I start to smile I think of Sammy – he'll never smile again – and ...' Her voice broke and she heaved a great sob.

Stella leaned over the back of her seat and put her arm around Maddy's shoulders, drawing her close. 'Maddy, darling, don't cry.'

'No,' Felix said. 'Let her cry. She needs to let it out. Cry as much as you like, Maddy, and for as long as you like, and we'll cry with you.'

'Oh, Felix,' Maddy said through her sobs, 'you don't really want to do that. Nobody does. They don't want to be upset, so they tell me not to cry.'

'No!' Stella exclaimed. 'I just don't like seeing *you* upset.'

'But I *am* upset. I'm upset all the time. "Not crying" doesn't change that – I just cry inside, or when I'm by myself.'

'And what you really want,' Felix said, 'is a shoulder to cry on. Someone to listen and share your tears. That's why you feel you can't go to the Hodges any more, because you think they're happy again – they've no more tears to shed. They have, of course, but it's true that life has changed for them now and you know that. And that's why we've come to fetch you back to Burracombe for a few days – so that you can cry as much as you like. And we'll be there to listen to all you want to say.'

Maddy stared at him and then burst into helpless sobs all over again. Stella cast Felix an anxious look and pulled Maddy even closer.

'I wish I could sit in the back with you, but that seat's too small. Let's get her home, Felix.'

He started the car again and Maddy found a hanky. She wiped her face and blew her nose, then gave them both a shaky smile. 'I'll be all right now. Till next time, anyway. But … I still want to say I'm sorry.'

'There's nothing to be sorry about,' Felix said, and Stella murmured her agreement. 'This is a horrible time you're going through, and you're doing very well.'

Maddy looked doubtful, but dried her eyes and the journey continued with only the occasional long, shaky sob from the back seat. Stella glanced over her shoulder a few times, and after a while, she whispered to Felix, 'I think she's asleep.'

'Good,' he said. 'That's another thing she needs. Sleep always helps.'

Stella was silent for a moment, then she said, 'How do you know all that, Felix? About letting people cry, I mean.'

'Well, I am a vicar,' he said drily, 'and vicars are supposed to know those kinds of things. But it's also something I've noticed for myself – something many of us tend to do. We ask someone who's been bereaved how they are, but we often don't really want to hear the truth. We don't really want the person to break down and cry and tell us how unhappy they are. What we really want is the brave smile, the stiff upper lip, and then we can feel that we've shown the proper sympathy without risking being drawn any further into the sadness. And the bereaved person, who longs to pour it all out, is cut off short.'

'But that sounds so callous. Surely people aren't really as hardhearted as that?'

'No, they're not, but a lot of us just don't know how to deal with grief. We're afraid of where it might lead, and we're afraid of breaking down ourselves – as if somehow we haven't as much *right* to grieve. When really all we need to do is listen, and give whatever comfort we can, by simply sharing the sadness.'

Stella considered. 'Perhaps we are afraid we *can't* give comfort. We think we'll just make things worse, and we don't know what to say. That's how I've felt myself, at times.'

'You don't have to say anything. Just be *there*. And cry too, if that's how you feel. It has to be better than turning away.'

She turned to him and put her hand on his knee. 'You're very wise, Felix.'

'I know,' he said with the grin that so often broke through when he had been serious for a while. 'I just hide it well!'

Over the next two days, Stella and Dottie took Felix's advice and listened as Maddy poured out her heart to the two people who knew her best. They wept with her when her sadness cast its shadow over their own hearts, and even smiled once or twice as she recalled the fun and mischief she and Sammy had shared as children. By Sunday evening, none of them was really sure that she felt better for it, but enough tears had been shed to fill a small swimming pool. When Felix came round after Evensong, he found three bemused faces awaiting him.

'Of course you all feel rather shaken just at the moment,' he said when Stella greeted him at the door with a half-hearted kiss. 'You've been through it all over again – at least, Maddy has, and you've shared it with her. It's like reliving the shock. Where is she, by the way?'

'Upstairs, lying down.' Stella turned as Maddy's footsteps sounded on the stairs, and said in a low voice, 'Honestly, Felix, I don't know if it's done any good at all. Isn't there a point when we've just got to put it in the past?'

'Yes, and you'll all come to it eventually. But you do have to go through this first. It's a catharsis.' He turned to greet Maddy. 'Maddy, sweetheart, how are you feeling?'

'As if I've been through Dottie's mangle,' she said with a wan smile. 'I don't seem to have any strength left.' She looked at her sister. 'I heard what you said, and I think you're right. I do have to put it in the past – eventually. But I don't think I can just yet. I'm simply not strong enough.'

'You're working towards it,' Felix told her. 'And you may not realise it, but you've just taken a step forward by saying that. I don't think you could have said it a few days ago, could you?'

Maddy looked at him in surprise. 'No – I don't think I could. But – oh, Felix, even by *thinking* it, I feel as if I'm betraying Sammy and then it all floods over me again. It's as if I feel guilty even to *think* I could be happy again one day. I don't have the right.'

'You do have the right,' he said gently. 'But all you need to take is one little step at a time. You don't have to rush. And now let's think about tomorrow. Why don't we all go out somewhere?'

'Can you?' Stella asked. 'You took Friday off, after all, and Maddy's going back to West Lyme tomorrow.'

'Well, I'm not thinking about going a long way. Just for a good walk, to clear the cobwebs away before we run Maddy back. I thought we could go to Pork Hill and walk up Staple Tor.'

'Goodness, it's ages since I've been up there,' Maddy said. 'It's a beautiful spot – the views are wonderful. Yes, let's do that. But you don't need to take me back, Felix. I'll go by train.'

'Oh, no—' Stella began, but Felix laid his hand on her arm and she stopped and looked at him enquiringly. He smiled at her and began to discuss what time train Maddy should catch, and how long that gave them for their walk.

'Why did you stop me?' she asked when Maddy had gone upstairs and Dottie was in the kitchen, preparing a snack for their supper. 'I thought we'd already decided to take her home.'

'Yes, but haven't we also decided that Maddy needs to start thinking for herself? Deciding to go home by train instead of depending on us is another step towards that.' He touched her cheek. 'You're the one who can help her most, you know – by letting her go.'

'You mean I've been doing too much for her? Mollycoddling her? But she's been through so much.'

'Yes, and she wouldn't have come this far without your support – yours and Dottie's. But now it's time to stand back a little. She's made her start, and the best thing we can do is support her in that – by not treating her like a little girl any more.'

Stella looked down and brushed her hand across her eyes. 'I suppose I've always done that,' she said a little shakily. 'She was my little sister and I used to look after her through all the bombing, especially after Thomas was born. When Mum was killed and we were evacuated, she depended on me even more. And then we were separated for all those years – and when I did find her again, she was still my little sister, even though she'd grown up and had a much more sophisticated life with Fenella than I'd had.'

'You never went through the growing-up period together,' he said. 'You'd have let go of her then and become friends, instead of big and little sister. It didn't really matter while everything was going well for you both, but now, it's got to happen rather too suddenly. She really does need to finish her growing-up now.'

Stella nodded. 'I see what you mean. All right – we'll have our walk and then put her on the afternoon train. And just hope that this weekend has done her good.'

Felix looked at her gravely. 'Don't expect miracles, darling. It's a long and weary road that Maddy has to travel, but she'll get there in the end.'

Stella smiled. 'Don't expect miracles? Felix, you're a vicar – a miracle is just what you *should* be telling me to expect! And perhaps one will happen – who knows?'

'Who knows indeed,' Felix said and got up to open the door for Dottie, who was pushing against it with a loaded tray in her hands. 'Now, that's what I call a Sunday-evening snack! Dottie, you've laid on a feast.'

'I thought you'd need a bite of summat after Evensong,' she said, setting the tray on the table. 'I don't suppose you had much before you went. And these two girls have been eating like birds all weekend.'

Felix eyed the tray. 'There still seems to be a lot here, for the four of us. Are you expecting someone else?'

Dottie blushed. 'Well, maybe I am. To tell the truth, Ted Tozer's brother Joe, that's over from America, said he might pop in, and I told him to bring his boy along as well. I thought it might be good for Maddy to see a couple of new faces in Burracombe before she goes back.'

'New faces?' Maddy asked, appearing at the foot of the stairs. She had washed her own face and put on just enough make-up to brighten her lips and colour her pale cheeks. 'Who's that, then?'

Her question was answered by a knock on the door, and a moment later Joe Tozer and his son were in the room. Stella and Felix, who had already met Joe, stood up and there was a flurry of introductions as Maddy shook hands.

Russ Tozer stood for a moment or two, looking down at her. For an instant, they were both quite still. It was as if everyone had stopped breathing.

Then Dottie bustled forward. 'Sit you down, do. You look as if you'm waiting for a bus. Joe, you sit in that armchair by the fire, and Russell, you have the one the other side. Felix and Stella had better have the settee, since they'm such lovebirds.' She surveyed them with satisfaction as Maddy took one of the only two chairs left and then jumped up again to help hand round the plates. ''Tis a pleasure to see you here at last, Joe and Russell. Pass them those meat patties, Maddy, there's a dear, while they'm hot from the oven.'

Maddy did as she was told. As she held out the plate to Russell, their eyes met and she felt a shiver run through her body. For the rest of the evening, she sat as far away from Russell Tozer as she could, and she made sure that their eyes did not meet again.

Chapter Fourteen

Jackie was coming to the end of her morning shift at the hotel reception desk, when she glanced up and saw two men standing in front of her. For a moment she stared, puzzled, and then she realised who they were.

'You must be Uncle Joe! And Russell.' Her colour rose with shyness and delight. 'Have you come all the way to Plymouth to see me?'

'Not only that,' Joe said, leaning across to give her a kiss. 'We're going to take you out to lunch. You're finished work for the day, I guess?'

'I'm off until seven this evening.' She looked from one to the other. 'Mum told me you might come. You really are like Dad, aren't you?'

'Sure – we were always like twins, Ted and me. And young Russ here's the younger version. Stop staring, Russ, and say hello to your pretty cousin.'

Russell laughed and shook Jackie's hand across the desk. 'It's a pleasure to meet you. I guess that makes the full set.'

'Full set?' Jackie asked.

'The whole family. We've got all the Burracombe ones and you're the only one to have made the break. Like Dad did.'

Jackie glanced at her uncle. 'Well, not exactly. I mean, he went to America – I've only got as far as Plymouth.'

'That's just the start,' Russell declared. 'I can see you're a girl who's going to go places. And why not America? There'd be a welcome for you over there, sure enough.' He tilted his chestnut head to one side and winked at her. 'Now, how about that lunch?'

Jackie felt her colour rise again. She stepped back, fiddling with the papers on the shelf below the desk. 'Well, I've just got to tidy up here, and then run up to my room to change. The other receptionist has to take over – oh, there you are, Sheila.' She felt a wave of relief as an older girl, wearing a smart grey suit, came through the inner door. 'I'm just about ready. Er – this is my Uncle Joe, from America. And this is my cousin – Russell.'

'Russ,' he said, with a warm smile. 'Pleasure to meet you, Sheila. Tell you something, if I'd known there were such pretty receptionists in Plymouth I might have decided to stay down here rather than at the farmhouse!'

Jackie blushed again and muttered something as she escaped from the desk. She had known, of course, that her uncle and cousin were likely to come to the hotel to see her, but she hadn't bargained for Russ being quite so good-looking. Why, he could be in films! Jackie was a connoisseur of male American film stars and considered him well up to the standard of James Stewart, James Mason or even Clark Gable. Those eyes! That crinkly, chestnut hair! And that *smile* ...

As swiftly as she could, she washed her face, replaced her make-up and brushed her hair. Thank goodness the hotel insisted on a high standard of dress in its staff – she could at least feel she looked her best as she slipped out of her grey costume and dithered for a moment over whether to wear her new autumn-coloured tartan skirt and tan jumper, or her blue dress. The autumn colours won, and she pulled the jumper over her head, aware of how it hugged her slim figure, and slipped her feet into her new brown court shoes. The whole outfit was new, bought only a week or two ago, and this was the first time she had worn it. Feeling the pleasure of being dressed entirely in new clothes, even if nobody but herself knew it, she pulled her best jacket round her shoulders and ran downstairs and into the foyer where her uncle and cousin were waiting.

'Well, there's a transformation,' Russ greeted her. 'From efficient businesswoman to glamorous young lady about town. Let me offer you my arm.' He crooked his elbow and Jackie slipped her hand through it, sliding a sideways glance at the other receptionist to see if she was watching. They sailed out through the front door and down the steps.

'I don't know where we can go for lunch at this time,' Jackie said anxiously. 'The cafés and restaurants will have stopped serving – not that there's much here anyway, they're still rebuilding after the war.'

'And making a pretty good job of it, too,' Russell said, glancing down to the wide thoroughfare of Royal Parade, with its big new department stores along one side and the old church of St Andrew on the other. 'But there's no need to worry. Dad and I thought of that and we made a reservation at the Continental. Reckoned you wouldn't want to eat in your own hotel – you can do that any day. It would be like eating at the works canteen!'

'Well, not quite,' Jackie said with a laugh. 'There's not much comparison between the Duke of Cornwall and a works canteen! But the staff don't eat in the restaurant. I don't think they'd like me going there, even in my time off.'

'That's what we thought,' Joe said. 'Best to be on different territory. And afterwards you can show us a bit of Plymouth, if you've got time.'

They walked across the road to Plymouth's other large hotel. Both had survived the terrible bombing of Plymouth during the Blitz, when scarcely one brick had been left standing on another over most of the city. St Andrew's church, too, had survived, even though as no more than a shell, and someone had nailed a piece of wood over its door the morning after it was hit with the word 'Resurgam' burned into it. It was almost impossible to imagine what it had been like then, even though there was still so much rebuilding to be done.

'We could see the light of the flames from Burracombe,' Jackie said as they stood at the door, gazing over the city. 'It was like the most amazing sunset you ever saw, with orange light spreading all over the sky and huge tongues of flame leaping across, and the bombs exploding like thunder. I was only about seven years old but I can remember it. Mum and Grandma were crying but Dad just stood there saying nothing. I shall never forget the look on his face. And next day we heard about it on the news. They didn't say it was Plymouth, of course, just "a town on the south coast". But we all knew they meant Plymouth.'

'It's unimaginable,' Russell said quietly. 'To think of waking up next morning – if you'd got any sleep at all, which I don't suppose many people did – and coming out of your house to find your city flattened. I don't know how people got through it.'

'They did, though. Mum's told me about it since – how shop girls picked their way through the rubble to get to work, if their shops hadn't been destroyed, and how people helped each other out. There was one little shop, blown almost to bits, and the owners had put up a sign saying "Temporarily Closed". It was terrible but it just made people more determined not to be beaten.'

'That's the British for you,' Joe said. 'Stubborn as mules. And Churchill was the most stubborn of the lot. He said out loud what everyone felt in their hearts but didn't know how to put into words. He gave 'em the courage to go on.'

They stood a moment or two longer, and then turned and went into the hotel. Although it was well after two, the restaurant was still serving lunches, and they sat at a table by the window and ordered roast lamb for Jackie and steak for the two men. Then they looked at each other, Jackie feeling suddenly shy again.

'So,' Russ said, a warm smile in his eyes, 'tell us all about yourself, Jackie. You prefer city life to the farm, I guess.'

'Yes, I do. It's not that I don't like Burracombe – it's my home. But it seems so small, and narrow. There's a big world outside, and I want to see it. I want to be *part* of it.' She stopped and blushed. 'I suppose that sounds silly to you.'

'It doesn't at all,' Joe said. 'It's exactly how I felt, back in 1919. I'd seen a bit of the world by then, mark you, but it wasn't the bit I had in mind – the mud of the trenches in France wasn't my idea of a good time.' He fell silent for a moment. 'It was good to be back home after that, but I wanted to see more. I always wanted to know what was round the next corner, if you get my meaning.'

'Yes, I do!' she cried. 'There's so *much* to see, so much to do. So many places and people … I don't think I even want to stay in Plymouth for long. I want to go to London. Or to Paris, or Rome. Maybe even …' She stopped again and Russell finished the sentence for her.

'Maybe even America?'

Jackie clasped her hands. 'I'd like to go there more than anywhere else on earth,' she breathed.

The waiter brought their food and they stopped talking to unfold their napkins and pass each other salt and pepper. When they had taken a few mouthfuls, Joe said with a twinkle, 'I guess when you say America, what you really mean is Hollywood. All the girls want to go there and meet the film stars – they think they'll run into Clark Gable or Gregory Peck on every street corner.'

Jackie grinned. 'Well, I can't say I wouldn't like that! Have you seen Gregory Peck's new film – *Roman Holiday*? It's *so* romantic.'

'I saw that,' Russell nodded. 'It's a great movie, shows a fantastic picture of Rome, and that new little actress, Audrey Hepburn, is a real honey.'

Jackie, who had been thinking of having her hair cut short, like Audrey Hepburn's, made up her mind to go to the hairdresser the first chance she got.

'Will you be going anywhere like that while you're over here?' she asked a little wistfully. 'Rome, I mean? Or are you going to stay in Burracombe for your whole visit?'

'No, I guess we'll be touring around a bit. I'd certainly like to see something of the Continent. You have to take these chances when they come, you never know if they'll happen again.'

Joe gave Jackie a quizzical look. 'And there's a lot more to America than Hollywood. You ought to come and have a look at us, in New York State.'

Jackie paused with her fork half way to her mouth. 'New York?'

'New York *State*,' he repeated. 'Not the city itself, although you'd enjoy that too, I guess. No, we live in Corning – a real nice little town about four hours' drive from the city. It's famous for making glass, but the original glassmakers came from England.'

'Yeah, you really ought to come over for a visit,' Russell urged her. 'The girls would love to meet you and I'd show you around – you'd have a great time.'

Jackie gazed at him. Going to America, which had long been a secret dream, suddenly seemed to be a possibility. And if she was going to be with family, how could her parents object?

She tried to remember the details of her American relatives. Until now, particularly as communication had been difficult during the war, she hadn't taken much interest in them and had only a hazy idea as to where they lived. Now, however, they had become very real and the idea of visiting them was like opening a door into a new and exciting world.

'It's too expensive,' she said at last, dismal reality setting in. 'I couldn't even afford the fare, and then there's all the expense of being there. Even if I was staying with you, I'd still need to pay for things. I'd want to be properly independent.'

'Of course you would,' Russell said. 'That's why you'd be coming. But you needn't be with the family all the time, if you don't want to. Save up the fare, and you can just stay with us till you find your feet. We could even find you a job.'

'A *job*?'

'Sure. Work for a few months, maybe a year or so, travel about a bit. Or have you got a sweetheart here you wouldn't want to leave?'

Jackie thought briefly of Roy Pettifer. 'No, there isn't anyone special at the moment.'

'Well, then,' Russell said, 'keep it that way until you come over.'

He spoke as if it were settled. Jackie looked at her plate, her thoughts whirling. Go to America? Work there for a few months, a year – maybe even *stay* there? Suppose she met someone really special . . . She might even meet a film star . . .

'Mum and Dad would go mad,' she said at last. 'They'd never agree.'

'Mine weren't too keen either,' Joe said. 'But heck, it was my life! So I went anyway, and I guess they came round in the end.'

Jackie thought of her grandmother, reading Joe's letters over and over again, writing back every week. 'I think Grandma always missed you.'

'Yeah, I guess she did,' Joe admitted. 'And maybe it was a bit different for me, being a man and having already been overseas. But things are different for women now, aren't they? You're a whole lot more independent than your ma could ever have been.'

'A bit, perhaps. The war made a difference – girls left home then to go in the forces or to be Land Girls, like Joanna. But since it ended – well, when the men came home, the women were just expected to go back to the way they'd been before, staying at home to be wives and mothers. Some have careers but there still isn't all that much they can do except be teachers or nurses, or have jobs like mine – hotel work, or an office. They can't really be properly independent; they can't get mortgages to buy their own houses, or that sort of thing.'

'It'll come,' Russ said with certainty. 'The changes are there – they've started. And it's young women like you, Jackie, striking out on your own, who'll make it happen.'

Jackie looked at him. Until now, nobody other than a handful of other young women – her sister Val, and Hilary Napier, who had encouraged her to leave her housemaid's job at the Barton and look for something better – had approved of what she had done. Now, she was beginning to hear a different perspective, and she felt excited by it.

'People have treated me as if I was doing something wrong,' she said at last. 'Mum and Dad never liked me coming to work in Plymouth, and my boyfriends weren't much better. They wanted to tell me what to do – they seemed to think they owned me.'

'You really should come to the States,' Russell told her. 'You'd find it different there.'

'Yes,' Jackie said thoughtfully. 'I think maybe I should.'

Maddy, too, had plenty to think about as she sat on the train taking her back to West Lyme. Felix's words and the patient understanding of her sister and Dottie, allied with the tears she had shed as she sobbed out all her heartfelt grief, had left her exhausted, yet somehow cleansed, as she had sometimes felt when recovering from a childhood illness. It was as if her body had been contaminated by a festering abscess that had been drained of its poison and was now finding its way back to health again.

I've been bottling it all up inside me, she thought. All those horrible feelings, that jealousy of Ruth and Dan, the bitterness because they could be happy again and I can't ... I couldn't really explain those feelings because they were so petty and nasty, and I thought everyone would hate me. I hated *myself*. But now they've gone – washed away – and I can begin to be myself again.

She knew that she would still have her grief. That would never leave her completely. She still wasn't convinced that she could ever find her own happiness again, wasn't sure she wanted to. It still felt like a betrayal of Sammy, even to think about it. But the bitterness and anger she had felt towards other people had begun to dissipate, and she felt, dimly, that she might soon even be able to be happy for the Hodges.

I must go and see them, she decided suddenly. I must make things right between us.

She gazed out of the window at the passing scenery – the wide mudflats of the Exe estuary, the red cliffs and tunnels of Dawlish, the rolling hills of East Devon and Dorset – and turned her thoughts to the newcomers in Burracombe: Joe Tozer and his son Russell. The evening spent in their company had opened a new window in her mind and she'd sat quietly in her chair, listening as they talked about their life in America, in the small town of Corning. It was a peaceful, contented place, they said, not at all like the America of gangster films, and centred around a glassmaking industry that had been pioneered by British glassmakers from Stourbridge, in the Midlands. Joe had been involved with the building of the new factory and had met the great Frederick Carder, whose work featured so prominently and who was now ninety years old and still a much-loved character in the little town.

'I saw him not long before we sailed,' he'd told them. 'Promised I'd make a trip to Stourbridge and take a few photos to show him what the old place is like now. May call in at some of the glassworks, too – Stuart Crystal, and Webb's – and see if there's anyone there who remembers the old guy.'

'I'm sure they'd know about him, even if there isn't anyone there old enough to remember him,' Felix had said. 'He sounds like one of our finest exports!'

Felix was a nice man, Maddy thought. Funny and unstuffy, but so wise and gentle when he needed to be. Stella was a very lucky girl to have found him. She wondered if she herself might ever be so lucky.

The idea brought her up short, and she gasped and put her hand to her cheek.

It was the first time since Sammy's death that she had entertained even the most fleeting thought of ever finding another man. Even now, a wave of guilt swept over her. I didn't mean it, Sammy, she thought frantically. I really didn't mean it. I don't want anyone but you – ever. I swear I don't.

But, even though she had driven it out of her mind the second it had entered it, the thought had been there, and she knew in her heart that it would return. Perhaps not yet, for she was armed against it now; but one day, when her guard was down, it would creep into her mind again and perhaps next time it would stay there, slowly wearing away the hard knot of grief tied inside her; slowly warming her heart into life again.

I'm not ready, she thought, feeling the tears well up inside her. I want to remember Sammy, and feel that he is with me, always. I don't want anyone else.

And yet ... if the healing had indeed begun, wouldn't that be an inevitable part?

Chapter Fifteen

'No letter from Robert again,' Gilbert Napier growled as he sorted through his post at the breakfast table. 'I'll ring Hubert after breakfast, ask him to look into it. The boy's housemaster should be seeing to it that he writes every week. Seems to me he's falling down on his job.'

'I'm sure he's all right,' Hilary said, waiting resignedly for her own letters. Looking through the post first was one of her father's ways of maintaining his position as head of the household, and much as she resented the fact that he saw her envelopes before she did, there was nothing to be done about it. 'We'd have been notified if there was anything wrong.'

'Of course I'd have been notified,' he snapped. 'That's not the point. Someone should be making sure the boy writes regularly.'

'I suppose he's writing to his mother,' she offered. 'Perhaps his housemaster thinks that's all he needs to do.'

'Well, it isn't! Hilary, I'm surprised that you take this so lightly. Naturally, he should write to his mother. That goes without saying. But I'm his guardian as well as his grandfather – I'm paying the fees, for God's sake – and I expect a weekly letter. It's not too much to ask, is it?'

Hilary thought it might well be, from a thirteen-year-old boy up-rooted from his own background and set down in a public school in a foreign country with no more ceremony than if he had been a dog changing masters. She remembered what Luke had said and felt rather guilty. I hope Rob's all right, she thought. I hope he's not miserable.

'Do you really think you should speak to the headmaster?' she asked as her father handed her a pile of letters at last. 'It might do more harm than good.' But she knew her words were falling on deaf ears. Her father was already reading his own post, and took no notice. She sighed and opened the first envelope.

'Goodness me!' she exclaimed, before she could stop herself.

Her father glanced up. 'What? Don't tell me he's written to you instead.'

Hilary shook her head. 'No, it's from a friend I met during the war. She and some others are having a get-together at the end of the month – a dinner in London. Staying overnight.'

'Oh.' He pushed his letters aside and poured himself some more coffee. 'Don't suppose you're interested in going.'

'Whyever not?' Hilary, who actually hadn't considered it possible, bristled. 'It would be fun to catch up with them again, talk over old times.'

'Thought you had too much to do here to go gallivanting about in London. That's what you always tell me, when I suggest you go up and see a few old friends, anyway.'

'By "old friends" you mean *your* old friends,' she retorted. 'Most of them widowers, looking for a younger woman to marry them and take care of them in their old age. These are *my* friends and I'd like to see them again. I shall write back and say yes, and book a room at the club. As for having too much to do here, I think I'm entitled to a little time off occasionally, don't you?'

He shrugged and ignored her question. They finished their breakfast in silence and Hilary took the dishes back to the kitchen before going to the office to see Travis and discuss the day's work.

Really, she thought, her father was becoming more self-centred by the day, and he was always grumpier when he was waiting for a letter from Robert. Not that the letters were particularly informative, but they were an indication that the boy was thinking of his grandfather. They afforded a glimpse, however slight, into his mind.

And a slight glimpse was all anyone had been given of Rob's mind, she thought. Apart from Stephen and Luke, who seemed to have managed to draw out a few of his thoughts and ambitions, nobody else seemed to know any more about him than they had on the day he had arrived. Which made it all the more difficult for Hilary to know what her own future might hold.

Maybe I should give in and marry one of Father's widower friends, she thought ruefully. Maybe that really is all that's left for someone like me.

Val was as interested as Hilary in the reunion. She wasn't included in the invitation, as she had been a VAD nurse and not in the ATS as Hilary had, but she had known a number of the army officers Hilary had chauffeured, both in England and, more especially, in Egypt. She recalled a few names as she and Hilary wheeled Christopher's pram through the village on his first real outing.

'Major Sutcliffe, do you remember him? He was rather sweet on you, as I remember. Mind you, most of them were – having a pretty young woman to drive them about must have a been a big bonus. Oh, and who was that tall, blond one? Colonel Farrant, wasn't it? All the girls swooned over him. We often wondered—'

'There was nothing to wonder about. He was a perfect gentleman,' Hilary said firmly. 'And so was Mark Sutcliffe. In fact, they all were. Well – except for one or two.'

'And no prizes for guessing who they were,' Val grinned. 'Captain Leonard Macintosh for one! Grubby Mac, we called him.'

Hilary laughed. 'Yes, it was a good idea to keep your distance. Luckily, I only had to drive him twice. The second time, I put a mousetrap on my knee.'

Val's words had given her pause for thought, however, and she wondered just who would go to the reunion. There were certainly a few people she would prefer not to meet. One name came particularly to mind, but she brushed it away at once.

It was unlikely that everyone would be there. And after all this time, there couldn't possibly be any reason to be concerned.

Their way through the village was punctuated by people wanting to stop and look at Christopher. Joyce Warren was the first.

'My, what a beautiful baby. You must be so proud, and after such a difficult pregnancy, too.'

'Yes, I'm very lucky.' Val felt a bit awkward. Mrs Warren had no children and while this might have been from choice, Val was conscious that the sight of young babies might be sad for her.

The older woman bent over the pram and touched the baby's face with a gentle finger. 'He's perfect. Let me give him a little present.' She fumbled in her bag.

'Oh, there's no need.'

'Of course there is. You should always give a new baby a piece of silver the first time you see him. Here you are, darling – half a crown.' She laid the coin on the pillow and straightened up. 'Do bring him to see me, won't you? Come to tea one afternoon next week. Let's see – what about Wednesday? At about three?'

'Well – yes. Thank you,' Val said, slightly stunned. She had never been invited to the Warrens' house before; the solicitor's wife generally considered herself a cut above the village people. They smiled at each other and then walked on.

'What do you think of that?' Val exclaimed as soon as they were out of earshot. 'Me, invited to tea with Mrs Warren! And it's all your fault,' she accused her sleeping son as she bent to retrieve the half-crown from the pillow. 'She would never have asked me if it hadn't been for you.'

'I've noticed before that she loves babies,' Hilary said thoughtfully. 'I wonder sometimes what her life was before she and Henry came to Burracombe – when was it, about two years before the war started? I don't think they'd been married all that long and she must be in her mid-fifties now. Maybe she was too old to start a family.'

'Everybody seems to have a story in their past,' Val said. 'And here comes another one – Ivy Sweet! You know what they say about her!'

'It's just gossip,' Hilary said firmly as the baker's wife stepped out of her cottage and closed the door behind her. 'I don't believe those stories about the Polish and Czechoslovakian pilots from Harrowbeer for a moment. Hello, Mrs Sweet,' she called, 'come and see the village's newest inhabitant.'

The woman hesitated, then walked towards them. She was always rather cool towards Val, owing to a long-standing animosity between her and Alice Tozer. Another story there, Val guessed, but her mother had always closed her lips firmly when asked. She peeped into the pram.

'Very fine baby,' she said, and felt in her purse. 'I'm glad you came through it all right.'

'Thank you,' Val said, watching as a sixpence was laid near the baby's head. 'That's really kind. And thank you for the flowers you sent, too.'

The woman shrugged. ''Twas just a few daisies from the garden. I thought they might brighten you up a bit, time you were waiting. My cousin's wife had to stop in bed for three months before her babby was born, so I know what 'tis like. Well, I must go, I want to catch the Tavi bus at the green.' She bustled off.

'I swear her hair's redder than ever today,' Hilary murmured but Val shook her head.

'What if it is? I know people say she's flighty and there's talk about that pub where she works, but she's got a kind heart for all that, and to my mind that's what matters.'

Hilary shot her a surprised look. 'All right – keep your own hair on. I didn't mean anything by it.' She thought for a moment. 'You're right, though, I *was* gossiping. Sorry. But you were too, you know!'

Val laughed. 'So I was. We're as bad as everyone else. It's what comes of living in a village – we're all far too interested in each other's doings.'

By the time they had made their way down to the little hump-backed bridge beside the ford, Christopher had amassed quite a little fortune in silver coins. Val gathered them up and put them into her purse.

'Three sixpences, two shillings, two florins and Mrs Warren's half-crown. That's ten shillings altogether for Christopher's money-box. We must come out more often,' she told her son. 'You could pay for your own keep at this rate.' She sat beside Hilary on the low parapet of the bridge and they gazed at the shallow water, rippling over the rocks and swirling into little pools and eddies.

'Is Luke getting any painting done these days?' Hilary enquired, and Val made a face.

'Not much, I'm afraid, what with having to look after me all that time I was in bed, and not being allowed up for the first ten days after the birth. And school keeps him busy, of course. But I'm hoping that once things are more settled he'll get back to it. He wants to have an exhibition, you know. It would be lovely if he could sell a few paintings and start to make a name for himself again.'

'He was doing quite well before, wasn't he? People must remember his name.'

'He was beginning to, yes. But the war took away several years, and he had to start all over again, even though he did work as a war artist during that time. He didn't want to go on painting that sort of thing, and it takes such a long time to achieve recognition. An exhibition is really the only way.'

'Well, let me know when he's putting one on,' Hilary said. 'I'll make sure all my friends attend and buy paintings, and hang them over their fireplaces so that everyone can admire them and want one of their own.'

Val laughed. 'That would be wonderful. And talking of painting, how's young Rob getting along now? Luke thought he showed quite a bit of promise.'

'Yes, he did seem quite keen.' Hilary frowned. 'To tell you the truth, Val, I'm not all that happy about Rob. I'm not sure he's settling down at Kelly. He hardly ever writes, although I suppose he must be writing to his mother. Dad doesn't seem too worried – he's rather put out that Rob isn't writing to him, but that's about it. But I keep thinking about what Luke said and wondering if we've been really fair to him.'

'When does he come home? They get what d'you call them – exeats – don't they?'

Hilary shook her head. 'The new boys don't get exeats until half-term. They're always later than the local schools for some reason. They get things called "Red-Letter Sundays" now and then, when they're allowed to go off for the day, but I don't think the new ones even get those. I just worry about whether he's being bullied, being French and so different from the others.'

'Well, there's nothing you can do about it until half-term,' Val said, wondering privately how anyone could bear to send children away to boarding school. She looked at her sleeping baby and felt thankful that she and Luke were not the sort of people – with the sort of income – who did that. A lot were forced to, of course – people who worked abroad or whose lives meant that they couldn't give their family a settled home – but that didn't really apply in Robert's case. There was a perfectly good grammar school in Tavistock. It was just that Gilbert Napier believed that only the education provided by a public school, and the friendship of the boys he would meet there, was good enough for his grandson.

She returned to the subject of the reunion. 'You are going to go to it, aren't you?'

'Oh yes. I didn't think I would at first, but then I thought – why not? It'll be fun to meet some of the old gang, and get me out of the rut a bit.' I hope it'll be fun, anyway, she thought.

'Do you really feel you're in a rut?'

'Yes, I do,' Hilary said. 'Or perhaps not so much a rut as a sort of limbo. I don't know where my life's going. Until Rob came on the scene, I was quite happy running the estate and thinking that was going to be my life. Steve doesn't want to inherit it, and even if he did, he'd be quite content to let me stay on and do it all. But now – well, it looks as if I'm no more than a caretaker after all. Father's leaving it all to Rob, as Baden's son, and I don't know what will happen.'

Val turned and looked at her in surprise. 'Really? But isn't he making any provision at all for you?'

'Oh yes. He's going to make it a condition that I have a home at the Barton for as long as I want it. Can you imagine what it'll be like, Val?' Her voice shook. 'Dependent on Robert for the rest of my life! Dependent on *Marianne*!'

Val stared at her. 'Don't you like Marianne?'

'Whether I like her or not doesn't come into it. It's the thought of being *dependent* on her – on either of them – to be allowed to stay in my own home. Where I've grown up, where I always felt I belonged. Where I thought I *counted* for something. I tell you, Val, if this happens I shan't be able to stay. I don't care what provision Father makes for me – I'll have to go. But where? And what will I be able to *do*? And the worst of it is, he expects me to stay and take care of it all until Rob's of age to take over. Then, I presume, he'll expect me to step gracefully aside. And you know how old I'll be then! Forty, at least. Almost too old to have children of my own – even if I could find anyone to marry me, which doesn't seem very likely. Too old to do *anything* with my life.' There was a pause, as she stared fixedly down at the hurrying stream and Val gazed at her in consternation. Then she added in a lower tone, 'And since you ask, no, I don't like Marianne. To be perfectly honest, I think she's a nasty, scheming little snake!'

'Well!' Val said after another pause. 'That doesn't leave much room for doubt, does it?'

Hilary turned and grinned reluctantly. 'Not a lot, no. Sorry, Val, I didn't mean to let fly like that.'

'It's all right. Why shouldn't you say what you feel? And who better to say it to? We've been through a lot together.' She thought for a moment. 'I can see just what you mean. It's a horrible position to be in. But you know, you don't have to stay in it.'

'Don't I? I don't see what else I can do.'

'You could just walk away. Wasn't that what you were going to do a couple of years ago, just before your father had his heart attack? You were going to go to London and become an air hostess.'

'I know, but it was different then. He was running the estate and there didn't seem to be any place for me. Then I took over and realised this was where I wanted to make my life, and I knew I could be good at it. I thought Father saw that too, until he brought Travis in.'

'And why did he do that?'

'Because he thought I wasn't good enough! And because he thought I ought to forget about running the estate and find a husband.'

'Yes, but you didn't want to do that, did you? So you and Travis agreed to work together. It doesn't alter the fact that your father thought a manager could do the work without you, and that was what he intended.'

'No-o, but—'

'Travis could do it on his own, couldn't he?'

'Yes, but—'

'So why not let him?' Val persisted. 'If you can't see any future in Burracombe, why not start to make your own life somewhere else? Why wait another eight or ten years? Travis is there, just as your father wanted – nobody could accuse you of leaving Burracombe in the lurch. You can just go. Maybe think again about being an air hostess, or maybe do something completely different. Travel a bit. See the world. It's easier now than it's ever been. Do what *you* want for a change, instead of what other people want you to do.'

'But what about Rob? Father's depending on me to help look after him.'

'Rob has a mother and a family in France and a grandfather here,' Val said bluntly. 'He's not your responsibility, Hil, and your father has no right to try to make you feel he is. And I'll tell you something else.'

'More?' Hilary asked, with a faint smile. She was looking dazed, and Val put a hand on her arm.

'Yes, one thing more and then I'll shut up. This reunion – I think it could be a beginning for you. Go to London. Stay a few days. Meet your old friends, go to a show or two, have a good time. And while you're away from Burracombe, just think about what you really want to do with your life. Because as far as I can see, Hilary, you can look at this situation in two ways – either as a trap or as an opportunity. And I know which I'd rather do.'

There was a short silence. Then Christopher stirred and began the little waking-up noises that Val recognised as the prelude to a demand for his next meal. She stood up and took the brake off the pram.

'I'll have to go home now. Look, Hil, I'm sorry if I've butted in. You don't have to take any notice of me if you don't want to. Forget what I've said.'

Hilary stood up too and brushed her skirt with her palms. 'No, I won't do that. I'll think about it. I'll think about it a lot. And – thanks.'

'Thanks?' Val echoed with a laugh. 'I don't know what you've got to thank me for!'

'For being a good friend,' Hilary said seriously, and laid her hand on the handle of the pram. 'And now, let me push my godson home. Just at the moment, that's my idea of a good time!'

But Val's words lingered in her mind. Why, indeed, shouldn't she walk away and let Travis take care of the estate, as he was well able to do? And suppose Val were right about the reunion as well – suppose meeting old friends and seeing a different view of the world, *did* herald a new beginning?

Chapter Sixteen

Val walked with Hilary as far as the track that led to her father's farm. She was going there for tea and was looking forward to seeing her uncle and cousin again. Since their arrival, they had been to Ted's Cottage for supper and she and Luke had been at the farm for Sunday dinner, but apart from that she'd seen little of them. They had been visiting other members of the family and Joe had been showing Russ his old boyhood haunts, as well as taking him to Plymouth.

She was surprised to find Jackie in the kitchen with the rest of the family.

'Hullo – is it your afternoon off? You don't usually come home during the week.'

Jackie coloured a little. 'Why shouldn't I?'

'I'm not saying you shouldn't,' Val replied, taken aback by her sister's tone. 'Just that you don't usually. It's nice to see you.' She manoeuvred Christopher's pram into the space at the bottom of the stairs. 'Is it all right if I go upstairs to feed him?'

'Yes, go up to Joanna's room – she's feeding Heather,' Alice said, coming over to peep at her latest grandchild. 'Look at the dear of him! And those tiny fingernails. I can never get over how small they are, like little shells you pick up off the beach.'

'I never knew you were such a poet, Alice,' Joe said, laughing, and she flapped her hand at him.

'You go on! You'm as big a tease as you always were. I was only saying.'

'And you were right,' he said, getting up to look at the baby in his turn. 'They *are* like minute shells, and he's like the song says – "mighty like a rose". There. You've got me at it now.'

'I think I'd better take him upstairs before he starts to yell and spoils the illusion,' Val remarked, opening the door to the staircase. 'You'll soon forget about poetry then.' She closed the door behind her and climbed the narrow stairs to Joanna's room, calling ahead of her, 'Jo, is it all right if I come in? Christopher wants his tea.'

'Mind you,' Alice said, returning to the table where she was splitting fresh scones and spooning jam and cream on to each half, 'our Val's right. It is a bit unusual for you to pay us a visit in the middle of the week, Jackie. Have you got some news for us, or something?'

'Honestly!' Jackie said, rolling her eyes. 'Anyone would think I'd come all the way from London. Whatever sort of news d'you think I'd have? I just thought I'd come home for an afternoon, that's all. I didn't realise it would mean an inquisition.'

'Leave the maid alone, Alice,' Minnie said. ''Tis plain to see why she'm here – come to see her uncle and cousin, and why not? They'll be on their way back to America soon enough and none of us will have seen as much of them as us would like.'

'True, I'm afraid,' Joe acknowledged. 'But we'll be here for Christmas. And I hope it won't be the last we see of young Jackie, even then.'

There was a sudden silence. Russ shot his father an exasperated look, and Jackie flushed. Alice looked sharply from one to the other.

'What's this, then? What are you three planning behind our backs?'

'We're not planning anything—' Jackie began, and at the same time Joe said quickly, 'Nothing's going on behind your back, Alice. It was just an idea—'

'An idea me and Ted would have liked to hear about, I reckon. Well, you'd better tell us now.'

'Mum, there's nothing to tell,' Jackie said. 'We were just talking, that's all, and Russ said it would be a good idea for me to go to America some time. And I think it would, too,' she finished defiantly.

Alice tightened her lips. 'Oh, you do, do you? And didn't any of you think it might be an even better idea to ask me and your father first?'

'There wasn't anything to ask. It just came up in conversation. We were talking about travelling and I said I'd like to see a bit of the world, and especially America, and Uncle Joe said—'

'So 'twas you!' Alice exclaimed, with an accusing glare at Joe. 'Not content with breaking your mother's heart, you want to break mine as well!'

'That's not fair, Alice! I never broke Mother's heart.'

'And how would you know? You weren't here to see it. You haven't been here all these years since, watching her look out for the postman, hoping there'd be a letter with an American stamp on it. And don't tell me she never said nothing about it in her letters – of course she didn't. She wouldn't want you to know how upset she was.'

Joe turned to his mother. 'I know I went a long way away, but you understood how I felt, didn't you, Ma? You knew there was no place on the farm for me. I had to make my own life and it wasn't here in Burracombe.'

Minnie looked from one to the other, her eyes distressed and her wrinkled lips trembling a little. 'Don't let's have an argument, not now we'm all together again.'

'Well, *I* certainly don't want any arguments,' Alice said, tossing her head. 'But I don't want no foolish notions put into my daughter's head, neither.'

'There's nothing foolish about it!' Jackie cried. 'I'm not talking about going off on my own – I'd be staying with family. Russ says they'll even find me a job, so I can afford to travel about a bit.'

'A *job*? And you're telling me that just "came up in conversation"? You're telling me you haven't been making plans?' Alice stood at the kitchen table, her hands on her hips, the platter of scones before her forgotten. 'You've got it all worked out between you – and me and your father the last to know. Just when us thought you were getting a bit of sense in your head at last, too. And as for you –' she turned to her brother-in-law and nephew, 'you ought to know better, the pair of you. Turning a young girl's head like that.'

Jackie opened her mouth angrily, but Joe shook his head and laid his hand on her arm. He spoke quietly to Alice.

'We're not turning her head, Alice, and you've no cause to say we wouldn't have talked to you about it. I'm sure Jackie came here this afternoon just to do that, but she didn't get a chance. I'm sorry I let the cat out of the bag, Jackie, but it never occurred to me there'd be any problem over it.'

'Well, it should have done,' Alice told him tartly. 'What did you think was going to happen, blurting out something like that? I dread to think what my Ted's going to say when he comes in from milking.'

'He'll say I can't go,' Jackie said sullenly. 'And if he doesn't, you will. Well, you needn't think I'll bother to come home on my afternoons off after this. If I can't go to America, I'll look for a job in London and you'll hardly ever see me anyway.'

'There's no need to be like that,' Alice began, and the row, which had shown signs of simmering down, broke out again. In the middle of it, two doors opened at once – the kitchen door from the yard and the door at the bottom of the stairs – and Ted at one, and Val, with Joanna close behind her, at the other, stood there bemused. At sight of her father, Jackie burst into tears, while Joe and Russ looked discomfited and Alice even more angry.

'What in the name of all that's wonderful is going on here?' Ted asked, staring from one to the other. 'I could hear the racket all across the yard. And what's our Jackie doing here on a Wednesday afternoon?' His eyes grew suspicious. 'You haven't gone and got yourself into trouble, have you?'

'No, I haven't!' Jackie shouted, leaping up. 'Trust you to jump to that conclusion! You never did trust me, did you? You've been expecting something like that ever since I went to work in Plymouth.'

'All right, all right, calm down,' said Alice, anything but calm herself. She turned to face her husband. 'It's your Joe,' she said accusingly, as if it must also be Ted's fault. 'Talking about taking our Jackie off to America, that's all. And not just for a holiday, neither – getting her a job, if you please, and not so much as a by-your-leave. That's what it's all about.' She turned back to the table and began slamming more jam and cream on the remaining scones, although who would feel like eating them now was a mystery.

'*What* did you say?' Ted stared at her, then turned to his brother. 'Is this right?'

'It is and it isn't,' Joe began uncomfortably. 'Nothing's been decided—'

'You're telling me it hasn't!' Ted began to take off his boots. 'Nor will it be, neither. If our Jackie goes off to America, it'll be over my dead body.'

Val and Joanna came further into the room and closed the staircase door behind them. Val shot a swift look at her sister and said, 'Come on, Dad, you haven't heard anything about it yet. None of us has.'

'I've heard enough,' he said grimly, padding across the kitchen. 'Where are my shoes? A man can't hold a conversation like this in his socks.' He found his indoor shoes and sat down in his armchair by the range to put them on while the rest of the family watched in silence. At last, he lifted his head and looked around the cluster of faces.

Jackie had stopped crying and was sitting with her elbows on the table, wiping her eyes and sniffing into a damp ball of handkerchief. Joe and Russ were looking decidedly uncomfortable, yet still defensive; Minnie was clearly upset, and Alice angry. Val and Joanna, still bewildered by whatever had been happening while they were upstairs feeding their babies, came over and joined the group sitting round the table, glancing uneasily from one face to another.

'Right,' Ted said, heavily, 'somebody better tell me what all this is about.'

Immediately, everyone began to speak at once, and he held up his hand and bellowed, 'One at a time, for pity's sake! How can a man make sense of all that gabble? And you'd better wait a minute – our Tom's coming over from the milking sheds and he'd better be in on it too. Us don't want to have to go through all this twice.'

'Once is too many times, if you ask me,' Alice said. 'The subject never ought to have come up in the first place.'

'Well, it has, and now it's got to be thrashed out.' He waited as Tom came through the back door and stared round at them. 'You'd better get your boots off, Tom, and come and hear this. Seems Joe here wants to take our Jackie back to America with him.'

'*Does* he?' Tom looked at his uncle and then at his sister. 'Sounds a good idea. Why's she crying? Doesn't she want to go?'

'Of course I want to go!' Jackie cried. 'They won't let me!'

Tom looked at his parents but before he could speak, Alice said bitterly, 'We might have known you'd take her side.'

'Look, there's no need for sides,' Joe broke in. 'We keep telling you, it's just an idea—'

'*Just an idea* that you're getting her a job? And how long is this supposed to be for? Once she's over there, she'll never come back – it'll be just like you, going over to "have a look round" and then stopping there. I know just what'll happen,' Alice went on, working herself up again. 'She'll meet some rich American and get married and never come back to Burracombe again. A letter every six weeks if we're lucky, and that'll be that.' Her eyes filled with tears. 'I don't know how you can suggest it, Joe. And as for you, Jackie, I don't know how you can even *think* about it. Leaving your family and all your friends who've loved you all your life, and going off to the other side of the world—'

'Mum, *stop* it!' Jackie screamed. 'Nobody's ever said anything about anything like that! It's just a *visit*, that's all. And anyway, what if I did meet someone and get married – shouldn't you be pleased for me? Isn't that what you've wanted all along?'

'In Burracombe, yes,' Alice retorted. 'Not halfway across the world where you've got no one of your own to look after you. And don't tell me—'

'Mum, calm down,' Val said, reaching up to take her mother by the arm. 'Sit down and let's talk about this sensibly. How about a cup of tea?'

'I'll make it,' Joanna said quickly, going over to the range where the kettle was in its usual position, waiting to be moved on to the hotplate to come to the boil. She warmed the big brown teapot and spooned tea into it, then brought it to the table, where cups, milk and sugar were already set out. The rest of the family waited while she poured out, and not until they each had a cup of tea in front of them did Ted speak.

'All right, then. We've all had a few minutes to get ourselves sorted out so now let's hear what this is all about.' He looked at his brother. 'Have you really asked our Jackie to go back to America with you?'

'Not in so many words, no, but in a way I guess you might say so. We were just talking generally, about travelling. Russ and I mentioned we were thinking of going over to have a look at one or two other places – Paris, Rome, and so on – and Jackie said she'd like to travel too, but most of all she'd like to go to America ...'

'So we said, why not come and stay with us for a bit?' Russ continued. He had remained silent during the argument, but now he gave Jackie a comforting glance and said, 'It seemed like a good idea. There's Dad and me, and the girls and their families – we'd all look after her. It's not like she'd be on her own. As for the job, it was only because Jackie said she wouldn't be able to afford it and we thought, why not stay for a few months and earn some money while she's there? Honestly, Aunt

Alice, it didn't seem anything that might cause trouble. That was the last thing we wanted.'

Ted cleared his throat and looked at his wife. Neither spoke, and Val said, 'Put like that, it doesn't sound unreasonable, does it? It would be a great experience for her.'

Alice gave a huff of exasperation. 'So now you're on her side, as well!'

'Uncle Joe's right,' Tom said. 'There's no need for sides. It just needs talking about, that's all. After all, what's the worst that could happen?'

His mother gave him a look. 'Any amount of things, as you well know, Tom. I don't need to spell them out, do I?'

'Things like that can happen anywhere,' Val pointed out. 'From what I can make out, Corning's a small place – more like Tavistock. She'd probably be safer there than in Plymouth.'

'I'm perfectly safe in Plymouth,' Jackie interjected, afraid of having her one opportunity for independence snatched away from her.

'I know you are. I'm just saying that Corning will be just as safe. Especially with family all around. Honestly, Mum, I don't think you need worry about that.'

'It's not a question of being worried. I just don't like the idea of her going so far away.' Alice looked at Joe. 'You don't understand what it's like, seeing your children leave you. It's bad enough having our Brian over in Germany, but at least we know he and Peggy will be coming home when he comes out of the Army. But to have our Jackie going to America ...' She shook her head. 'I can't countenance it. I'm sorry, I just can't.'

Joe looked at his own mother. 'Did I really break your heart?' he asked softly. 'I never meant to.'

Minnie gazed at him across the big scrubbed table. Her eyes were wet with tears and her wrinkled hand trembled. She pressed her lips tightly together, then answered in a steady enough voice, 'I'm not saying it was easy, Joe, but you have to let your children make their own lives. Like you say, there weren't nothing for you here, with Ted ready and willing to take over the farm.'

'I'd have worked with him, if need be,' Ted broke in. 'There weren't no need for him to go on my account.'

'It seemed to me there was,' Joe stated quietly. 'When I came back after four years in the First World War, there didn't seem to be much of a place for me any more. I didn't want to spend the rest of my life milking cows.'

'There ain't nothing wrong with milking cows,' Ted began, his face reddening.

'For goodness' sake, everyone, *stop* it!' Val exclaimed. 'You're raking over old ground and there's no need for it. This whole visit will be spoiled if you go on like this. Look, surely the main thing is whether Jackie ought to go to America or not, and it seems to me that's something that needs to be thought about and talked over quietly and calmly, without getting all het up about it.'

'As head of the family—' Ted began, but this time Joe butted in.

'You're not head of *my* family, Ted. I know we're just visitors here now, and got no rights, but you got no call to pull rank over me.'

'Would everyone listen to *me* for a minute?' Jackie demanded loudly, and at the sound of her voice they all stopped and turned towards her. She waited a moment, saw that she had their attention, and went on more quietly, 'All right, I'm only nineteen, but I won't be for ever. You might be able to stop me doing what I want now, but in two years' time I'll be able to do whatever I like: get married, go to London, go to America, if that's what I want. And I *will*. So what's the point in stopping me now? What's the point in stopping me doing *anything*?'

She paused and looked around again. They were all staring at her – her mother and father angry but now baffled as well; her sister half surprised, half approving; her brother grinning. Joe's own anger seemed to be subsiding, while Russ was looking amused and admiring, and Joanna seemed more concerned with whether all the noise had woken her baby.

After a long silence, Minnie spoke again.

'The maid's right. You'll not be able to do a thing about it in two years' time. You got to make up your mind to it, Alice and Ted – youngsters these days got minds of their own and wants to live life their own way. The world's changing all the time, and it's changed a lot since Joe went away. And young women got their independence during the war, travelling about and doing all sorts of men's jobs. They're not going to give it up now. Why, isn't that how we got our Joanna here, coming to be a Land Girl?' She looked at her son and her expression softened. 'You never broke my heart, Joe,' she said softly.

'You might have cracked it a bit when you went away, but as long as I knew you were all right, you never broke it. That's all any mother wants, when it comes down to it – to know that her children are all right. Wherever they are, and whatever they be doing.' A tear slipped from her eye and made a path for itself down the deep-set wrinkles of her cheek. 'And if they comes back to you in the end – why, like the Good Book says, 'tis a joy past all understanding.'

Chapter Seventeen

Stella Simmons felt quietly confident about her own future. There was still a lot to plan for the wedding but the main things had been decided, most of the bridesmaids chosen and Dottie had already begun to sew her wedding dress. Stella had finally picked a simple princess-style in oyster satin, with a stand-up collar and long, pointed sleeves. The back dropped to a swirling train and Jacob had offered her his mother's Honiton-lace veil, which Jennifer Kellaway had worn at her wedding to Travis only a month ago.

'Have you decided which little maid is going to be your last bridesmaid yet?' Dottie enquired as they ate their breakfast that morning.

'No. We're going to do it today.' Stella sighed. 'I'm not really looking forward to it, to tell you the truth.'

'Because you might have to choose one you don't really want?'

'Well, partly, but also because all the others are going to be disappointed. But Felix has come up with a very good idea to make sure we can't be accused of favouritism. We're going to let the children themselves decide.'

Dottie gazed at her. 'How be you going to do that, then?'

'We'll give them each two slips of paper. On one, they can write their own name – some would do that anyway! On the other, they write the name of the girl they would like to see as bridesmaid if it's not them. Then we collect them all in, discard one of each name and see who gets most votes. Even if they cheat and write their own name twice, that'll only be one extra vote, so it shouldn't matter. With luck, there'll be a clear winner.'

'That *is* a good idea,' Dottie said. 'Trust Felix to think of it. And I dare say they'll all come to the church anyway.'

'Yes, and we're going to have a party at the school the day before, so they don't feel they're being excluded from the reception. It's quite a good opportunity to teach them about weddings, too. We're thinking of having a sort of little play – choosing a bride and groom and acting out the whole ceremony. Felix says he'll officiate.'

'Be that such a good idea?' Dottie asked with a worried frown. 'I mean, they won't actually *be* married, will they? What with having a proper vicar and all?'

'Of course they won't be,' Stella said with a laugh. 'They're not old enough, for a start! But since the playground is already full of weddings going on between dolls and teddy-bears, and some of the girls have started to bring bits of white material to wear as veils, we thought we might as well make use of the craze. It'll bring the boys in as well. They're all pretending to be very uninterested at the moment.'

She set off for school, walking down the village street between cottage gardens filled with dahlias, chrysanthemums and Michaelmas daisies. The trees were turning colour in earnest now, with the beeches tinged with gold and the oaks a burnished bronze. In one garden a Japanese maple almost twenty feet high spread a canopy of deep, purplish red which was echoed by two weeping cherries on the other side of the road.

It still seemed strange to Stella that soon she would have left this street behind – left the whole village behind, in fact – and be living over the river in Little Burracombe. I shall miss it all so much, she thought, and the children especially. But as long as Felix is happy for me to help out when one of the permanent teachers is ill or away, I can at least keep in touch. I might even go to other schools in the area – that would be interesting. And life will be busy enough in other ways.

The children had been enthusiastic about the idea of choosing Stella's bridesmaid themselves, and sat eagerly at their desks waiting for their slips of paper to be handed out by Betty Culliford. There had been some discussion about whether the boys should be involved in this, and it had finally been decided that they should. Since they would not be voting for themselves, they were given only one slip of paper each. Stella gave the word when they were allowed to begin, and forty heads bent over their desks while forty pencils scrawled industriously on their papers.

'You may collect the papers now, Betty,' Miss Kemp said, and the little girl went around the room, picking up the pieces of paper and taking them to the head teacher's desk. Stella eyed them nervously, wondering who she would end up with. However hard she tried not to have favourites, there were bound to be some girls she'd rather have than others. She watched as the headmistress sorted the slips into forty, and saw that there were several names that had more than two. She hoped there wouldn't be a draw and they'd have to vote again.

At last there were two names with obviously the most votes, and Miss Kemp counted them.

'Seven in one, and eleven in the other,' she said to the waiting children. 'And I'm only going to tell you the winner, so that all the rest of you can consider yourselves equal. And the girl that most of you want for Miss Simmons' bridesmaid *is* . . .' she smiled around the room '. . . Janice Ruddicombe!'

There was a little gasp, half of disappointment, and half of pleasure, and Stella was conscious of a feeling of both surprise and delight. Janice Ruddicombe was the newest girl in her own infants' class, one of the 'babies', and the youngest in the school. Stella beckoned the little girl out to the front.

'There, Janice,' she said, bending to give her a kiss. 'What do you think of that? More people wanted you to be my bridesmaid than anyone else. And you're going to look so pretty in your frock, as well.'

Janice gazed up at her. It was true that she was a pretty child, with the dark hair, large brown eyes and slightly olive skin that could 'take' orange, but it was a surprise that the other children had chosen her, and Stella felt a thrill of warmth at their compassion. For Janice had suffered with infantile paralysis when she was only two years old. Her legs had grown unevenly and she wore callipers and a heavy surgical boot, which had to be renewed every few months. Her gait was slow and irregular and both Stella and Miss Kemp had been anxious about how she would manage in both the classroom and the playground. To their relief, the other children had shown a caring and helpful attitude, looking after her and making sure she was included in their games. One or two of the bigger boys had jeered at her to begin with, but they had quickly been sorted out and Janice was treated tenderly as a china doll.

'But I won't be able to walk fast enough, Miss,' Janice said. 'I won't be able to keep up. And I won't be able to wear pretty shoes.'

'We shall all walk slowly,' Stella promised. 'People do at weddings. And you'll have a long frock on – nobody will see your boot. Now, tomorrow after school I'll take you to see Miss Friend. She's going to make your dress, and she'll need to measure you, so tell your mother I'll bring you home.'

Janice nodded shyly and stood before the class, looking almost too tiny to be at school, her face flushed with joy, her large eyes brimming with tears. Stella felt a wave of love for her, and for all the children who had voted so unselfishly. Some, she could see by the number of slips, hadn't even voted for themselves once but had used both their votes for other girls.

'I wish I could have you all as bridesmaids,' she told them. 'But since I can't, I'm really pleased to be having Janice. And you're all invited to the church, and to our very own party the day before. I'm going to miss you all so much.'

To her dismay, her voice cracked on the last words and tears came to her own eyes. She dashed them away with the back of her hand and then George and Edward Crocker, the identical twins, stood up and marched out to the front. She noticed that, against all rules, they were wearing identical jerseys.

'Please, Miss,' said George (or it may have been Edward), 'can we be pageboys and wear skilts?'

'Only we saw some at a wedding in Tavi the other day,' Edward (or perhaps George) added, 'and they had daggers in their socks. We wouldn't mind wearing skilts, if we could have proper daggers in our socks.'

Stella felt her lips twitch.

'No, boys,' she said firmly. 'I'm afraid I'm not having any pageboys, and if I did they would not wear skilts – *kilts* – and they certainly would not have daggers. It's very kind of you to offer, but that's all there is to it.'

She paused, uncertain what to say next, and Miss Kemp came to the rescue.

'Go back to your places, all of you, and open your desks quietly to get out your school hymnbooks. We're going to spend the rest of the morning planning our own little wedding here, and thinking about what the words of the service and the hymns mean. If you really want to be pageboys, George and Edward, you can do so then – but unless you can persuade your sister to lend you her skirt, you'll have to wear your school shorts, and, as Miss Simmons says, there will be *no* daggers. No,' she said firmly as they opened their mouths, 'not even toy ones!'

Joe and Russell had taken up Dottie's invitation and had gone to her cottage several times to drink tea and eat rock cakes or scones in her cosy little room. On the day after the quarrel, Joe went alone and it wasn't long before Dottie saw that there was something wrong.

'What's the matter, Joe? You look as if you've lost a shilling and found sixpence.'

He smiled ruefully. 'I could never keep anything from you, Dottie. Oh, it's just one of those family disagreements. It'll blow over, I guess.'

'A family disagreement? That's a pity, when you've only been back five minutes.' She regarded him thoughtfully. 'You look as if it's a bit more serious than that, mind. I know 'tis none of my business, but if you wants to talk about it, you know it won't go outside these four walls.'

'I know, Dottie. You're not one of the village gossips.' He hesitated, then explained what had happened at the farm. 'Honestly, we never meant to set the cat among the pigeons like that. It just seemed a good idea for young Jackie to see a bit of the world and take advantage of having family to go to. But Alice seemed to think we were whisking her away to the other end of the earth and she'd never come back again.'

'Well, you can't really blame her, seeing as it was what *you* did,' Dottie pointed out. 'And Jackie's a pretty girl – suppose she met someone and wanted to get married over there?'

'That's what Alice said. But Russ and me – we just thought of her coming for a few months, not long enough for anything like that.'

'A *week's* long enough for something like that, sometimes,' Dottie said drily. 'But I don't suppose you and Russell gave that a thought.'

'No, we didn't. It just never struck us there might be complications – but, oh brother, we soon found out there were!'

'So what's going to happen? How was it left?'

He shrugged. 'It sort of settled down a bit and we had tea together, and then Jackie said she had to go back to Plymouth and no more was said – then. But Ted took me outside afterwards and tore a real strip off me. Said I ought to have had more consideration, and thought about what it would do to Alice if she lost her youngest. And he said something else.' Joe gazed into his cup for a moment, then looked up suddenly into Dottie's eyes. 'Dot, I didn't really break my mother's heart when I went to America, did I? He and Alice both reckon I did.'

Dottie met his gaze. 'What does your mother say?'

'Oh, she says not, but then she would, wouldn't she? She wouldn't want to make me feel guilty after all this time. It's not as if I can put things right. But you've known her all your life – what do you think?'

Dottie was silent for a moment or two, then she said quietly, 'No, I don't think you broke your mother's heart. She was upset to think you'd gone so far off, not long after you'd come back from the war, but she understood why you went. And she didn't know then that you'd be gone so long, did she? She didn't know it was for life. No, it wasn't your mother's heart you broke.'

Joe's brows creased. He put out his hand and laid it on Dottie's.

'What do you mean by that, Dottie?'

The silence continued. Dottie was looking down at the table and the hand beneath his shook a little. Then, as she drew in a breath and seemed about to speak, Joe's fingers tightened.

The back door opened and a cool draught blew in from the garden. Stella came whisking in, her eyes bright and her cheeks flushed. Joe swiftly drew back his hand but Stella was too full of her own news to notice.

'You'll never guess who those dear children have chosen to be my bridesmaid! Little Janice Ruddicombe! Isn't that kind of them? I couldn't be more pleased.'

'Oh, the lambs,' Dottie said, getting up and speaking very quickly. 'Did you hear that, Joe? Janice is Bill Ruddicombe's granddaughter – you remember Bill, don't you? She've been poorly the last two or three years with that nasty infantile paralysis that they've got some other posh name for—'

'Polio,' Stella said. 'Poliomyelitis.'

'That's it. Caught it when they took her to the seaside on an outing, poor little scrap. Stuck in bed for months, her was, and they didn't think her'd ever walk again. Even now, the bones haven't growed proper.'

'She has to wear callipers and a surgical boot,' Stella told him. 'I think she'll have to have them all her life. But she gets about and she's such a happy little thing; everyone loves her. I really didn't think they'd pick her for my bridesmaid, though.'

'Well, that's grand,' Joe said, although he would have preferred Stella to have arrived rather later with her news. He glanced at Dottie but she was busy with the kettle and teapot, and avoided his eye. He fiddled with his teaspoon, feeling out of place. Dottie had been just about to say something important, he was sure, but whether she'd ever say it now seemed doubtful. She'd kept it quiet all these years – if it even existed – and she might decide to go on keeping it quiet. From the way she was bustling around, chattering about bridesmaids' dresses and wedding cakes and so on, it seemed she was thankful they'd been interrupted.

He sighed and shook his head when Dottie offered him another cup of tea.

'I guess I ought to be getting along. Leave you two to your plans.' He smiled and nodded at Stella. 'It all sounds real exciting.'

''Well, it is to me,' she admitted. 'But I can see it's not for you. Don't go yet – we've never had a proper talk.'

'I'll come again, don't worry. There'll be plenty of time before Russ and me go back to the States.' A shadow crossed his face, then he lifted his shoulders and smiled again. 'We're not sailing until the middle of January.'

'Why, you'll be here for the wedding, then!' Stella exclaimed. 'You will come, won't you? I'll put you on the list. Yes, of course you must come,' she went on, brushing aside his demurral. 'The whole village will be there. I can't leave you out.'

'Well, then, we'd be delighted. And thanks very much.' He turned to Dottie. 'I'll drop in again soon – maybe we can pick up where we left off.'

Dottie glanced at him quickly, then looked away. 'Yes, maybe,' she said offhandedly. 'You drop in any time, Joe. You and Russ.'

He lingered for a moment in the doorway, then let himself out and the two women sat down at the table.

'What did he mean – pick up where you left off?' Stella asked. 'I didn't interrupt anything important, did I?'

'No,' Dottie said, pouring the tea. 'You didn't interrupt anything at all.'

Chapter Eighteen

It had taken all Maddy's resolve to reach this point. For weeks, she had been battling with her feelings – the misery of her still sharp grief over Sammy, the sense of betrayal she had felt on hearing that Ruth was to have a baby, the shock of Felix and Stella's words to her and, finally, a sense of shame – and even a touch of resentment towards the people who had, it seemed, caused her to behave badly.

Gradually, however, as time passed, she had begun to come to terms with her conflicting emotions and to realise that the resentment itself was a childish reaction which had to be overcome before she could deal with the rest. And once that was done, and she could forgive herself, she knew that the next step was to ask forgiveness from Ruth and Dan. She still could not feel any joy that they were to have another child, and she didn't think she ever would. But that was something that must be kept hidden. She would never again hurt them as she had done when they had first told her their news.

I have to go and see them, she told herself as she came through yet another sleepless night. I have to make things right, and it can't be done by letter. I have to see them face to face, and hope they won't turn me away.

She had set off on the morning train. It was a Saturday and Dan would be home from the forge for his midday meal, and then free for the afternoon. Usually, he and Ruth would then spend the afternoon with seven-year-old Linnet, either taking her for a walk and perhaps a picnic in the forest, or at the farm with Ruth's sister Jane and her family. Whatever it was, Maddy would probably be able to join them, and if not she could visit some of her old friends, made first when she had been evacuated to Bridge End as a child and renewed when she and Sammy had begun to see each other.

That, she reminded herself as she sat in the train, was if Ruth didn't slam the door in her face – which she'd have every right to do, after the things Maddy had said to them both.

As the train drew nearer to Southampton, she found herself growing more and more nervous. In all her life, Maddy had never been rejected and she had no idea how she would be able to bear it if Ruth and Dan turned her away now. Stella and Felix are right, she thought, gazing out of the window at the wooded scenery of the New Forest. I've had a cushioned, cosseted life. Stella must have had many more knocks than me – she was taken to an orphanage and stayed there until she left school and went to college. I know the matron was kind to her, but it couldn't have been the same as it was for me, being adopted by Fenella and then living with Dottie. I've had a very easy, comfortable life – until now.

Perhaps, she reflected, that was why she'd taken Sammy's death so hard. Any girl would have been devastated by such a horrible accident, happening right in front of her eyes, any girl would have felt as bereft, but a girl who had learned to deal with sorrow in the past might have recovered more quickly, mightn't she? And yet, nobody could say that Maddy hadn't had her share of bereavement as well, losing both her parents and her baby brother in the war ...

She sighed and gave up. It was all too difficult, and maybe all this soul-searching wasn't a help anyway. Maybe it was better to do as someone – Felix? Stella? Dottie? – had suggested: to start thinking of other people and to put the past behind her. Maybe it was time to move forward, even if her progress did seem painfully slow. One step at a time, Felix had advised her, and even if the steps were very small, they were still steps. They still, eventually, got you to where you wanted to go.

The only problem is, Maddy thought as the train steamed into the station and she gathered up her small overnight bag and stood at the compartment door, I don't know yet where it is I do want to go.

She only just caught the bus that went to Bridge End and sat aboard it as it trundled through the lanes. The hedges were glowing with autumn colour and beech trees arched a coppery canopy overhead. As they entered the village, she felt a pang of familiarity. This was where she had spent part of her childhood; yet for years, as she'd lived in Burracombe and then travelled on the Continent with Fenella, she had almost forgotten it. Now, those days came rushing back to her – long days spent in the garden of the vicarage where she and Stella had lodged with the Budd boys, Tim and Keith, looked after by the eccentric old vicar who had bought their sugar ration at – what was it? A halfpenny a teaspoonful? – and his housekeeper, kindly Mrs Mudge. They might have stayed there until the end of the war if the wise old man hadn't died suddenly in his chair and a woman who Keith Budd had described as looking like a brown settee had come to take them away.

That was when she'd first known Sammy, the timid little boy who had also lived in April Grove in Portsmouth, where the Budds had lived. He'd been sent to Ruth Hodges and had gradually come out of his shell to become Maddy's best friend. She remembered the day she'd almost bullied him into bringing Ruth's beloved parrot, Silver, out to the forest for a picnic, and how they'd almost lost the bird. She'd got him into trouble on other occasions too, although never as badly as that. And then she'd been taken to the orphanage, separated from Stella, and during the years that followed she had almost forgotten the fair-haired little boy – until Rose Budd's wedding day, when they'd met again and fallen instantly in love.

The bus stopped and the passengers climbed out. One or two of them had been vaguely familiar to Maddy, but she hadn't had time during the brief romance to get to know the villagers well again. They departed their separate ways, and she turned to walk along the lane to Ruth's cottage.

Her heart was hammering against her ribs. This was the moment she had been dreading. If Ruth did shut the door against her, there would be at least two hours to wait until the bus came again. What would she do? She could hardly bear to think about it – the shame of having ruined a lovely friendship, of having hurt a woman who had herself been bereft. And Dan, too. He had always seemed so tough and hard, hiding his feelings, but he'd lost his son – both his sons, in fact – and her accusations must have struck at his heart. How could I have been so cruel and thoughtless? she thought miserably as her footsteps dragged. How could I have hurt them so much, just because I was unhappy myself?

At last she was at the gate. She paused, her hand on the latch, her fingers trembling. It wasn't too late to turn and walk away. Ruth and Dan need never know she had been here. She could just go back to West Lyme, forget she had ever come, forget any of it had ever happened. She did not have to risk the rejection she feared so much.

Except that she couldn't turn away. She couldn't live for the rest of her life with the knowledge that she had behaved so selfishly. And leaving now would be even more selfish than when she had run from here the first time, because she'd had time to think and she knew what she must do. Leaving them the first time had been the impulsive, unthinking action of grief. Leaving now would be the action of a coward.

She opened the gate and walked on shaking legs up the short path to the front door. She knocked, timidly at first and then more loudly. There was a moment of breathless waiting, and then it opened.

'*Maddy*...'

For a long half-minute, Ruth Hodges stood absolutely still, staring at the young woman at her door. Then she opened her arms wide and Maddy, bursting into tears, almost fell into them.

'Maddy,' Ruth said wonderingly. And then, opening her arms wide: 'Oh, *Maddy* ...'

They cried together in each other's arms, perhaps for the last time – the last time, at least, that there would be quite such a storm of weeping. There would always be moments when a sudden memory brought tears, but never again would it be like this. It was as if all their common grief had been released at last and they had turned a corner in their recovery.

'I'm so sorry,' Maddy gulped at last, feeling for yet another handkerchief. 'I didn't mean to do this. I meant to just – to just say how sorry I was for the way I behaved, and then go away again. If you didn't want me to stay, I mean.' She looked at Ruth through swollen eyelids. 'Would you like me to do that anyway?'

'Go away?' Ruth echoed, gathering her close again. 'Of course not! I'm just so thankful you're here. Oh, Maddy, these past few weeks have been dreadful. I didn't know what to do about you. I wanted to write to you, but knowing how you felt, I was afraid to make things worse. The only thing I could do was wait, and hope that one day you'd walk back through the door – and I can't tell you how happy I am that you have.'

Maddy looked at her and laughed shakily. 'I am, too – but nobody would think so, the way we've been carrying on. What a sight we must look.' She blew her nose. 'I've been so miserable, Ruth, but what's worse is that I made you miserable, too – you and Dan – just when you should have been happy again. I don't think I'll ever be able to forgive myself for that.'

'Of course you will,' Ruth said. 'Because *we* can forgive you – we already have. We were just so sorry that you were upset. We shouldn't have told you the way we did.'

'How else could you have told me?' Maddy wiped her eyes again. 'Oh dear, I don't seem to be able to stop these tears. They just keep coming ... Honestly, Ruth, I've thought about it so much and I can't see what else you could have done. Once I'd talked to Stella and Felix, and Dottie, about it all, I began to see how selfish I'd been—'

'No!' Ruth exclaimed. 'You weren't selfish at all! It was a shock—'

'Yes, it was, but I didn't have to behave the way I did. I didn't have to be so unkind. And I *was* being selfish – and childish. Felix made me see that. He's really very wise.'

Ruth had only met Felix briefly, at Rose Budd's wedding, and she remembered him as rather a light-hearted young man, quite unlike her idea of a vicar. But then, what actually was her idea of a vicar? Old Reverend Bennett, who had looked after Maddy when she'd been an evacuee, wasn't most people's idea of a vicar either, and now she came to think of it, he'd probably been very like Felix as a young man.

'I think we could both do with a cup of tea,' she said, getting up. She went out to the scullery and Maddy heard her working the pump over the sink. A minute or two later, she came back with the kettle and set it on the range. She sat down beside Maddy and took both her hands in her own, rubbing them gently as she had rubbed Sammy's when he was a little boy and came in with chilled fingers.

'I can understand how you felt,' she said after a minute or two. 'You've lost your sweetheart, in the most awful way, and you feel as if your world's come to an end. And here were Dan and I, who you thought were just as upset as you, having another baby – just as if we didn't care a bit.'

'I shouldn't have said that,' Maddy whispered. 'I know you care.'

'Yes, of course we do. It's one of the worst things in the world, to lose a child. Even though Sammy wasn't really mine, I'd had him since he came to me as a little eight-year-old evacuee, and he was like a son to me – especially after Dan and I got married. I thought I'd never have any children of my own.'

'And now you'll have two,' Maddy said, but the bitterness had gone from her voice.

'Yes, I will. If all goes well.'

Maddy turned her head sharply. 'Why do you say that? There's nothing wrong, is there?'

'Not as far as I know, but we have to remember my age, Maddy. I'm forty-eight years old. That's quite old to be having a baby.' The kettle began to sing and she started to get up.

Maddy jumped to her feet. 'Oh, how could I be so thoughtless? You should be resting – let me make the tea. And I'll get supper ready as well, if you'll tell me what to do.' She stopped suddenly and said, 'I can stay the night, can't I? You wouldn't rather I went back to West Lyme?'

'Of course you can stay here. Dan will want to see you as well – and Linnet. She's been up at the farm all morning and he's gone to collect her – they'll be back soon. Don't look so worried, Maddy, and you don't need to fuss over me either. I'm as strong as a horse and don't forget, I was a midwife. I know how to take care of myself *and* the baby.' She smiled at the younger woman. 'Make the tea, now you're on your feet, and then sit down again.'

Maddy did as she was told. She left the tea to brew in the fat brown teapot while she got out cups and saucers and went to the outside safe for milk. As she closed the small netted door, she heard the click of the garden gate and turned to see Dan and Linnet coming through, hand in hand. They stopped and stared, and then Linnet ran forward and flung herself into Maddy's arms.

'Maddy! Where have you been? Why haven't you been to see us? We've missed you!'

Maddy scooped her up and hugged her, feeling the peach-soft skin of her cheek against her own and breathing in the scent of her hair. She closed her eyes, feeling yet more tears trickle out, and Linnet tilted her head back to look into her face.

'You're crying,' she accused. 'Why are you crying?'

'Because I'm so happy to see you,' Maddy said, a tremulous smile on her lips. 'Haven't you ever cried because you were happy?'

Linnet considered for a moment. 'I cried when Daddy mended my dolly,' she said at last. 'She had a china face and she got broken when I dropped her. Has somebody mended something you'd got broken?'

The question was so near to the truth that Maddy felt her whole body shake and the tears threaten to burst forth again. She drew in a deep breath and held it for a second or two, then said quietly, 'Something *was* broken, Linnet, but I think it is being mended.' She put the little girl down on the path. 'Now, take this milk indoors while I talk to your daddy.'

Linnet took the jug and carried it carefully through the back door. It closed behind her and Maddy turned to face the big, dark-haired man standing quietly by the gate. He regarded her silently and she hesitated, then went to him and laid her hand tentatively on his arm.

'I'm sorry for all those things I said, Dan. I knew even then that they were wrong, but I didn't seem able to help it. I was just so surprised. So ... shocked, I suppose.'

He nodded. 'That's all right, girl. Me and Ruth have talked it all over and she got me to see what it must have been like for you. I'm sorry I let off at you like that myself. I reckon it came as a shock to all of us. A lot of people might think just the same as you – that we didn't really care about Sam.'

'But I don't think it! I didn't even then – not really. It was just – oh, I don't really know what it was. I felt all muddled up about it. For ages. I didn't honestly know what I thought.'

'Well, I'll tell you what I think now,' he said, and put his hands on her shoulders to draw her close for an awkward kiss. 'I think we'll go in and have some tea. Come on. And then maybe we'll have a round or two of cards. Linnet's getting quite good at Sevens – you have to watch her like a hawk.'

They went into the cottage together but Maddy stopped for a moment at the door. She turned to look back at the garden where she and Sammy had played as children, and whispered a silent goodbye to the childhood they had shared. The memories would always be there, but she knew now that she would be able to move forwards in her life at last. She felt a lightness about her shoulders, as if someone had quietly removed a burden she had carried for too long.

A raucous voice split the moment, and she turned again, smiling. It was the first utterance she had heard this afternoon from Silver, the African Grey parrot that Ruth's first husband, Jack, had brought back to her many years before and, as so often happened with Silver, it was uncannily appropriate.

'Born in a field, were you?' he yelled. 'Shut the bloody door, before we all freeze to death!'

Chapter Nineteen

Half-term arrived at last and Hilary collected Rob from Kelly College early on Friday morning. He came out, seeming rather isolated in the crowd of boys, and she felt a sudden pang of compassion for him. He looked small and defensive, as if he expected to be set upon at any moment, and she wondered again if he had been bullied.

'All boys have to go through some sort of initiation when they start school,' her father had said when she broached the subject a few weeks ago. 'Toughens them up. It's over soon enough and then they're all right. He'll have forgotten all about it by half-term, you'll see.'

Hilary wasn't so sure as she watched Rob, walking apart from his fellows and showing little enthusiasm for her. He climbed into the front seat of the car and sat staring out through the window.

'Didn't you bring anything with you?' she asked. The other boys all had a bag or satchel, presumably containing books or treasures they had collected or made at school.

He shrugged. 'I don't need anything from school. I have enough clothes at your house.'

Your house, she noted. 'Yes, you can change out of your uniform as soon as we get home. There's no need to wear that again until you go back on Sunday evening. And there are plenty of books and things for you to do.'

He said nothing and her heart sank as she saw his closed expression. His lips were pressed firmly together and he clearly didn't intend to speak again. She let in the clutch and the car moved down the drive and out on to the Tavistock road.

'I've got a bit of shopping to do in town,' she told him. 'It's market day. Shall we have some coffee and a bun somewhere?'

Rob shrugged again, as if it didn't matter either way, and Hilary sighed, wishing Stephen had agreed to come home this weekend. He had been the only person who seemed able to get anything out of Rob during those early difficult days when he and Marianne had first arrived at the Barton. Perhaps Luke would be able to help, she thought. He'd said she could send Rob down to him at the charcoal-burner's hut that he used as a studio. A few hours with someone not connected with either family or school was probably just what the lonely French boy needed.

We're failing him, she thought as she parked the car in Tavistock and they both climbed out. We haven't taken proper note of what he needs. It's all been what Father wants for him – and from him. It's as Luke says – we've been treating him like an object instead of a person in his own right.

They went into the big pannier market, which was crowded with stalls of all kinds selling fruit, vegetables, cakes and bread, and household goods as well as bric-a-brac and second-hand books. Hilary bought what she needed, then went through to the main street where she gave an order for greengroceries in Roland Bailey's shop. Then she walked along to Creber's, the grocer's on the corner, for cheese and freshly ground coffee. Robert stayed outside, kicking desultorily at the kerb. He had followed her all the way like a dog, taking almost no interest in his surroundings, and she felt her anxiety increase.

'Where would you like to go for coffee?' she enquired, guessing that the Bedford Hotel would not be to his taste. She indicated the café on the corner opposite Creber's. 'Goode's, or Perraton's?'

'Oh – Goode's, please.'

'All right.' She led the way through the door and they sat down at one of the tables. Hilary distributed her shopping bags on the spare seat and smiled at him. 'What would you like? A bun? Or a doughnut? I dare say you're hungry. Stephen always seemed to be at starvation point when he came home from school.'

'A doughnut, please.'

Having answered her, he closed his lips and seemed unlikely to say more. Hilary gazed at him, feeling helpless. She gave her order to the waitress and tried again.

'So how are you settling down? You haven't told us much in your letters. I don't think you liked it much at first, did you?' He looked at her but said nothing and she went on, disconcerted by the expression in his eyes. 'Your grandfather says it always takes a little while to get used to school, but you'll enjoy it then.'

'I shall never enjoy it,' he said flatly.

Hilary blinked. 'Oh, I don't think you can say that. The other boys enjoy it, don't they?'

'Oh yes,' he said with a touch of bitterness. '*They* enjoy it.'

'Well, then ... You'll enjoy it too, you'll see. It's natural to feel a little homesick at first, and especially for you. It really will get better.'

'It won't,' he said in the same flat, uncompromising tone. 'It won't ever get better.'

Their coffee and doughnuts arrived. Hilary watched as he picked his up and bit into it. Jam oozed out and he licked it into his mouth, yet he didn't seem to be eating with the relish Stephen had always displayed when he came home from school. It seemed as if he ate almost out of duty, or a need to stay alive.

'Of course it will get better,' she said. 'Look, Rob, I'm really sorry you're finding it difficult, but I promise you it *will* get better. You'll make good friends there. You must have made one or two already.'

'No,' he said. 'I have no friends.'

'But you've been there for weeks now! You must have found some boys you like.'

'I don't care for any of them,' he said coldly. 'They are *barbare*.'

'*Barbare?*' she echoed doubtfully, and saw him cast about in his mind for the English translation.

'Barbaric,' he said at last. 'They are barbarians.'

Shocked, she stared at him. 'Rob, that's a dreadful thing to say. Of course they're not. They're just ordinary boys.'

He gave her a look as if to say *that's what you think* and closed his lips again. He had finished his doughnut and Hilary looked down at hers, which she hadn't touched, and passed it across to him.

'Here, you have it. I'm not all that hungry.'

At least his appetite didn't seem to be impaired, and he even showed a glimmer of enjoyment as he ate the second doughnut. Hilary watched in silence, unable to think of anything else to say. Was he really unhappy, or just being sulky because he couldn't have his own way? Her father had said some boys took longer than others to settle, and she knew, from her own experience of boarding school, that this was true. But although girls could be difficult, even spiteful, she didn't think she would ever have called her own schoolmates 'barbarians'. She wondered if Stephen would have done.

We don't have the right to take this boy's life and shake it to pieces, she thought as they finished their coffee and went out into the street again. And somehow, over the next couple of days, I've got to find out what's really been going on at that school. If Rob is truly miserable something will have to be done about it.

'*Miserable?* Of course he's miserable,' Gilbert barked when she tried to talk to him about it later that evening. Rob had gone straight to his room when they had arrived home, coming down only for lunch, and had then disappeared for a walk. Hilary had a suspicion he had gone to the village, perhaps to look for his friends Micky and Henry, but she had refrained from asking him when he returned. He had eaten his dinner almost in silence, answering in monosyllables when his grand-father questioned him about school, and had then said goodnight and gone back to his room.

'All boys are miserable when they first go to school. I've told you that before. It's part of the whole process of growing up, learning to be a man. It's a *necessary* part. It's why we send them away in the first place. How can a boy toughen up and learn to take his place in the world if he's tied to his mother's apron strings?'

'Rob's hardly that,' she pointed out. 'His mother's in France – they'd have to be pretty long apron strings.'

'That's the sort of facetious comment Stephen would have made,' he said coldly. 'The fact is that if Robert is going to be any use around here, he has to learn English ways, and there's no better place than a decent school. I take it you won't dispute that Kelly *is* a decent school?'

'I always thought so, yes,' she returned. 'But if it's producing bar-barians, I'm not so sure.'

'Barbarians!' he snorted. 'That's the most utterly ridiculous thing I've ever heard. Normal, high-spirited schoolboys enjoying a bit of fun, that's all. The trouble with Rob is that he doesn't understand the English sense of humour. Once he gets used to that—'

'But can we be sure it *is* just high spirits and fun? Suppose he's really being bullied?'

'Hubert would never countenance bullying in his school,' Gilbert said flatly.

Hilary shook her head. 'I'm not saying he would – if he knew about it. But, Father, you know as well as I do that the boys aren't under supervision every minute of the day – or night. *We* weren't, at the abbey. There were quite long periods when we could go for walks in the grounds, or were left on our own in the common rooms, when bullying could go on. And so it did.'

'*Girls* went in for bullying? I don't believe it.'

'Maybe not the sort of bullying that boys do – knocking each other about. But they could certainly be very nasty. I remember one girl who got picked on by everyone.' Including me, she thought guiltily, until I realised how much we were upsetting her and put a stop to it. 'People either ignored her or followed her about in a crowd, staring at her. Nobody ever touched her, or even said anything unpleasant, but it was enough to reduce her to tears at night.'

'And you think that's what's been happening to Robert? Well, if that's all there is to it, it simply bears out what I've been saying – the boy needs toughening up. If he can't deal with being stared at—'

'I didn't say that's what's been happening. I don't *know* what's been happening. But I'm as sure as I'm sitting here that something has happened, and it's making him very unhappy. And it's up to us to find out what it is. We can't just send him back to school having done nothing about it. He's in our *care*, Father. We can't just shrug it off.'

'I'm not shrugging it off. I'm simply telling you that it's nothing out of the ordinary. It's what every boy who ever went to school has had to deal with, and it happens for a purpose. For God's sake, every tribe of savages has its initiation rites, when a boy becomes a man. It's part of the natural way of things.'

'So you're saying that schoolboys are savages?' Hilary permitted herself a small, grim smile. 'Well, I don't think I'd argue with that! And what exactly is the difference between savages and barbarians?'

Her father glowered at her. 'Now you're trying to be clever. You know perfectly well what I mean. Look, take it from me, however miserable Robert thinks he is now, he'll feel completely different by the time he comes home again at Christmas. He'll have settled down, made friends and forgotten all about "being miserable". Wait and see.'

Hilary said no more. But as she said goodnight to her father and went to bed, she felt doubtful. Rob's misery had seemed to her to go deeper than a few minor humiliations inflicted by fellow schoolboys as a form of initiation, and not only did she doubt that it would be resolved by Christmas, she felt deeply uneasy at the thought of sending him back to endure more.

She washed, brushed her teeth and then stood at her window for a few moments, looking out over the moonlit lawn. There was no denying that Burracombe was one of the most beautiful places on earth. But beauty had little to say to a young boy, far from home, torn from his family and thrown headlong into a completely alien way of life. Rob needed comfort and reassurance, yet who was the one most able to give it him?

Not me, I'm afraid, she thought, and turned away from the window.

Chapter Twenty

The argument that had flared up at Tozers' farm over Jackie's plans to go to America had been calmed by Minnie's words, and by the time she'd left to return to Plymouth, Jackie and her parents had been more or less reconciled. They all knew, though, that the matter hadn't gone away and when Russ had driven her back to the main road to catch the bus, he had made it quite clear that she was welcome in Corning whenever she wanted to come.

'Now, or in two years' time,' he'd said, smiling. 'It's not *so* long to wait, after all.'

Jackie didn't want to wait even two years. She had never been very patient, even as a child, always longing for Christmas or birthdays to come quickly, and demanding everything 'now'. As her mother had often remarked, once Jackie got an idea in her head she wanted to get on with it straight away, never mind whether it was sensible or not.

Back at the hotel, her head was filled with visions of herself in America. Whatever her uncle and cousin said about Corning being a small, quiet town, it was still America and therefore, to her mind, it must be glamorous and exciting. The people would be glossier and more polished – better dressed, with good jobs and more money. And I could get a job there easily, she thought. They must have hotels where I could work. It doesn't even have to be in a hotel. I could be a receptionist in a big office, or a doctor's surgery. And I can do typing and shorthand – I could be a secretary. There are lots of things I could do.

She dreamed of America and the people she would meet there, the exciting things she would do, and determined to get up early and start making plans. The first thing was a passport. How did you go about getting one of those? But when she woke in the morning to see the dawn send a sliver of grey light through a crack in the curtain, a fresh thought struck like a shard of ice to her heart – would she need her parents' permission to have one?

Jackie sat up and put both hands to her cheeks. Almost certainly, she would. She thumped her fist on the eiderdown in frustration. You couldn't do anything without your parents' permission, until you were twenty-one. You couldn't get married, or vote, or do anything adults did at all, even though you could be out at work, earning your own living, and if you were a boy you could go and fight and even die for your country. But you couldn't live your own life as you wanted to live it.

They'll never give permission, she thought. They can stop me going just like that. They can stop *everything*.

And her dreams seemed to shatter around her, like fragile glass.

'I think it's a shame,' Russ said as he and his father climbed up the hill to the Standing Stones, the little ring of ancient megaliths silhouetted on the hillside above the village. 'The kid's bright and smart, and keen to see the world. And she'd be with family – we'd look after her. Why are her ma and pa so against the idea?'

'They think she'll go away and never come back,' Joe said. 'Like I did. You can understand it.'

'I'm not sure I can. It's her life, after all. She ought to be able to live it the way she wants. And like she says – in two years' time she'll be able to do whatever she likes, so why stop her now?'

'Because in two years' time, she might have changed her mind. That's what they're hoping – Alice especially. By then, she could be married and settled down, maybe even have a baby on the way. And she'd be somewhere near Burracombe. They'd have her nearby for life, and that's what they want.'

Russ paused for breath and turned to look down over the village, dreaming in its wooded valley. 'Well, if you ask me, that's darned selfish. OK, they're living their lives the way they want to, and it's a good life, I can see that. But to insist on it for your children, whether it's what they want for themselves or not – no, that's plain selfish, no other word for it. And it's not as if Jackie's their only child. They've got Brian – I know he's in Germany just now but he'll be back home one day when he leaves the army. And Tom lives in the same house with them, and Val's in the village.' They began to climb again, each occupied with his own thoughts, and then he said, 'Say, Dad, suppose it was me wanting to stay here in England – would you stop me?'

'Tell me how I could,' Joe said drily. 'No, of course I wouldn't, any more than my ma and pa stopped me. But it's different for a girl.'

'I don't see why. I truly don't see why.'

They reached the stones and stopped again. Joe gazed over the countryside he had known so well as a boy and a young man, before war had broken out and torn Europe apart, spreading its canker over the rest of the world. This was what he had fought for – to keep England as it was, to make it a land fit for heroes to live in. He had returned to find that, in the cynical words of one of his friends, you had to be a hero to live there, and had decided to seek pastures new in America. It had been the best decision he had ever made – that, and marrying Eleanor – and he had never regretted it. Yet since returning for this visit, he had begun to realise how hard his decision had been for his mother, and probably his father, too. Minnie had said he hadn't broken her heart, but it had obviously hurt her deeply to see her son leave his home and family. He knew that if Russ did leave him, he would find that just as hard, and while he knew that he would never prevent the boy from living his own life, he also understood the feelings Ted and Alice had about Jackie.

'Logically, I don't see why, either,' he said at last. 'But logic don't always come into it, Russ. Not when it's your kids involved. Especially not when it's your daughter.'

Russ sat down at the base of one of the stones. 'So what do we do?'

'Nothing we can do.' Joe squatted beside him. 'It's between young Jackie and her family now. Best for us to try not to get too deeply involved. I don't want any quarrel between us. Ted may be right – she may forget the idea. But if she doesn't, and if she manages to win them round – or if she waits the two years and then comes over – well, we'll give her all the support we can, and make sure Ted and Alice realise we'll look after her. I think they pretty well know that already.'

'Seems a pity she can't come back with us, though. It'd be good to have her along with us when we get home.'

'Well, it could happen yet. There's still a while before we go back.

'We've got our trip on the Continent ahead of us, and then we'll be back here for Christmas and young Stella's wedding to the vicar before we head back to the States. It's good of her to invite us along to that.'

'She seems a real nice young woman. And I like Felix, too – a different cut from what you expect of a vicar. Not that Basil Harvey's not a grand chap as well. I suppose it'll be a pretty big do.'

'I guess so,' Joe said. 'Both villages will be there.' He smiled. 'Funny to think of that – Burracombe and Little Burracombe have been at loggerheads ever since I can remember. If there's a fence they can get on opposite sides of, you can bet they'll be there, glaring at each other over the top. And now here they are, having to set it all aside for the vicar's wedding. And Felix was curate of Burracombe before he crossed the Clam, you know.'

'Yeah. Before they know it, they'll all be bosom buddies.'

'I doubt that.' Joe grinned. 'Give it three days and they'll find something else to argue about.'

There was a short silence, then Russ said, 'I guess Stella's sister will be there too – Maggie, was it?'

'Maddy,' Joe said. 'Sure to be. Another nice young lady, but had a bit of tragedy, I hear.'

'That's right. Pretty hard, to lose her fiancé in a road accident. Nice-looking girl like that won't be on her own for long, though.'

Joe glanced sideways at his son. Russ was gazing out over the valley, watching a buzzard riding the thermals high over the distant tors. He looked distracted, as though his thoughts were elsewhere. Joe waited, but nothing more appeared to be forthcoming and after a moment he went back to the subject of their visit.

'We'll have to be thinking about where we want to go next. London first, maybe, and then the Continent. I don't mind which, so long as we're back for Christmas.'

'Yeah, I'm looking forward to Christmas in Burracombe,' Russ agreed. 'It sounds a real ball.'

'It is. Carol singing in the snow... a candlelit church service at midnight on Christmas Eve ...'

'Little rosy-cheeked children singing "Rudolph the Red-Nosed Reindeer" and "I Saw Mommy Kissing Santa Claus".' Russ suggested, grinning.

'Yeah, that too, I guess. And a big family Christmas party, with crackers and paper hats and games like Postman's Knock and Pass the Scissors.'

'That sure sounds exciting stuff,' Russ observed, and his father gave him a push that sent him sprawling on the grass. 'Well, have you *listened* to yourself!'

'It's good old-fashioned family entertainment,' Joe told him severely, 'and I don't want anything happening to spoil it. I'm serious, Russ.'

'Yeah, I know. So am I. It's OK, Pa – we won't upset the applecart now. Like you say, it's between Jackie and her folks and we'll just wait for them to come round. And in the meantime, I mean to enjoy some more Devon country life before we set off on the next part of our travels.'

'France,' Joe said thoughtfully. 'I want to pay a visit to some of the places I saw when I was over there during the Great War. Pay my respects, I guess, to the mates that never came home. And then we'll take a look at Switzerland or maybe Italy. It's the tour of a lifetime for me, Russ. I don't want to waste a minute of it in family arguments. And I don't want to waste my family, either.' He let his gaze travel slowly over the scene before him – the cottages, clustered together in the valley, the glimpse of sparkling water tumbling over rocks between the burnished colours of the trees, the purple moors and the grey, dreaming tors in the distance. 'It's only now, coming back after all these years, that I realise just how much they've meant to me.'

Val and Luke were discussing Jackie's plans, too. They talked about the idea that evening as Val gave Christopher his six o'clock feed. Luke had brought home a pile of drawings made by his pupils in that day's art class, and was sitting at the table going through them as they chatted.

'How do you feel about it?' he asked. 'You're pretty close to Jackie. D'you reckon they ought to let her go?'

'I don't quite know what to think,' she answered thoughtfully. 'On one hand, I can see Mum and Dad's point – Jackie is very young, and she's young for her age, too, although she's grown up quite a lot since she's been in Plymouth and had more independence. But they can't see that, of course – they still think of her as a little girl. I don't think they really like to see her being more independent and making her own decisions – it's almost as if it frightens them.'

'I suppose it does, a bit. After all, if she makes the *wrong* decision ...'

'Well, we all do that, at times,' she said quietly, and their eyes met as they remembered the time when they had first known each other, in Egypt, and the disastrous end to their affair then. 'Being over twenty-one doesn't necessarily make any difference to that.'

There was a brief silence, and then he said, 'But *you* went away from home before you were twenty-one. Most girls did – the war took them. There was nothing parents could do to stop that.'

'I know, and perhaps that's why they try even harder to hold them back now. I thought of trying to say something like that to Mum – about me going into the army as a nurse, and going abroad. But how can I do that, now that she knows about Johnny?' She looked down at the baby at her breast. 'Maybe I shouldn't have told her I'd already had a miscarriage, on the way back from Egypt, but I did. And although I don't suppose she'd remind me, I know she'd think it's proof that she's right – that girls shouldn't leave home and go so far away.'

'So that's one hand,' he said, squinting at one of the drawings. 'Talk about a budding Picasso! I can't even see which way up this one's supposed to be ... What's the other hand?'

'The other hand? Well – it's Jackie's point of view, of course. And she knows I went away when I was much the same age as she is, and *she* sees it as proof that she could do the same. Not that she probably even thinks of it like that – Jackie's mind doesn't work that way. She just believes that whatever she wants to do is the right thing for her, and she's confident enough now to believe she can cope with whatever happens.'

'Even travelling around America on her own?' He caught her startled glance. 'Well, you're not telling me she'll stay in Corning very long! She'll take whatever job's offered, save up a bit of money and then go off to the next place that takes her fancy. Jackie's what your cousin Russ would call a *go-getter*.' He scribbled a quick '2 out of 10' on the paper before him and then got up and went over to her, his fingers lightly touching the soft cheek of his son as he fed. 'To be perfectly honest, Val, I believe your parents really do have something to worry about. They're afraid that once Jackie goes to America she may never come back – and I think they could very well be right.'

Chapter Twenty-One

'I don't want to go back,' Robert said, dragging his feet across the grass. 'I don't like it there. I *hate* it.'

Hilary stopped and looked back at him in despair. She had brought him out for a walk on the moor with the dogs, hoping it would cheer him up before they had high tea and she took him back to Kelly College. At least, she thought, he might talk to her. But as the afternoon progressed, he had become more and more silent and now his face was sullen, with that closed expression she had come to dread.

'Rob, you must go back,' she said. 'It can't be that bad, surely? All the other boys don't hate it.'

'How do you know?' he asked, and she had to admit she didn't.

'I really don't think they do. If everyone felt like that, the parents would do something about it. They wouldn't send their boys to school if it was that bad.'

'English parents would,' he said bitterly. 'I think the English don't like their children much, or they would keep them at home, as we do in France, and not send them away. It's like going to prison.'

'Rob, it isn't! And the English do love their children. That's why we want them to have a good education.'

'But there are other schools. There's a school in Tavistock – Micky and Henry go there. Won't they get a good education?'

'Yes, I think they will,' Hilary admitted. 'It's a grammar school, and they're very good. But you need to make friends—'

'Micky and Henry are my friends. Why can't I go to school with them?'

Because Micky and Henry are sons of the village blacksmith and a farm labourer, Hilary thought, feeling ashamed. She knew that the two boys were also bright, intelligent and the equals of many public-school pupils. But that was what it boiled down to – keeping children within their own class. Gilbert Napier, a landowner and army colonel, did not wish his grandson to mix with the village children. He had made this very plain after the escapade during the summer, when the two boys had taken Rob down one of the old mine adits on the moor.

'Your grandfather wants you to go to Kelly,' she said. 'It's a very good school, Rob. You'll realise that later on. You'll get an excellent education and you'll meet the sort of people he wants you to meet.'

'*Those* sort of people?' Rob exclaimed. 'Does he know what sort of people they are, *Tante* Hilary? Do *you* know?'

She stared at him, nonplussed. 'I know what you called them the other day, but they can't be that bad, Rob. They're sons of good families, they're—'

'Barbarians,' he said contemptuously. 'Yes, that's what I called them, because that's what they are. Do you know what they do to new boys there? These "sons of good families"? Shall I tell you?'

'Yes,' Hilary said, thinking that at last they were going to get to the crux of the matter. 'I think you better had.'

They sat down on a rock. It was the sort of thing Hilary had often done herself – come up here, to sit in a quiet place with the beauty of Dartmoor laid out before her, to think over some problem and come to some conclusion. She had almost always returned home feeling better for the respite. Perhaps the tranquil, yet wild, atmosphere would work its magic on Rob as well. She looked at him, and waited.

'First,' he said, 'the new boys are called "new ticks". *Ticks*! As if we were some nasty little pests who fasten themselves into the skin of a dog! That is to humiliate us, of course, but it's just the start. Then we are given a test – a long list of facts about the school, which we must learn.'

'Well, that doesn't sound too bad,' Hilary said. 'After all, there must be a lot to learn and get used to. What sort of facts?'

'Facts such as who scored most tries in a rugby match about twenty years ago,' he said scornfully. 'Or who won the third-form hundred yards race on sports day in 1939 – as if anyone cares. Those sort of facts.'

She looked at him doubtfully. 'The teachers give you this list?'

'No, the boys do, but the teachers know about it. They know *all* about it – otherwise why should they not look into in the common room when the punishment is carried out?'

'Punishment?'

'Nobody can learn all that is on that list,' he said. 'There isn't time, and anyway, who would want to? So the next day, all the new boys – the *ticks* – are brought into the Junior Common Room and tested. And then, because they don't pass the test, they are punished.'

Hilary was beginning to feel deeply uneasy. She knew that boys could be very hard on each other, but had never really believed that it amounted to cruelty. This sounded like real bullying.

'How are they punished?' she asked at last.

'There are two ways,' Robert said. 'First, you are taken to the bathrooms, where the water pipes are always hot. They are *very* hot – almost boiling, I think – and they are quite high above the floor. You are made to stand on a chair and reach up to hold on to the pipes. And then the chair is taken away.' He looked at his hands. 'It seems like a very long time, when your hands are burning and you're afraid to let go.'

Hilary stared at him. 'But you have to let go, surely!'

'Yes, but if you let go too soon, there is another part to the punishment, and that's worse. So you try to hold on for as long as you can.' He looked at his hands again. 'I had large blisters, but because I am French and the headmaster knows my grandfather, I was made to hold on longer than the others. And even that was not enough.'

Hilary grasped his hands and examined the palms. There were indeed patches of shiny new skin where blisters had healed.

'So then what happened?' she asked, feeling sick.

'Then there is *boxing*.'

'Boxing? Well, at least you have a chance to win then – although I don't suppose you've learned much boxing, have you?'

'Not that sort of boxing,' he said scathingly. 'In the common room, there is a large box. It's kept for rubbish to be thrown into, a sort of big waste-paper basket, and there's a division down its length so that paper rubbish can be kept separate from things like apple cores or orange peel. First, you are put into this box. You have to bend over the division, so that your legs and feet are one side and your head and arms the other. It's just the right size for a *new tick*.'

'And then?' she asked, knowing there had to be more.

'Then the common-room table is lifted over you. It's just the right height, so you're folded over and pressed down a little. It is very uncomfortable.' He put one hand on his stomach and Hilary thought of the wooden divider, pressing into a boy's abdomen. 'You cannot move. And then the other boys climb on to the table and begin to jump on it, and dance. They make a lot of noise. And the teachers know what is happening. They must know.'

'How long did this go on for?' Hilary was feeling faint now. That this had been happening, just a few miles from the Barton, while she and her father were thinking complacently that their charge was simply having a little difficulty in settling down! She thought of his description of them as barbarians.

'About an hour, I think. It seemed a very long time. And then they all went out of the room and left me.'

'*Left* you?'

'Yes,' he said. 'I didn't know when they were coming back.'

Hilary thought of the boy – cramped into the most uncomfortable and, by then, painful position under a heavy table, then left there for goodness knows how long – and made up her mind. 'Rob, you must tell your grandfather all this. We can't allow you to be bullied in this way. You're right – it's barbaric.' She hesitated, half afraid to ask the next question. 'Was there any more?'

'That's the worst. There are a lot of small things, too – a shoe missing, a tie stained, pencils taken from the desk – things that will get you into trouble. I've been in quite a lot of trouble like that.'

They might sound small in comparison with the pitiless 'punishments' meted to the defenceless new boys, but Hilary knew that such harassment could be equally cruel. She looked at the French boy and saw that his face was hard with bitterness and resentment.

'Come on,' she said. She stood up, holding out her hand. 'Let's go back. I think you must tell your grandfather all this, before you go back to school.'

'Back?' he repeated, and got up slowly, ignoring her hand. 'You are still going to send me back?'

'Well, yes,' Hilary said, rather at a loss. 'I'm afraid you do have to go back. For the time being, at least.'

'But I've told you – I don't *want* to go back.'

'I know,' she said gently, 'but it's not that easy. You have to go to school – it's the law of the land. And you have a place at Kelly. You can't just leave – we'd never get you in anywhere else at this stage, halfway through the term.'

'You said Tavistock Grammar is a good school.'

'Yes, so it is, but you can't just *go* there – you'd have to pass the 11-plus exam and—'

'I would pass that,' he said with certainty. 'I am not stupid.'

'No, of course you're not, but – well, it would all take time, and there might not be a place. You might have to go to the other school – the secondary modern.'

'So what is wrong with that?'

'Nothing,' Hilary said, floundering desperately. 'But you wouldn't learn so many subjects. Latin and Greek – French – science and mathematics. It's different there. They do different things, like woodwork and metalwork—'

'Engineering!' he exclaimed, his face lighting up. 'That's what I want to do! I could go to that school and learn to be an engineer.'

'Not as well as you would at Kelly,' she said. 'In any case, Father will never let you. I'm sorry, Rob, but you have to go back to school this afternoon. Perhaps we could have a word with the headmaster.'

'And make everything much, much worse,' he said grimly. 'No, thank you, *Tante* Hilary. Well, if I have to go back today, I will. But I won't stay there, you know. And if I can't go to another school in Tavistock, I'll go back to France. I'll go home.'

As he spoke the last few words, he turned away, so that she could not see his face. She watched him for a moment, deeply disturbed. There was no doubt that he meant it.

'Rob,' she said gently, touching his arm and turning him to face her. 'I'm truly sorry that you're so unhappy. But please will you try again? I'm sure things will get better, as time goes on. And *I'll* talk to your grandfather about it.' She too had a very good idea what her father would say, but surely once he knew what Rob had been enduring … 'I'll do my very best for you,' she promised.

Their eyes met and she was struck all over again by his resemblance to Baden. It wasn't just his looks either, she thought – there was a steeliness in those blue eyes that spoke of a hidden determination never to give in, a will to win over whatever odds. She had seen her brother look like that frequently, from the time he was a toddler, refusing to let go of his toys, to the day when, as a man, he had marched away to war. If he had passed that resolute fortitude to his son, Robert would surely come through whatever indignities his schoolmates had to offer.

She would keep her promise to speak to her father, though.

'Not stay at Kelly?' Gilbert laid down his knife and fork and stared at her across the dining table. 'What in heaven's name are you talking about?'

'Exactly what I said, Father. He's unhappy there – that's why he hasn't been writing. He's being bullied—'

'Nonsense!'

'It isn't nonsense. He told me all about it.' Hilary described what Robert had told her, but her father snorted and shrugged it aside.

'Those are just the normal rituals that all new boys go through. Toughens them up. If he doesn't like it, all he has to do is fight back. Once they've got a bit of respect for him, they'll leave him alone.'

'I don't think Rob is the "fighting back" sort,' Hilary said.

'Then he'd better learn to be. A few bouts with his fists behind the gym and he'll soon show the rest of 'em what a Napier is made of.'

'And suppose he can't do that?'

'Are you saying Baden's son is a coward?' he demanded, his heavy brows drawing together.

'No, I'm not, and I don't believe he is. But I don't think he's a fighter – not in that way. And he doesn't understand the way an English public school works. He doesn't like it.'

'I didn't like it either, not at first. I doubt if Baden liked it, or Stephen. But we soon *learned* to like it. I tell you, Hilary, once the other boys respect him he'll be all right. I dare say he's all right *now*. The first half-term's over, and they'll have forgotten all about tests and punishments, and be more interested in who gets into the rugger team.'

Hilary wasn't so sure. With Robert, she felt, grudges ran deep. The other boys might forget his humiliation, but he wouldn't.

She said, 'It's more difficult for him, though. You and Baden and Stephen had all been to prep school. You had older brothers or friends with older brothers, who gave you some sort of inkling about what would happen, and you probably had friends at the main school already – boys who'd been with you at prep. Rob didn't have any of that. He's just been flung in, willy-nilly, with no idea about what it would be like. And there's the fagging, too. He's got to fag for one of the older boys.'

'Perfectly normal. Teaches the young'ns their place.'

'I know, but apparently the boy he fags for is a real bully. And Rob's not used to having to run errands and act like a servant.'

'Do him good,' Gilbert said unfeelingly, and picked up his knife and fork again. 'Look, Hilary, all boys go through this. It's nothing out of the ordinary, and the masters keep an eye on it so that it doesn't go too far.'

'Do they? According to Rob, none of them came near the common room while all this was going on.'

'Because they *knew* it was going on! They'd have been on the spot soon enough if it had got out of hand, believe me.' He gave her a straight look. 'You say Rob called them savages—'

'Barbarians.'

'Barbarians, then. Well, in effect, he's right – that's what boys are. All of 'em. A tribe of savages, or barbarians if you like, with their own rules and their own rituals. Once you learn what they are, you're all right. And there's nothing to be done about it – it's what boys are like. You can't change them, so you go along with them and gradually impose your own set of rules until you can turn them into something resembling human beings. That's what a good school does, and that's why the masters won't interfere. It's all part of the process.'

Hilary said no more. It was clear that her father had fixed ideas on this, as he had on so many things, and his mind would not be changed. She finished her meal and then went outside and stood on the terrace, gazing at the stars.

I hope Father's right, and Rob does settle down now, she thought. But what if he really does make up his mind that he isn't going to stay at school? What will he do then?

Chapter Twenty-Two

Hilary was still worrying about Rob when she set off for the reunion in London a few days later. She caught the train in Tavistock and sat beside the window, watching the purple moors disappear behind her and the softer green hills and coppery woods of east Devon take their place, and wondered how he was getting along. Were there other rituals to go through, other humiliations and 'punishments'? And was her father right in saying that it not only did no harm, but was actively good? She sighed and shook her head. Whatever the answers, she could do nothing about it now and might as well turn her mind to the weekend ahead. She still wasn't sure it had been a good idea to come, and once again she wondered just who would be there.

She cast her mind over the names she and Val had recalled. Major Sutcliffe ... Colonel Farrant ... 'Grubby' Mac ... And others she'd known as well, that Val had either not known or forgotten, but Hilary had not. John Brewer ... David Hunter ... She smiled a little, wondering if she would even recognise them after all these years, and then knew that she would. Some faces would never be forgotten.

They probably wouldn't be there, though. In fact, she told herself as she caught a sudden glimpse of a white horse carved into the hillside, she hoped they wouldn't. She certainly hoped that at least one of them wouldn't.

The club she was staying in was near Marble Arch – an elegant house at the end of a terrace in a quiet back street. She went through the doors and was greeted by the young woman at the desk and given the key to her room. After unpacking her small suitcase and tidying herself, she went down to the lounge.

'Hilary!'

A small, dainty woman of her own age rose from one of the chairs and came forward to embrace her. They gazed at each other, taking in the changes since they had last met, laughing a little.

'Dorcas! You don't look a day older.'

'Flatterer! Of course I look older. I was nothing but a silly child when we went out to Egypt. I grew up there, though!' She grinned wickedly and Hilary laughed.

'I think we all did. Are any of the others staying here?'

'Vanessa is, and Liz. I don't know about the others. Isn't this fun! We'll get a taxi together to go to the party. How long are you staying? We could go to a show one evening.'

'Only the two nights. I thought I'd do some shopping as well. I don't often come to London these days.'

'Oh yes! *Lots* of shopping!' Dorcas tossed her head in glee. Her pale gold hair had been cut in a shorter style, Hilary noticed, and curled all over her small head. Her china-blue eyes were just as bright and laughing as ever, and her small mouth coloured with rose. As usual, Hilary felt tall and gawky beside her petite figure.

Dorcas took her by the arm and led her towards a group of armchairs. 'Come and tell me what you've been doing, burying yourself down in Devon all this time. Have you got a gorgeous husband? And lots of marvellous lovers? Don't tell me you've got half a dozen children clustered round your knees!'

'None of those,' Hilary admitted, laughing despite herself. She was quite sure that Dorcas had all of these – well, perhaps not half a dozen children, not with a figure like hers, but certainly the gorgeous husband and, if she were running true to form, one or two lovers as well. 'Still not married, no lovers, but quite happy running the estate for my father.'

'Running the estate? You mean *farming*? And no men in your life? I don't believe it! Hilary, we must do something about this at once.'

'There's no need to do anything about it. I told you, I'm quite happy.' Well, I was until recently, she thought.

'You can't be,' Dorcas said positively. 'Oh look, here's Liz. Liz, look who I've got here – it's Hilary, and you simply won't *believe* what she's telling me!'

'Honestly, Dorcas, there's no need to broadcast it everywhere,'

Hilary protested, and kissed the newcomer. Liz, her long blonde hair tumbling in waves to her shoulders, was even taller than she was, but Hilary was sure she would never feel gawky. She had the looks and grace of a catwalk model. 'You look more like Barbara Goalen every time I see you,' Hilary told her.

'I wish it were true.' Liz studied her. 'You look pretty good yourself, Hilary. Country air obviously suits you.'

'That's just what I'm *telling* you,' Dorcas interrupted. 'Hilary's turned into a *farmer*! She probably even gets up early to milk *cows*. Do you, Hilary? Please tell us you don't!'

'I don't,' Hilary said obligingly. 'And I haven't come all the way to London to talk about them either. Tell me what you two are doing. It has to be more interesting than my life.'

They sat down, ordered tea, and began to tell each other about their lives since the end of the war. All of them had intended to keep in touch, but civilian life and the many changes that had taken place during the six years of war had soon swept them into a different world and communication had dwindled to little more than Christmas cards or the occasional holiday postcard. There was a lot to catch up on.

While they were doing it, the fourth member of their group arrived. Vanessa was even more glamorous and well-groomed than the other two, dressed in a dark blue suit that even Hilary could see was a Dior creation, with a silver fox fur draped carelessly around her neck. She unwound it and tossed it on to the back of a chair, kissed them all, and sat down, crossing long legs encased in sheer nylon. Her dark hair was artfully styled, with a deep wave sweeping up past her ears to a pile of curls on top of her head. She opened her handbag and took out a silver cigarette case, offering it round.

Hilary shook her head. 'Thanks, but I don't.'

'You never did, did you?' Liz borrowed Vanessa's lighter. 'You never drank much either, from what I remember. No vices at all?'

'I told you,' Dorcas said, lighting up. 'She *farms*. Don't you, Hilary?'

'Yes, I do, as a matter of fact.' Hilary was beginning to feel a little nettled. I don't belong here, she thought. I've forgotten how to be a society girl – if I ever knew. 'I run quite a large estate. We have a manager, too, because my father doesn't believe in women having careers, but before he came I ran it on my own.'

'Careers?' Vanessa said, blowing a languid smoke-ring. 'Is farming a career?'

Hilary glanced at her and remembered that she had never liked Vanessa much. But things had been different when they were all ATS officers and working together. It was true that the others had been doing mostly administrative work, while she had been a driver, but glamour hadn't been a big part of their lives in those days – although they'd made a pretty good effort for the dances and balls that were held in the mess.

'What do you all do?' she asked, looking round the little circle of faces. 'Do you have careers?'

Dorcas gave a squeal of laughter and Liz smiled. Vanessa looked down her nose.

'A career? No, darling, I had enough of that in the war. I have enough to do looking after the house, and my husband, of course.'

'Yes, you married Tim Standrick, didn't you? I remember getting an invitation. I was sorry I couldn't go, but it was when my mother was ill. D'you have any family?'

'Two,' Vanessa said. 'Pigeon pair, duty done. Vaughan is five and Constance is two.' She flicked ash from the end of her cigarette.

'And I've got three,' Liz said, grinning. 'Didn't mean to, but the second one turned out to be twins! All boys, so of course everyone wants me to try again, for a girl, but I'm holding out against it.'

'I should think so too,' Dorcas said, and shuddered. 'The very *thought* of having a baby terrifies me. Thankfully, Artie feels the same – not terrified, of course, since he wouldn't be the one to go through it, but he doesn't want children any more than I do. We like to live our own lives.' She blew a smoke-ring to rival Vanessa's and smiled a secret smile.

'Didn't you marry, then?' Vanessa asked Hilary. 'I know your fiancé was killed, but surely there've been a few chances.' *Even for you*, her look added.

'No,' Hilary said shortly. 'I didn't, and I don't suppose I will now.' To their sympathetic expressions, she added, 'I don't actually *want* to. I'm perfectly happy as I am. And as I've already told you,' she added to Dorcas, 'I don't have lovers, either.'

Liz laughed. 'Then your life must be a lot simpler than Dorcas's! How she manages to keep so many pots boiling, I can't imagine.

Anyway, we're not here to discuss husbands and children – we're here to relive the old days and kick over the traces a bit, like we used to in Egypt. Do you remember when …?' And she began to talk about the days when they had lived and worked under a baking sun in the desert near Cairo. One reminiscence led to another and, before they knew it, it was time to go and change for dinner. They parted and went to their rooms, agreeing to meet in an hour's time and go by taxi to the Café Royal, where tonight's dinner was to be held.

Hilary lay in her bath, wondering why she had come. She had nothing in common with these women, she thought. Liz was all right – she'd always been friendly and down to earth – but Vanessa was a supercilious snob and Dorcas an empty-headed butterfly. It was a pity Val wasn't here, but Val hadn't been invited and wouldn't have been able to come anyway. Still, there were others coming to the dinner who had been closer friends, and she was looking forward to meeting them.

The reunion wasn't only for the ATS officers. There were men coming too, from the regiment, and the Saturday night was to be a dinner-dance. Hilary, who seldom went to such affairs now, had been to Exeter to shop for an evening dress and felt quite pleased with her purchase, which was a dark red velvet with a deep boat neck and long full skirt. For this evening, which was to be less formal, she had brought a black cocktail dress that Dottie Friend had made for her two or three years ago. The hemline wasn't the sixteen inches from the floor decreed by Dior, but she felt quite satisfied with her reflection in the long mirror and drew her mother's fur coat around her shoulders before going down to join the others.

Vanessa, of course, was dressed like a film star, while Liz didn't seem able to help looking as if she'd just stepped out of a fashion plate. Dorcas, her waist as tiny as a child's in her tight-fitting gold cocktail dress, seemed to shimmer from head to foot. They made no comment on Hilary's attire and all went out together to the taxi that was waiting outside.

I wish I hadn't come, Hilary thought as they drove through the London streets. This just isn't my world any more. I've nothing in common with any of them – even Liz, who I used to be quite friendly with. Their lives are different from mine and I want no part of them.

She felt suddenly very lonely. In staying at home, first to look after her mother and then her father, and then to take on the estate, she had turned her back on 'society' life. She was no stranger to it – she had done her season as a debutante, mixed with dukes and duchesses, met Henry and got engaged. But now all that seemed to have happened in another life. There had been a war since then; she had travelled abroad, seen its effects at close hand, taken on responsibilities she had never dreamed of. It had changed her, and she found that she didn't want to change back.

My place isn't here, she thought as the taxi drew up outside the Café Royal. But it doesn't seem to be at Burracombe any more, either. So where do I belong?

Inside, everyone was standing with a drink in their hand, greeting each other like long-lost friends – as most of them indeed were. Hilary accepted a glass of champagne from a waitress, and waited for Liz and the others to return from the cloakroom. She knew most of those in the room, and was already talking to a small group of girls she vaguely remembered from an office somewhere, when a hand fell lightly upon her shoulder.

'Hilary,' a quiet voice said in her ear, and she spun round, almost spilling her champagne.

He was there. She had done her best to put him out of her mind, to convince herself that he would not come. Her breath seemed to leave her body, and she stood very still.

For a long moment, she stared at him, her eyes taking in his height, the deep brown of his eyes, the lean, chiselled planes of his cheekbones and the achingly familiar, faintly wicked contour of his mouth. There was a slight touch of silver at the temples in the eagle's-wing curve of his dark hair, and his expression held a gravity she did not remember. She wondered briefly what the years had done to him, and then her memory swept her away from the Café Royal and into a night under the stars in the Egyptian desert, with the sound of a band playing dance tunes in the officers' mess and the soft whisper of palm leaves moving gently above.

'*David* ...' she breathed, and the world spun about her head.

'Champagne on an empty stomach,' she said with a little laugh to the cluster of anxious faces. 'That's all. I'm quite all right, really.'

'Thought you were going to pass out on us,' said a red-faced man with a ginger moustache whom Hilary could not remember ever having seen before. 'Just caught you before you toppled over.'

Someone handed her a glass of water, and she sipped it, feeling the strength return. 'I'm all right now. Thanks.'

The little crowd hovered for a moment, as if not wishing to seem callous, then dispersed gratefully to their own small gatherings. The man with the ginger moustache seemed disposed to linger, but she smiled at him dismissively and he moved reluctantly away. Hilary and David were left alone.

'I didn't think you'd be here,' she said at last, taking another sip of water.

'I hoped *you* would be,' he returned, and she caught her breath again.

'David—'

'Hilary, I want to talk to you. There's so much to say.'

'No,' she said. 'There isn't.'

'There is. But not here. Tomorrow – what are you doing during the day?'

'Shopping, probably. Some of the others and I – we're staying at the club, near Marble Arch...'

'Meet me,' he said in a low, urgent voice. 'We'll have lunch together. Walk in Hyde Park. Please, Hilary – just for a few hours. Just for one day.'

She looked up and met his eyes. The pupils were wide and black; the dark brown of the irises had almost disappeared. Their urgency caught at her heart and, almost against her will, she nodded.

'All right. I'll meet you at Speaker's Corner, at twelve o'clock.'

'Make it eleven,' he said. 'Make it ten.'

She laughed despite herself. 'Ten thirty.'

They exchanged a long look and then she stood up and put her glass on the tray of a passing waiter. Someone touched her arm and she turned to find Dorcas beside her, shimmering in her gold cocktail dress, her china-blue eyes alight with laughter and curiosity.

'Hilary! Where have you been hiding? I've been talking to so many people, you'd never guess ... And who's this gorgeous man? Aren't you going to introduce me?'

Reluctantly, Hilary smiled back. 'Of course I am. Dorcas, this is

David Hunter. David, this is Dorcas …' But as she turned, she found that there was nobody there. David had melted into the crowd and vanished.

Chapter Twenty-Three

'I just couldn't face that predatory little female,' he said next morning. 'And I knew there'd be no chance of getting you alone again for the rest of the evening. The thought of having to make small talk for about three hours when I had so much to say to you was too much for me.'

'So you just left? You didn't stay at all? But there must have been other people you wanted to meet.'

He shrugged. 'I'll see them tonight. But it was you I really wanted to see.'

They were in Hyde Park, strolling beneath huge, copper-leaved trees towards the Serpentine. Pigeons and squirrels vied for possession of crumbs thrown by other walkers and, as they drew nearer to the blue water, ducks and geese waddled across the grass towards them. Two or three riders on horses cantered along one of the walks, and the sun shone with weak November warmth on Hilary's bare head.

The dinner the evening before had passed in a haze. She was conscious of having met numbers of people she remembered and others she did not. She had laughed and talked, and drunk more champagne than she was used to, and had been glad to sit down to a meal she had only toyed with. She had conversed with the men on either side of her, with little recollection of what they had talked about, and she had finally returned to the club with the other girls, barely hearing their excited chatter and going straight to her room to lie awake half the night, seeing only those deep brown eyes and curving mouth. And when she had fallen asleep at last, it had been to dream of starry Egyptian skies and the snuffling of camels under the whispering palms.

'David,' she said abruptly, stopping on the path. 'I'm not sure this is a good idea.'

'What? Walking in Hyde Park?'

'Walking anywhere. *Being* anywhere ... together.'

He looked at her gravely. 'Why not? What harm can it do?'

'I don't know,' she said. 'I just ... it doesn't feel right.' She glanced up at him. 'It's all so long ago. Things have changed – *we've* changed. We know so little about each other now.'

'Then let's find out.' He guided her to a bench facing the water, and they sat down, side by side. 'Tell me what's been happening to you during these eight or nine years. Did you marry – what was his name? Henry?'

'No,' she said quietly. 'He was killed.'

'I see. I'm sorry.' He was silent for a moment. 'But I'm sure you've found someone else. You *are* married?'

'No.' She paused, then added, 'No one else.'

She kept her gaze fixed on the water, watching a flock of ducks battle over some crusts of bread. At last, she said, 'And you? Did you marry Sybil?'

'Yes,' he said, and a little cloud seemed to pass across the sun. 'Yes, I did.'

'Well, there you are, then,' Hilary said after a moment. 'As I said, this isn't a good idea.'

She began to get up. David caught at her arm and pulled her back beside him. His fingers felt like fire through her sleeve and sent a tremor to her heart. She turned to him in protest, but as their eyes met the words died on her lips and she was transfixed.

'David ...' she whispered. 'David, don't ...'

'Hilary,' he said, 'I have to talk to you. I have to.'

'We can't ... There isn't anything ... David, please let go of me.'

'Just one day,' he pleaded. 'That's all I'm asking. One day with you. *Please*, Hilary.'

Hilary struggled with herself. The thoughts of those nights in Egypt, thrust out of her mind for so long, boxed away in her memory, never allowed to surface, were now swarming around her like bees. She turned her face aside, desperate to escape the burning hunger in his darkened eyes, aware of an answering need in her own heart. I didn't want this, she thought despairingly. I didn't ever, ever want this ...

'Just one day,' he murmured, and he slipped his hand down her arm so that his thumb moved gently on her bare wrist.

Hilary jerked her arm away. 'No! Don't do that! You've no right.'

Instantly, he moved back. 'I'm sorry. Of course I haven't.' His voice sounded stilted and she felt a pang of regret, knowing she'd hurt him.

'It's all right. Only – please don't do it again.' She hesitated, then said, almost against her will, 'All right. Just one day. Just one.'

His face was transfigured. A glow lit his eyes and his mouth widened in the smile she had never been able to resist. He gripped both her hands and shook them, then let go as if they scorched him. 'Sorry! I'm just so relieved. Oh, Hilary, I thought you were going to send me away.'

'I should do,' she said ruefully, although she felt his delight infecting her too. 'I still don't think it's a good idea.'

'It's just one day,' he insisted. 'A day for you and me. It'll harm nobody.' He jumped up and held out his hand. 'Let's walk again.'

Hilary laughed and rose from the seat. He kept her hand in his as they began to stroll again, walking along the shore of the lake and, after a moment of mental struggle, she let it stay there. The sun threw a shimmering veil of translucent gold, bronze and auburn silk over the trees, while ducks fought and squabbled in the water and swans drifted amongst them like tall ships in full white sail. Two pelicans strutted beside the water, their bills sagging like a news-vendor's empty pouches. It was all a world away from wartime Egypt.

'So, tell me what you're doing now, if you didn't marry,' he said after a while. 'You're not the type to stay at home arranging flowers. Are you a frighteningly efficient businesswoman? There are a few about, I believe. Or a pillar of the local community?'

'I suppose I could be both, if you think about it,' she said thoughtfully, and began to tell him about Burracombe and the estate, ending – although she hadn't intended to mention it – with Robert's arrival.

'So he's your brother's son? Legitimate?' He whistled. 'That must have put the cat among the pigeons.'

'It has, rather. Father's determined to make him his heir. He says – quite rightly – that Robert would have stood to inherit if Baden had lived, and he's entitled to his birthright.'

'And where does that leave you?'

'In the same position as I would have been, I suppose.' She hesitated, then added, 'Except that I wouldn't have spent the last few years putting my heart and soul into the place.'

David gave her a quick look. 'You sound rather bitter.'

'Do I? Well, I suppose it's because I don't know where I stand. My father's not in good health – I told you, he had a heart attack a couple of years ago and is supposed to take care, not that he does unless it suits him – and if anything happens to him, Rob will inherit everything. Oh, I am to be *provided* for, and I'm to have the right to live in the house, but I shan't have any other rights. And we don't even know that Rob really *wants* to continue with the estate. He's only thirteen years old. He could bring his mother and all his family over to live there. He could sell it all off. It's all happened too suddenly and Father's rushed into changing his will, without proper consideration. And there's no arguing with him – although I find myself doing so with monotonous regularity.'

David smiled a little. Then he said soberly, 'I can see it's a problem for you, Hilary. Have you had any thoughts about what you might do?'

Hilary shrugged. 'Plenty. My brother Stephen is talking about emigrating to Canada when he comes out of the RAF. He's suggested I join him – and I may just do that.'

'I hope not,' David said. 'Not just when I've found you again.'

There was a short, brittle silence, then Hilary asked with an effort at a light tone, 'And what about you? How has life treated you since the war ended?'

'As well as I deserve, probably,' he said a trifle bleakly, and Hilary shot him a startled glance. 'There's not much to tell, really. Came out of the army, went back to work in the practice with Dad, which I'll be taking over when he retires in a year or two, got married … That's about it.'

'There must be more to it than that, surely. Do you have any children?'

'No. No children.'

There was another silence and Hilary said, 'I think you owe it to me to tell me more than that, David. You insisted we meet, you wanted me to tell you all about myself, you can't just leave it at that.'

'No, I can't, can I?' he said with a sigh. 'All right, then. Sybil and

I got married within six months of me leaving the army. It was the biggest mistake of my life and I thank God on my knees every day that we had no children.' He stopped and turned to Hilary, gripping her hands again, and said with sudden passion, 'It ought to have been us, Hilary. You know that as well as I do. We knew it back in Egypt, both of us, and we should have had the courage to carry it through. All this time, all these years – we ought to have been together.'

She stared at him, shaken. 'David—'

'Don't say you don't know it!' he exclaimed. 'Why else have you never married?'

'Because – because Henry was killed—'

'Don't tell me you've had no other chances! A lovely, attractive woman like you – there must have been men who wanted to marry you.'

'Well, maybe one or two.' She thought of Felix Copley, who had nursed a brief infatuation for her when he'd first arrived in Burracombe, and of Travis, who she'd thought could make her a satisfactory mate. But she knew that neither they nor any of the other men she'd met since the war had come anywhere near as close to her heart as had the man standing before her now. 'But I never ...'

'You never really fell in love,' he said. 'Because you were still in love with me. You always were. You still are. You always will be.'

'You can't possibly say that!'

'I can see it in your eyes. I can hear it in your voice. I saw it last night, when you almost passed out because you saw me. Why else did you come to this ridiculous reunion, if not in the hope of seeing me?'

'You have a very fine opinion of yourself!' she flashed. 'I came because I felt like a break. I needed to get away from Burracombe for a few days, and it sounded like fun to meet a few of the old gang. I never dreamed you'd be here.'

'Why not? Why shouldn't I be here?'

'No reason,' Hilary said. 'Except that I've managed quite success-fully to forget you. I didn't even give you a thought.'

The silence this time was longer. They stood facing each other on the path. A woman with a pram tried to walk past them, and they stepped aside for her without taking their eyes from each other's faces. Then David said quietly, 'Is that true? Had you really forgotten me?'

'Pretty well, yes. Most of the time, anyway. What was the point of remembering? I didn't think I'd ever see you again. I thought you'd be happily married to your Sybil and have half a dozen children by now. We said *goodbye*, David, remember? And I meant it. I put you out of my mind and didn't let you in again.'

Except sometimes in the small hours of the morning, she thought. Except when she'd wondered bleakly what life held for her, where she really ought to be. Except when she and Val had talked about their time in Egypt.

But Val had never known about David. She had been too wrapped up in her own romance with Luke and, on the voyage home, in the sad consequences of their affair.

'But now I am in again,' he said. 'I don't think you'll be able to push me out a second time.'

Hilary drew her hands free and turned away. Walking on along the path, she said, 'I have to. There's nothing for us, David, nothing. It's too long ago.' She turned her head and met his gaze. 'And you're married.'

They walked miles that day, talking, arguing, reminiscing and sometimes silent. At some point, Hilary discovered that their fingers were again entwined; his grasp was warm and familiar, bringing both excitement and comfort, and she let her hand stay in his. After all, it was only for one day. A day that was already half over. And she couldn't quite bear to let it go.

The Serpentine was a blue sapphire, glistening in the dying warmth of the early November sun. They stopped at a café and drank coffee. Hilary thought afterwards that they had probably eaten something too, but she could not remember what it was. With every moment, the years fell away and the barrier between them grew thinner and frailer; with every moment, she felt the pull of this man towards her, and knew that she was stepping into peril; and with every moment, she cared less about the danger.

He leaned across the little round table and folded both her hands in his, and once again she did nothing to stop him. Her heart was thudding as she looked into his eyes and she glanced swiftly away, then back again. He held her gaze.

'You know what's happening, Hilary, don't you?' he said quietly.

'David. We can't ... We must stop ...'

'It's too late,' he said. 'It's already too late – you know that as well as I do. Nothing is any different between us, nothing. Not one single thing has changed.'

'If we hadn't met again ...' she began desperately.

'If! If! But we *have* met again. It was always going to happen, Hilary, and we can't walk away from each other a second time.'

She shook her head. 'No, David. This is impossible. We have responsibilities. You're married—'

'A farce!' he exclaimed, so loudly that people at other tables turned and glanced at them. 'A sham! She knows it as well as I do. But she's done something about it – something I've never done.'

'What do you mean?'

'Other men,' he said tersely. 'Lovers. It's a charade, Hilary, the whole of our marriage. It always has been.'

'Then why ...?'

'Because it's suited us both, I suppose,' he said in a tired voice, looking out of the café window at the water and the people walking by. 'Or, it suited Sybil. I just didn't have the energy to do anything about her affairs. I didn't have the motivation.' His eyes returning to her face. 'Until now.'

Hilary shook her head again. 'No, David. This is too sudden. And I can't be involved in – in what you're suggesting. Not like this.'

His grip tightened. 'Then how?'

She tried to pull her hands away. 'Not in any way. I've already told you, I have obligations. My father—'

'He sounds a lot more robust than you think. And he'd have to do without you if you married one of his rich widower friends.'

'The estate—'

'Being efficiently managed by your estate manager, and you're probably not going to inherit it anyway. In fact,' he said brutally, 'you may well be kicked out, to all intents and purposes. Next?'

'Robert – he's just a child—'

'But not your child. He has a mother, grandparents, aunts, and a grandfather who's willing to shower the world on his little French head. Hilary, *none* of these are your responsibility now. None of them cares about you, not really – well, I'm sure your father does, but not in the way you want – and none of them is going to take your real needs into consideration.' His fingers tightened again. 'None of them even knows your real needs,' he said softly. 'Not as I do.'

Hilary felt as if she were drowning. The waters were closing over her head and there was nothing she could do about it. For a third time, she shook her head. 'It's too quick,' she murmured again. 'We only met again last night. Truly, David, I'd done my best to forget you.'

'But now,' he said, 'you've remembered again. Haven't you?' And she could only nod mutely and look down at their entangled hands. A tear fell from her eyes on to his fingers.

'Let's walk again,' he said, getting up, and she followed him from the café and into the late afternoon, where the sun was dipping below the trees and a cool breeze of premonition was cutting across the chilly waters of the lake.

Chapter Twenty-Four

'So where have *you* been all day?' Dorcas greeted her when she returned to the club, her arms noticeably bare of purchases. 'I thought we were all going shopping together.' She went on without waiting for an answer: 'I simply *must* show you the darling little hat I've bought. And Vanessa has got the most *sumptuous* chiffon blouse. I'd have killed her for it if it hadn't been two sizes too big for me. What did you buy?'

'I didn't buy anything.' Hilary had been hoping to slip in unobserved but Dorcas had evidently been on watch in the lounge, with a good view of the front door. 'I didn't go shopping. I – I went for a walk.'

'A *walk*? You can do that at home! Where on earth did you go?'

'Hyde Park,' Hilary said reluctantly. 'I walked round the Serpentine.'

Dorcas gazed her, her cigarette lighter held beside her face, her eyes narrowed slightly in the smoke. 'Just around the Serpentine? All *day*? All by yourself?'

'Not *just* the Serpentine, no,' Hilary said quickly, glossing over the last question. 'Green Park as well. And St James's. And we stopped and looked at Buckingham Palace, of course, and—' Too late, she realised her mistake. Dorcas pounced.

'*We*? Oh – *ho*.' Her chin lifted a little and her glance became appraising. 'So there *was* another attraction. The handsome man you were so wrapped up in last night, perhaps?'

'I wasn't wrapped up in him!' Hilary flashed, and bit her lip as Dorcas laughed. 'Oh, all right, then – yes. He's someone I knew in Egypt – before your time, I think. We decided to spend the day together, for old times' sake. And that's all,' she added firmly, aware of her rising colour.

'Is it really?' Dorcas said sceptically. 'Well, if you say so ... Anyway, we'll all meet him this evening, won't we? I'm looking forward to it already.'

Hilary turned away to hide the flush of scarlet in her cheeks. 'I'm going upstairs to have my bath,' she said abruptly.

As she lay in the warm water a little later, staring out through the tiny square of window at the blue sky, she tried to come to terms with her feelings. Their strength had taken her by surprise. If I'd believed for one moment he'd be here, she thought – and then argued with herself: it wouldn't have made the slightest difference to her own decision to come. It was all over, part of a distant past. If they had come face to face, they would simply have said a polite hello, maybe shaken hands and then moved away. And she would have felt nothing.

Or so she would have told herself. *Had* told herself ...

Instead, at the first sound of his voice as he spoke her name, she had experienced a rush of emotion that made her dizzy. It was as if the world had fallen away from her, the room at the Café Royal ceased to exist, and the noise of talk and laughter faded to no more than a blur of sound. When she turned and looked at his face, meeting those dark eyes, the years had swung away and she was once more beneath the stars of an Egyptian sky, moving into his arms in the heat of the night, her blood scorching her skin and the power of her longing invading her body.

This can't happen, she told herself now. I don't want it. We said goodbye and we thought it was for ever. And he's married.

It's *over*.

The longing swept over her again and she turned her head restlessly, as if to escape it. It had been a mistake to meet again today, to walk through the park together, to talk and laugh and reminisce. To rediscover.

For that was what had happened. The passion that had lain dormant all these years had torn aside the closed doors of her heart and this time it refused to be shut away.

He'd been right when he'd stated that she had never properly fallen in love again, because he had always been first in her heart. She had never allowed herself to think of that, had rarely allowed herself even to think of him – had always suppressed any thoughts that might have come to her mind. But a heart that is filled with one person can never fully allow another to enter. There had been only a small space in Hilary's heart for someone else, and it had never been enough.

It would not have been enough even for Henry, the man she had been engaged to. For the first time in many years, she wondered what would have happened had he not been killed. Would she have married him, knowing that she didn't really love him? And if she had, what would their life have been like?

A lie, she thought, facing the truth. It would have been a lie, and we would have destroyed each other. And then, even more honestly – *I* would have destroyed Henry, for it would not have been his fault.

And now, what could be done?

David had made his feelings quite clear. Yet she was not sure what he wanted from her. A divorce on his side, and then marriage, with all the scandal that would entail? She shuddered to think of her father's reaction. There would be no question of any inheritance then – he would cast her out, like the Victorian he had been born. Most of the villagers would take the same attitude, and Burracombe would no longer be her home.

And if not divorce and marriage, what then? An affair? Hole-and-corner meetings, lies and excuses for trips to London, nights in sleazy hotels that didn't ask questions? Hilary shuddered again, this time on her own account. I won't be involved in anything so sordid, she thought. I can't. We'll have to say goodbye, and mean it.

The water had gone cold. She got out, shivering, and wrapped her towel around her, hugging it to her with crossed arms and peering at her dim reflection in the steamy mirror. She looked no different from yesterday, yet she felt a thousand years older and a world away from the Hilary who had boarded the train in Tavistock to meet old friends and do a little shopping. What had she been thinking of, not to realise that David would be here? But she had spoken the truth when she had told him she had pushed him to the back of her mind. It had been a deliberate act, born from guilt and achieved only with much determination. And once blocked out, the memories had remained buried – until last night.

Now, she thought, dispiritedly rubbing her skin dry with the towel, she had the whole weary work to do again, and this time it would be much, much harder.

Once again, the four of them shared a taxi to the hotel where the dinner-dance was to be held. The other women chattered excitedly, discussing their day's shopping as well as the old friends they had met the night before and would see again that evening. Hilary sat silently in her corner, aware of Dorcas's eyes upon her, dreading some remark that would focus the attention on her. But apart from a few inquisitive glances, Dorcas said nothing; she was too interested in her own affairs.

Affairs! Hilary thought. Well, if she wanted advice in that direction, Dorcas was the one to ask, by all accounts. But the kind of advice she wanted – on how to resist a man who had the magnetic power over her that David Hunter had – wasn't the sort Dorcas was likely to give. Dorcas would simply think she was mad to pass up the chance of a little fun and flirtation.

Except that it wouldn't be 'fun', Hilary thought, and it certainly wouldn't be a flirtation.

The hotel foyer was bright and welcoming. It had been almost completely destroyed during the Blitz and only recently reopened, and was now decorated and furnished in the latest style. Strangely shaped furniture – chairs like eggs, a sofa that looked like a pair of glossy red lips – stood in groups on the black-and-white chequerboard floor, and the reception desk was a swooping curve of shiny wood with a black leather buttoned front. A signboard directed them to the function room where their event was to be held, and the girls went to the cloakroom to hand in their coats.

'I needn't ask who you'll be dancing the night away with,' Dorcas murmured in Hilary's ear as they waited. 'I saw him just outside, waiting for you. *Very* handsome.'

'Did you?' Hilary asked, trying to sound casual. She had seen him too, the moment they walked in, but had refused to meet his glance. 'Well, you can dance with him if you like. I told you, I'm not interested.'

Dorcas gave her a glimmering look. 'Be careful, darling, or I might just do that. He looks to me like a plum ripe for picking.'

Hilary felt a prickle of annoyance. As if David could be seduced by any pretty little flibbertigibbet who looked his way! Alarmed, she detected a touch of possessiveness in her reaction, and turned her head quickly away. Dorcas's shrewd blue eyes saw too much.

'I don't suppose either of us will have much chance,' she said shortly, leading the way back to the foyer. 'The dinner will go on for hours, what with all the speeches and so on, and I don't suppose I'll feel like staying too late.'

'Of course, you farmers keep early hours, don't you?' Dorcas said sweetly. 'Up at dawn for the milking, with all those husky cowhands and everything.'

'It's not exactly the Wild West,' Hilary began, and stopped as a hand touched her arm. She did not need to turn her head again to know who it was. The fingers felt almost as familiar as her own.

Dorcas grinned wickedly. 'Well, talk of the devil!' She put out her hand, her small golden head held prettily on one side. 'You must be the delicious Major Hunter. Hilary's told me *all* about you.'

Hilary cast a swift, agonised glance at his face but his expression told her nothing. He took Dorcas's hand and looked down gravely at the uplifted face, taking in the rose-tinted mouth and made-up blue eyes. A smile touched his lips.

'I'm not sure about "delicious" and I'm no longer a major, since I left the army, but I can't deny I'm David Hunter. And you must be one of Hilary's friends from her time in the service.'

'That's right. I'm Dorcas Somerville. I was Sandiman when we were in Egypt, but I don't think we met then. We *almost* met last night, but you were very *naughty* and disappeared just as Hilary was about to introduce us. But you won't get away now.' She was still holding on to his hand. 'I'm going to make *sure* of that!'

'Oh, you'll be surprised,' he said easily. 'They didn't call me the Houdini of the officers' mess for nothing, you know.' He regained his hand and turned to Hilary. 'I've looked at the seating plan and it seems we're on the same table, so may I have the honour of escorting you into dinner?'

He crooked his elbow and Hilary, too bemused to reply, put her hand on his arm. The tingle that had once been so familiar and now absent for so long fired through her blood, and she felt her legs tremble and tried to withdraw her hand, but he tightened his arm around it.

Hilary glanced back and saw Dorcas standing alone and staring after them. She began to speak, but he cut her off.

'Yes, maybe it was rude, but she'll not be alone for long. She's not the kind.'

They followed the slow procession of people going into the dining room, and then David suddenly swerved aside, taking Hilary with him. They slipped between two pillars and through a doorway, finding themselves on a deserted landing.

'David, where are we going? What—' But before she could finish, he had taken her in his arms and his lips were on hers, soft, sweet, gentle and sensuous. Hilary struggled for a moment, then gave way. Her senses were whirling when he stepped away, his hands still on her arms.

'*David* ...' she whispered, barely able to speak. 'What are you thinking of? Anyone might come along ...' She tried to pull away. 'We must go back.'

'No,' he said in a low tone, 'we mustn't. Hilary, this is our only chance. Tomorrow you'll be going back to your country estate and I – I'll be going back to Sybil. We can't waste the time sitting at a dinner table making polite conversation. Come on – let's get away before someone notices we're not there and comes to look for us.'

'But we can't just leave. What will they think?'

He was already tugging at her hand, leading her along a carpeted passage. 'What does it matter what they think? We haven't seen any of these people for years, we may never see them again. They don't matter a jot to us, Hilary, nor we to them.'

'We'll matter to Dorcas,' she said ruefully. 'She's a gossip, David, and she'll make a mountain out of a molehill.'

'You can only do that,' he said, 'if there's a molehill to start with. This doesn't feel like that to me, Hilary. This is a mountain already.'

They came to the foyer and he began to head for the main entrance.

'My coat!' Hilary exclaimed. 'I have to collect my coat.'

She went back to the cloakroom and produced her ticket. She was shaking as she held it out, and the girl eyed her curiously as she fetched the coat and handed it over. She hesitated a little, and Hilary said quickly, 'It's all right. I just have to leave early, that's all. Some news from home ...' She grabbed the coat and fled.

'I'm sure she thinks I'm stealing it,' she said as she rejoined David. 'I look so guilty. And I feel it, too. David, this is dreadful. Can't we go back? It's not too late – we could make some excuse. My shoe, or something.'

'No,' he said, and took her hand again firmly. 'I'm not letting you go again. This evening is ours, Hilary, and I don't intend to waste a moment of it.'

Chapter Twenty-Five

'**G**ee, it's a helluva busy place,' Russ said, as he and his father stood in Piccadilly Circus, staring at the traffic. 'And it all looks such a muddle – all these streets heading off in different directions. Why didn't they build it on a grid, like New York, and even Corning?'

Joe laughed. 'Because they started building London over two thousand years ago, that's why! And it's just grown up since, as and when they needed to spread out. That's what gives it its character.' He looked up at the figure of the naked, winged archer, perched on one foot above the fountain, shining in the headlights of cars and red double-decker buses. 'That's Eros. They took him away during the war but he's back now. One of the most famous statues in London.'

Russell gazed up at the façades of the big buildings. 'I guess those are neon signs up there. Bovril ... Kodak ... We ought to come back tonight and have a look-see. It must have been pretty dreary here during the Second War, with everything switched off.'

'Not so dreary during the Blitz, when bombs were falling,' his father commented. 'You can still see a lot of the damage. It'll take years to rebuild everything.' He looked about him at the crowds and chuckled. 'You know, they say that if you wait long enough in Piccadilly, everyone you know will eventually pass by!'

'Well, I don't think I'll wait for everyone I know in Corning to come over,' Russ said with a grin. 'What else do you want to show me?'

'Don't forget, I don't know London well myself,' Joe confessed, leading the way into the Haymarket. 'I was just a farm boy when I went to war in 1914, never been further than Exeter – I've only been here a couple of times in my life. It's as much an adventure for me as it is for you. But I do remember coming here one night when I brought your mother over, and seeing all the advertising signs lit up.'

They sauntered together down to Trafalgar Square and spent some time sitting by one of the fountains, looking up at the lions and at Nelson far above on top of his column, and watching people feed the pigeons. After a while, Russ said, 'You know, Pa, I had a distinct feeling that Aunt Alice and Uncle Ted weren't too sorry to see us go this morning. You reckon we outstayed our welcome?'

Joe grimaced slightly. 'I don't think it was that, son. It's this bother over young Jackie that's upsetting them, and I guess they lay the blame for that at our door. She'd never have thought of going to America if we hadn't put the idea into her head.'

'She'd have thought of something, though. A smart girl like Jackie's not going to be satisfied with working as a hotel receptionist in the back of beyond for long.'

'You'd better not let Ted and Alice hear you call Plymouth the back of beyond,' Joe advised with a grin. 'It's the big wicked city, as far as they're concerned. And it's not as if we come from the great metropolis ourselves – Corning's not much bigger than Tavistock.'

'It's got the glass industry, though. It *could* be big – it just likes to keep its small-town atmosphere.'

Joe inclined his head in acknowledgement. Corning was a pleasant place to live, with wide streets and nice houses, and a crime rate of almost nothing. Its atmosphere was contented, almost sleepy.

'I don't know that it would suit Jackie as much as she thinks,' he said thoughtfully. 'She's got this glamorous image of America and she doesn't realise it's not all like Hollywood. A few months there, and I reckon she'd be getting itchy feet again and wanting to move on.'

'But nobody's talking about moving on. It's just a visit – a month or two. Maybe not even that.'

Joe glanced sideways at his son. 'Don't you fool yourself,' he advised. 'That girl's got her sights on more than a holiday. She wants to see the world, starting with America. Or maybe America will be enough. But she won't want to stay in Corning long, mark my words.'

Russ let out a long, low whistle. 'You reckon her ma and pa know that?'

'They might not have said so in as many words,' Joe said quietly, 'but I reckon they know it inside. And that's why they're so set against it. They know their daughter, and they know that once she's got a passport in her hand, she'll be away, and they won't know what she's doing or where she's going, or whether they'll ever see her again.'

That evening, the family gathered for supper and, inevitably, to discuss the subject once again. Alice, in particular, couldn't leave it alone.

'She's too young,' she stated flatly as she sat down after serving a large enamel dish of toad-in-the-hole. 'Going over the other side of the world at her age! I never heard of such a thing.'

'It's not that unknown, Mother,' Val said mildly, helping herself to cabbage. 'Lots of us did it during the war.'

Alice shot her a look and Val coloured, knowing that she was thinking about the affair she had had with Luke while they were in Egypt. I shouldn't have told her, she thought. It upset her at the time and it's probably been on her mind ever since. But it was done now, and there was no taking it back. 'Of course,' she added, 'we did have supervision.'

'For what that was worth,' Alice said darkly, and turned to her husband. 'And I dare say your Joe thinks he'll be supervision for our Jackie. But how can he be? He don't have no rights over her, and once she's there, out of our influence ...'

'I know,' he said heavily. 'She's a high-spirited young woman and she'll go her own way, no matter what Joe says.'

'But that's just the point, surely,' Joanna put in. Until now, she had tried to keep out of the discussion but had decided that if it were to continue being talked about at every mealtime she had a right to speak as well. 'Jackie's a young woman, not a little girl. And she's already quite independent anyway, living in Plymouth. You don't know what she does there in her time off, do you?'

'I don't know what you'm suggesting ...' Alice began ominously, but Joanna shook her head.

'I'm not suggesting anything. I'm just saying you don't know so you have to trust her. And she seems to manage perfectly well there, after all. If you trust her in Plymouth, why not trust her in America?'

'It's a bit different, that's why. She can come home in an hour from Plymouth, or we can go there if her's in trouble. I should have thought that was obvious.'

Joanna persisted. 'Well, as Val said, a lot of us left home during the war. I wasn't much older than Jackie when I came here as a Land Girl.'

'But *you* were coming to a family.'

'And Jackie will be going to a family, too. Her own family. And not all Land Girls were as lucky as I was, you know – some of them went to horrible places and were treated like slaves.'

'All that's beside the point,' Ted said, losing patience. 'The point is, Jackie never even thought about going to America before our Joe and his boy came here, and the point is that us don't want her to go now, and if you ask me there didn't ought to need to be no more argufying about it. I'm still head of this family, as far as I know, and what I says goes. I'm putting my foot down over this.'

'That's just it, Dad,' Tom said, poking about in the dish for another sausage, and scraping the crispy bits of batter from the sides. 'I don't think what you say does go now, as far as our Jackie's concerned. She's tasted a bit of independence and she likes it. You might as well face up to it – she's not going to take much notice of you putting your foot down when she's not here to see it.'

'All right, but her'll not go abroad,' Ted said angrily. 'You need a passport for that, and that's one thing she *can't* get without my say-so. And your mother agrees with me, don't you, Alice?'

'That I do, Ted,' Alice agreed. 'The girl's under our jurisdiction until she turns twenty-one and she might as well make up her mind to it. And 'tis no good you looking at me like that, our Tom. 'Tis for her own good. If her still wants to go in two years' time – well, I'll not say she'll have our blessing, but at least us won't put nothing in her way. She'll be two years older and wiser by then, and ten to one she won't want to go at all – have other fish to fry by then, I dare say.'

'Perhaps,' Val said. 'But I don't envy you when you tell Jackie that. She might decide she doesn't want to come home any more.'

There was a short silence. Then Alice said, 'What do you mean, Val? What's Jackie been saying to you?'

'She hasn't said a thing. But I know what she's like, and so should you. She's always wanted her own way, and she usually finds a way of getting it. I wouldn't put it past her to cut herself off, that's all. And none of us wants that.'

'Her'd never do that,' Alice said uneasily. 'Not cut herself off from her own family.'

'Well, I hope not,' Val said. 'But don't say I didn't warn you if she does.'

The thought had already occurred to Jackie. She was on morning shift that day and after she had finished she walked up to the Hoe and leaned on the railings, gazing down at Tinside swimming bath. Although early November, there was still some warmth in the sun and a few hardy little boys were splashing about in the rock pools. Beyond them, the sun sparkled on the blue waters of the Sound and Drake's Island seemed to float like a magical green fairytale islet above the waves.

Not much fairytale for me, she thought bitterly. Here I've got a chance to go to America and see a bit of the world, but I might as well be in prison for all the good it'll do me. If Mum and Dad had their way, I wouldn't even be in Plymouth – I'd still be working as a housemaid at Burracombe Barton, or stuck at home on the farm helping Mum feed chickens. And I want more than that! I want a *life*.

People were passing her by, admiring the view and chatting to each other. She heard little snatches of conversation – remarks about the Eddystone Lighthouse, just visible like a faintly drawn pencil on the far horizon, or the red-and-white striped Smeaton's Tower on the Hoe itself. And then a few words seemed to sound more clearly, almost as if they had been spoken directly into her own ear.

'You'll find it's not such a disaster,' a woman's voice said. 'There'll be a way round it if you just think hard enough – there always is.'

Jackie felt her blood freeze. For a moment or two, she was unable to move; then she turned quickly, almost as if she wanted to capture the speaker and ask her what she meant. But the woman and her companion had already moved away, lost in a throng of other people, and Jackie couldn't even tell who it was that had spoken.

Slowly, she turned back and stared out to sea once again. The words echoed in her mind. *Not such a disaster ... always a way round it, if you just think hard enough ...* And she felt a sudden lightening of her spirit, as if a burden had been lifted from her shoulders and the way ahead was clear.

I know what to do, she thought, and she could almost sense the sparkle coming back to her eyes. I know what to do, and I *will* go to America.

After a day's sightseeing, Joe and Russ were ready for dinner in their hotel and an early night, but they had promised themselves a visit to Piccadilly Circus after dark, to see the neon lights, so when they had eaten they took themselves out and made their way back.

Once again, the streets were thronged with sightseers. Since the Festival of Britain, two years earlier, tourists had begun to come to London again to see the great city that had been so heavily bombed during the war, and although there was still much evidence of damage, all the most prominent features remained. Whitehall and Downing Street, where Joe and Russ had gone after their pause in Trafalgar Square; the Houses of Parliament, and the great clock tower that housed Big Ben; the slow-moving Thames, busy with tugs and boats of all kinds; Westminster Abbey; the Embankment – all these were on the tourist 'route' they had so dutifully followed, and tomorrow they would take it to more famous sights: St Paul's Cathedral, the Monument, Fleet Street. The city seemed to be a bottomless well of historic spectacle and beauty.

'We'll never get to see everything,' Russell lamented. 'It's a job to know which to choose. I wanted to go to Hampton Court Maze – and Windsor Castle. There just isn't time for it all!'

'There'll be other trips,' Joe said with a smile. 'Not for me, maybe, but there's nothing to stop you coming over again. Now you know the family, you'll be welcome.'

'Not if young Jackie leaves home!' Russ said wryly. 'I don't see Aunt Alice laying out the welcome mat for me if she thinks I've encouraged her daughter to emigrate.'

'Who's talking about emigrating?' Joe asked, and then stopped suddenly. 'Well, take a look at that. What did I tell you this morning?'

'I dunno. What *did* you tell me? About Jackie, you mean?'

'No, not Jackie. About meeting everyone you know if you just stand long enough in Piccadilly Circus.' Joe nodded his head at the crowd near the foot of Eros's plinth. 'See what I mean?'

Russ followed his glance. The darkness was only dimly lit by the street lamps but the flashing of the neon signs cast a brief and colourful illumination on the people who had come to see them. He scanned the faces of the people in the middle of the Circus, and was about to shake his head when his eye was caught by a woman standing almost opposite, with a tall man who had his arm around her waist.

'Why, it looks like Colonel Napier's daughter – Hilary, isn't it? – from the Barton,' he said. 'Whatever's she doing up in London?'

'I guess she's entitled to come here if she wants to,' Joe said with a grin. 'But I wonder who the fella is. Alice told me she'd never married and didn't show any signs of wanting to – married to the estate, she reckons. But she looks pretty friendly with that guy, wouldn't you say?'

Chapter Twenty-Six

'This is crazy,' Hilary said, laughing a little as they stood looking up at Eros. 'Utterly crazy. Why have you brought me here?'

'Because Eros is the God of Love, and it's the right place to begin.' He slid his arm around her waist. 'This is our night, Hilary, and I want everything to be perfect.'

Startled, she turned her head and looked at him. His eyes were dark, his face lit by the colours of the neon signs, his expression grave. She felt her heart kick, and caught her breath.

'David—'

'Let's find somewhere to eat,' he interrupted. 'Somewhere small and quiet, where no one will know us.'

'I'll stick out like a sore thumb,' Hilary objected, looking down at her dress. 'I was expecting a dinner-dance, not a little café.'

'I didn't say a café. I know a nice place where there'll be tables and music and we can even dance a little if you want to.' His arm tightened. 'Let's get a taxi.'

Hilary started to protest again, but his arm was like a band of fire around her waist and she was helpless to escape. She didn't want to escape, she realised. She didn't want to go and have dinner either, nor listen to music, nor dance. She would have been happy to stand here for ever, the swirl of people parting around them like water around a rock, with her body close to his and the flame in her heart answering the blaze in his eyes.

Without knowing quite how, she found herself in a taxi, sweeping through the crowded streets. David kept his arm about her waist and when his hand tightened against her ribs she turned her head and let her lips part. His kiss was hard and brief, and she let her head droop against his shoulder, almost unable to breathe for the thudding in her breast.

In moments, it seemed, the taxi was drawing to a halt outside a small restaurant, its windows darkened by drawn curtains, in a street that Hilary did not recognise. She glanced interrogatively at David, but he simply smiled and came round to hold the taxi door open for her. He ushered her up the steps to the front door, which stood hospitably open, and she entered a little uncertainly.

'It's all right,' he said, taking her coat from her shoulders and handing it to a dark-haired, swarthy man in a black dinner-jacket who stepped forward as they came in. 'It's perfectly respectable. It's run by a Greek family. This is Andreas, the proprietor. I come here whenever I'm in London.' He spoke briefly to the man, who led them through to a room with perhaps eight or ten tables and seated them in a corner, near the window and away from the door. The tables nearest them were unoccupied and the others were busy with what looked to Hilary like Greek families, all talking and laughing loudly together.

'Nobody will take any notice of us here,' David said as she sat down, still a little doubtful. 'And nobody will hear what we say.'

'I'm not sure we'll be able to hear what we say ourselves,' she commented, but in fact although the other diners were making a great deal of noise they were far enough away for her and David to be able to hear each other quite comfortably. And any lull in the conversation would be filled with the Greek music playing in the background.

'It's not quite what I expected when you mentioned music and dancing,' she remarked, and David grinned.

'The dancing comes later, when the waiters start to demonstrate their national customs – including some plate-throwing! But –' his eyes sought hers, 'we may not want to stay that late.'

'No, I don't think we will,' Hilary agreed, and went on rapidly, 'I'd rather like to be safely in my room before the others get back to the club. They're going to want to know just why I wasn't at the dinner – and I haven't the faintest idea what to tell them.'

David reached for her hand across the table. 'You don't have to tell them anything. You don't have to go back.'

Startled, Hilary drew back and stared at him. 'What do you mean? Of course I have to go back.'

'Well, not tonight,' he said. 'This is our night, Hilary. Our night for love.' He bent a little closer. 'Come back with me. Come back to my hotel.'

Hilary tried to speak, swallowed and shook her head. 'No,' she whispered at last. 'No, David. We can't.'

'We can. Why not?' His fingers gripped hers again. 'All these years, Hilary, I've thought of you, dreamed of what might have been – what *should* have been. If I'd known you were single all that time ... I'd never have married Sybil, if I'd thought there was any chance for us. Why didn't you let me know your fiancé had died?'

'How could I?' she cried, and bit her lip as one or two heads turned in their direction. She went on in a lower tone, 'How could I do that? You were engaged! I had no reason to think—'

'You had *every* reason to think! You knew as well as I did that we were meant to be together. Whatever reason either of us had for getting engaged, we both knew we'd made a mistake. I shall always regret not having the courage to go back and say so. Marrying Sybil has just meant years of misery for her, as well as me.'

'And having an affair with me will just make it worse,' she retorted, and flushed scarlet as she realised that the Greek proprietor was standing at their table, waiting for their order. They hadn't even looked at the menus but David gave a quick order, and the man nodded and melted away. He returned a moment later with two glasses of wine and set them down.

'It won't make it worse,' David insisted as soon as he had gone. 'How can taking a little of the happiness that ought to have been ours make it worse?'

'Because she'll never know, you mean? David, I'm not going to get into a hole-and-corner affair – it's sordid. All right, if we'd both broken off our engagements we could have got married and lived happily ever after, but we didn't, and that's the end of it. How could I have done that, anyway? Henry and I may not have been madly in love, but we had committed ourselves, and he was away from home, fighting a war. How could I write to him and tell him it was over? At least he died knowing I'd been true to him.'

'But you hadn't,' David said softly, 'had you?'

Hilary felt tears sting her eyes. 'That's a horrible thing to say.'

'It's true, though. Face facts, Hilary. The minute you met me, you began to lie to Henry. You've lied ever since. And now you're trying to lie to me.'

'What do you mean?'

'You've spent the last nine years trying to pretend it never happened. And now you're trying to pretend things have changed between us. But they haven't, have they?' He leaned closer, his fingers so tight around hers that she gasped. 'It's all still there, Hilary,' he murmured. 'All the love and passion ... all the desire ... It's all still there. You can't deny it, can you?' When she didn't reply he said again, more insistently, '*Can* you?''

'Please, David ... don't ...'

'This is our only chance,' he said. 'If we don't take it while it's here ... we may live out the rest of our lives in regret, wondering what could have been.'

Hilary met his eyes. She could find no way of denying what he said. If she did not take this chance now – if she did not follow his lead – she would regret it for the rest of her days.

'But you're married,' she protested weakly, grasping at the one immutable fact.

'I know,' he said soberly. 'And believe me, my darling, I'm *not* asking you to embark on some hole-and-corner affair. I'm not going to suggest frequent trips to London so that we can meet, with all the lies that would involve. I have more respect for you than that.' He paused, then went on, 'But I *could* ask Sybil for a divorce.'

'A *divorce*?' Hilary stared at him. 'But – on what grounds?'

'Infidelity, I suppose. Mine, of course.' He grimaced. 'It doesn't sound pleasant, and I wouldn't involve you in any way – but these things can be arranged.'

Hilary looked at him a moment longer, then withdrew her hand. At that moment, the waiter arrived with their food and set the plates down in front of them, talking volubly and flourishing his napkin. They waited until he had gone, returning his expansive smiles with pale imitations. Hilary picked up her knife and fork but made no attempt to use them.

'Arranged?' she repeated. 'You mean you'll pay some woman – a prostitute, presumably – to spend the night with you and be "discovered" by a chambermaid next morning? David, that's just squalid.'

'It's the only way. You know perfectly well what the laws are.'

'Not as well as you do, apparently. But then I've never had cause to think about them much.'

'Please!' he said, reaching across the table again and gripping her wrist so tightly that she dropped her knife on the table. 'Darling, please don't speak to me like that. Don't look at me as if I disgust you. I wouldn't be thinking about them either, if I didn't want this so much.' She was silent and he went on, more urgently. 'I told you, I've thought about you, longed for you, all these years. I can't let this chance go by. I *won't*.'

'It's *not* a chance! We met at a reunion – that's all. We say hello and goodbye and go home again. *And that is all*.' She picked up her knife again. 'I'm sorry, David, but you have to see how impossible it all is – even if I agreed to what you're suggesting. A divorce would be in the newspapers. Everyone would know – your friends, my friends, every-one in Burracombe. I'd never be able to show my face there again. My father would have nothing more to do with me – and he needs me too. I just can't throw it all away. I *can't*.'

The silence stretched between them. Hilary tried to eat her food. After a few moments, she laid the cutlery down.

'I can't eat this. I'm sorry.'

'Neither can I.' He put down his knife and fork as well and looked at her. 'Hilary, I'm sorry. I didn't mean to rush you like this. I simply couldn't help myself. Let's start again, shall we?'

'Start what?' she asked miserably. 'There's nothing *to* start, as far as I can see.'

He touched her hand again. 'The whole evening. From when we stood by Eros and looked up at the God of Love, with his bow and arrow. Remember what I said? Our night for love. Let's have that, if we have nothing else. If we have to say goodbye in the morning and walk away from each other for ever, let's at least have that.' Again, his eyes sought hers. 'Come back with me tonight.'

Hilary looked down at their hands. Hers was lying palm downwards on the white tablecloth, his rested lightly over it, his fingertips tiny flames on the sensitive skin of her wrist. She thought of the implica-tions of what he was saying: a night of forbidden love, with all the memories it would bring of those other nights under the Egyptian stars; the yearning of the past nine years, assuaged at last; the fresh yearning that would begin the moment they said their goodbyes. The guilt.

Could it be worth it? Could one night, just a few brief hours, be worth what must follow? Yet even as she asked herself that question, she knew that at this moment, in the intensity of their longing, there was no answer. Tomorrow must do as it would. Tonight was a moment out of time. Tonight, as David had said, was theirs.

'My things ...' she murmured, making one last feeble attempt to salvage her honour. 'I'll have to go back to the club first to collect my things.'

He shook his head. 'I'm not risking you getting back to your room and never coming out again. We'll collect them in the morning.'

She looked down at her evening dress. 'Dressed like this? How can I do that?'

'Nobody would bat an eyelid,' he said confidently. 'They'll just think you went on to a night-club or something after the dance, and ended up having breakfast somewhere. Plenty of people do that.'

'Dorcas will know what's happened,' she said gloomily, and he laughed.

'And she's the very one who is least likely to bat an eyelid! She'll probably be doing the same thing herself. You don't have to worry about Dorcas.'

'But I'm not like Dorcas!' Hilary exclaimed, stung. Then she looked at him and her mouth twisted ruefully. 'Or maybe I am. I'm certainly not fit to sit in judgement over her, or anyone else.'

David leaned forward again. 'Darling, stop worrying about other people. This is our night, remember? Don't think about anyone else but us. Just for a few hours. Please.'

She met his dark eyes and turned her hand over, so that it clasped his, palm to palm. The touch of his skin tingled up her inner arm like an electric shock.

'All right,' she said at last. 'I won't think about anyone else but us. At least, until tomorrow.'

'Tomorrow may never come,' he said. 'And if it does, it will look after itself.' He turned his head and gestured to the waiter. 'I'm sorry, we can't finish our meal. We have to go.'

'There is something wrong?' the man began in dismay, but David shook his head and took out his wallet.

'Nothing's wrong. We just ... have to go.' He paid quickly and the proprietor brought Hilary's coat. David took it and draped it around her shoulders. They went outside and within a few minutes were sitting in a taxi.

'You won't regret this, darling,' David said, cupping his hand behind her head and turning her face towards him. 'I promise you, you'll never regret this.' He laid his other hand lightly on her breast, and she shivered and closed her eyes.

'I don't know what I'm going to feel,' she whispered as his lips touched hers. 'I only know that I want you more than I've ever wanted anything in my whole life. More even than I wanted you in Egypt. You're right, David. This is our night.'

Chapter Twenty-Seven

'This is our day,' Felix said, as he and Stella sat together at his desk in the vicarage study, 'so we must have it just as we want it. It's something we'll remember all our lives. And I especially want you to have what *you* want.'

'Including seven bridesmaids!' Stella said wryly. 'To be honest, Felix, if we had it just as *I* wanted, we'd be walking to the church on a spring morning and getting married with just our closest family and friends to wish us well, and then having lunch in the vicarage garden before going off with knapsacks on our backs to walk across Dartmoor.'

'Sounds idyllic,' Felix said wistfully. 'But you know, that's really what we're doing – getting married in front of our closest friends and family. It's just that we have a lot of friends, including all the children at the village school, and I happen to have rather a large family!'

'I know. And we can't have the reception in the vicarage because there isn't room, and we can't walk off with knapsacks on our backs because it'll be January and the moor will probably be deep in snow.'

He gazed at her. 'Is this really upsetting you, darling? I meant it when I said everything should be as you wanted it, and now it seems as if *nothing* is going to be as you want it. We really don't have to do all this if it's going to make you miserable.'

'Of course it's not going to make me miserable.' She flung her arms around his neck and kissed him. 'I'm being silly. I know you don't want to wait until the spring, and neither do I, really. The problem is, I want two different things: I'd really love a spring wedding, a simple service and reception and a honeymoon just walking in the countryside – but I also want to be married to you as soon as possible. And that's the thing I want most, so January it is, with seven bridesmaids dressed in all the colours of the rainbow and as many guests as we can cram into the church!'

'That's all right, then,' he said, laughing. 'To tell you the truth, the sort of wedding you want is just what I would like too, but we seem to have an awful lot of other people to consider.'

'Even though it's *our* day?' she asked wickedly, and he sighed.

'That must have been wishful thinking. But we'll make it ours as much as we possibly can. And really, all those things are just trimmings, aren't they? The real meaning of it all will be ours. Those few moments standing at the altar, while my father makes us man and wife – those are ours and nobody else's.'

'And then we have the rest of our lives,' she said. 'It's not too much, is it, to share the first day with people who love us?' She turned back to the pile of envelopes on the desk. 'So we'd better get on with writing these invitations. There seem to be an awful lot of them.'

'Well, they won't all come,' Felix said optimistically. 'Great-Uncle Hubert and Great-Aunt Agatha live in Edinburgh; I'm sure they won't want to travel all that way in January. And we've barely heard a word from Great-Aunt Josephine for years. She fell out with the rest of the family in 1947 over some squabble about an apple pie.'

Stella looked at him. 'An *apple pie*? How can anyone fall out with a whole family, a family the size of yours, over an apple pie? You're having me on.'

'I am not,' he said with dignity. 'I don't know how you can make such an accusation. Honestly, Stella, it was an apple pie. At least, I think it was. It might have been rhubarb. Anyway, she fell out with everyone else over it and nobody's heard from her since, so I don't suppose for a minute she'll want to come to our wedding.'

'And you're supposed to be a Christian family,' Stella said, reaching for the first envelope.

'We're human too,' he said. 'And *she's* heard from *us*. Christmas cards, birthday cards, letters … none of them answered, but we keep soldiering on. You can't accuse *us* of not being forgiving.'

'No, all right.' She began to write an address from the long list before them. 'Who's Uncle Algernon?'

'The Bishop of Colchester. He might come, if the weather's not too bad.'

'How many bishops actually are there in your family?' she asked.

'I'm not really sure. It changes, you see, with some retiring and others being promoted. Usually, it's around five or six. We'll have to make sure the Bedford Hotel has plenty of whisky.'

They wrote steadily, and the pile of invitations and envelopes slowly diminished. Although Felix's parents had offered to pay for the entire wedding, Stella was guiltily aware that a lot of the expense would normally be borne by the bride's family so, as she had no family of her own and certainly no money to meet the kind of bills she feared were going to mount up, she had insisted that the least she and Felix could do was make as many of the actual arrangements as possible. Since they were also on the spot, Felix's parents had agreed to this practical solution, so the printed invitations and their white envelopes had been delivered to the Little Burracombe vicarage to be filled in and posted six weeks before the wedding date.

'How's Dottie getting on with the dresses?' Felix asked after a while.

'Janice has been for a fitting and hers is almost finished. I still can't get over the children's generosity in choosing her. Even those who didn't vote for her seemed pleased. I had a letter from Jess Budd this morning, saying that Maureen's is almost done too. Dottie's doing mine at the moment – so you'd better let us know in advance if you're coming over to the cottage, I don't want you walking in one day and finding me trying it on!'

'I wouldn't mind,' he said solemnly, and she hit him with one of the envelopes. 'But I know I mustn't see it until the day, so I'll do my best to remember. What about the others?'

'I've not heard about the ones from your family – Pearl (I refuse to call her Button) and Vivienne and Julie – and Dottie's waiting to make Val's until we're sure she's got her figure back. That just leaves Maddy.' She frowned and bit the end of her fountain pen.

'Yes,' he said quietly. 'Maddy. Have you heard any more from her?'

Stella looked at him with distressed eyes. 'No. I'm really worried, Felix. I'm afraid we really hurt her. Suppose she's decided to cut herself off from us for ever!'

'Stella, don't be silly,' he said, pushing his work aside and taking her hands. 'Of course she hasn't done that. Don't you remember how much better she was when she left here last time? I knew she cried all weekend – we all seemed to cry a lot that weekend – but it was a good kind of crying. A lot of hurt and sadness was released with those tears. And when she went back to West Lyme, don't you remember how good it was that she decided to go by herself, on the train? It seemed as if she'd turned the corner at last.'

'I know you thought that,' Stella said despondently. 'I was never really sure. 'And I've hardly heard a thing since then – just scrappy little letters, saying nothing of any importance. And not even those for the past ten days or more.'

'I'm sure she's still working through her feelings,' he said. 'She can't say anything important because she's still not sorted things out properly in her own mind. And there's something she needs to do before she can really do that, you know – something very important indeed.'

'What's that?'

'She needs to make her peace with the Hodges. Whatever she said to them has been eating at her heart, and until she's put that right, she'll never be able to move any further. But I'm sure she'll do it – and when she's done it, she'll write you a proper letter again. You'll see … She might even be doing it at this very moment.'

'I hope you're right,' Stella said. 'I really, really hope you're right.'

'I don't like to say it,' Alice Tozer said, taking a large casserole of rabbit stew from the oven, 'but I'm not sorry we're on our own again for a while. I'm fond of your Joe, Ted, as you know, and Russell's a nice young chap, but their ways are different from ours.'

'Joe's a proper Yank now,' Ted agreed. 'Not surprising, mind, since he've been over there most of his life. It's been good to see them again, mind.'

'Oh, I'm not saying it hasn't. I'm just saying it's good to have a bit of breathing space before they come back from their travels to spend Christmas with us. And it'll give our Jackie a bit of time to settle her ideas down again, too. Pass me your plate, Tom.'

'I'm not sure it'll do that,' Ted observed, helping himself to winter greens and carrots. 'If you ask me, we've got an uphill job with that young lady. Still got stars in her eyes.'

'And if you ask *me*,' Tom said, although nobody had, 'you might as well give it up straight away. Jackie's made up her mind to go, and you know what she's like when she's made up her mind.'

'And I know what I'm like when I've made up mine,' Ted growled. 'I'm not going to be told by a bit of a girl like our Jackie. What she does when she's of age will be her own business, but until then she stays here.'

The staircase door opened, and Minnie came in and took her seat beside Joanna. 'You'm not still chewing the fat over whether that maid goes to America or not, are you? I thought with Joe and Russell off in London we'd get a bit of rest from that.'

Ted looked at his mother in surprise. 'You sound a bit sharp, Mother.'

'To tell the truth,' Minnie said, accepting a plate of stew, 'I think you're being a bit heavy-handed with the maid. She might be a bit headstrong, but her head's screwed on the right way round and I think it's time you put a bit of trust in her. She've been living in Plymouth a while now, with nothing untoward happening to her—'

'As far as we know,' Ted muttered darkly.

'And if you ask me,' Minnie went on, unaware that she was the third person to offer an opinion in this way, 'it's better for her to go where there's family to keep an eye on her than just go off on her own where she don't know nobody at all. And I'd have thought you'd think so too.'

The meal continued in silence. Ted glowered at his food and Alice pursed her lips. After a few minutes, Robin, who had been quiet as he ate his dinner, announced, 'We'm having a wedding at school. I'm going to be a pageboy.'

They all looked at him. Joanna said, 'I don't think so, Robin. Miss Simmons told me she's only having bridesmaids. She's having one of the girls at school, though, isn't she?'

Robin shook his head. 'Not *that* wedding. This is at school. It's going to be before the Christmas holidays.'

'After Christmas,' Joanna corrected him. 'And it'll be in the church. You're having a party for it at school.'

'It's a *wedding*,' he insisted, beginning to turn red. 'There's going to be a bride in a white frock, and a gloom—'

Tom burst out laughing. 'I bet there's many a man would agree with that!'

'Thank you, dear,' Joanna said, giving him a look. She turned back to her son. 'It's a groom, Robin, not a gloom. And I think you're getting mixed up. Miss Simmons is getting married to Mr Copley, after Christmas. That's right, isn't it?'

'Yes,' he answered, in the patient tone he had heard Stella use when she was explaining something to one of the less able children, 'but we'm having *another* wedding, in school. Shirley Culliford's getting married to Billy Madge, and me and Edward Crocker are going to be pageboys. And there's going to be bridesmaids as well,' he added offhandedly.

'Oh, I remember now!' Alice exclaimed as they all stared at him. 'Dottie did tell me, Stella said they were going to have a little play with a wedding, and Felix is going to do it all properly, just like a real wedding. She and Miss Kemp thought it would be a good way to teach the children about weddings, and what they mean—'

'Not everything they mean, I hope,' Tom murmured, and earned another reproving glance, from his mother this time, before Alice continued: 'It would also stop them being disappointed at not being able to go to her own wedding. Except for Janice, of course – although they'll all be able to see her go into church, which they'll probably enjoy more anyway.'

'Janice's parents will have to be invited too,' Joanna remarked. 'It's going to be a big wedding, from what I can make out.'

'Bound to be,' Alice said. 'The local schoolteacher marrying the vicar! I know he's not our vicar, but he was our curate. And there's going to be bishops and all there. So when is this wedding at school going to be?' she asked her grandson. 'I suppose they want to get it in before they start getting ready for Christmas. And that reminds me, us'd better start sorting out what fruit and stuff we need for the cake and puddings. With our Joe and Russell here this year, we want to make a good do of it.'

She seemed to have forgotten her earlier mild resentment of the American visitors. All she'd wanted, as she said to Minnie later, was a bit of rest and to have the house to themselves again for a while. Joe and Russell would be as welcome as the flowers in May when they returned.

The old woman nodded. 'I'm not looking forward to them going back to America in January, I don't mind telling you. But there, now our Joe's made the effort once I reckon he'll make it again. And I don't think it'll be the last we see of young Russell.'

'What do you mean?' Alice asked, but Minnie shook her head and smiled.

'We'll see. Let's just say I've noticed things. But you know what I always say – time will tell.'

Chapter Twenty-Eight

'So I had to come and tell you myself,' Maddy finished as she sat in the morning-room of Felix's vicarage. 'It seemed too important to write in a letter.'

Stella got up from the settee and came over to give her sister a hug. 'I'm glad you did. We both are. And we're really, really pleased that you've put things right with the Hodges – aren't we, Felix?'

'We certainly are. It was making you very unhappy, wasn't it, Maddy?'

'Yes, it was. And it was stopping me from feeling better about Sammy. Not that I've stopped feeling sad about him,' she added quickly, 'but it's different, somehow. It sounds peculiar, but being upset with Ruth and Dan seemed to spoil what I was feeling about him. Yet how can grief can be "spoiled"? It doesn't make sense.'

'It make perfect sense,' Felix declared. 'Grief is like any other emotion – it has to be honest. Yours was getting muddied by your feelings about Ruth's new baby. It was tainted—' He stopped, but Maddy finished for him.

'By jealousy. That's what it was really, wasn't it? I was jealous that they could find something to be happy about, when I couldn't. And it was meanness too, that I begrudged them their happiness. I'm not a very nice person at all, am I?'

'Now, don't start that again,' he said severely. 'You're as nice as any of us, and a lot nicer than some. You just got mixed up for a while, that's all, and now you've had the courage to put it right. Only a very nice person indeed could do that.'

'So we don't want to hear any more about how selfish you are,' Stella told her. 'What I do want to hear is how Ruth is. And how about Linnet? Does she know yet she's going to have a baby brother or sister?'

'Not yet. I think they're going to tell her soon. And Ruth is absolutely blooming. Honestly, she looks lovely – shiny hair, beautiful skin – and she hardly shows at all.'

'When is the baby due?'

'In April. The twelfth, they think. And Ruth told me they don't mind what it is. I thought they'd want a boy, but she says they'll just be happy if it's healthy. Dan treats her like porcelain. He says she's got to be careful – she's quite old to be having a baby. But Ruth just laughs at him and says she's a nurse so she knows what she can and can't do. She's not going to take any risks.' Maddy was silent for a moment, then she added quietly, 'I really am happy for them now. And I'm going to go to Bridge End to see them as often as I can. It's an easy journey from West Lyme – I can do it in a day, so I don't need to stay overnight.'

'That's lovely news,' Stella said. 'So now we can invite them to the wedding, can't we?'

'Yes, of course. I never thought of that. Weren't you going to, then?'

'Well, we couldn't if you were still upset, could we? But now there's no reason why not. And don't start saying how selfish you've been, again. We'll ask Ruth and Dan, and Linnet, too, of course. And the Budds are coming, since Maureen's going to be a bridesmaid, so it will be nice for them to see each other again.'

'We've still got to decide who's giving you away,' Felix said. 'Have you had any thoughts about that?'

Stella nodded. 'As a matter of fact, I was wondering whether to ask Frank Budd. He and Jess were so kind to us when we were there during the war, and they knew our father, too. In fact, Frank's known me longer than any other man I can think of, and Jess was like a second mother to us after our own mother was killed.'

'I think that's a marvellous idea,' he said warmly. 'You'd better write to him. Who else in the family will you want to invite?'

'Well, I think Rose has moved away, now she's married. I don't suppose the two boys – Tim and Keith – will be interested.'

'Of course they will,' Maddy exclaimed. 'And I'd like to see them again, too. The last time was at Rose's wedding.' She stopped suddenly as they all remembered that it was at Rose Budd's wedding that she and Sammy had met again and fallen in love. 'Anyway,' she went on determinedly, 'we stayed in the same billet with them at Bridge End as well – they were like brothers to us, so of course they should come.'

'That's two more for your side of the church, then,' Felix said to Stella. 'You see? You didn't think there'd be any. At this rate, you'll have more than I do.'

'Is there a prize for who has most guests?' Maddy asked innocently, and they all laughed.

Felix stood up. 'I don't know about you two, but I think we should have a little celebration. A glass of ginger wine all round – what do you say?'

'I say yes!' Maddy said. 'But what are we celebrating?'

'You,' he said, already at the sideboard where he kept a decanter of sherry and one or two other bottles. He poured three glasses of ginger wine and brought them over on a silver tray one of his uncles had given him for a Christmas present. He held the tray in front of Maddy and as she took the glass, their eyes met. 'I don't need to say any more than that, do I?' he said quietly. 'Just – you. Our dear, lovely Maddy, back with us again.'

The rest of the weekend passed more happily than Maddy could re-member for many months. Although, perhaps 'happily' wasn't quite the right word, she thought, still almost afraid to admit that she could ever feel truly happy again. Perhaps 'at ease' was more accurate. After a long period of turmoil and doubt, she was at peace with herself. She would always grieve for Sammy but it was now, as Felix said, an honest grief, untainted by sour emotions. She could feel it without shame, and could begin to live her life again, carrying her sorrow beside her instead of as a heavy, oppressive load on her back.

It would be a slow process, though. As they talked in the vicarage that evening, Felix warned her not to expect too much, too soon. 'You feel better now, and you might even feel happy – a sort of euphoria – but that's just because you've been so sad. Don't expect those times to last for long at first. There are bound to be times when you feel down, and you mustn't be too disappointed or worried, because they won't last either. It'll be a bit like the Big Dipper at the fair – up and down. But it will all settle down eventually, and as long as you hold on to your faith that you will come through, you'll be all right. Just take it gently.'

Maddy nodded. 'I do feel that now, Felix – that I'll come through. There's still a kind of guilt, that I'm alive and might be happy again, while poor Sammy is dead and will never know all the lovely things we could have done together. But there's nothing I can do about that, and I know he wouldn't have wanted me to spend the next fifty years or so being miserable and a burden to everyone else.'

'The guilt is natural too,' Felix said. 'One of my uncles was the only one who survived out of his whole unit when he was in France during the war. They were going to hear Vera Lynn sing at a nearby army camp, and he opted out at the last minute because of a stomach upset. They hit a mine on the way there and everyone was killed. It took him a long time to come to terms with not being killed alongside them. It was as if he felt he ought to have been, and it was wrong that he wasn't. But eventually he decided that God must have wanted him to survive and he's spent the years since then working with men who were badly injured and never able to work again, almost as a sort of reparation.'

'Do you think I ought to do something like that?' Maddy asked doubtfully, and he laughed and hugged her.

'No, of course not – unless you really feel you want to, of course. But I think it will be enough if you're just the happy, lovely girl you really are inside. Let her out again and you'll make a lot of other people happy too, just by being you. I think that's probably good enough.'

After supper, they walked back across the Clam to Burracombe, and Felix left them at Dottie's gate. Maddy went on indoors to give him and Stella some time alone together, and he took Stella in his arms and said, 'I hope I've said the right things. She does seem happier now, doesn't she?'

'Yes, she does. And you said exactly the right things. Maddy's always seemed rather a butterfly, flitting through life without a care in the world, but this has changed her. She's a more thoughtful person now, more sensitive to others, but I've begun to catch a glimpse of the old Maddy peeping out, and it's good to see. I don't think she'll ever be quite such a butterfly again, though.'

'I think she's going to grow into a fine person,' Felix said. 'Rather like her sister, in fact!'

Stella punched his arm and laughed. Then she said, more soberly, 'I think you could be right. And although I don't think she'll do what your uncle did, I'll be surprised if she doesn't follow his example and find something valuable to do with her life.'

'More valuable than working for an Archdeacon?' he asked in a shocked voice. 'Really, darling, I'm surprised at you. Anyway –' he gathered her closer, 'let's stop talking about your sister now and think about ourselves. Are you going to write to Frank Budd and ask him to give you away?'

'Yes, I'll do that tomorrow. I'm sure he'll say yes, and that means Jess can be the "bride's mother" and sit in the front pew.' She hugged him. 'It's all beginning to seem quite real!'

'Of course it's real – you didn't doubt it, did you?'

'No, I didn't doubt it, but it seemed somehow more like a dream than something that was really going to happen. But now we've written all the invitations and the dresses are being made, and we've chosen our hymns and everything – well, it seems as if nothing can stop it now.'

'Nothing could ever stop it,' he said. 'You're going to be my wife and if anything tries to get in our way, it will have me to answer to!'

Maddy had gone straight upstairs to bed. Her window faced the back of the cottage, so she did not hear Stella and Felix talking about her, but her thoughts ran on very similar lines. Until now, she thought, I've never really taken much notice of real life. I was such a child when Fenella adopted me, and then I lived very happily with Dottie until the war ended and Fenella could take me abroad with her. Even though we were bombed out twice and I lost all my family, I've always been looked after and cosseted. I've never really had to deal with it myself.

Now, I can understand a little of what everyone has to experience at some time – real pain and grief, and real love, too. Not just Sammy's love, but the love of all these other people – Stella and Felix and Dottie; Ruth and Dan; the Archdeacon and Mrs Copley, and all the other people I know so well. And they must love me, or how could they have put up with me all these months?

Now is the time to start repaying their love, by becoming the sort of person they'll be happy to know. By making them proud of me.

Somehow, she thought, gazing out at the moonlit fields and the dark silhouette of the moors, I've got to find something to do. Sammy has lost his life, but I was allowed to keep mine, and I must make good use of it.

She undressed and got into bed without drawing the curtains, so that she could gaze out at the moon as it sailed across the indigo sky. The answer wasn't there yet, but she had the feeling that it would come to her soon, maybe when she was least expecting it.

Chapter Twenty-Nine

Ishouldn't be doing this, Hilary thought as she boarded the train. I'm sliding into deception: telling Father, not exactly lies, not yet, but letting him think what isn't really true. Letting him think I'm meeting a woman friend in London for some Christmas shopping, letting him think this is an innocent visit, when in truth I am guilty of words I don't even like saying to myself.

Adultery. She'd looked up the word in her dictionary and found that it applied not just to the married partner in such a liaison, but to the unmarried one as well. Even though she had never been married, she was guilty of adultery. She felt a hot wave of shame, yet she knew that even this wasn't enough to prevent her from going to London to meet David Hunter again.

Ever since the night of the reunion, he had filled her thoughts. She woke in the morning to his name, and she carried her memories with her through the day, to relive in passionate detail at night. Now, with only hours to go before meeting again, her heart was already beating wildly and her body tingling with anticipation.

'Off to London again?' her father had asked in some surprise when she'd told him. 'That reunion seems to have done you some good – showed you there's life outside Burracombe. Well, you go, my girl, meet your friends and do a bit of shopping, see a show or two. *The Times* gave a good review of that new musical – doubt if you'll be able to get tickets now, though.'

'Well, it doesn't matter,' Hilary said. 'We haven't made any firm plans.'

'As long as you don't forget your responsibilities here,' he added with a touch of sternness. 'Can't afford to have you gadding about too much, with Robert to think of.'

Hilary gave him a look but decided not to respond. It would only end in an argument, and she didn't feel like clashing with her father just now. She was too full of the excitement of a new love – no, a rediscovered love – to want to quarrel with anyone, and she needed all her energy for exploring feelings that were not exactly new to her, but which had lain dormant for years.

She had never felt this way about Henry, her fiancé. She'd known, even then, that their relationship was not, and never would be, a great romance. It would be comfortable enough, almost middle-aged before it had properly begun. They would have lived in Henry's family home in Dorset, a house not unlike Burracombe Barton, raised a family of three or four children, and grown old together without ever having experienced the heady exhilaration of what she was feeling now. And perhaps there was a good deal to be said for that. It was the way many of England's families had been produced – something not far short of an arranged marriage, with two people who had met each other from within a fairly tight social circle, introduced during the Season, when girls were presented to the Queen – or, in Hilary's day, the King – and then embarked on a summer of parties, balls and dances where they would meet the suitable young men from whom they would choose a husband. That was how it was done.

All that had been changed by the war. Young men like Henry had been called up for active service and never returned. Young women like Hilary had left their homes to take on jobs they would never have dreamed of, and returned as different people. And they had met men they would not normally have met, and some – like Hilary – had fallen in love with them.

David Hunter had been a doctor, working in his father's practice in a country town in Derbyshire when the war started. In the normal way, he and Hilary would never have met, never have fallen in love as they had done in Egypt. But everything had been different there – senses and emotions heightened by danger, by the feeling that every time you saw each other it could be for the last time, by the need to make the most of the life you had while you still had it. And temptation, on that last, hot night under a canopy of glittering stars, had been almost impossible to resist.

It was only the thought of Henry that had kept Hilary from that final step. Now, there was no Henry – but there was Sybil. And there was Burracombe.

David was married. It was, he said, an unhappy marriage, one that should never have been made, but nevertheless he was married. Her heart should be filled with guilt, yet all she could feel was this tremulous excitement, this deep thrill of anticipation. She could not look ahead to consequences, could not even begin to imagine what they might be. It was sufficient to be here now, on this train, alive and speeding towards him, towards love.

David was waiting at the barrier at Paddington Station. She saw him as soon as she got off the train but her legs would not move fast enough, and she ended up almost running into his arms. They clung together, oblivious of the swirl of people around them, conscious only of the warmth of each other's bodies, the beating of each other's hearts. Hilary was trembling, almost in tears, and he held her so tightly she was afraid she would break. It seemed impossible to be close enough.

Eventually, they drew apart, smiling rather shakily at each other. She searched his face with her eyes, as if trying to detect the minutest difference since they last met. There was a tiny shaving cut on his chin, but the brown eyes were just as kind and steady, the mouth just as firm. She kissed it, to make sure.

'Oh, Hilary,' he said. 'It's seemed like a lifetime.'

'I know.' She took his hand as he picked up her case. 'And I thought, at the last moment, that I wasn't going to be able to get away.'

'Why not?'

'Rob. He suddenly telephoned home to say he had an exeat this weekend. We thought it wasn't till next week. Father took it for granted that I'd stay – he was quite taken aback when I said I wasn't going to. But I pointed out that he would be able to have Rob to himself for the whole weekend, and he agreed that that was a good idea. They can spend the entire time looking at old photographs and Baden's school reports.'

David smiled. 'That doesn't sound much fun.'

'Oh, I expect he'll escape at some point and slip down to the village to see his friends. Dad doesn't approve of them – they got into rather a scrape in the summer. Anyway, don't let's talk about them – don't let's talk about home at all. This is *our* time and I want to make the most of every moment. What are we going to do?'

David slid his eyes sideways and she laughed. 'Apart from that, I mean! I can't come to London and not have anything to tell Father when I go back. He expects me to go to at least one show.'

'And so we shall. I've got tickets for the Theatre Royal in Drury Lane – *The King and I*.'

'You haven't!' Hilary clapped her hands. 'That's marvellous! But it's only just opened – how did you manage it?'

He tapped the side of his nose and looked mysterious. 'I have my ways. Anyway, I thought you'd like to see it. They say Valerie Hobson and Herbert Lom are excellent as Anna and the King of Siam. And everyone's humming the songs.'

'I know. How lovely.' They were walking briskly through the streets to their hotel, which stood opposite Hyde Park. The trees were showing their late autumn colours at their best now, and Hilary felt a brief pang of guilt as she followed David up the steps, reminded of the trees around Burracombe and the people there, who would have been shocked and disbelieving if they had known where she was now. As David signed the register, her guilt deepened and she caught the receptionist's eye and looked away hastily, sure that the woman knew the truth. But David's manner was as normal and natural as if they had been married for years as he took her arm and guided her to the lift.

'Anyone would think you were quite used to doing this,' Hilary said with a little laugh as he pressed the button for their floor, but David's face was serious.

'I've never done it in my life. Believe me, Hilary, there's been nobody I would have wanted to do it with, only you.'

She nodded, still ill at ease. When she had gone back with David to his hotel on the night of the reunion, it had been spontaneous and unplanned, something that might have been regretted afterwards but just possibly excused and not repeated. This time, it was deliberate, an act of decision from which there was no going back. The joy of meeting him again, of being in his arms, evaporated, leaving her cold and uncomfortable.

The lift stopped and they stepped out into the corridor. David led the way along to their room and unlocked the door. They went inside and he closed the door behind them. They stood just inside, looking at each other.

'What is it, darling?' he asked quietly. 'What's gone wrong?'

Hilary shivered, then laughed again. 'Oh, nothing really. Just a goose walking over my grave.'

'No,' he said, 'something's happened to you, Are you regretting this? Do you want to go back?'

Hilary glanced at him, then looked quickly away. She walked over the window and stood looking out at the park opposite, the trees with their cascading leaves of gold and auburn, the glimpse of the blue waters of the Serpentine. They had walked there together, talked and rediscovered their feelings for each other. It was like a dream to remember it now, but it had happened, only a few hundred yards from where she stood now. And, later, they had gone together to the hotel where he was staying, and they had shut themselves away from the world and taken the night for their own.

David came softly behind her and laid his hands on her shoulders. His touch was gentle but it shot a searing flame through her body, and she quivered. She turned to face him and looked into his eyes, seeing them darken with an expression that seemed to drive straight into her heart. She lifted her arms and wound them around his neck, drawing his lips down to hers.

'Oh, Hilary ...' he murmured at last. 'I thought you were having second thoughts. I thought you were going to say no, and leave me for ever.'

'I'm sorry,' she whispered. 'I just realised what we were doing. What people would say, if they knew. Oh, David ...'

'Don't think about it,' he urged. 'Don't think about *them* – whoever they are. They don't matter. This is what matters – us, and the fact that we've found each other again. We can't let it go this time.'

'But what are we to do?' she asked. 'I can't see into the future at all. I can't see any future for *us*. We *can't* be together. Only like this – meeting in hotels, spending the odd day together, telling lies.'

'You know that's not what I want for us—' he began, but she cut in on his words.

'It's not what either of us wants. But it's all there is for us. We *can't have* what we want. Oh, I'm sorry.' She let her head droop against his chest. 'I didn't mean this to happen, the moment we were on our own. I meant us to be so happy.'

'And so we shall be. So we are. Come here.' He took her hand and led her to the wide double bed. He sat down and drew her down beside him. 'Listen, darling, you don't have to do anything you don't want to do. I'm not going to force you, I'm not going to beg or plead – much as I want to. You can go now if you want to – though I hope very much that you won't – or I'll book another room and we can spend a chaste weekend together, just enjoying each other's company. We'll take it as slowly as you like. It's entirely up to you.'

Hilary took off her gloves and looked down at her hands. On her right hand she wore her mother's engagement and wedding rings. Her left was bare, as it had been after she had finally removed Henry's ring, a year after he was killed. She wondered what her life would have been if she had given way to David's pleading all those years ago and been wearing his ring during that time. For they would have married, she knew that. They would, perhaps, be celebrating their tenth wedding anniversary about now. They would have had children …

'So much time has gone by,' she whispered through the lump in her throat. 'We can never get that back.'

'But there's time ahead of us too. Time for us to begin again. To marry – to have the family we ought to have. Don't you feel it, as I do? We've been given another chance.'

'You know it's not as easy as that. There's too much still standing in our way.'

'No,' he said, 'there's not. You're seeing everything as an obstacle, like a huge wall we can't climb over. Well, we can't demolish it all at once, but we *can* remove one obstacle at a time, brick by brick. We can do it, Hilary.' He paused and looked gravely into her eyes. 'I won't let you go again. We're meant to be together. You know we are.'

There was a long silence. Hilary felt as if he was looking into her heart, and that she was looking into his, and what she saw there slowly began to calm her. She felt her fears ebb away and passion begin to take their place.

She slid her hands away from his and began to unbutton her jacket and then his shirt. She slipped her hands inside, feeling the warmth of his skin, and the flame he had lit earlier suddenly flared into life again and this time it would not be denied.

Chapter Thirty

'So that's it, and all about it,' Jackie announced defiantly. 'If you don't let me have a passport and go to America, I'll get a job in London and stay there until I'm twenty-one, and *then* I'll go. And you won't be able to do a thing to stop me.'

'And suppose I put a stop to you going to London?' Ted demanded. 'I've still got some say in what you do and don't do.'

'No, you haven't,' she retorted. 'You can stop me getting married or going abroad, but you can't stop me leaving home. And anyway, I already have, *and* it was with your agreement, so nobody's going to make me come back. There's not much else you can stop me doing, when it comes down to it. You can't even stop me having a baby,' she finished, her colour rising.

Ted and Alice stared at her. Alice found her voice first.

'Jackie! You're not telling us you're in trouble!'

'No, of course I'm not. I'm just saying that you can't really stop me living my life, that's all. At least, you can, but not for ever, so you might as well give in and let me go to America now, and stop all this arguing.'

'The arguing would stop if you remembered your place and took notice of what your mother and father told you,' Ted told her. He turned to Alice. 'I knew it would come to this. Didn't I say it would lead to trouble, letting a maid like her go off and live in Plymouth? Us should have put our foot down in the first place and said no. She was perfectly happy working as a maid at the Barton, but once her started to get ideas above her station it was bound to end in tears.'

Alice agreed with him, but she didn't think he was going the best way about putting things right. She looked pleadingly at her daughter.

'Us have got your best interests at heart, maid. It's not so bad you working in Plymouth, but London's different. It's too big, there's too many people, and they'm not like us. There's too many ready to take advantage of a young girl.'

'Let me go to America, then,' Jackie said implacably. 'I'll be in a small town there, with family. And they won't take advantage of me.'

Alice sighed and looked helplessly at her husband. He scowled at the newspaper he'd been reading when Jackie had come in.

'What makes you think you'll get a job in London anyway? I don't suppose they're two a penny, specially for a young girl up from Devon who's never been to London in her life.'

'Yes, I have. I went to the Festival of Britain with the village coach trip.'

'Well, that's hardly experience, is it! You never went on the Underground or anything like that. You didn't really do anything except go to the Festival. I tell you what I think – you find yourself a job, that's what, and *then* we'll think about whether you can go to London, or anywhere else, for that matter. And I reckon it'll be a while before you do that.'

'Well, it won't,' Jackie said triumphantly, 'because Miss Millington says she's got a friend in one of the big London hotels and she might be able to find me a place. It won't be a receptionist, not to start with, but I can work my way up, same as I have at The Duke. All I have to do is go up one day for an interview and then I can give in my notice at The Duke and start in a couple of weeks. And I will.' As Ted's head came up, she met his eyes boldly. 'And once I'm there, I shan't be coming home again, so there.'

'Jackie!' Alice cried in dismay. 'You don't mean that! Not come home again – not to see me and your dad and the family? Not to see your gran or the babies? Of course you don't mean it.'

'I do,' Jackie said, but her voice wavered and tears came into her eyes. She looked at her father and said in a smaller voice, 'Please, Dad. Please let me go to America with Russ and Uncle Joe. I want to so much and I promise I'll be sensible. And I *will* come home again. I really will.'

There was a long silence. Ted's eyes dropped and then he looked at his wife. Alice moved over to him and put her hand on his shoulder. He chewed his lip, sighed deeply and said, 'I'll think about it. That's all I'm saying. I'm not promising nothing, mind –' as Jackie's mouth opened with a squeal of delight, 'I'm not saying anything either way, not till I've had a good long think about it, and talked to your mother and to your uncle. I need to get a lot sorted out in my mind before I says any more. But I'll think about it.'

'Oh, Dad,' she whispered, and flung herself on her knees beside his chair. She threw her arms around his neck. 'Dad, if you just let me go to America now I'll do whatever you want for the rest of my life!'

Ted gave a snort of laughter. 'Well, I won't hold my breath for that! I reckon once you turn twenty-one you'll do whatever *you* want, same as you always have. But as to America – well, we'll see. That's all.'

But Jackie and her mother both knew that when Ted said he would see, it was more than halfway to a yes. Jackie's face was flushed with excitement as she scrambled to her feet, and Alice looked relieved, but still anxious. She put her hand out to her daughter and said, 'You will be careful, won't you? Take notice of what your Uncle Joe tells you. And your cousins too – they'll look after you, I'm sure. It's a long way away, though, and they might be family but they don't know you like we do.'

'I will,' Jackie promised. 'And I'll write every week, and—'

'Now you just hold your horses,' Ted interrupted. 'I've not said yes yet. There's a long way to go before us starts thinking about getting a passport or anything like that.'

'Passport!' Jackie said. 'Yes, we really ought to find out about that. I don't know how long it will take, but—'

'*I haven't said yes yet!*' Ted shouted, but neither of the women took any notice of him and he sank back in his chair, shaking his head. When Minnie opened the door, Jackie was looking in the dresser drawer for paper and Alice was rooting for a pencil. She looked at them all in surprise.

'Whatever be going on? I could hear the noise all the way upstairs. You'm not still argufying over this America trip, are you?'

'No, we're not,' Jackie told her, still pink with excitement. 'Dad's said he'll think about it. We're just making a list of all the things we've got to do.'

Minnie looked at her son. 'Be this true, Ted?'

'Yes, it is,' he said with resignation. 'And that's *all* I said – that I'd think about it. Young Jackie seems to think that's a definite yes.'

'Well, it is, isn't it?' she asked coaxingly, coming over to wind her arms around his neck and lay her cheek against his. 'It's what you meant really, wasn't it? You just didn't want to say so straight away.'

'I don't reckon it matters what I *meant* to do,' he grumbled, shaking his newspaper. 'It seems to be what I done. Well, all right, then, you can go.' He raised his voice over her cries. 'Go on – make your list and you'd better find out about this passport as well. And now, perhaps, I can have a bit of peace to read my paper. Unless there's anything else you want me to say? Not that you'd take any notice if I did.'

The women laughed. Jackie's excitement was infectious, carrying them all along with her, and when she caught sight of Joanna in the yard, she dashed out to tell her the news. The three in the kitchen looked at each other.

'Well, that seems to be that,' Alice said. 'I must say, it's a long time since I saw our Jackie looking as happy as she do now. It's almost worth the worry.'

'And you know why she looks so happy, don't you?' Ted growled. 'Because she's got her own way, that's why.' He opened out his newspaper and stared at it, wondering what he'd been reading about before all this started. 'I just hope we won't be sorry for it.'

Chapter Thirty-One

'Hope you won't be bored, rattling about in the house with just your old grandfather for company,' Gilbert said as he collected Robert in the silver Armstrong Siddeley. 'Your Aunt Hilary's gone up to London for the weekend. She'd have stayed home if we'd known you had an exeat, but it was too late to change her plans. Meeting some friends there.'

'It doesn't matter,' Robert said. 'I will amuse myself.'

'Thought we might look through a few more of the old photographs,' Gilbert went on. 'And this afternoon you can spend an hour or two with Mr Kellaway if you'd like, going round the estate. He'll be about until five or so.'

'That would be pleasant. Perhaps I could go to Wood Cottage and visit Mrs Kellaway and the new puppy.'

He talks like an old man, Gilbert thought a shade impatiently, but he only said, 'That's a good idea. You can ask him now – I've just seen the Land Rover going round to the yard.' He drove the big car around the side of the house to the big stable yard, where Travis was parking the Land Rover. 'Kellaway – here's my young grandson, wants to spend a few hours with you, if that's all right. Says he'd like to see your good lady and the dog.'

Travis turned and grinned at Robert. 'Certainly. I dare say you want to change into mufti first. I'll be here for a while.'

'Mufti?'

'Home clothes,' Gilbert translated. 'And he'll want a spot of lunch, too. An hour's time suit you?'

Travis nodded and Gilbert shepherded Robert indoors, where Mrs

Ellis had just finished laying the table in the dining room. She put her hands on her hips and beamed at the French boy.

'Well, you're a sight for sore eyes, I must say. We've missed having you around the place. And how are you getting along at the school?'

'I don't like it,' Robert stated flatly. 'I am not staying there.'

Mrs Ellis looked surprised, and Gilbert scowled.

'We'll see about that. You don't seem to realise what a good chance this is for you.'

'I liked my own school,' Robert said stubbornly. 'In France.'

'It's bound to seem different at first,' the housekeeper said uncomfortably. 'You'll soon settle down. There are some nice boys there for you to make friends with, aren't there?'

'No,' he said. 'There are no nice boys there, none at all.' He turned towards the stairs. 'I will change now into ... mufti.'

He clattered up to his bedroom, leaving Gilbert and Mrs Ellis looking at each other. The housekeeper shifted uneasily, aware that Colonel Napier was not accustomed to discussing his family affairs with a servant. She said, 'I expect the poor lamb's a bit homesick, that's all.'

'Yes, I dare say,' he said gruffly, turning away to go into the dining room. 'Better give him ten minutes or so and then serve lunch. He'll be out all afternoon, might stop over at the Kellaways' for tea. It'll do him good.'

He shut the door behind him and went to stare at Baden's portrait over the fireplace. The blue eyes met his with the steady gaze that he had seen in Robert's eyes. It was primarily that gaze that had convinced him that the boy was his true grandson, and fit to be heir to the Burracombe estate; but now he wondered if, in Robert, it didn't also contain more than a hint of stubbornness.

Well, there was nothing wrong with a touch of stubbornness. That was what kept men treading the path they believed to be right. It was when their path was wrong that it became dangerous.

And that was just why Robert, who had not had the benefit of an English upbringing, with prep school and the right sort of friends to show him the way, must be treated with extra care – made to understand what his path must be, that the boys he was mixing with now were the right sort, the friends that would last him all his life. As Mrs Ellis said, he was probably no more than homesick. Well, that would pass and mustn't be given in to. What he needed now was a firm hand, the reassurance that whatever he was enduring at school at the moment (and Gilbert knew very well that new boys did endure a good deal in their first term or so) would help build a strong, firm character – the kind of character a Napier should have to enable him to take his rightful place in the world.

To Gilbert Napier, landowner and Army colonel, that meant being in charge. Running an estate, or running a country, it made little difference. It was an obligation as well as a right, and those who were destined to take this path must be properly prepared.

It was his duty to see that Robert was so prepared, in order to take his place as a fitting heir to Burracombe.

At Wood Cottage, Jennifer was giving Tavy, the puppy, a training session. Already, the little dog could sit and lie down to command and was learning to 'stay', although she grew anxious if Jennifer went too far away or disappeared from her sight. She was nearly four months old now, and almost house-trained, with only the occasional accident if she became over-excited. She was excited now, by Robert's arrival, and had to be carried outside hastily to squat in the corner of the garden that Jennifer had designated as 'her spot'.

'She's nice,' Robert said as she scurried back to him. 'I wish I could have a dog. Grandfather's dogs are old now, and don't want to play.'

'Time he had a new couple,' Travis said. 'Selsey and Bart are getting too decrepit to be of any use in the field, and the Colonel still likes to do a bit of shooting. He'll be wanting to take you along pretty soon, too, Rob.'

'Yes, he says he will ask you to teach me,' the French boy said. 'We have *chasseurs* in France too, of course, but I have never been hunting.'

'Do you have a dog at home?' Jennifer asked, throwing an old ball for Tavy to rush after. They all laughed as the puppy tripped over her own legs in her eagerness to pick it up and then came back to drop it at Jennifer's feet.

'No, we have only a cat called Grisette, because she is small and grey. I miss her.'

Jennifer looked at him sympathetically. 'You must miss all your family. You didn't really expect to stay here so long when you first came over, did you?'

'We did not know what to expect,' Rob said, and he threw the ball for Tavy. It rolled into the bushes, and he ran over to help the puppy look for it. Jennifer glanced at Travis.

'I suppose I oughtn't to ask him family things, but he has such a lost look about him sometimes, and it doesn't seem right to pretend they don't exist. He has a brother and sister as well, doesn't he? And the grandmother and aunt live with the family too. It's no wonder he feels lonely.'

'I don't think he's settling down at all well at school,' Travis said. 'He hasn't said much, but that's a bad sign in itself – a boy of his age who's enjoying life and has plenty of friends never stops chattering about them.'

'He made friends in the village, though, didn't he? He spent a lot of time with Micky and Henry during the summer.'

'And look where that led!' Travis said with a grin. 'Those two rapscallions aren't at all the Colonel's idea of suitable friends for his grandson. It's a pity – they're good boys at heart, they just let their enthusiasm run away with them at times.'

'Is he seeing them over the weekend?'

'Not if his grandfather has anything to do with it!' They watched as the boy and dog played together, Rob's laugh ringing out as it hadn't done for weeks. 'It's a pity, because it would be the best thing for him, to spend some time with the boys he gets on well with. But it's not for me to interfere. The Colonel has his own ideas about how he should be brought up, and presumably it's the way his father and Stephen were brought up – well-to-do English boys, cocooned from the lower classes. I just hope that where Rob's concerned he's not making a big mistake. A child's a bit like a half-grown tree – you can't just uproot it and transplant it in a completely different place and expect it flourish without a lot of extra care.'

They went indoors, leaving Rob to play with Tavy and mooch about the garden and woods on his own. Jennifer opened the oven door and took out a tray of scones and another of saffron buns.

'We'll take these out into the garden,' she said, putting the kettle on to the range. 'There won't be all that many days when we can still eat outside. We'll probably be snowed up by Christmas.'

'Will you mind that?' he asked. 'It could be difficult for you to get into the village. I'll be able to use the Land Rover, but when I'm not around you'll be a bit isolated.'

'I shan't mind. I'll have Tavy for company – I'm looking forward to seeing her first experience of snow – and I really enjoy being in such a quiet place after living in Devonport. And it'll only be for a few hours each day, after all.'

'Still, you need to see your friends,' he persisted. 'You ought to make some sort of arrangement with Val Ferris and go in to see her once or twice a week. It's not good for you to be on your own too much.'

'Yes, I could do that. I can walk into the village, or if the weather's bad you could take me in after dinner and then fetch me at teatime. And I've got some other ideas too – I'm going to start doing tapestry, and embroidery. Dottie Friend's going to teach me. And then there's Christmas to think about. Alice Tozer has asked me to go carol-singing and help with the WI Christmas tea, and I'm looking forward to decorating the cottage. I want you to bring me lots of holly and ivy from the woods. And mistletoe, of course.'

'Of course,' he agreed. 'Not that we need mistletoe.' He leaned over and kissed her and she laughed.

'We'll have some, just the same. And we mustn't forget Stella and Felix's wedding, only a week or so after Christmas. Honestly, Travis, you don't need to worry. I won't be lonely, and I certainly won't be bored.'

They looked up as Rob came in, carrying the puppy. 'I think she wants to go to sleep,' he said, laying her on the old cushion in the cardboard box that was her bed. He saw the cakes on the table. 'Those look very good. Almost as good as *Maman* makes at home.'

Jennifer smiled. 'Well, that's a compliment! I was just going to bring them out to have tea in the garden. Put them on those plates, will you, Rob, while I make the tea, and here's some cream and jam for the scones.' She poured boiling water into the big brown teapot while he loaded the tray. Travis went ahead to clear the wooden garden table of fallen leaves and they set out the crockery and food. Travis had made benches to sit on, and they settled down.

'It's like being in a magic place,' Rob remarked after a while. 'Just a cottage in the woods, with nothing but trees and birds, and animals rustling amongst the bushes. I wonder if there are wolves. Or bears. We have them in some of the forests in France.'

Jennifer smiled. 'Probably not, but we could imagine them if you like. Friendly bears, I think, don't you?'

'Oh, no – dangerous ones. Very frightening. We would have to fight them off.'

'They'd be coming for the buns,' Travis observed solemnly, and when the other two looked at him, he said, 'Don't you know the rhyme? *And wandering bears would come with buns, And steal the bags to hold the crumbs.* Well, they must get the buns from somewhere!'

'This conversation is getting silly,' Jennifer declared, spooning jam and cream on to a fluffy scone. 'Rob, we were wondering if you'd like to see Micky and Henry while you're here.'

'I would, but I don't think Grandfather wants me to, and there won't be time tomorrow. I have to go to church in the morning, and then we're going to look at my father's old photographs and school books, and I have to go back to Kelly at four o'clock.' He spoke without enthusiasm, and Travis and Jennifer glanced at each other.

'Well, next time, perhaps,' Jennifer said. 'If you let us know when you've got another weekend at home, we'll ask them over here for tea. I'm sure your grandfather wouldn't mind that.'

'I'm sure he would!' Travis said, after he'd taken Rob home and returned to find Jennifer listening to *In Town Tonight* on the wireless as she knitted him a new winter pullover. 'I assume you don't expect Rob to tell him about this plan.'

'That's up to him,' Jennifer said equably, taking out a new skein of wool. 'But least said soonest mended, so I don't think we need mention it. Anyway, I can't see what harm it could do for him to meet them here. They're perfectly decent boys. If the Colonel had any sense, he'd invite them to tea at the Barton, where he could keep an eye on them himself.'

Travis threw up his hands in mock horror. 'What? Invite the villagers to tea? You've surely been in Burracombe long enough now to know that that simply isn't done.'

'Well, perhaps it's time it was done,' she said, taking advantage of his upraised hands to hook the wool round them. 'Hold this while I wind a new ball ... And I think Hilary would do it, if she'd been at home. After all, in France Rob's the son of the equivalent of George

Sweet, the village baker. Colonel Napier's not only uprooted him from his family, he's taken him out of the circle he naturally belongs to. It's no wonder he gets along better with Micky and Henry than he does with the boys at Kelly College.'

'And that's just what the Colonel is trying to change,' Travis said soberly. 'He wants Rob to forget his roots and become an English gentleman, but I'm not at all sure it's going to work. That boy's got other ideas in his head – or I'm a Dutchman!'

Chapter Thirty-Two

'We'll have to get up soon,' Hilary said, raising herself on one elbow and looking down at David's face. She traced the small lines around his eyes with one fingertip. 'It's ten o'clock – we have to check out by eleven.'

'No, we don't,' he said, running his fingers down her spine. 'I booked us in for tonight as well.'

'But I've got to go back this afternoon. And surely you—'

'You don't have to stay here tonight, much as I'd like you to, but I shall. I've got some paperwork to do – I'll stay here and do it, if I can keep my mind on it. Sybil's not expecting me back till tomorrow evening, not that she'd care either way. But it means we don't have to leave until the last minute. We can stay in bed all morning and most of the afternoon!'

Hilary laughed. 'You're a wicked man, David Hunter.'

'I know,' he said with a grin. 'Nice, isn't it!'

He pulled her close against him and they laughed together, but soon their laughter turned yet again to passion and it was a while before they began to talk again. This time, they spoke more soberly.

'What *are* we going to do, David? If I keep coming to London like this, someone's going to get suspicious. Even Father will never believe I'm just coming to meet women friends that I haven't seen for years.'

'Let's not think about it too much,' he said. 'Not this weekend, anyway. We're just discovering each other again. I want to have a perfect weekend to look back on during the dark days when we're apart. We can do our thinking then.'

'We need to talk as well, though.'

'Next time,' he said. 'I promise we will next time.'

Hilary sat up, the sheets falling away from her shoulders. 'Next time ...? There wasn't even supposed to be *this* time, David. I never meant this to happen, you know. I always thought I was above this sort of thing – secret meetings, weekends in hotels, having a secret lover. And I suppose now I'm a *mistress*. I never expected to be that. I thought I had more self—' she hesitated.

'More self-respect?' he asked quietly, lying on his back and watching her face.

'More self-control. But I haven't – not where you're concerned. It's come as rather a surprise.'

'That's because you're leaving love out of the equation,' he said. 'It doesn't go too well with self-control. Not when you've waited as long as we have.'

She turned and looked down into his eyes. 'I didn't even realise I was waiting.' She thought of the men who had caught her fancy during the past few years: Felix, who was about to marry Stella; Travis, who had married Jennifer. And others, even earlier. In each case, she'd wondered if this could be the man for her, had played with the idea of marrying, but had been only faintly disappointed when they'd turned away from her. Perhaps that was why their own interest hadn't been strong enough – they'd known, somehow, that she could not give them her heart. All these years, when she'd thought him out of her life for ever, it had still been reserved for David.

'We were both waiting,' he said. 'Even though I was fool enough to marry Sybil, I was really waiting for you.'

'But you did marry her,' she said in a flat tone. 'And she's always going to be there, between us. You're always going to go home to her.'

'She's not going to be between us this weekend,' he said, and sat up with sudden energy. 'Come on – let's go for a walk in Hyde Park. We'll have lunch, and then come back to say a lingering goodbye before you have to catch your train.'

'Not too lingering,' she said. 'Father's coming to Tavistock to meet me, so I mustn't be late. I wonder how he's got along with Rob over the weekend.'

Hyde Park was popular that morning with people walking their dogs, people pushing prams, people just walking and enjoying the unexpectedly warm November sunshine. Couples strolled along arm in arm, as Hilary and David were doing, or sat on the benches overlooking the Serpentine. An armada of swans drifted by, their wings unfurled and held aloft like the broad white sails of proud schooners, while their half-grown, mottled cygnets came behind and mallards, teal and dabchicks circled around them like a flotilla of lesser ships, breaking away in a flurry of glittering foam when someone scattered bread for them from the bank. Hilary and David paused on the bridge to look down into the clear water and saw a crested grebe swimming below the surface, its neck stretched out as it snatched at a shoal of tiny, fleeing minnows. A squirrel ran across the parapet, stopping as if startled to see them, and Hilary laughed.

They ate lunch at a café, talking about the show they had seen the night before. The songs had already caught on, brought across from America, while *The King and I* was on Broadway with Gertrude Lawrence and Yul Brynner, and Hilary had had one of them running through her head all morning.

'They all seem so appropriate,' she said now. '"Hello, Young Lovers" – though we're not so very young now! – and "Getting To Know You". That's what we're doing, isn't it? Getting to know each other. And "We Kiss in the Shadows".' She looked down at her plate. 'That's what we're doing, too. Kissing in shadows, because we can't let ourselves be seen in broad daylight.'

David reached across the table and took her hand. 'Don't think like that, darling. Not this weekend. Just remember those other songs and "whistle a happy tune". And do you know what my favourites are?'

Her eyes misting with tears, she shook her head and whispered, 'No.'

'"Something Wonderful",' he said. 'And "I Have Dreamed" – because for years dreaming was all I could do and now, just as in the song, I know what it's like to be loved by you. And it's something very wonderful indeed.' He lifted her hand to his lips and she felt her head swim.

'David ...'

'Why, hullo, there,' a voice exclaimed just behind her. 'It's Miss Napier, isn't it? What a coincidence – we saw you in Piccadilly Circus too, a coupla weeks ago.'

Hilary froze. She saw David raise his eyes with no recognition in his expression, and turned slowly. The American accent had already told her who this was, but her heart sank as she looked up into the faces of Joe and Russ Tozer. They grinned down at her, clearly with no idea that this was an inopportune meeting, and Joe glanced at David.

Hilary sighed. 'This is David Hunter, an old wartime friend,' she said, wondering if they had seen him kiss her hand. 'David, this is Joe Tozer and his son Russ. They've come over from America to visit relatives in Burracombe.'

'Good to meet you,' David said, standing up to shake hands. 'Won't you join us? We've had lunch but we're about to have coffee. I'll ask the waitress for some extra cups.'

'Sure,' Joe said, and sat down beside Hilary. Russ took the chair on her other side. 'So are you here for the day or the weekend?' he enquired pleasantly.

'The day,' Hilary said, at the same moment as David said, 'The weekend.' She felt herself grow scarlet and bit her lip. 'I mean, I'm going back this afternoon, on the four o'clock train.'

'Why, so are we,' Joe exclaimed. 'Maybe we can travel together. Russ and I have been over to France,' he went on, turning to David. 'Visited one or two of the places I was in during the First World War – the Abbeville area, mostly. I was at the Battle of the Somme but I was one of the lucky ones. I guess you were in this last lot.'

'That's right,' David said. 'I was in Egypt part of the time. That's where I met Hilary. We ran into each other again at a reunion – I expect that's when you saw us in Piccadilly, on the way to the dinner.'

'Yeah, I guess so,' Joe said, but something in his tone made Hilary wonder just what he had seen. She cast her mind back to the evening when she and David had stood looking up at Eros on his plinth. David's arm had been round her waist ... She wondered what Joe was making of this second meeting and, again, if he had seen her hand at David's lips a few moments ago.

'Did you go anywhere else on the Continent?' she asked Russ. 'I thought I heard you were planning to see Switzerland as well.'

'We just hopped over the border,' he nodded. 'Too much snow to go travelling unless you've got skis! Anyway, we didn't want to be away too long.'

'I expect your father wants to see his family again, especially his mother.'

'I reckon that's it, really,' he said. 'She's a tough old bird but she's getting on, and I've got an idea he feels a bit guilty for not having seen her for so long. Mothers miss their sons.'

'Yes, I think they do,' Hilary agreed, wondering how badly Marianne was missing Robert. And she was sure that Robert was missing his mother, and the rest of his family – indeed, everything that was familiar to him.

'I think Dad also wants to makes things up a bit,' Russ went on. 'We left under a bit of a cloud, you know, on account of young Jackie wanting to come back to the States with us.'

'Does she?' Hilary asked. 'I hadn't heard about that. It would be a good idea, though – she's a bright girl, an experience like that would be excellent for her. And Alice and Ted wouldn't have to worry about her if she were going to be with family.' She stopped and looked at him enquiringly. 'Or don't they see it that way?'

'I don't think they do,' he said ruefully. 'They were pretty annoyed, to be honest. It's been niggling at Dad's mind a bit and he wants to set things right.'

Hilary nodded. 'I hope it works out. Jackie used to work for us, you know, in the house, and it was partly due to my encouragement that she decided to find a job in Plymouth. I don't think I was especially popular with them over that!' She glanced across the table and caught David's eye. 'I really think I ought to go now, though. I've got to collect my things from our – from my hotel. Perhaps I'll see you at Paddington.'

'We'll look out for you,' Joe said, and watched as David and Hilary got up and walked away together. He turned to his son. 'Well, what do you make of that?'

'They seem pretty good friends,' Russ said, without much interest. 'She's never been married, has she? Maybe they met again at this reunion they were talking about, and just clicked.'

'Maybe,' Joe said. 'But if they did, I reckon they'd rather it was kept quiet for a while. So we won't mention it, back in Burracombe, OK?'

'Sure,' Russ said absently. He drank his coffee. He wasn't especially interested in Hilary, although she seemed a nice enough woman, and quite attractive for her age. He was more concerned with who else they might bump into, once they were back in Burracombe.

That pretty little schoolteacher's sister, for instance. He'd only met her once, but her face had stayed in his mind and he wouldn't at all mind getting to know her better.

'Oh dear,' Hilary said as she and David walked back to the hotel. 'Who would have thought we'd run into someone from Burracombe in the middle of Hyde Park? *And* they said they saw us at Piccadilly Circus, the other week.'

'Well, you know what they say about Piccadilly,' he said. 'If you stand there long enough, everyone you know will walk by.'

'Yes, but it doesn't have to be true,' she retorted. 'And it doesn't have to happen the first time you go there. I suppose now it'll be all round the village that I've been meeting a man in London.'

'I doubt it. They didn't strike me as the gossiping kind, and anyway, I don't suppose they're all that interested. They'll be more concerned with their own family.'

'Yes, I expect you're right,' Hilary agreed, still a trifle uneasily. David took her hand in his and after a moment's hesitation she let it stay there. The warmth of his fingers around hers was both exciting and reassuring. A wave of desolation swept over her and she said, 'Only another hour, and I'll be on the train.'

'I know,' he said. 'When will you be able to come again?'

'I don't know. I told you, Father will get suspicious if it's too often. And I've insisted so much that I take an active part in the estate, I can't just drop it now. It's my livelihood.'

'But not for ever, if young Rob takes over.'

'We can't be sure of that. Stephen says he wants to be an engineer, but he's only thirteen – boys of that age want to do half a dozen things before they settle down. And I can't see Marianne letting him do that when he could be inheriting an estate like Burracombe.'

'You love it, don't you?' he said soberly. 'Have you thought what you'll do if he does? Will you be able to bear to leave it?' He stopped and put both hands on her shoulders. 'Will you be able to leave it to come to me?'

Hilary stared at him with tormented eyes. 'You can't ask me that, David. You know it's impossible.'

'It needn't be. Suppose I *make* it possible?'

'How?' she asked. 'No – don't answer that. There's only one way, and I've told you, we can't do that. The scandal would kill my father. I mean it, David – he's got a weak heart and I can't do something that I know will affect him so badly. I really can't. I wouldn't be able to live with myself.'

He sighed and dropped his hands. They walked on and up the steps of the hotel. The receptionist gave him their key and they went up to their room.

'I'm sorry, David,' Hilary said as they reached their door. 'I don't think I can do this any more. I'm just not used to it. The way that woman looked at me – and the way she said "Mrs Hunter" in that sarcastic voice. I'm sure she knows. I saw her look at my left hand when I took my gloves off. It makes me feel ...'

'Dirty?' he said quietly, turning the key, and she shook her head violently.

'No! Of course not. I don't really know what I mean. I just don't feel I can do it again, I'm sorry.'

He closed the door behind them and took her in his arms. She rested her face against his chest and let the tears flow, while he held her closely and stroked her back. At last, she looked up again and said shakily, 'I can't do it again and I can't *not* do it. Oh, David, this hurts so much. Knowing I've got to say goodbye – knowing that while I'm back in Devon, you'll be in Derbyshire. We're so far apart. I don't know how I'm going to bear it.'

'We have to meet again,' he said into her hair. 'We have to take what happiness we can find. Maybe not London next time – maybe Bristol, or Gloucester, or Cheltenham. Don't you have any friends in those places?'

'Probably,' she said dismally, 'but it means more lies, and more chance of being found out. I don't know what to do.'

He was silent for a few moments, then he said, 'I'm going to talk to Sybil. There must be a way. She has so many lovers herself and she doesn't care a jot for me, not really. If I let her have the house and a decent sum of money ... Maybe I could move to another practice somewhere, and you could come to me there. Nobody would know we weren't married.'

'It wouldn't work. You know it wouldn't. People always find out, somehow, and you're a doctor. You're expected to be "respectable". You might even be struck off. And how could we ever have a family?

Besides, it would still kill my father and I'd still be letting down the estate.' She shook her head. 'It has to be above board or we can't do it at all. And that means no sordid little encounter in a seedy hotel with a woman you pay to stay in a room with you overnight. I couldn't bear it, David.'

'And I couldn't bear to ask it of you.' He sighed and drew her closer. 'Let's stop worrying about it now. Something will happen, to show us the way. And now – you really do have to go. Oh, my darling ...'

Ten minutes later she was in a taxi, on her way to Paddington Station. At the last minute, he had said he was coming with her, but she refused to let him. Joe and Russell would be there, looking out for her, and she would not be able to hide her feelings as she and David parted. They kissed one last time, and then she was away.

Her last sight of him was that of a solitary figure, standing at the edge of the pavement, one hand lifted in farewell.

The journey back to Burracombe seemed interminable. At any other time, Hilary would have found Joe and Russ's company interesting, but today all she wanted to do was gaze out of the window, alone with her thoughts. After a while, the two Americans seemed to realise this and fell into conversation between themselves, leaving her alone.

Not that her thoughts were very good company, she soon discovered. For they were running about in her head like ants whose nest had been disturbed. Her suddenly reawakened feelings for David – reawakened and, it seemed, given extra strength by their long period of being buried somewhere in the recesses of her heart – were like a horde clamouring at a city gate to be let in, and any defences she might have left were powerless against them. It was no use telling herself, as she did repeatedly, that the whole situation was wrong, that it could come to no good end, that she should never have allowed it to get so far, should never have allowed it to start in the first place. I knew David might be at that reunion, she thought, I tried to pretend not to know, I tried to pretend I'd forgotten him, but I knew he'd be there, and what's worse, I *hoped* it. I told myself I didn't, but really and truly I wanted to see him again. I wanted to know if he still loved me. I wanted to know if I still loved him.

Well, now she did know, and the power of her emotions had taken her by surprise. Pent up for so long, instead of weakening they had gathered strength and now the walls had been broken down, the gate breached and there was no turning back. It was like Canute trying to stem the tide.

So what was she to do now? If she asked anyone for advice, they would tell her to stop, to tell David there must be no communication between them, no more meetings, no more weekends like this one, spent in a passionate haze of love such as she had never dreamed possible. Write to him; repeat her arguments about the impossibility, the scandal, the harm it could to do her father; tell him again about her responsibilities and obligations, responsibilities she could not turn her back on. End it now, lock it away again in her heart, a pearl to be encased in soft, thick velvet, maybe to be taken out one day when she was very old, too old to want any more than memories, to be stroked and fondled and caressed. It could be as easy as that.

It was not easy at all. It was impossible. As impossible as continuing along the path she and David had begun to tread.

She leaned her forehead against the glass of the window and a tear trickled from beneath her closed eyelids. Russ, sitting opposite, noticed and glanced questioningly at his father but Joe shook his head. It was clear that something was very wrong with Hilary Napier, and he had a very good idea that it must be connected to the man she had left behind in London, but it was not for them to interfere, not now. Whatever her secret was, whatever her trouble, it must remain hers.

One day, perhaps, he would drop a hint that she could confide in him if she wished, but he doubted if she would. She had her own friends in Burracombe, and Joe knew very well that friends in Burracombe were friends indeed.

The train rattled through Okehampton and turned south towards Plymouth. When it had passed the little halt at Mary Tavy, Joe and Russ got up and lifted their luggage down from the racks. Russ took down Hilary's case as well, and Joe bent to touch her on the shoulder.

Hilary had dropped off to sleep, tired out from passion and sorrow. She woke with a start and looked at them uncertainly before remembering where she was.

'Oh – thank you, Mr Tozer. I'm sorry to have been so unsociable. Look, my father will be in the station yard at Tavistock. You must let us give you a lift back to Burracombe.'

'That's kind of you, Miss Napier, but I reckon our Ted will be there, or maybe Tom. They know we're coming.' He helped her down to the platform and they made their way out of the station together to the yard. 'My stars, as our Alice would say, it's turned cold. Yeah, there's Tom. Well, it's been good to share the journey with you.' He hesitated, then decided to say it anyway. 'And if you ever need … well, just to have a talk at any time, I'd be happy to help.' He smiled at her and then turned away with Russ, who gave her a surprised sort of grin and followed his father over to the farm vehicle that Tom Tozer had driven in to meet them.

Hilary made her way over to the Armstrong Siddeley, feeling rather shaken. Clearly, she hadn't been able to hide her turmoil from Joe Tozer, and if he – who barely knew her – had been able to see it, surely everyone else would too. Somehow, she must now gather herself together and behave normally, as if nothing had happened, as if she had indeed spent the weekend with a woman friend. As if her entire world had not been turned upside down in two short days.

Gilbert Napier was in the driving seat. As she came closer, she saw with a sinking heart that his face was like thunder and knew that something had seriously angered him. In this mood, he would be unlikely to notice anything different at all. She could arrive with her hair dyed red or her head shaved, and he still wouldn't notice.

'Hello, Father,' she greeted him, somehow injecting cheerfulness into her voice. 'How has your weekend been? Did Rob have a good time? Is he settling down at school now?'

'A good time?' Gilbert growled. 'Don't ask me! He spent all yesterday afternoon with the Kellaways, and now he's disappeared altogether. God knows what the little fool thinks he's playing at.'

Hilary stared at him. 'Disappeared? What on earth do you mean?'

'What I say, of course. I took him into Tavistock this morning to go to that blasted Roman Catholic church and he told me not to bother to come and fetch him because he would catch the bus back to the Burracombe turning and walk from there. Showing a bit of independence, I thought, and when he was late for lunch I assumed that he'd missed the bus and would have to wait for the next one, and you know what the Sunday buses are like. Aggravating, when I'd hardly seen him, so when I judged he'd have arrived at the turning I went out to pick him up. No sign of him, but I could see the bus disappearing in the distance. Obviously he hadn't been on it. I was starting to get worried by then, so I came home and rang up the RC priest. And you'll never credit what he told me.'

'What did he tell you?' Hilary asked, feeling ominously that she knew.

'Why, the boy never went to church at all! Slipped away as soon as my back was turned and nobody's seen him since. Thinks he can persuade me to let him stay at home and not go back to Kelly. Well, he's got another think coming. As soon as he turns up, he goes straight back to take whatever punishment the headmaster sees fit to hand out to him.'

'As soon as he turns up?' Hilary echoed in dismay. 'But, Father, what makes you think he *will* turn up? Don't you realise what he's done?'

'What are you talking about?' her father demanded impatiently. 'Of course I realise what he's done – I've just told you.'

'No,' she said, getting into the car. 'You *don't* realise. He's run away – from school and from us. He's going to try to go home – to France.'

Chapter Thirty-Three

Gilbert Napier still did not believe the truth until they were back at the Barton and had searched Robert's room. Hilary slid the last drawer closed and turned to face her father.

'You see? His school clothes here – thrown in that corner because he knows, or hopes, he'll never need them again – and his passport and Post Office savings book gone. And no money in this tin, where I know he used to keep whatever he had. There was some there last week when I got his room ready – I know, because I picked it up to dust and it rattled.'

'He might have taken some to spend in Tavistock,' Gilbert said, still unwilling to accept it.

'Where? All the shops are closed.'

'For his church collection, then.'

'He didn't *go* to church!' Hilary exclaimed in exasperation.' Father, haven't you been listening? Rob was unhappy at school, we both knew that, and you just dismissed it – and I'm as much at fault because I didn't do anything about it either. He was bullied, he felt out of place, he hated it there, and we let him – no, we *made* him – go back. It was cruel. On top of taking him away from his real family – yes, Father, his *real* family, the one he'd grown up in – it was unforgivable. Honestly, it's not surprising he's run away. He wants to go back to his real home, and I can't say I blame him.'

'Well, he won't stop there,' Gilbert said angrily. 'I'll have him brought back straight away, and his mother will agree with me. She won't be pleased to see him coming home again. She's too sensible – knows which side *her* bread's buttered, and his as well.'

'That's certainly true,' Hilary said grimly. 'But that's not important now. What is important is that Robert is trying to make his way back to France and we've got to find him. He's only a child, Father – we can't just shrug our shoulders and wait for him to reach his home. He may never get there. Anything could happen to him.'

Gilbert hesitated, then nodded reluctantly. 'You're right, of course. Not that he'd get very far anyway. Probably gone to Plymouth to cross by sea.'

'I'm not sure he'll be able to do that,' Hilary said. 'There are hardly any ferry crossings, and they don't go to the right part of France. If you remember, he and Marianne came via Dover, and I think he'd go back that way. He probably caught the first train to London and heaven knows how we'll find him there. In fact, the more I think about it, the more anxious I feel. I think we ought to contact the police.'

'And have some local village bobby nosing into our affairs?' Gilbert snorted. 'We'll handle this ourselves. Robert's a sensible boy and he's done the crossing before – he knows the ropes of travelling. We'll send someone down to Plymouth to see if he's trying to get a passage there, and I'll telephone a friend of mine in Dover and ask him to get the port authorities to look out for him. He won't have got very far – it's only a few hours since he left. In fact, if you're right and that's where he's making for, he might not even have got to London yet. Where's the train timetable?'

They went downstairs to the office and Hilary found the book and looked through it. 'Lucky there are fewer trains on Sunday – he couldn't have got one to London before two o'clock. You're right, he won't even be at Paddington yet. Perhaps we can get the stationmaster to look out for him.'

'Better if we could ask someone we knew.' Gilbert snapped his fingers irritably. 'Trouble is, all my old friends are likely to be in the country. I wonder ...'

Hilary felt her heart quiver. 'I know someone who might be able to do it.'

'You do? Who's that, then?'

'Just a friend,' she said, hoping he would not probe further. 'I could telephone him – her – now.' She felt her colour rise and wondered if her father had noticed the slip. Not that it mattered if the friend were male or female, it was only her guilty conscience that made it seem significant. She turned towards the door. 'I'll go and look up the number.'

'You'd better be quick,' her father said. 'It's almost five; the train gets to Paddington at six. Lucky it's a slow one.'

Hilary went to the hall, where she'd dropped her bag, and found her diary. With trembling fingers, she turned to the page where she'd written the details of the hotel where she and David had stayed. Back in the office, she found her father waiting and realised that he was going to hear her ask for Dr Hunter and, unable to think of any other way to get him out of the room, said hastily, 'I'm gasping for a cup of tea, Father. Would you mind very much going to put the kettle on while I do this?'

Never before could she remember asking him to do such a thing, but to her relief he nodded and left the office without a word. Amazing what an emergency will do to people, she thought wryly, and asked the operator for the number. In a moment, she was through and the receptionist confirmed that Dr Hunter was in his room.

'David? David, it's me.' She spoke rapidly. 'Yes, I'm home … Yes, dreadfully – but we've got a bit of a flap on here and I need help. Could you possibly go to Paddington Station and see if Robert, our French boy, gets off the train? He seems to have run away and we're afraid he might be trying to go back to France … Yes … thirteen years old, not very big for his age, dark hair and very blue eyes. I shouldn't think he'd have much luggage, maybe just his haversack … Well, he should be easy enough to pick out, I don't suppose there are many thirteen-year-old French boys travelling alone. Oh, thank you, thank you. And will you ring me as soon as you've found him? Or if he *doesn't* get off the train? It's the 2 p.m. from Tavistock – it started at Penzance, around noon, I'd guess. It should be there about six … Yes, all right, we can decide what to do once we know if he's there. Yes … yes, me too.' She was uncomfortably aware that her father had just come back, carrying a tray with a cup of tea on it. 'Thank you. I'll wait to hear from you.' She put down the phone.

'Is she going to go there and get him?' Gilbert asked, and Hilary realised she couldn't continue with the pretence that this was a woman friend. Still, at least he didn't know she'd been ringing a hotel. She took the cup of tea and sipped before answering.

'Thank you, Father. Yes, he's going straight away. It's a man who was at the reunion,' she went on swiftly as her father raised his eyebrows enquiringly. 'One of the officers. I just hope he'll be able to pick Rob out if he is there. And that Rob agrees to go with him. He might not, you know. He might think he's being kidnapped.'

'Not if this man knows his name and where he's come from. Well, I suppose there's not much else we can do until we hear. We'll have to think how to get the boy back, if he has gone to London. Best thing will be for you to go and fetch him, Hilary.'

'Yes, it probably will,' Hilary said. 'But I can't go until tomorrow, there are no more trains. What is David – Dr Hunter – supposed to do with him overnight?'

'Take him home, of course. I don't suppose that's a problem, do you? He can put the boy up for a few hours?'

'It's a lot to ask,' Hilary murmured feebly. 'But you're right – it's Rob we've got to think about. If he *is* on that train – which we don't know – we've got to think about bringing him back, and if he isn't we've got to think where else he might be. I could go to Plymouth and see if he's there, but I ought to wait for David to ring back. Honestly, I really think we should ring the police. They'll know what to do.'

'And I've already said, we're not doing that unless we're sure he's actually missing. If he gets off the London train, as I think he will, we'll have had them poking their noses into our affairs for nothing, not to mention the gossip there'll be in the village if a police car's seen coming up our drive. Perhaps Kellaway could go down to Plymouth. I'll give him a ring.'

'No, Father. It's not fair to involve Travis in this. It's not his job to start searching for Rob on a Sunday evening.'

'He might be able to tell us if the boy gave any hint about what he planned to do while he was there yesterday,' Gilbert argued, and she sighed and nodded.

'Yes, all right, but I'll ring him. You shouldn't be getting too upset about this, it's not good for you. Sit down and have a rest.' She looked at him anxiously, noting that his colour had changed and he was beginning to breathe rather heavily. Don't have a heart attack now, she prayed, please don't have a heart attack now ... She dialled Travis's number and waited while it rang.

'Jennifer? It's Hilary Napier here. I'm really sorry to bother you on a Sunday evening, but we're a bit worried about Rob. He seems to have disappeared ... Yes, since this morning, he was supposed to be going to church in Tavistock but he didn't go and he didn't come home again ... Yes, we think he may be trying to go back to France. He took his passport ... We wondered if he'd said anything to you yesterday ... No, please don't ask him to do that, it's his day off ... Well, if you're sure, we'd be very grateful. Thank you, Jennifer.' She put down the phone. 'Travis is coming over straight away.'

'Told you he'd want to help,' said Gilbert, who had said no such thing. 'Perhaps he'd be willing to drive up to London to collect the boy.'

'We don't know that he's there,' Hilary said tiredly. She leaned her head back against her chair and closed her eyes. It was almost too much to bear, having this anxiety thrust upon her so soon after she had left David, and with her thoughts already in turmoil. And now David was drawn in as well. It could be dealt with relatively easily, of course. He could take Rob to the hotel and put him on a fast, non-stopping train tomorrow – if there was one, which she doubted – or she could go up to collect him. But she had a nasty feeling it wouldn't be that simple. David, who she had hoped to keep separate from her life in Burracombe, was now involved and already she had had to evade her father's questions. There was no knowing where it might lead.

Oh, what a tangled web we weave, she thought ruefully, and then jumped as she heard a knock on the door and Travis came in, with Jennifer close behind him.

'What's all this about? Jennifer says Rob's disappeared.'

'He seems to have run away,' Hilary said wearily, and went through the story again. 'I've rung a friend in London who's going to meet the train we think he might have used, but we really wondered if he'd said anything to you yesterday. Did he seem to be planning anything like this?'

'Not really,' Travis said doubtfully. He turned to Jennifer. 'Did you notice anything?'

'Only that he seemed very unhappy about going back to school,' she said, a little apologetically. 'I felt rather sorry for him.'

Hilary shot her father a quick glance. His colour had risen and his expression tightened. She said, more to him than to Jennifer, 'We already knew that. We were hoping that he'd settle down as the term went on.'

'Boys usually do,' Gilbert said gruffly, a defensive note in his voice. 'No reason to suppose he wouldn't. It's a good school, turned out some fine young men.'

'The question now,' Hilary said, not wanting to be sidetracked yet again, 'is what do we do if he isn't on the train? David will telephone as soon as he knows, but we ought to have some plan in case Rob isn't there. He may have caught an earlier train, or not caught a train at all. He might even be trying to hitch-hike.'

'Did he have enough money for the fare?' Travis asked, and she nodded.

'We think so. He had his Post Office savings book – although he wouldn't be able to use that until tomorrow – and he also had some money here. Not much, but enough to get him to London, I should think.'

'And he took his passport?'

'Yes, so it seems pretty certain he meant to go to France. They came via Dover in June, so I'd expect him to go back that way, since it's familiar to him.'

'Have you contacted the police?'

'I don't want to do that,' Gilbert said abruptly. 'Not unless it's absolutely necessary. Family matter.'

Travis glanced at him. 'You may have to, if Rob isn't found quickly. His mother would have to be notified, too.'

'Cross that bridge when we come to it.' Gilbert glanced at the clock. 'It's nearly six anyway – we should know soon, one way or the other.'

An uneasy silence fell. The minutes ticked by. Six o'clock came and went; the hands moved on to three minutes past, five, seven ... Gilbert stirred restlessly.

'What in God's name is your friend thinking of? Either the boy's there or he isn't. Why doesn't he ring?'

'He can't do it straight away,' she said. 'He's got to find Rob first, then persuade him that he's a friend – Rob might just run away from him. And even if he does, he's got to find a phone. It all takes time.'

Gilbert grunted and Jennifer gave Hilary a troubled glance. 'Are we in the way? We'll do whatever we can to help, but if you'd rather we went—'

'No, please don't go,' Hilary said quickly. 'Four heads are better

than two, and you did see Rob yesterday. If there's anything he said
– any hint at all ...'

'I can't think of anything.' She looked at Travis. 'He did seem
rather miserable, but he cheered up as time went on. He was enjoying
playing with Tavy – the puppy. He said your dogs are too old to want
to play now.'

'That's easily dealt with,' Gilbert said. 'Time we had a couple of
new gundogs anyway. The boy could have a pup of his own, keep him
occupied in the holidays.'

'I don't think the holidays are any problem, Father,' Hilary said
quietly. 'It's the school he's running away from, not us.' As she said
it, she had a momentary stab of doubt. Perhaps Rob *was* running away
from them, as well as from the school. He'd clearly intended to go
back to France and at thirteen he must surely still miss his family and
friends there. Perhaps, when he had found himself at the school, he
had suddenly realised what it all meant. A summer, spent in a large
country house with a new family, was one thing. A complete change of
life, from one country to another, with his future apparently planned
for him without consultation, was quite another.

We rushed into this far too quickly, she thought for the hundredth
time. Father went completely overboard. And yet ... and yet ... Rob
is the legitimate heir. It couldn't just be ignored.

The ringing of the telephone shattered the silence and they all
jumped. Gilbert stretched out his hand but Hilary snatched up the
receiver. 'Yes?'

'Hilary, it's all right. He's here.' Her sigh of relief was echoed by
the three in the room with her. 'Got off the train a quarter of an hour
ago. I had a bit of a struggle to persuade him that I was a friend, but I
think he was a bit scared by what he'd done by then, and glad to have
someone take over. What do you want me to do with him?'

'Well, we'd better get him back as soon as possible. I suppose there
aren't any trains this evening?'

'No, I've looked at the timetable. Look, he can stay with me at the
hotel if that's all right with you, and I'll send him back in the morning.
There's a train that only stops at Reading and Exeter before going on
to Penzance. I could go as far as Reading and then change for Derby,
so if you could meet him at Exeter ...'

'Yes,' she said quickly. 'Yes, that would be fine. What time does it get there?'

'About one o'clock. Are you sure that's all right?'

'It's marvellous,' she said in heartfelt tones. 'Thank you *so* much, David. I can't tell you how grateful I am.'

'Tell me in person next time we meet,' he said, with a smile in his voice, and she knew she was blushing. 'Now, d'you want to speak to him?'

'Yes, please,' she said, and heard Robert's voice, very small and uncertain. 'Hello, Rob. Are you all right?'

'Let me,' Gilbert said, stretching out his hand again, but she shook her head and held the receiver out of his reach.

'I'm all right,' Rob said, and she thought he was probably crying. 'I'm sorry, *Tante* Hilary. I've caused you a lot of trouble.'

'That doesn't matter. The main thing is that you're all right. Now, you stay with Dr Hunter – he'll look after you – and we'll see you tomorrow. You won't do anything else silly, will you? I mean, you won't try to run away again?' She paused and said more softly, 'We'll sort it all out when you get back, Rob. But don't worry – you won't go back to school if you don't want to.'

She heard a muffled 'Thank you' and then put down the phone, turning somewhat defiantly to face her father.

'Why on earth did you say that?' he demanded. 'Of course he'll go back.'

'I said, we'll sort it out when he gets here,' she said. 'But if you do try to send him back, you'll have me to contend with. Me and his mother. I can't believe she wants him to be unhappy. We've been unkind to him, Father – to be honest, I think we've been downright cruel.'

'*Cruel?*' Gilbert half-rose from his chair, then sank back, breathing heavily. Hilary looked at him in alarm, afraid she had gone too far, and Travis quickly picked up a glass of water from the desk and held it to his lips. Impatiently, Gilbert waved it away. 'Leave me alone. Perfectly all right. In fact, you might as well go back home now, nothing more to do here. Grateful you came, but we'll be all right now.'

Travis hesitated, then shrugged. He glanced at Hilary, who grimaced slightly.

'You might as well,' she said. 'Father's right, there's nothing more any of us can do tonight. And we'll have to talk to the school as well. His housemaster's already been on the phone, asking where Rob is. We'll see you tomorrow.'

'You won't, actually,' he said. 'I've got that meeting with the fellow in Somerset we're buying those rams from. I'll be leaving early in the morning.'

'Oh, yes, I'd forgotten that. Well, that's all right. There's nothing urgent for me to do – I'll go and meet Rob at Exeter and see you later.' She looked at them both. 'Thank you very much for coming. It's been a great help, having you here.'

Travis nodded and opened the door. Jennifer looked back and said, 'I'm really sorry about all this, Hilary. I didn't feel we were really much help, but if there's anything we can do … You can always send Rob down to me for a few hours if you think he'd like that. He did seem to enjoy playing with Tavy.'

'Yes,' Hilary said. 'Thanks.'

The door closed behind them and she turned back to her father. 'Well, that's that. Rob's safe and well, he'll be back tomorrow and then we've got to make some decisions. I meant what I said. I won't have him sent back. The public school regime might suit a boy who's been prepared for it, but it's not fair simply to throw a child like Rob into it and expect him to survive. We've got to have a long think about this, and do whatever's best for him.'

'That's exactly what I've been doing—' he began, but she cut him off sharply.

'No, you haven't. You've been doing what you think is best for Burracombe, not what's best for Rob. It might have been best for him if he'd lived here since he was born, been to prep school, already knew a few boys at Kelly and knew what was in store, but that isn't how it is for him. He's different and we've got to take all the differences into account.'

'So what do you suggest?' he demanded truculently. 'Send him back to an insignificant little town in France? Let him go back to the local school, forget he had an English father, forget he could inherit and be responsible for an English country estate?'

'If that's what's best for him, yes. We're dealing with a human being here, Father, not a puppet. If you want my opinion –' she fixed a steely gaze on him, daring him to say that he didn't, 'this could be the best thing he could have done. He's made us stop and think about him, instead of some figure we'd conjured up in our minds. He's made us think about Robert Aucoin, the person, instead of "Robert Napier" –' and here she gave his name the English pronunciation '– the heir to Burracombe.'

Chapter Thirty-Four

It was barely light when Hilary took Beau for an early-morning ride next day but as they reached the brow of the hill she could see the sun rising behind a silky grey mist, lighting it with soft apricot that seemed to flood across the frosted valley. A few birds were singing, even now when winter was beginning to show its claws, and she could see a cluster of Dartmoor ponies against the stone wall that divided the moor from the fields. They had been rounded up in the 'drift' a few weeks before and some of the foals sold at St John's Fair, in Tavistock market. The mares were well into foal again, their bellies beginning to swell, and she hoped the winter would not be too hard for them. Soon, farmers like Ted Tozer who owned them, would have to start taking out bundles of hay to supplement the grass that by now had stopped growing.

She paused at the top to take in the scene before her. A ribbon of soft grey mist followed the line of the river, shimmering as it slowly evaporated in the pale winter sunlight. As she watched, a heron lifted from a pool somewhere in the fields and flapped its great wings with effortless strength to disappear in search of breakfast, and a buzzard floated high overhead. There was not a breath of wind, but the air was cold and Beau stamped his foot impatiently, wanting to be off.

Hilary was stabbed by her love for this place. The house, the land, the village, the farms had been part of her all her life, bred into her bones from the moment she was born. Her mother, who had come to it as a young bride, had loved it too, had tended the gardens and known every villager by name. She had been a true lady of the manor, old-fashioned by today's standards and never desiring a career or life of her own as Hilary did, yet Hilary knew that essentially they were alike in their passionate devotion to this place.

Yet even they, perhaps, had not known quite the same profound depth of attachment that her father had. His was almost frightening in its intensity, deepened by the loss of his eldest child, the son he had expected would inherit all that he had worked for. Baden had been more than a son to him, he had been almost a mirror image of Gilbert, and his loss had been a greater blow than anyone could have realised. It wasn't surprising that Robert, arriving so unexpectedly, looking so like his father, should have seemed the answer to all Gilbert's prayers. It wasn't surprising that he should have lost sight of the fact that, even at thirteen years old, Robert was a person in his own right, who deserved to be considered: that what his grandfather thought best for him might turn out to be the worst.

And now we've got to decide what to do next, Hilary thought, letting Beau amble along the ridge at his own pace. As if I didn't have enough to think about at the moment ...

David. What was she to do about this love that had suddenly erupted into her life? She knew that the affair had gone too far to be stopped now. Even if she wanted to draw back, to finish it, David would never accept it. He had set his heart, set all his being, on their coming together, and while her own heart trembled at the thought, while she was blinded and confused by the almost insurmountable difficulties that must lie ahead, she knew it was what she most longed for too. Yet how could it ever be achieved, without having to turn her back on everything she knew and loved, on all the people she had grown up with – her family, the village, the farms, her friends? What sort of life would they have together, isolated and shunned by all they had known?

Hilary was still struggling with the two dilemmas when she finally brought Beau down from the hill and clattered into the yard. There was ice on the cobblestones and the sound of his hooves rang like bells in the clear, cold air. She slipped off the horse and removed his harness, rubbing him down and settling him before going indoors. Her father would be up by now and in the breakfast room, reading the newspaper while the two old dogs slumbered by the fire Mrs Ellis would have lit. He would be impatient to see his grandson again.

She was in the gun room, washing her hands in the small basin, when she heard footsteps running along the corridor and Mrs Ellis burst in.

'Oh, there you are, Miss Hilary! I'm proper thankful to see you. It's your father – been took bad just as he was coming in to breakfast. I've sent for the doctor but I heard you come into the yard and I thought best to fetch you right away.' She was running back through the house as she spoke, Hilary coming after her with her hands still clutching a towel. 'I thought he looked a bad colour when I saw him come down the stairs,' the housekeeper went on, puffing for breath. 'And then he sort of staggered, and put out his hand to hold on to the door-jamb, and then just toppled forwards. Fell on the carpet, thank goodness, and he's still breathing, but— Oh, there's the doorbell, that'll be Dr Latimer. I'll go and let him in.'

By now, they were at the door to the breakfast room and Hilary saw her father lying sprawled on the carpet. She dropped to her knees beside him, noting with anxiety the blue tinge about his lips, and turned him gently into the recovery position she'd been taught in first-aid classes. His breathing was loud and stertorous, and anxiety unfurled within her like a gigantic and grotesque flower.

It's been too much for him, she thought. All this anxiety over Rob – it's just the sort of thing I've been trying to avoid for the past two years. It *would* happen when I was away. And now what are we going to do?

The thought slid into her mind: *What will happen if he dies now?*

Angrily, she pushed the thought aside. Her father was not going to die. He would not be *allowed* to die.

'Hilary – my dear ...'

She looked up quickly and moved out of the way as the doctor came in and knelt beside the unconscious man. Swiftly, he examined him and then opened his bag and took out a small bottle of pills. He shook one into his hand and slipped it into Gilbert's mouth.

'Do you want some water?' Hilary whispered, but he shook his head.

'No, I want it to dissolve under his tongue. How long has he been unconscious?'

Hilary turned her head to look up at the housekeeper, who gabbled her story out again. The doctor looked at his watch.

'Less than fifteen minutes. Well, we'll soon know if this is working.'

They waited, their eyes fixed on Gilbert's ashen face, listening to his difficult breathing. Then, to Hilary's relief, the painful sounds began to ease a little, and gradually become more normal. The colour began to return, although he was still pale, and after a few more minutes his eyelids fluttered and he opened his eyes and looked at the little ring of faces hovering above him.

'What ... what in God's name ...?'

'Don't try to talk, Father,' Hilary said quickly. 'You're all right. You're at home, in the breakfast room. Stay still.'

He turned his head and the familiar scowl began. 'I'm ... on the ... *floor*. What ...?'

'You've had a small angina attack,' the doctor said calmly. 'It's nothing to worry about but you need to stay quiet for a few minutes. I've given you a pill and you'll be all right soon, but I want you to rest for a couple of days.'

'Rest? Nonsense.' Gilbert began to struggle to get up, but the doctor pressed him back on to the cushions Mrs Ellis was busy packing around him. 'Can't possibly rest ... to much to do ... got to fetch Robert back from Exeter ...'

'You're not fetching anyone from anywhere,' Charles Latimer told him sternly. 'You're staying here. I don't even want you going upstairs until I'm satisfied with you. Hilary, you can make up a bed down here for him, can't you? That big sofa in the drawing room would do.'

'Yes, of course.' She glanced at the housekeeper, who left the room and could then be heard running up the stairs. 'And you don't have to worry about Rob,' she told her father. 'I'll collect him. Unless you think I ought to stay here?' she added to the doctor.

'I'd prefer you not to leave him. Is it urgent? What's young Rob doing in Exeter, anyway? I thought he was at school.'

'He is, but ... it's a long story. I must say I'd rather not leave Father in this state. I'll have to find someone else to go. Travis – oh no, he was going to Somerset; he'll be gone by now. Oh, who else is there in the village with a car?' She bit her lips in frustration.

'How about Felix?' the doctor suggested. 'He'll be in the school this morning. They're having some sort of "wedding" party there today. Basil told me about it when he and Grace had dinner with us last night. I'm sure he'd be willing to help out. Monday's his day off, so he may be free after that.'

'That's a good idea,' Hilary agreed in relief. 'Oh, thank you, Mrs Ellis,' as the housekeeper returned with an armful of blankets and pillowcases. 'Let's get you settled now, Father, and then I'll see if I can get hold of Felix before he leaves the vicarage.'

Between them, they got Gilbert into the drawing room and laid him down on the sofa that Mrs Ellis had transformed into a comfortable bed. He protested a little, then lay back, clearly still feeling weak. Hilary gazed at him anxiously.

'You're sure he's going to be all right?' she asked the doctor as they left the drawing room. 'It's been rather a worrying weekend – Rob was home for an exeat but he seems to have taken the opportunity to run off and try to go back to France. We've managed to intercept him at Paddington, and he's being put on the train this morning, but it doesn't stop at Tavistock – that's why someone has to fetch him from Exeter.'

'I see. Well, I'm sure your father will be fine after a few hours down here. I'll slip in again at lunchtime and I should think he'll be able to manage the stairs then, to go to bed. But I don't want him doing anything strenuous, or indeed anything at all, for at least two or three days, and I don't want him worrying over this grandson of his.'

'That's easier said than done,' she said gloomily. 'But it will be a tremendous help if Felix can fetch him. I'll have to think what to do with him once we've got him home. Oh, why does everything happen at once?'

'It's the way of the world, my dear. Now, will you be able to manage? Why not get Val Ferris to come up and be with you? I'll call in on my way back home, if you like. I'll have to go soon anyway – it's almost time to open the surgery.'

'Yes,' Hilary said. 'That's a good idea. Thank you so much, Charles.'

Mrs Ellis appeared again. 'Will you be wanting your breakfast now, Miss Hilary? It's all ready.'

'Breakfast?' Hilary rubbed her hand across her face. 'It feels like the middle of the day. Yes, please, I'd better eat something.'

She went into the breakfast room, feeling depressed. Too much had happened too quickly, and suddenly she seemed beset by crises. The weekend she had spent with David, filled with emotions she needed time to assimilate, had been superseded by the anxiety over Robert, and her father's sudden illness was the last straw. Her mind was in a frenzy, and she scarcely knew which dilemma to tackle first.

'The best thing to do,' Val Ferris advised her, when she arrived to find her friend staring blankly at a plate of congealing bacon and egg, 'is to take one step at a time. First,' she swept the cooling plate away, 'you've got to eat properly and keep up your own strength. I'll ask Mrs Ellis to do you some scrambled eggs on toast – that'll just slip down without too much effort. And then we'll make sure that Felix will be able to collect Rob from Exeter. Have you tried to contact him yet?'

'Yes, but he must have left the vicarage because he didn't answer the phone, and there's nothing I can do until he arrives at the school.'

'No, but you can go to the school and ask him once they've finished this wedding thing. I'll stay here with your father while you do that.'

'Would you? Oh, yes please. And I could probably manage some scrambled eggs. I just couldn't face this, somehow. But what about Christopher?' She put her elbow on the table and rested her head on her hand. 'I feel so tired, Val!'

'It's shock,' Val said, pouring her a cup of tea. 'Now, you drink that and I'll see to everything. Christopher's in his pram in the kitchen – Mrs Ellis is in her element with him. I'll stay all morning and make sure your father's all right until Dr Latimer comes again. But I'm sure he'll be fine. He just needs to rest.'

Hilary nodded, smiled at her rather weakly, and sipped her tea. But when Val had left the room she let her head drop once more on to her hand, and the thought that she had pushed away so angrily earlier came sliding back into her mind.

Suppose her father were *not* all right? Suppose he died, and the will he had made so hastily came into force, leaving the estate to Rob. What would it to mean to the family? To Stephen and to Rob? To herself – and to David?

'And I now pronounce you man and wife,' Felix intoned over the two young people before him. 'You may now kiss the bride.'

Billy Madge, dressed to kill in his best Sunday School blazer and grey flannel shorts, turned and looked at his bride in dismay.

'You never said I had to kiss her.'

'I don't want you to kiss me anyway,' Shirley Culliford retorted. 'So there!'

Robin and Edward, who had found being pageboys rather boring, fidgeted and sighed noisily. 'Is it playtime now?' Edward asked. 'Can we have our milk?'

'Yes, the wedding's over,' Felix began, but Stella intervened firmly. 'No, it isn't playtime yet, Edward, as you know perfectly well. But you can all go back to your seats and then we'll have a little talk about what a wedding means. Mind you don't get crayon on your dress, Shirley, and I don't want to see you drawing on her back either, George. Now, who will start? Wendy Cole, your auntie got married a little while ago, didn't she? Can you tell us why you think she did that?'

'My mum said it was because she was expecting a little stranger,' Wendy said. 'But I haven't seen no one round at their house yet, so I think she got it wrong.'

'Go on,' George Crocker scoffed as Felix turned away to hide his twitching lips, 'that's what a grown-up says when they'm having a baby. And I've seen your auntie – she's getting ever so fat, so that proves it.'

'Well, has anyone else been to a wedding lately?' Stella asked a little desperately. 'Linda Martin, didn't you say you'd been to one in Mary Tavy?'

'Yes, but that was my grandad and Mrs Treadwell from up Horndon, so that don't count.'

'Why not?' Stella asked, thankful that this at least couldn't have been a case of 'having to get married'.

'Well, because they'm old, miss. And she never wore a white frock or nothing, just a costume, and she didn't have no bridesmaids neither, and no proper party afterwards, just a ham salad dinner in our house.' Linda's tone showed quite clearly what she thought of this travesty. 'They didn't even go away on honeymoon, just a holiday down Torquay, and now we've got to call her Grandma.'

'All right,' Stella said, wondering what difference there was between a honeymoon and a holiday in Torquay, 'we'll forget that and think about weddings in general. Now, why do you think people really get married?' She hoped there would be no more mention of little strangers and brides suddenly putting on weight and, to her relief, was able to guide the conversation along the lines she wanted. Felix settled himself on the edge of her desk and joined in, adding the religious perspective to the more practical one of setting up home and raising a family together, and together they brought the discussion to a neat conclusion by saying that the most important part of all was that the bride and groom must love each other.

'I'm sure all your parents love each other,' she said, 'or they wouldn't have got married. And that's what you all have at home, even if you don't realise it – two parents who love each other and love their children, whatever difficulties they might have.'

'I don't think our dad loves me and George,' Edward Crocker said gloomily. 'Fiends from hell, he says we are.'

'He loves you just the same,' Felix said firmly. 'But perhaps if you weren't quite so naughty, you'd give him more chance to show it.'

'And now it really is playtime,' Stella announced, and the children leaped to their feet. 'Shirley, Billy, Edward and Robin, you'd better change into your ordinary clothes before you go outside.'

The children poured out into the playground in a stream of chatter, and she and Felix helped the four participants to shed their finery. Alone at last, they looked at each other and Felix grinned.

'I must say, you manage them very well.'

'They can still pull a few surprises out of the hat,' she said ruefully. 'I know they're country children and used to seeing animals mate, but I'm never quite sure if they relate that to human behaviour as well. Probably not – if they find kissing each other so disgusting, they certainly wouldn't want to think about anything more!'

'Well, they seem happy enough with the idea of a wedding,' he said. 'And now that this is over, I suppose you'll need to start thinking about Christmas.'

'Yes, indeed – there's not many weeks to go now and the children will want to make paper-chains for the classroom, and cards for their families, not to mention the Nativity Play and all the usual fuss over who's going to be Mary and Joseph and the Three Wise Men. Miss Kemp likes to have the older children for those parts – my class generally get shepherds, with a few angels thrown in for good measure.'

Felix grinned. 'You'd better make sure you've got enough dressing gowns and tea-towels to go round, for their costumes. And why not have a real donkey this year, instead of that moth-eaten old pantomime horse Mrs Warren keeps dragging out of the stock of clothes she has for the drama group?'

Stella gave him a look. 'Because we all know perfectly well what donkeys are like. They never do what you want them to do, and they always do what you don't want them to do.'

'I went to a performance of *The Desert Song* once where they had a donkey,' Felix reminisced. 'You could hear it stamping and hee-hawing behind the scenes, and they had to drag it through the curtains to the stage, where it stood perfectly still and refused to move a muscle until they hauled it off again and you could hear it stamping and braying again. It was the best part of the entire show.'

'Well, we're not having one here,' she said firmly. 'Nor any sheep, either, so it's no use suggesting it. Woolly toys are quite good enough. Anyway, we needn't start thinking about it today, we've only just had the wedding.'

'As Mary said to Joseph,' he murmured wickedly, and then glanced out of the window. 'Hullo – there's Hilary coming into the playground. Wonder what she wants?

'... And so I wondered if you could possibly go to Exeter and collect him?' Hilary finished, after telling them the story of Robert's defection. 'It's an awful lot to ask, I know, and I'm sorry to be a nuisance, but I just can't think of anyone else and I really can't leave my father until we know he's on the mend.'

'Of course you can't,' Felix said. 'And of course I'll go. The only thing is, I don't really know Rob very well. It would be better if Stella could come too – he spent a few days in school last term, didn't he, darling?'

'Yes, that's how he got to know Micky Coker and Henry Bennetts. I saw him a few times in the holidays as well. But I can't go until school's over this afternoon.'

'Yes, you can,' said Miss Kemp, who had also been listening to Hilary's tale. 'I'll take both classes for the rest of the day. I think this counts as an emergency. We can't let the poor child be passed around amongst comparative strangers like a parcel nobody wants.'

'That will be a great help,' Felix said in relief. 'We could give him some lunch on the way back. But we'll have to go soon if we're to be in Exeter by one.'

Hilary looked at them both with gratitude. 'I can't tell you how thankful I am. When I think of what might have happened to him ...'

'He's going to be all right,' Felix told her comfortingly. 'Once he's back, you can start to consider what ought to be done next. The important thing is to bring him back, safe and sound. And now, darling, we'd better go.'

'We'll be back by teatime,' Stella said, and they went out through the playground to where Felix's sports car was parked opposite the school gates.

'He's a good man,' Hilary said to the head teacher as they watched Mirabelle disappear towards the Exeter road. 'He'll be a good husband to Stella.'

'And she'll be a good wife,' Miss Kemp said. 'I shall miss her dreadfully, and so will the children, but those two will make a good life together. I hope everything goes well for them. They deserve it.'

Chapter Thirty-Five

Back at the Barton, Hilary hurried into the drawing room, where Gilbert was still lying on the sofa, wrapped in blankets but now fully awake and complaining fretfully to Val.

'Perfectly all right now. Charles Latimer's an old woman – I've said it before, I'll say it again. No need at all for all this fuss.'

'Well, I'm sorry, Colonel Napier, but he and Hilary have left me in charge, and I daren't let you move until they say so,' said Val, who had plenty of experience of dealing with difficult patients. 'And you may feel perfectly well lying there, but it could be a very different story if you start putting demands on your heart before it's ready. You don't want another collapse.'

'Treating me like a child,' he grumbled. 'Be telling me to drink up my milk next.'

'And that's a very good idea,' Val observed. 'I'll ask Mrs Ellis to bring some in.'

Hilary crossed the room to her father and looked down at him. 'How are you, Father?'

'You'd better ask this young woman. She seems to think I've regressed to childhood. Won't let me move.'

'Good,' Hilary said unsympathetically. 'Nor will I, not until Charles gets here. Now, I've asked Felix to go and meet Rob off the train, and Stella's going too. They'll have some lunch on the way and be here around four, I should think.' She turned to Val. 'Thanks so much for coming over, Val. It must have disrupted your morning.'

'Not really,' Val said cheerfully. 'I was only going to wash nappies – as usual! I can do that later. And I'd already put a lamb's heart casserole in the oven for Luke's dinner, so there's nothing to do when I get home except the cabbage and potatoes. I'll bake a couple of apples for pudding. Still, I'd better go now, unless you need me to stay. Christopher will be wanting his feed.'

Hilary nodded. She looked at her father again.

'Will you be all right by yourself for a few minutes? Or is there anything you need?'

'Bit of peace and quiet would be good,' he growled, and then glanced towards Val. 'Not that I'm not grateful to you, mind. Good of you to come over and sit with an old man. Sorry if I've been a bit churlish.'

'That's all right. I was glad to be able to help.' Val stood up. 'Don't forget, if you need me any time, just send down to the cottage and I'll come up right away. But I don't think you'll have any more problems. I expect Dr Latimer will just order a couple of days in bed to make sure, and then you'll be right as rain.'

They went out together and made their way back to the kitchen, where Mrs Ellis was preparing lunch and Christopher was beginning to stir in his pram, which had been pushed into a corner. Val bent over him and he opened his eyes, smiled and stretched out his arms.

'The dear of him,' Mrs Ellis said fondly. 'Been as good as gold, he has, sleeping over there. You can leave him with me any time, Val, if you wants to go shopping or anything.'

'You wouldn't believe how many offers I have like that,' Val said, sitting down on a kitchen chair with the baby in her arms. 'Is it all right if I feed him here, Hilary? Nobody's likely to come in, are they?'

'I shouldn't think so. Travis is away for the day and if you sit over there nobody will see you if they do come in. I'll make some coffee.' She went to the sink to fill the kettle, asking over her shoulder, 'What's the situation with Jackie now? Is she still at loggerheads with your parents about going to America? Russell mentioned it to me.'

'No, it's all sorted out now. She more or less told Mum and Dad that if they didn't let her, she'd go to London and they'd never see her again! It was bluff, of course, but they couldn't take the risk and agreed to her going back with Uncle Joe and Russ, if it can be arranged. Dad even said he'd pay her fare!'

'Goodness,' Hilary said, getting cups and saucers out of the cupboard. 'That can't be cheap.'

'It's not, but Uncle Joe says he'll stump up half, and Gran said she'd put a bit towards it as well.'

'She's a very lucky young woman, then,' Mrs Ellis commented. 'I can't see many young maids Jackie's age being allowed to go off to the other side of the world and helped with the fare as well.'

'I think they realised she really wanted to go, and they hope if she goes now she'll get it out of her system and be content to settle down at home when she comes back.' Val unbuttoned her blouse and inserted a nipple into Christopher's mouth. 'I'm not so sure, myself. Our Jackie's always been a restless sort – I wouldn't be surprised if she just goes on travelling, once she starts.'

Hilary made the coffee and brought two cups to the table for Val and Mrs Ellis. 'I'll take mine and have it with Father. Not that he's having coffee – hot milk for him.' She paused at the door. 'Val ... you do think he'll be all right, don't you?'

Val glanced up, aware of the edge of anxiety in her friend's voice.

'Yes, I do,' she said. 'Don't worry, Hilary. This is more like a warning. He may have to be more careful in future, but he'll get over it. The main thing is to make sure he doesn't overdo things. And he really mustn't worry, or let himself get angry.'

Hilary nodded and went through the door. But as she made her way back to the drawing room her face was grave.

Making sure her father didn't overdo things was possible, especially now that Travis was here. But not to worry, or get angry?

With not only Rob's problems increasing, but her new relationship with David impossible to keep secret for long, she could foresee him getting very angry indeed.

It was a subdued, slightly truculent Rob who got off the train at Exeter and was met by Felix and Stella. He looked at them suspiciously.

'I thought *Tante* Hilary was going to meet me.'

'She couldn't come. Your grandfather isn't very well. And Mr Kellaway's gone to Somerset, so we were called in as a last resort.' Felix spoke cheerfully as he glanced at the rucksack on Rob's shoulder. 'Is that all the luggage you have?'

'Yes. I didn't need to take much.' He followed them out of the station, his head drooping and feet dragging. He looked tired and rather pale, with dark shadows under his eyes, and he was shivering in a thin jacket he must have brought with him in the summer from France.

Stella touched his shoulder. 'Do you feel all right, Rob? Did you have breakfast?'

'Yes, at the hotel. Dr Hunter said I could have everything I wanted.' His voice wobbled a little. 'I said I just wanted to go home, but he said I had to go back to Burracombe.'

'Well, you must for the time being, at least,' Stella said uncomfortably, not sure quite how to handle the situation. Poor Rob, she thought, he's still only a child and he's had so many changes in his life. No wonder he looks so lost and bewildered. 'But there are a lot of people who want to help you,' she went on. 'And there's no great hurry to get you home now – we may as well enjoy ourselves. We thought we'd go back across the moor and have lunch somewhere. Would you like that?'

He nodded, without much enthusiasm, and didn't even show a lot of interest in Felix's sports car, Mirabelle. He got into the little dickey seat at the back without comment, and Felix started the engine. They weaved their way out of Exeter and on to the Moretonhampstead road. It was still cold on the moors, with black ice in the shady patches and hollows of the twisting road, and Felix drove carefully. For a while, nobody spoke, then at last Rob asked: 'Is my grandfather very angry with me?'

Stella considered her words before replying. 'We haven't seen him ourselves. It was Hilary who came to the school to ask us to meet you. But I think he was quite upset.'

'He thinks I am a coward,' Rob said gloomily. 'I am not fit to be his grandson and a Napier.'

'Oh Rob, I'm sure he doesn't think that,' Stella exclaimed in distress. 'He's upset because you've been so unhappy.' She hoped this was true. Hilary had given her the impression he was very angry indeed, and that this might even have caused his collapse, but it wouldn't do any good for Rob to know that, and anyway it wasn't her place to tell him. 'Has it been very bad for you?' she asked gently.

'I won't go back there,' he stated flatly. 'I won't go back to school.'

They were nearing the little moorland town of Moretonhampstead and Felix turned off the road and drove along a narrow lane. 'There's a nice little place here for lunch. We don't want to go anywhere grand, it's really not much more than a farmhouse but Mrs Dodd does very good food – Stella and I have been here several times. They're not normally open at the beginning of December, but I rang up Mrs Dodd before we left, to ask if she could feed us.'

He drew into a parking area in front of a long, low building that did indeed look like one of the old Devon longhouses typical of the area. The door opened as they got out, and a comfortable-looking woman rather like Alice Tozer came out to greet them.

'There you be, then. Come along inside, 'tis master cold out here. I've got a nice steak and kidney pie in the oven for you, and bread and butter pudding for afters. So this be the young man, is it?' She looked kindly at Rob. 'You look fair shrammed with cold in that draughty old car.'

'I have had the hood up,' Felix said, 'but I admit Mirabelle's a bit draughty in winter. Don't you have anything warmer with you, Rob?'

He shook his head. 'I only had my summer clothes. I did not want to take anything that wasn't mine.'

Stella gave a small exclamation of distress. 'But all the things your grandfather has bought you are yours, Rob. He wouldn't want you to leave them behind.'

Rob closed his lips and said nothing, and Felix put a hand on the boy's shoulder and pushed him gently ahead of them into the big farmhouse kitchen, where a table was already laid. 'Come on. Let's go and get warm by the fire and have some hot food. We'll all feel better after that.' He met Stella's gaze and shook his head slightly. Lowering his voice, he said, 'The poor child's terrified. We must try to take his mind off it for a while, and maybe you could have a word with Hilary. Do you think she realises?'

'I think she has a good idea,' Stella said quietly. 'Poor Rob. Obviously this whole situation is going to be a lot more difficult than Colonel Napier thought. But it was never going to be simple, was it, taking a child into a completely different environment and treating him as if there'd been no change. It was all done far too quickly.'

Rob was sitting at one side of the big inglenook fireplace, holding his hands out to the blaze. Stella and Felix joined him, warming themselves thankfully. After a few moments, Stella asked: 'Did you let your mother know you were planning to go home, Robert?'

He shook his head. 'No one knew. I didn't know myself – I didn't expect an exeat this weekend. I decided as soon as I knew about it.'

'Well, that's one thing to be thankful for,' she remarked. 'Your mother won't be worrying about you. But you'll be seeing her soon, won't you? I thought your aunt told me she and your brother and sister were coming over here for Christmas.'

'But I still won't see my *Tante* Ginette, or my two *gran'mères*. And there are all my friends. They will have forgotten all about me.'

'I don't think they'll forget that quickly,' Felix said, but he knew that if Robert did not go back and take up his life in France again, he would be forgotten remarkably quickly by his peers. No wonder the poor child was lonely, he thought. He'd been torn away from all that was familiar, discouraged from his friendship with Micky and Henry, and thrown into the company of boys who apparently did not accept him, and showed it with the brutality than only boys could display. He obviously missed his family desperately, and now he was afraid that his old friends would have forgotten him. Felix felt a jarring bolt of anger and determined that, interfering or not, he would have to speak to Hilary or even Colonel Napier about it. The whole thing amounted to cruelty, and he could not, would not, stand by and let it go on.

Their meal was brought in and they moved to the table to eat. Rob seemed uninterested at first, but after a few bites of flaky pastry and savoury meat he began to eat with more appetite, and even asked for more mashed potato. After two helpings of bread and butter pudding so fluffy and light Felix thought it ought to be weighted down, he had recovered his normal colour and even his eyes looked brighter. As they left, he smiled at the woman who had fed them so royally, and thanked her.

'It was the best meal I have had since I went to school,' he told her. 'I wish I could come here and live with you!'

'Rob!' Stella exclaimed, laughing. 'Only half an hour ago you were saying you wanted to go home to France!'

'Well, I wish Mrs Dodd could come and live with us there,' he said. 'She could work in our *patisserie*.'

'I think I'm too old to go and live in furrin parts now,' Mrs Dodd said, smiling. 'But you'm welcome here any time you like, young man. And next time I'll make some of my gingerbread cake for you.'

They crammed themselves back into Mirabelle and set off. Now that they were really on their way back to Burracombe, Robert's good spirits deserted him again and he lapsed into a gloomy silence. Stella too was beginning to feel anxious, and Felix, aware that the light was fading and the temperature dropping under gathering clouds, wished they hadn't stayed so long. It would be dark before they reached home, and Mirabelle's lights had been behaving erratically lately. He reproached himself for not having taken her to the garage in Tavistock to be looked at.

As they passed the Warren House Inn, on the highest part of the moorland road, the sun was dipping from sight. The clouds were like bruises in the sky, their leaden grey stained with a dirty yellow which deepened to an angry, flaring orange as if someone had lit a gigantic fire of oily rubbish somewhere below the horizon. The flames spread higher, their scarlet tongues licking at the lowering clouds and turning the sky to a blazing inferno. The three in the car were transfixed by the sight and Felix murmured softly, 'You can understand the idea of a chariot of fire coming from the sky to carry Elijah up to Heaven, can't you? Maybe I'll ask in next week's sermon if anyone else saw this amazing sunset and use it to tell his story.'

The sky continued to blaze as they drove along the high road, but was fading into darkness by the time they reached Princetown. The dimpsy light, as Devon folk called it, was gathering its shadows around them like a dark cloak, and the sheep and ponies that wandered on the moor and sometimes across the road were like phantoms drifting in the cold air.

'Will we be home soon?' Rob asked somewhat plaintively, as they left Princetown, with its grim fortress of a prison, behind them. 'I'm feeling cold again.'

'I'm not surprised,' Stella said, although she had wrapped a blanket around his knees before they set off. 'It's like an icebox in here. I wish cars had heaters.'

'Another ten minutes or so, I should think,' Felix said. 'We're just coming up to Devil's Elbow. It's a nasty double bend, this, but once we've – *what's that?*'

'Ponies!' Stella cried at the same moment. 'All over the road! Felix, be careful – there's a black one there, you can hardly see. *Ohhhhh!*'

The ponies loomed up before them, their long faces staring in terror at this monster that had come so abruptly out of the fog that filled the hollow of the double bend. For a few seconds they stood in panic-stricken immobility, then they turned and skittered away, their hooves slipping on a patch of ice. One slid to its side on the road and the two nearest the car reared up, their front legs flailing the air, caught in Mirabelle's faltering headlights. Felix wrenched the steering wheel uselessly, but the front wheels lost traction and, as Stella and Rob screamed again, the windscreen seemed filled with the staring whitened eyes and bared teeth of the black pony, its high, whinnying shriek adding to the clamour. There was a crash of splintering metal and glass as it came down again, unable to avoid the car that was screeching to an uncontrollable skidding halt, and as its head smashed through the windscreen Mirabelle lurched on to its thrashing body, stopped for a brief second, as if poised on top, and was then shrugged off, rolling over into the soft, marshy ground at the side of the road to lie still and silent. And then the only sound was that of the pony's agonised squeals, and the galloping of hooves as the rest of the herd made their terrified escape.

Chapter Thirty-Six

'R an into a herd of ponies on Devil's Elbow, that's what I heard,' Bernie Nethercott told the regulars at the Bell Inn that evening. 'Car all smashed up, poor young Stella Simmons half-killed and the young vicar nearly out of his mind. And that boy of Colonel Napier's, the French tacker, he was mixed up in it too, God knows why. I thought he was meant to be up at Kelly College.'

''Tis terrible,' Ted Tozer said. He was there with his brother and Russell, who had decided to stay in Burracombe until they returned to America. Family meant more than jaunting about on the Continent, Joe had declared when they'd returned on Sunday, especially as Ted and Alice had now agreed to let Jackie go back to America with them. There was a lot to arrange ... 'What were they doing out there anyway?'

'Don't ask me,' Bernie said, filling Jacob Prout's pewter tankard with ale as he saw the old man come in. 'Colonel don't take me into his confidence. Anyway, the upshot is that the poor young schoolteacher's in Plymouth hospital and the vicar's with her, and they don't know whether her's going to live or die.' He handed the tankard across the bar. 'Have you heard any more, Jacob, as you come through the village?'

Jacob gave him the money and took his pint to the inglenook, which was his favourite seat. He shook his head gloomily. 'I knocked on Dottie's door as I come by, but there weren't no answer. I thought she might be here, but seein' as she ain't I reckon she've gone down to the hospital too.'

'That's right,' Bernie said. 'Come over in a right old state, her did, soon as Miss Hilary went down to tell her, and said she were going with Miss Hilary in the car. She said she'd ring up soon as there was any news, but we ain't heard nothing yet. Looks bad to me.'

'What about Felix and young Rob?' someone else asked. 'Were they hurt too?'

'Don't know. I don't think they were, or not as bad as poor young Miss Simmons, anyway, but they all went in the ambulance, so Dottie said. I suppose the doctors will want to give 'em a look-over. It were a nasty smash, evidently.'

'A pony can do a lot of damage,' Norman Tozer said, filling his pipe with tobacco. 'I remember when I ran into—'

But nobody was interested in his reminiscence, for at that moment Jacob took his tankard from his lips, leaving a frothy white moustache, and said, 'What about young Maddy? Have anyone let her know?'

Bernie and his customers looked at each other in consternation.

'Dottie never said nothing,' Bernie said doubtfully. 'She'd be the one to think of it. But she went straight off with Miss Hilary.'

'Well, someone ought to do something,' Jacob said. 'She's her sister.'

There was an uncomfortable silence. Then Bernie said, 'I dunno what us *can* do, Jacob. Young Maddy lives nearly a hundred miles away, in Dorset somewhere. And 'tisn't really up to us anyway, is it? Us can't interfere.'

'I don't see as it would be interfering to ask, though,' Ted said. 'I don't mind going up to the Barton to see if the Colonel knows aught.'

'Yes, but the Colonel was took ill himself this morning,' Jacob objected. 'Saw Dr Latimer going there myself, around eight o'clock. Us can't go bothering he.'

'You're right,' Ted nodded. 'Our Val spent the morning there with Miss Hilary. Well then, seems to me it wouldn't do no harm to ask the doctor what he thinks us should do. I don't suppose he've gone to the hospital as well.'

'If it's any help,' Russell said, as Ted moved towards the door, 'I'd be happy to go and fetch her. We've got the car standing out there doing nothing, and it would only take a few hours, there and back.'

The others turned and looked at him. Ted said doubtfully, 'You've only met the maid the once, though.'

'I don't think that matters. It's an emergency, ain't it? The main thing is to get her here as soon as possible.'

'I dunno,' Ted said. 'First thing is to find out if anyone's let her know. I don't even know where she is, to be exact. Works for a rector or summat, don't she? But I don't know which one.'

'Archdeacon,' Jacob said. 'That's who he be. And our vicar'll know his address, bound to. Come to think of it, I reckon he'll know if anyone's been in touch with her. Doctor will have told him about the accident. He might even have rung her up himself.'

'I'll go round to the vicarage right away,' Ted declared, and Russell and his father both put down their glasses and said they'd go with him.

Basil Harvey answered the door, his round, rosy face creased like a baby's with worry. 'I'm glad you've come. Dr Latimer's only just been on the phone. He's at the hospital with them. He says Maddy must be told at once.'

''Tis bad, then?' Ted asked anxiously, and the vicar sighed and shook his head.

'Poor Stella's badly hurt, I'm afraid. Felix and the boy seem all right, though very shaken, of course. They're still at the hospital. The car's completely wrecked.'

'We come to see if there's anything we can do,' Ted said as Basil led them into the house. 'Russell here says he'll go and fetch young Maddy if need be.'

'Would you really?' Basil asked, turning to the young American in relief. 'Well, that would be a great help. There's no one else in the village with a car, except for Henry Warren, and he's out at a Rotary Club dinner.' He thought for a moment. 'Look, I'd better ring the Archdeacon and ask him to tell Maddy – that would be better than breaking it over the phone – and then we can decide what to do. Better wait in the parish room – there's not room for us all in my study.' He showed them into the large sitting room he used for parish meetings and they sat uneasily on chairs while he went to his study to use the telephone.

'He's going to tell her at once,' Basil said when he returned. 'And he says there's a train she can catch in about an hour's time – it'll be at Exeter by nine. She could change there for Plymouth, but it takes a long time to go that way, along the sea route through Dawlish and Teignmouth, and down the estuary. It would be quicker to go by car ...' He looked at Russell. 'If you could meet here there ...?'

'Sure I will. I'll take her straight to Plymouth. You'd better tell me how to find the hospital.'

'Best go back to the farm for half an hour or so,' Ted said. 'Have a bite to eat before you go. It could be a long wait down there.'

The three men waited until the Archdeacon had rung back to say that Maddy would be on the train, and then left. A bitter wind had sprung up and as they hurried home, a few drops of icy rain struck their faces. Russell shivered.

'Nasty night for a road accident. I wonder how long they were there before help came along. I guess there's not a lot on those roads at night.'

'One of them might have gone back to Princetown,' Ted surmised. 'Though I don't suppose Felix would have left Stella, not in that state, and he couldn't have sent the boy in the pitch dark. Someone must have come along.'

They were all silent, imagining the nightmarish situation. The car, wrecked and on its side, Rob frightened, Stella badly hurt and unconscious, and Felix beside himself with fear for her. And an injured and terrified pony to contend with as well. How long had they waited there?

'Well, thank goodness someone did come,' Ted said at last, as they opened the farmhouse door and crowded into the kitchen. 'It could have been even worse.'

Alice, who was sitting by the kitchen fire, mending a pile of socks, looked up in surprise. 'You'm home early.' And then, as she saw their faces, 'What's the matter? What could have been worse? What's happened?'

'Accident out at Devil's Elbow, on the Princetown road,' Ted told her briefly as he took off his coat. 'Stella Simmons has been hurt – her and Felix and young Rob Napier are all down in Plymouth hospital. Vicar's sent for Maddy, and Russ is going up to Exeter to meet her.'

'What?' Alice was on her feet and Minnie, who was sitting at the table working out some new Christmas harmonies for the handbells, dropped her pencil. 'How bad is she? Are the others hurt, too? However did it happen?'

'Run into a pony, apparently,' Joe said. 'That's all anyone knows at the moment but Felix and the boy don't seem to have been hurt. The young teacher sounds in a bad way, though.'

'Oh, that's awful,' Alice said, her hand at her mouth. 'The poor young things. And them just getting ready for their wedding, not to mention Christmas almost on us. What can we do? Does Dottie know?'

'She's down at the hospital too; went with Hilary. I don't think there's anything we can do at the minute, Alice. You could put up a few sandwiches, for young Russ here – he ought to have a bite to eat before he goes off, or take summat with him.'

'I'll make some for Maddy, too,' Alice said, going over immediately to the larder. 'And if you'm going down to the hospital you can take some for the folk there, I dare say they'll need some sustenance as well.' She began to slice and butter bread. 'I'll put in some of that ham we had left over from supper yesterday, and there's some good sharp cheese here and a bit of pickle. Folk need something tasty when they'm upset.' She paused suddenly, the knife held up in front of her. 'If Hilary's gone to the hospital, who's stopping to look after the Colonel? Our Val said he'd been took poorly this morning. She was there till dinnertime.'

'Well, they won't have left him on his own,' Ted reassured her. 'Perhaps Mary Ellis has stayed on, or they might have got Travis Kellaway to go over with Jennifer. I don't think us needs to worry about him as well. Russ, if you'm going to be at Exeter in time to meet that train, you ought to be going soon. You don't want to go racing over the moor and ending up in hospital yourself. And get a hot drink inside you, too, it's bitter out there.'

'I'll make you a cup of cocoa,' Minnie said, moving the kettle over on the range. 'I'll fill up the Thermos flask as well, and you'd better take some blankets for poor Maddy – the car'll be like an icebox.'

The family bustled about, getting Russell ready for his journey, and when he set off the back seat was piled with blankets, cushions and a box full of food, with Ted's Thermos flask filled with hot cocoa. Both Joe and Ted offered to go with him, but it was decided that he'd be better to go alone in case the extra seats in the car were needed to bring anyone back from Plymouth.

They all stood in the yard to wave him off, and then went back into the house. Alice sat down suddenly.

'Oh, that poor little maid!' she said, wiping her eyes. 'I wish now I'd gone with Russell. She needs someone she knows with her.'

'He'll look after her,' Joe said comfortingly. 'He's got a good head on him in a crisis. And Uncle Ted's right, he can bring anyone back who needs to come home. They can't all stop at the hospital.'

'Come on, my bird,' Ted said, patting her shoulder. 'Make us a cup of tea. I reckon us all needs one after all this excitement.'

Alice nodded and refilled the kettle. Her face was sad and her mouth working a little.

'It's such a shame, though. Just as if the poor dear soul hasn't had enough trouble this year, what with losing her sweetheart, and now her sister lying there at death's door. I know Miss Forsyth adopted her and did a lot for her, but she don't see all that much of her now. Stella's the only real family she's got in the world. I don't know what she'll do if she loses her too.'

Russ was on the platform several minutes before the train steamed in, and he saw Maddy the moment she stepped off. He waved and ran towards her and she looked at him blankly for a moment before her face cleared.

'You're Ted Tozer's nephew – Russell, isn't it? The Archdeacon said you'd be here to meet me. It's very kind of you.' Her face was pale, her voice tired, and the words seemed to be spoken automatically.

'It's no trouble at all,' Russ said. He took her bag and steered her towards the exit. 'This must have been a terrible shock for you.'

'Do you know how she is?' Maddy asked, but he shook his head.

'I came pretty soon after Mr Harvey had called you. I don't think there's been any more news.' He glanced at her with pity. 'Try not to worry too much. We'll get there as soon as possible and you'll see for yourself.'

She nodded but didn't speak again until they were in the car. Russ wrapped a warm, soft blanket about her and slipped a small cushion behind her head. She smiled tremulously as he climbed into the driver's seat and closed the door.

'Thank you. I really am grateful that you came all this way. I could have changed and gone on to Plymouth by train, but it would have taken much longer at this time of night. I don't—' Her voice shook and she paused, took a deep breath, and finished, 'I don't know what

I'll do if – if …' But she couldn't finish, and the breath turned into a sob as the tears trickled down her cheeks.

'Oh, Maddy,' Russ said, and turned to put his arms around her. He held her close, and she wept against his chest. With one hand, he stroked her hair, feeling its silkiness beneath his palm. Her slender curves seemed to fit perfectly against his body and a wave of tenderness for her swept through him. He wanted to hold her like this, protecting her from the cruelty of life, for ever.

'I'm here, Maddy,' he whispered, hardly knowing what he was saying. 'I'll look after you. Whenever you want me, I'll be here.'

Whether she heard him through the storm of weeping, he didn't know, but after a few minutes he felt a tremor run through her, and she drew away slightly and sat up straight. He looked at her in concern and she pushed back a damp lock of hair with one hand and made a little sound, not quite a laugh but not a sob either.

'I'm sorry. Crying all over you like that. I don't know what you must think …' But her voice faded, and after a moment he said, 'All I think is that we must get to Plymouth as soon as we can. But I may not be able to go very fast, Maddy. The roads are icy – we don't want another accident.'

'No, we don't.' She sat back in her seat, looking determinedly ahead. 'I'm all right now. Let's go.'

Neither spoke again for the entire journey. Russ concentrated on the dark, unfamiliar road, his attention focused on the need to reach Plymouth safely. Beside him, Maddy strained her eyes anxiously through the darkness until her weariness overtook her, and her eyelids drooped. After a while, Russ risked a glance and saw that she was asleep.

If only it weren't such a desperate journey, he thought, he would have liked it to last for ever. Just himself and Maddy together, speeding through the night, cocooned against the rest of the world. Just himself and Maddy, alone.

Chapter Thirty-Seven

'However long can it take?' Hilary whispered, agonisedly. 'They've been hours in there.'

'They'll tell us as soon as they know anything, flower,' Dottie murmured. 'And at least you know Rob's all right. They're just keeping him in for observation overnight, to make sure he didn't bang his head.'

'If anything happens to him ...' Hilary worried. 'I don't know how we're going to tell Marianne as it is. She was furious when he hurt his ankle down in the mine with Micky and Henry in the summer.'

'She was willing enough for him to stay here,' Dottie pointed out. 'She must have known you wouldn't keep the boy in cotton wool.'

'Yes, but he ran away from school, Dottie. He was so unhappy there, and he told us he was, but Father – we – took no notice. We've been unkind to him, and he was in our care.'

Dottie was silent. She knew that families of Hilary's class thought nothing of sending children as young as eight years old away to school, but she didn't hold with it. Children should be at home in their own families, and bringing that boy all this way from France and then sending him to a big public school and expecting him to settle down had been, in her opinion, little short of madness. But she didn't say so to Hilary. She had a feeling she didn't need to.

The hospital corridor was bleak and empty, with just a few hard chairs placed along the wall. At the far end was a door leading to a ward, where visitors had come out at the end of visiting hour soon after Dottie and Hilary had arrived, and the doors along the corridor were firmly closed. Felix, Robert and Stella were behind them somewhere, but since a nurse had taken some details from the two women and told them to wait, they had seen and heard no more of them.

'I don't think Felix was badly hurt,' Hilary went on. 'But Stella ... I didn't like the look on that nurse's face, Dottie. Oh, I wish they'd just *tell* us something.'

At that moment a door opened and a doctor in a white coat came out and walked briskly towards them. They looked up at him, half eager and half afraid, and he said, 'Miss Napier?'

'Yes,' Hilary said. 'And this is Miss Friend. Miss Simmons lodges with her.'

The doctor nodded. 'Well, you'll be pleased to know that Mr Copley is quite unhurt – just a few bruises and scratches. The little boy, too – he's very shaken but unless he develops signs of concussion he'll be able to go home in the morning.' He paused. 'I'm afraid the news about Miss Simmons is not so good.'

'She ... she's not ...?' Hilary could not finish the sentence. The doctor shook his head, although not as quickly as she would have liked.

'No, she's holding her own at the moment. But she has a number of injuries, some possibly internal, and I'm afraid that until she regains consciousness we won't be able to tell the extent of them.' He paused again. 'There's some damage to the spine.'

'The *spine?*' Hilary echoed in dismay. 'But – does that mean—?'

'We can't tell yet what it means. It may be that there will be some paralysis.'

'Oh, poor Stella!' Hilary exclaimed, and heard Dottie utter a sob beside her. 'Does Felix know?'

'Mr Copley is with her now. We're having some difficulty in persuading him to leave her.'

'Can't he stop there?' Dottie asked. 'Even if the poor maid's unconscious, it'll do her good to have him near.'

The doctor glanced at her briefly. 'We're allowing him to stay for the time being, but once we've decided how to proceed he'll have to go. And he ought to have some rest anyway. He might not have been hurt, but he was certainly very shocked.' He paused again. 'Does the young lady have any other relatives?'

'A sister,' Hilary said. 'She lives near Lyme Regis.'

'It would probably be a good idea to send for her,' the doctor said, and a weight of horror seemed to settle in Hilary's breast.

He hesitated, as if debating whether to say more, then gave them a brief nod and turned away. Hilary half rose from her chair and caught at his sleeve.

'Please – can't we see her? Just for a moment?'

'Perhaps in a few minutes,' the doctor said. 'It might be better if you have a word with the boy.'

'Of course,' she said at once, ashamed at not having asked this already. The doctor opened another door and put his head in.

'Visitors for you, young man,' he said cheerfully, and withdrew as Hilary and Dottie went in.

Rob was sitting up in bed, almost as pale as his hospital nightgown. There was a bruise on his forehead but otherwise he appeared to be much as usual. He gave Hilary a faint, rather sheepish grin as she came in and said, 'Hello, *Tante* Hilary. I have been a nuisance, I think.'

'You've given us all a bit of anxiety,' she acknowledged as she sat down on another hard chair. 'How are you feeling? The doctor says he wants you to stay in overnight.'

'That's because I bumped my head. It aches a bit, but that's all. Will my grandfather make me go back to school? I don't want to go back, *Tante* Hilary.'

Hilary looked at him in astonishment. Wasn't he even a little concerned about Stella and Felix? 'I'm afraid I haven't thought about that,' she answered a little sharply. 'And your grandfather isn't at all well. He was very worried about you, you know.'

Rob looked abashed, and at once she felt sorry. Hadn't she only just admitted to Dottie that she felt that they had been unkind to him? She said more gently, 'I don't think you'll have to go back immediately, anyway. We need to think about it, and we ought to talk to your mother as well.'

'And Miss Simmons and Mr Copley?' he asked. 'Are they staying here tonight as well? I would like to see them, to say I am sorry for causing so much trouble.'

It dawned on Hilary that he hadn't been told anything about their condition. She hesitated, then said carefully, 'Mr Copley's all right, I think. But Miss Simmons may have to stay in a bit longer.'

He looked alarmed. 'She's hurt?'

Hilary glanced at Dottie, wondering how to answer him, but at that moment the door opened and the doctor looked in again. 'Miss Simmons' sister is here.'

'Maddy?' Hilary jumped up. 'But how?' She hurried out into the corridor, with Dottie close behind her. 'Maddy! How did you get here so quickly? We were going to send for you—'

'Mr Tozer went to the vicar and he rang the archdeacon. I caught the train and Russ met me at Exeter.' Maddy spoke quickly, her words tumbling over themselves. She was pale, her eyes red-rimmed and her hair tousled and the man with her was holding her arm firmly, as if he felt she would fall without his support. Hilary held out her arms and Maddy went into them, bursting into tears.

'I'm sorry, I keep on crying, I can't help it. Poor Russ has had to put up with me all the way from Exeter … Oh, Hilary, what's been happening? Where's Stella? I want to see her.'

The doctor stepped forward. 'If you'd like to follow me … Just for a few minutes, mind, we need to do some tests … Mr Copley's with her now. Please be very quiet.'

They followed him into a small side ward. There was one bed, surrounded by drips and other equipment, with a nurse on each side. Stella was lying very flat and very white, with tubes attached to both arms, and a streak of dried blood on one cheek. Felix was beside her, his face almost as white as the sheets. He raised his head as they came in and Hilary's heart was stabbed by the lost look on his face.

Maddy moved forward with a quickly stifled cry, and he put out one hand to her. She gripped it tightly and crouched beside the bed. 'Stella. Oh, Stella, darling, can you hear me?'

But the figure in the bed did not move or make any sign. One of the nurses said quietly, 'She's deeply unconscious, I'm afraid.'

The tears were pouring down Maddy's cheeks and Hilary felt her own eyes brim as well. She glanced at Dottie and saw the same anguish in the working mouth. She could find no words of comfort for any of them.

'I'm afraid you can't stay any longer,' the nurse said in the same quiet tone. 'The doctor will be here in a moment to examine her again.'

Hilary half turned to go, then put out a hand to touch Maddy's sleeve. 'Come on, Maddy. We'll wait outside. The doctor will tell us as soon as he knows anything.' She hesitated. 'Felix?'

'I can't leave her,' he said brokenly, but the nurse put her hand on his shoulder.

'Wait outside with the others, please, sir.'

After a moment, he got slowly to his feet and, with a last look at the still figure, followed them outside. They moved back to the chairs and sat down in a silent, unhappy row, and Hilary said, 'Can you tell us what happened, Felix?'

He rubbed a hand over his face. 'I hardly know. It was so dark and Mirabelle's lights weren't very good. We saw these ponies all over the road – there was ice, as well. I tried to avoid them, but the wheels skidded and then it all seemed to happen at once. The ponies – they *screamed*, Hilary, the most awful sound. I felt us hit one – its head came right through the windscreen, it seemed to be almost in Stella's lap. I saw its eyes, its teeth ... We turned over and rolled into the ditch and we were on top of its body, it kept on screaming and screaming ... I didn't know horses could make that noise ... I had to crawl out of the car, and Rob was thrown on to the grass ... He got up after a minute and crawled over to me, but the lights had gone out and it was so dark, we couldn't see anything at all ... I called Stella's name and managed to get her door open, but she didn't answer me, and when I touched her face I could feel blood ... Hilary, I don't know what I shall do if she dies.'

'She's not going to die,' Hilary said steadily. 'They won't let her. *We* won't let her.'

But Maddy stamped her foot angrily and cried, 'How can you say that? You don't know – none of us knows. People *do* die. My mother and father died. My baby brother died. *Sammy* died. How do you know Stella won't die as well?' And she broke into a storm of noisy weeping and turned away.

Russ moved forward quickly and took her in his arms, talking to her in a low, soothing voice. Hilary glanced uneasily at Felix and he said miserably, 'She's right, Hilary. We don't know.'

'Then we can *believe*,' she said fiercely. 'We can pray. Felix, you know how to do that. If you've ever prayed for anything in your life, this is the time to pray as hard as you can.'

'And don't you think I've been doing that all the time?' he asked, and his eyes were filled with despair. 'But we don't always get what we pray for, Hilary, if it isn't what God wants for us. And Maddy is right: people do die.'

'Die?' a small voice asked, and they all turned quickly. Rob was standing there, looking very young and very frightened in his white hospital gown. His eyes were huge and almost black as he turned them from one face to another. 'Is Miss Simmons going to die – and all because of me?'

Chapter Thirty-Eight

The news went round Burracombe like wildfire next morning. Those who had heard it at the pub told their families, who passed it over their garden fences as soon as it was light, or hurried to the village shops where knots of people gathered, their faces drawn with anxiety.

'And just before Christmas, too,' Jessie Friend lamented. She had been up a stepladder, putting up paper-chains when she heard, and looked down woefully as the customers came in. 'The poor young vicar must be at his wits' end. Does anyone know how Miss Simmons is?'

'Hovering between life and death, that's what I heard,' replied Mabel Purdy. 'Well, that wedding won't be happening, that's one thing certain.'

Jacob Prout, who had come in for his morning packet of Woodbines, turned on her sharply. 'Don't say that, Mabel. It might have to be put off for a while, but they can do wonderful things these days, what with penicillin and all. What were they doing out at Princetown anyway? Is it true that young French kiddy was with them, that's supposed to be the Colonel's grandson?'

George Sweet, who had brought over a few loaves of bread before he started his delivery round, nodded. 'That American nevvy of Ted Tozer's brought Dottie Friend and young Maddy back at about midnight. I stepped outside for a minute and Dottie told me they'd all been sent home bar Mr Copley and the boy – keeping them in for observation, whatever that might mean. There weren't no point in the rest of them stopping there all night. And Hilary Napier was worried about her dad, too, so he brought her as well.'

'That's right, took bad yesterday morning, squire was,' Bert Foster chimed in. 'Mary Ellis told me that when she popped in for some bacon. She was going back straight away to stop the night, when poor Miss Hilary was called away to the hospital. Proper do all round, it seemed to be.'

'Why does everything happen at once?' Aggie Madge wondered. 'It were the same when my Bob was took, and Uncle Fred had a stroke the same day. Us didn't know which way to turn.'

'But that still don't explain why the French tacker was there as well,' Jacob said. 'I dunno, it sounds a bit funny to me. Still, it won't do no good standing here chewing the fat over it, I got work to do.' He paid for his cigarettes and went out.

At the vicarage, Basil Harvey and his wife Grace were equally worried. After sending Russ to Exeter to meet Maddy, there had been nothing more they could do, and they'd gone to bed hoping for news in the morning. So far, they'd heard nothing but as they sat eating their toast they heard a knock on the front door.

Basil got up and hurried out. Grace heard voices and a moment later Ted Tozer came in, carrying his cap in his hands and looking anxiously at his feet, encased in much-darned socks. 'Excuse my feet, Mrs Harvey, I walked over and 'tis a bit muddy, my boots were a big clagged up ...'

'Don't worry about that, Ted,' Basil said. 'Just tell us what's happening.'

'Well, young Russ come back in the early hours. He brought Maddy and Dottie Friend back, in a right state they were, the poor maid half wore out with crying, and Dottie in a real tizzy. Our Joe's gone down to see her and if she wants to go back to the hospital he'll run her down there with Maddy, if her's fit to go. Russ thinks she ought to have a good rest before she goes again but you know what it is, Stella's her sister and she's going to want to be with her. Apparently it don't look too good.'

'Oh, Ted!' Grace cried in distress, and then, seeing how upset he looked, added, 'Do sit down. What about the others? How bad are they?'

'Not bad at all, it seems. A bit bruised, and they wanted to make sure the boy didn't have no concussion, but nothing worse than that.

It was poor Stella who got the worst of it – the pony's head come right through the windscreen and done I don't know what damage.'

'It's dreadful.' Grace poured him a cup of tea. 'Drink this, Ted. You look quite shaken yourself. Did you and Alice get much sleep?'

'Not a lot,' he admitted, taking the cup. 'Thank you, Mrs Harvey. We laid there for a bit, wondering what was going on, and then Russ came back so us all got up again and had a cup of tea in the kitchen while he told us as much as he could. He brought Hilary back, too – she was worried about her dad. Russ didn't think she ought to drive back on her own, so she left her car down there and now she've gone in with Joe this morning.' He rubbed a large hand over his face. 'It's all a proper muddle. I don't hardly know who's where.'

'How's Maddy? And Dottie?' Grace asked. 'They must be frantic. And what about Colonel Napier?'

'Haven't heard nothing about the Colonel. Joe went up to the Barton to pick Hilary up and he went straight off then. But Russ said Maddy's in a real taking, and Felix is beside himself with worry. They let him stop in, since he was pretty shook up. The boy's upset too, blaming himself apparently for causing it all, though I don't see as the accident were his fault. Still, 'tis true that if it wasn't for him they wouldn't have been there ... Dottie's hoping he'll be sent home today. What we've arranged, as much as we could arrange anything at all since we don't know what's happening, is that if the young chap is let out, Hilary can bring him back, and then Joe can stop with Dottie if need be. They need someone down there with a car, since Felix's has been wrecked.'

'I think I should go, too,' Basil said. 'I'll look in at Dottie's cottage in an hour or so and see if Maddy's ready to go back. She won't want to stay in Burracombe while her sister's so ill. It sounds as if they could do with some more support.'

'That would be good of you, Vicar,' Ted said gratefully. 'I'd go meself, or send our Tom, but us have only got the truck and it's a bit mucky at present ... Well, I reckon that's about all I can tell you now. I just looked in to see if you had any more news, really.'

Basil shook his head. 'No, we've heard nothing. Thank you for coming in, Ted. I'll try to telephone from the hospital when I get there, to give you the latest news – if there is any. I'd better try to arrange something about Felix's services too. And I'll slip into the school before I go, to let Miss Kemp know, although I'm sure she'll have heard by now.'

Miss Kemp had indeed heard the news but, when he arrived to find the children practising Christmas carols, she was grateful to hear it from Basil's lips. According to the many garbled reports she'd been given by the children, Stella, Felix and Robert had all been half-killed in a road accident involving three lorries, injured in a fight with a gang of escaped Dartmoor prisoners (anything that happened near Princetown was automatically put down to escaped prisoners) or attacked by a large wild dog that she suspected had its origins in the Sherlock Holmes tale of the Hound of the Baskervilles which she had seen at the cinema before the war. Although even Basil only knew the bare bones of the story, she called all the children together in the big classroom.

'You all know that Miss Simmons isn't here this morning, and we've heard lots of rumours about what's happened to her,' she began. 'Now, we don't know very much yet but Mr Harvey has told me that she and Mr Copley had an accident in Mr Copley's car near Princetown last night, and Robert Napier was with them. They were all taken to hospital in Plymouth to be looked after. Robert and Mr Copley weren't badly hurt, and we're hoping they will be able to come home today. But I'm sorry to say that Miss Simmons will have to stay a little bit longer. And that's all we know for the time being. But if you hear anyone say that they were attacked by escaped prisoners, you can tell them it's not true, and there were no lorries or other cars either.'

'Miss, my dad told me that Mr Coker told him they run into some ponies,' Shirley Culliford said, putting up her hand. 'And that must be true, because Mr Coker had to go out and shoot one of them.'

Miss Kemp felt a little faint. Whatever had happened out there, in the icy pitch darkness? 'Well, it sounds as if that's true, then,' she acknowledged as the rest of the children uttered little gasps and cries of horror. 'But I don't think there's any use in us worrying about it until we know. The best thing we can do for Miss Simmons is get on with our lessons. I'm hoping we can get a teacher to come out and take the infants' class, but until then you'll all be together in here and I think the little ones can draw some nice pictures for Miss Simmons to look at when she's better. Betty, you can take round some paper, and Linda, you can take the crayons.'

'Can us make paper-chains too, Miss?' Shirley asked. 'It'd be nice for Miss Simmons to see the classroom all decorated up when her comes back.'

Miss Kemp hesitated. From all she'd heard, it seemed unlikely that Stella would be back in time to see the Christmas decorations but, despite the grisly rumours they had brought into the school, there was a limit to what bad news children should be expected to bear.

'Yes, when you've drawn your pictures I think you can all make paper-chains,' she said. 'We don't usually decorate the classroom until the last week before Christmas, but it would be nice to do it early. And if Miss Simmons isn't out of hospital by then, we could send in a few for her to put round her bed, with the pictures.'

Subdued by the thought that their beloved teacher might not be back before Christmas, the children began to settle to their work, but Janice Ruddicombe had another question.

'What about the wedding, Miss? Will I still be able to be bridesmaid?'

The children immediately broke into a babble of questions and answers and Miss Kemp, feeling further dismay, rang the bell for quiet. She looked at them all gravely.

'That's something we'll have to wait to find out, Janice. There are still a few weeks to go before the wedding, and we must all hope that Miss Simmons is quite well again by then and that it will all happen just as planned. And in the meantime, we must work as hard as we can, so that she knows we've been thinking of her and doing just what she would have wanted, even though she's not here.'

They settled down again at last and, with all the heads bent industriously over either drawings or the sums she had set the older children to do, she moved to the window to gaze out at the village street. It was cold and grey out there, with a spattering of frozen snow still on some of the roofs, and looked more cheerless than she had ever known it.

An accident with a pony, which had to be put down. And poor Stella lying in hospital, badly hurt.

What an appalling thing to happen, so near to Christmas and so near to the wedding Stella and Felix had planned so joyously.

Hilary had also reached home after midnight. She had told Mrs Ellis to use the spare room to sleep in once her father was settled for the night, but as she'd let herself wearily in through the front door, the housekeeper had appeared from the kitchen, her face anxious.

'Whatever happened? Are they all right?' She took in Hilary's exhausted face and said, 'Come along in here, and I'll make you a hot drink and something on toast.'

'I couldn't eat a thing,' Hilary said, but the housekeeper took no notice and got out the breadbin while the kettle began to boil. Hilary sank down on a chair, leaned both elbows on the table and rested her forehead against her fingertips. She gave a deep, shuddering sigh and Mrs Ellis rested a hand on her shoulder for a moment.

'Don't try to talk yet. Tell me when you're ready.'

Hilary lifted her face and tried a wobbly smile. 'I'm all right. It just swept over me for a minute. They seem to have run into some ponies and smashed the car up. Felix and Rob are both all right, though pretty shaken, but Stella ...' Her voice shook. 'Stella's hurt.'

'Badly?' Mrs Ellis asked quietly, and Hilary nodded.

'Yes, I think it is quite bad. She – she's unconscious and they can't tell exactly what damage there is until she comes round. But there are some broken bones, and some internal injuries of some sort, and – and they think her spine's been damaged.'

'Oh, my dear Lord,' Mrs Ellis said, and sat down in one of the other chairs. 'Oh, that poor maid. And Mr Copley, too. He must be almost out of his mind with worry.'

'Yes, he is. He can't bear to leave her. We saw her for a few minutes. Oh, Mrs Ellis, she looked so small and white in that bed. There's nothing of her. And they sent for Maddy – Ted Tozer's grandson went to Exeter to meet her off the train. She was distraught. It was Russ who brought us back – I don't think I could have driven myself. He'll take us back in tomorrow, or someone from the farm will, and I can collect Rob.'

'And what about him? He's the one who caused all this trouble. Running off like that and frightening us all to death!'

'We mustn't blame him, Mrs Ellis,' Hilary said quickly. 'He's just a little boy and he's had a difficult time for the past few months. He told us he was unhappy at school, but we didn't really take much notice of him. Father said all boys go through that, the first term.' She watched as the housekeeper got up again and started to slice bread, laying it in the wire toast-holder and setting it on the hotplate of the range. 'He's blaming himself anyway. Poor little boy – I shall never forget the look on his face when he asked if Stella was going to die because of him. It's a terrible burden for a child to bear.'

'Well, I suppose it wasn't his fault they ran into a pony,' Mrs Ellis acknowledged. She went to the larder and took out some eggs which she began to beat together in a bowl.

'And how's my father?' Hilary asked. She had been so taken up with answering the housekeeper's questions that she hadn't had time until now, and she'd assumed from the woman's manner that he was satisfactory. 'I hope he hasn't been a trouble to you.'

'Not a bit of it,' declared Mrs Ellis, who had been a children's nanny in her time and treated the Colonel as if he were one of her charges. 'The doctor came in to see him about eight o'clock and gave him something to settle him down, and I haven't heard a peep out of him since. I looked in a few times and he was sleeping like a baby. Doctor says he should be able to get up for a while tomorrow, but he's not to start doing anything for at least a week. It weren't a serious attack, just a bit of a turn, but he've got to take notice. A sort of warning, the doctor said.'

'Yes, that's what I thought,' Hilary agreed. 'Well, that's one thing to be thankful for. I don't know how I would have managed if he'd been really ill.'

Mrs Ellis turned from the range, where she was stirring the eggs in a small saucepan. 'You'd have managed, because you're a person who always does manage, Miss Hilary. And you'd have had all of us to help you. But now you need to get some rest – you look tired to death.' She took the toast from the wire and put it on a plate, buttering it generously before tipping a pile of creamy scrambled eggs over the top. 'Now, you get this inside you and then you're to go straight to bed. I'll not wake you in the morning – you need your sleep before you go back to Plymouth. I don't suppose that young chap will be round here too early to collect you, not if Alice Tozer has any sense.'

Hilary took a bite or two of the scrambled eggs to please the housekeeper, and then found she could eat a little more after all. Within a few minutes the plate was empty and she looked at it with some surprise.

'I didn't realise I was so hungry! Thank you, Mrs Ellis, I feel much better now. It was very good of you to wait up for me. I'll go to bed now, and you must, too. I'll just peep in at Father first.'

As Mrs Ellis had said, he was sleeping like a baby. His colour was better and he looked his old self. She withdrew quietly and tiptoed along to her own room, undressing and slipping into bed with a sigh of relief.

She hadn't thought she would sleep either, but to her surprise, when she opened her eyes after what seemed no more than a few minutes, it was broad daylight and there was a cup of tea on the table beside her.

It was almost cold. The housekeeper must have brought it and put it down before stealing away again without waking her. Hilary looked at her watch and saw that it was past nine o'clock. The events of the previous day flooded back into her mind and she leaped out of bed.

Stella! Had she survived the night? And what about poor Felix, sitting beside her bed, praying that she would recover from her terrible injuries? Maddy, too, who had already lost so many people and now had only her sister left. And Rob, Baden's son, with his ashen face and huge, piteous eyes, asking if it were all his fault.

I must go to them, she thought, scrambling into her clothes. If no one from the farm can take me, I'll catch the train. But I must be there ...

Chapter Thirty-Nine

Hilary could not, however, leave the Barton at once. First, there was breakfast, at Mrs Ellis's insistence, which Hilary acknowledged to be sensible, and then she had to speak to her father, who was sitting up in bed waiting impatiently for Dr Latimer to call and give him permission to get up.

'Why I have to wait for that old woman's say-so I don't know,' he grumbled as Hilary came into the drawing room. 'And I dare say when he does allow me out of bed it will only be to sit in the chair by that window. Lot of fuss about nothing.'

'I'm glad to see you're taking notice of him anyway,' she said, sitting down on the chair beside the make-shift bed. 'We don't want to lose you yet, Father. There's a lot for you to do before you hand over Burracombe to – whomever you're handing it over to.'

'I've been thinking about that,' he said. 'Wondering if I've been a bit hasty.'

Hilary looked at him in surprise. She waited and, after a moment, he went on.

'Young Rob. What do you think? Will he be up to it?'

'Taking on the Barton, and the estate, you mean?' She considered. Here was a chance, if she cared for it, to convince her father that he should leave the inheritance as it had been before – between herself and Stephen, albeit with a reasonable bequest to Rob. Even Marianne might be content with that. But was it a chance she should take? Was it morally right, to take advantage of her father's weakness and disappointment? And she knew quite well that that was what she would be doing.

And, sliding into her mind like a bright, narrow sword, came the thought of David. She could not, at present, see where this was heading or where it would end, but she knew that, one way or another, her life was about to change, and Burracombe's place in it would change, too. Was it possible that she might even be thankful to hand over the responsibility?

'Of course that's what I mean. I don't mind telling you, Hilary, I feel he's let us down. Running off like that. Trying to go back to France. With never a word to us—'

'That's not quite fair,' she interrupted. 'He told us how unhappy he was and you – we – just shrugged it off. If we'd taken notice of him then, he wouldn't have done it.'

'I told you before, all boys go through these initiations. It's a rite of passage. Happens in all societies. Happens in primitive tribes.'

'Yes, but we're not primitive,' Hilary said sharply, and then caught herself up. Whatever happened, she must not allow this to develop into an argument and upset her father all over again. She wondered a little bitterly if he didn't sometimes use his heart condition as a form of blackmail, but his collapse yesterday had been real enough. She said more calmly, 'Rob's an intelligent boy, and I don't believe he's a coward. He spent his early childhood with Germans in the house, seeing his mother and grandparents harbour British servicemen at risk of their own lives. If he decided to leave Kelly, it was because he didn't believe the other boys had the right to treat him as they did, and decided to stand no more of it. And he didn't believe we would support him. I'm sorry to say, he was right, too. But it wasn't the action of a coward. He planned it from the start and he'd have done it, if it hadn't been for the fact that we could intercept him in London.'

'Yes. I'd like the address of your friend, Hilary, by the way.'

'David's address?' she asked, his name startled out of her.

'Why not? Must write and thank him. Presume you can give it to me.'

'Yes,' she said faintly, thinking of her father's letter arriving at David's home in Derbyshire. Would Sybil see it? But she could not worry about that now. There were more immediate things to be dealt with.

'You still haven't answered my question. D'you think Rob's up to it? Not just Burracombe – all of it. School … Kelly … learning about the land, about our way of life. And eventually taking it on.' He looked at her and she was saddened by the expression in his eyes, almost of defeat. Gilbert Napier wasn't used to defeat; it must be wounding him more than she could imagine.

'He's Baden's son,' she said carefully, aware that if she were not fair to the boy now she would regret it for the rest of her life. 'You've always said he was the rightful heir.'

'I know. And *you've* always said that I can leave the estate to whomever I choose. But now ...' He lifted his shoulders, looking suddenly old and weary. 'I don't know, Hilary. I just don't know. After all the work you've put in, too ... Am I being fair?'

Hilary felt a twinge of alarm. She had never before heard her father give way to self-doubt. He seemed so dispirited, as if he were ready to give up. He was wound down like a clock about to stop and she wondered in abrupt panic whether the collapse had been worse than they thought.

'Father, I don't think we should make any decisions now. We need to think carefully about the situation and then decide what to do. We have to think what is best for the estate and the family; but most of all, we have to think what is best for Rob. He's Baden's son, and he has the right to inherit, but if it isn't the right thing for him after all, maybe we shouldn't force it on him. Maybe we should just wait and see what *he* wants.'

'But he's just a child,' her father said fretfully. 'How can he know what he wants?'

'Precisely. He can't – especially after all this upheaval. He can only look a little way ahead. And it seems that he's done that and doesn't like what he sees. Father ...' Her thoughts were clarifying themselves now, setting themselves in order, and she went on more confidently, 'Why don't we let him go back to France and finish his education there, in the system he knows and understands, with his own family and friends to support him? Perhaps he could come back when he's – oh, say, sixteen and more able to cope – and finish his schooling here, maybe go to university as Stephen did. He could come here for his holidays and learn about the estate gradually, just by being a part of it, as we did. And if by that time you think he should inherit, it will be because you know he's "up to it". What do you think?'

'And if I don't live that long?' he asked wryly. 'You're looking quite a few years ahead, Hilary. A lot can change in that time.'

'Yes, it can.' She thought fleetingly of David. 'But you will live longer than that, Father, if you take proper care. You've been well for a long time now – it's just all this worry that's been too much for you.'

'And my will? The inheritance?'

'It might be better to make some changes there,' she said carefully. 'Obviously Rob must be looked after, but ... Perhaps you'd better ask John Wolstencroft to come back and go through it again – just until you know what you really want to do. And you know, I believe that once we have the question of Rob settled and you know that *he's* happy, you'll feel happier too. After all, you do care about him a lot, don't you?'

'Yes,' he said after a moment, his voice gruff. 'I do care about him. He seemed to come out of nowhere – the grandson I'd always longed for. The grandson I thought I'd never have – Baden's son. And you're right, Hilary, I can't have him being unhappy.' He thought for a while, then said, 'Very well. I'll consider what you've said, but it seems to be the right thing to do. Maybe I've rushed the boy too much. As you say, he's only a child. And I think you're right – he's not a coward. No son of Baden's could be a coward.'

Hilary thought that Marianne might have quite a lot to do with it too – however much she might dislike the French woman, she would never have accused her of cowardice. She leaned forward and kissed her father, then stood up.

'I'll have to go now. I'll bring Rob in to see you as soon as we get home. He'll need some reassurance that you're not angry with him ... You're not, are you?'

'Not any more,' he said, and she knew that he would give Robert what he needed. 'And if he asks, you can tell him there's no question of his going back to Kelly. He wasn't ready for it – I can see that now. Maybe in a few years' time – but only if he wants it too.'

Hilary smiled at him and slipped out of the room. She closed the door behind her and leaned against it, breathing deeply.

It had gone better than she'd expected. The situation now was becoming more manageable. Rob might still inherit Burracombe, but only if he really did become a fitting heir. And meanwhile ...

Meanwhile, there was David. But he was her problem, and she could not even begin to think about him now.

She heard a car draw up outside the house, and ran to the front door.

The sky had cleared during the night and it was a bright morning, with frost riming the stone walls of the cottage gardens and outlining leaves with a sparkle of ice. But there was little warmth to soften the hard brightness of frozen puddles, and Hilary had brought the warmest clothes she could find for Robert to wear, guessing that the clothes he had worn for his escape would have been soiled and torn in the accident. And the ice in her heart – as she thought of Stella, still lying immobile in that hospital bed, and Felix keeping anguished watch beside her – seemed colder than any frost.

Maddy was waiting at the cottage gate, her face still white and her eyes shadowed, when the car Joe Tozer had hired drew up beside her, with Hilary already inside. As it came to a halt, Dottie appeared on the doorstep, wrapped in the winter coat she'd had since before the war.

'Is there room for me, too? I've been worrying all night about that poor maid, but I know Maddy wants to be there so if you can't fit me in ... There's a few bits and bobs in this basket, if you wouldn't mind taking it along.'

'Of course there's room for you. I'll put the basket in the trunk. Get in the back, both of you.' Russ got out and held the door open. Dottie got in first, then Maddy, and Russ slid in beside her. Dottie saw that his father was driving, with Hilary beside him.

'But how will us get back?'

'It's all right, Dottie,' Hilary reassured her. 'My car's already there. I'll probably take Rob home as soon as they let him go. And if you need transport, either to take you there or come and fetch you home, you have only to telephone the Barton. I'll come at any time.'

'That's proper good of you, Miss Hilary,' Dottie said gratefully. 'But us can get the bus or the train if need be.'

'Only if absolutely necessary,' Hilary said firmly, and Russ, sitting beside Maddy, agreed.

'Dad and I are pretty free. We'd like to make ourselves useful. You just call on us whenever you need.'

Maddy turned her head slightly to look at him, and he seemed to sense her glance and looked back. Their eyes met and she remembered how he had held her last night, consoling her as she wept. She had had a strange sense of homecoming and, even as her tears began to dry, she hadn't wanted to leave the shelter of his arms.

An odd little shiver ran through her body and she turned away quickly, but she was now sharply aware of the warmth of his side against hers. She looked down at his hands, lying loosely on his lap, and thought what a nice shape they had, slender yet strong. A musician's hands. She wondered if he played any instrument, and realised that she knew almost nothing about him. So why this sense of familiarity – as if they had met before, in another place, another time?

A deep guilt rushed over her as she remembered the reason for this journey. How could she have forgotten her sister, even for a moment? And all her fear swept back as she wondered what the morning would bring.

'I rang the hospital before I left,' Hilary said, as if answering her thoughts. 'There's been no change, I'm afraid, but at least that doesn't mean she's worse.'

Maddy gave a little sigh, half of relief, half anxiety. 'She must be terribly badly hurt to have stayed unconscious all this time. Oh, why do these things happen? Why do they always happen to *us*?'

Dottie took one of her cold hands and held it between her own. 'There, there, my pretty, you mustn't worry too much. 'Tis the body's way of resting when it's had a shock. She'll wake up when she'm ready.'

Maddy felt the tears prick her eyes. She looked down at the clasped hands and whispered, 'I know I'm being selfish. Terrible things happen to other people as well. It's just that … if I lose Stella, I don't know what I'll do. And it's so soon after Sammy …'

'I know, my bird, I know. It don't seem fair. But you haven't lost her yet and us mustn't lose hope. Stella's a strong and healthy young woman, and she'll fight all the way. Us'll have her back as good as ever, never you fret.'

Maddy sighed again. She didn't know whether she could believe Dottie but it was comforting to hear the words spoken in that warm, burring voice. She felt the warmth of Russ and Dottie cocooning her on either side, and she closed her eyes and let herself rest in their strength and love.

'And how about you, Dottie?' Joe asked from the driver's seat. 'Did you manage to get any sleep?'

'I didn't do too bad, thanks, Joe. Reckon I was pretty tired when us got home last night, so Maddy and me went straight to bed with a cup of cocoa and mine was still there when I woke up.' She didn't mention that it had been three o'clock when she woke up and she'd not been able to sleep again for visions of Stella, so still and white in the hospital bed. For all her reassuring words to Maddy, Dottie was sick with fear over her lodger. She had seen enough during her time to know that unconsciousness that lasted for several hours, indicating a bad bang on the head, together with broken bones and a possible spine injury, boded ill, and she was as fond of Stella as she was of Maddy herself. Like daughters they are to me, both of 'em, she thought. I couldn't have had better ones if I'd made their pattern myself, like making out a pattern for a frock.

Her eyes went to the back of Joe's head. Since the evening when he'd come to see her and they'd been interrupted by Stella, he had visited her several times, and they'd sat talking over the old days in the village, but he had never again approached the subject of their own relationship. She sighed. She'd felt that night as if he was about to say something important, something she wasn't entirely sure she wanted to hear, and she hadn't been sorry to be interrupted; but she'd thought about it often since then and wished he would say whatever it was. Until it was said, it felt like a loose thread hanging from a favourite cardigan; something that needed to be pulled through and made tidy again.

Dottie let her mind drift back to the days of her girlhood when she and Joe Tozer had been in love. They'd known each other since they were babies, of course; grown up in the same village – Joe at the farm, and Dottie in the cottage where she lived now – and went to the village school together. As they got older and left school to go out to work, they'd hung about in the evenings with the other boys and girls on the bridge by the ford, larking and chatting and gradually pairing off until it was accepted that certain pairs were 'walking out' together. And Joe and Dottie had been one of those pairs.

We were true sweethearts, she thought wistfully. But then, in July 1914, war – the war to end all wars, it had been called – had been declared and Joe had volunteered for the army, even though he was underage at the time. They'd written all through the war, of course, and he'd come home a few times on leave, but she'd never dared agree to marry him until it was over. She'd felt almost superstitious over it, as if to put a ring on her finger would have made her a widow, and she couldn't bear to think of her Joe dying out there somewhere in France.

Well, they hadn't married, and Joe hadn't died, although they'd all had a bad scare when he came home at the end of it all and almost immediately caught that terrible flu. And then, when he'd recovered from that, he and Dottie had gone for a walk along the Burra Brook together and he'd told her he was planning to emigrate to America.

'America?' she'd exclaimed in dismay. 'But whatever do you want to do that for, Joe?'

'There's no place for me here now, Dottie. Our Ted's more or less running the farm with Dad, and now he's married, him and Alice are bound to take over. There's not room for two families. And I don't feel like playing second fiddle, not after all I've been through. I want to make a new life for myself and I reckon America's the place to do it.'

'But it's so far away,' she'd said. 'The other side of the world. You'd never come home again.'

'Of course I would. I'd come home for visits. It only takes a week on one of the big liners. And a chap can earn good money in America, Dottie. We could have a good life there together.'

'We?' she echoed, stopping on the grassy bank and staring at him. 'You and me, you mean?'

'Course I do. You didn't think I'd go without you, did you?'

Dottie walked on, her thoughts tumbling in her head. Go to America! She'd never dreamed of such a thing. Why, she'd hardly been out of the village.

'I don't know as I could,' she said, her voice trembling a little. 'It's all right for you, Joe, you've travelled a bit, but I've hardly ever been further than Plymouth. Us did go to Looe once on a church outing, but that's all.'

'I don't know that the Somme counts as travel, exactly,' he said grimly, 'but I suppose you're right in a way. But it's nothing to worry about, Dottie. We'd be together. I'd look after you.' He stopped and took both her hands in his, gripping them tightly, and she saw his eyes blaze with excitement. 'Think of it! A new life, away from all this talk about the war. I'm sick of hearing it, sick of thinking about it. I just want to push it out of my mind for ever. Dottie, we've waited all this time, we've always been sweethearts. Tell me you'll come with me. Tell me you'll marry me and come to America with me.'

'Joe ...'

'Please,' he said, and began to kiss her. His lips were hard and passionate and she felt herself melt against him. He drew her down beside him on the grass and stroked her hair and her body with hands that shook with yearning, and Dottie felt her own desire, kept in check for so long, sweep through her body.

'Please, Dottie,' he whispered again, and this time she knew he was asking for something different. Not for America, not for the future at all, but for the here and now – for the joy of the present and the consummation of a love that had waited too long.

Chapter Forty

Maddy had decided to try to fend off her fear by thinking of something else. Dottie herself had taught her this when she was a small girl, crying herself to sleep over the loss of her parents and her baby brother and the separation from her sister. 'If it can't be helped, you must just try to let it go, my flower,' she would say, sitting by the bed and smoothing Maddy's damp brow with a gentle hand. 'Let your mind go to another place – a nice place, where you can feel happy. It'll rest your mind. Tell me about the things you liked when you were little, but don't let them make you feel sad again.'

And Maddy would talk, hesitantly and with fresh tears at first, about the days she and Stella and their parents had spent on the beach at Southsea before the war. Sunday afternoons, after church and Sunday School in the morning, when Kathy and Mike had cycled there from their home in North End, with the two little girls in seats on the backs of their bikes, the bottles of orange squash and a tin box of sandwiches in the old haversack on Mike's back, and the swimming costumes and towels in Kathy's basket on the front. They would find a spot somewhere amongst all the other families, near South Parade Pier, and struggle out of their clothes, squirming under the biggest of the towels so as not to reveal too much of their decency, and then rush headlong into the waves. Mike was always first in, entering the water like a whale and sending up huge clouds of spray, with Kathy following more slowly and the two girls squealing and jumping as the smaller waves at the edge made little circles of icy cold ever higher up their legs. But eventually they would all be thoroughly wet and not noticing the cold any more, and then Mike would take them far out on his broad back, and after that he and Kathy would teach them to swim, with one hand under their stomachs and the other beneath their chins. And eventually, when they were shivering but still insistent that they weren't cold, Kathy would decree that they must go back to their towels, and she would rub them dry and they would sit with their arms around their knees, waiting while she got out the orange squash and tomato sandwiches and slices of home-made fruit cake for tea.

To begin with, the memories made her cry all the more, but gradually, instead of pushing them out of her mind because of the pain they brought, she came to treasure them, to see them as bright spots in the sadness of her life and find comfort in them. As Dottie said, when she saw that this was happening, to put them out of her mind was almost like saying they had never happened, and that would mean that the happy family life she remembered had never been; that she had never had a loving mother or father or older sister ...

Maddy had been too young then to put all this into words, but she knew that it was so; and she knew now that it would help her to remember other brightness in her life. And the brightest part of all had been Sammy.

Sammy had come into her life as swiftly as a shooting star, and had left it with the cruel, shattering abruptness of an explosion. Just as it had been an explosion that had taken her mother and baby brother ... But while he was there, he had lit her days with love and laughter. Their love had been innocent and true, with no blemishes to tarnish the memory she would always carry in her heart, and nothing could mar it now. It was with her for ever, and she found to her surprise that she could allow herself to explore her memories with a tentative feeling of warmth rather than the sharp pain of grief.

Her eyes still closed, she was aware of the man next to her, the warmth of his body comforting her through the thickness of her winter coat. She remembered the first time she had met him, the strange feeling she had experienced when their eyes met and her determination not to let them meet again. When she had got off the train yesterday and seen him on the platform, her heart had given a peculiar twist, as if trying to sink and leap at the same moment and for a minute or two she hadn't known how to respond. She'd tried to remain in control of herself but there had been something about him that had reached out to her and touched her, so that she could not hold back the tears; and indeed, had not wanted to, for she knew somehow that he would be able to comfort and support her.

Comfort. That was what Russ Tozer was offering her now. Yet she knew, somewhere deep in her being, that he could offer her much more, and she knew that one day she would have to consider whether she wished to accept it.

Hilary's thoughts were divided between her father and her nephew. As far as her father was concerned, she felt sure that a reasonable compromise had been achieved, but she did not really know whether it was enough, now, to allay Robert's misery. They might have done too much harm for him to recover quickly, and his shock at the accident, together with his guilt at having caused it, even indirectly, might be very hard for him to deal with.

He mustn't go back to school, she thought, not even for the rest of the term – *especially* not for the rest of the term. Heaven knows what the other boys would do to him. He needs time to get over it all, and he needs to be back with his own family.

But Marianne and her other children were supposed to be coming to Burracombe for Christmas. It was not much more than a fortnight to go now. There should be no problem in keeping Robert at home – she was sure that Charles Latimer would agree he was not fit to go back – but would he want to stay at Burracombe for Christmas, or would he rather go back to France? She sighed, knowing that this was yet another decision to be made.

And when was she to have time to think about her own life? When could she think about the changes that had come to her in the past few weeks? The love that had been rediscovered, that had flowered so powerfully and refused to be denied for a second time? When could she examine her own feelings about the difficulties that must lie ahead if she didn't reject David; if she agreed that somehow, whatever it might mean in terms of scandal, of disrupting his marriage – and even though he said it had become a meaningless marriage, he had still made his vows to Sybil, and Hilary's whole being revolted against the breaking of such vows – they must find a way to be together? Could she really go through with it? Could she turn her back on Burracombe, as David would have to turn his back on his own home and medical practice and start anew somewhere unfamiliar to them both? Did their relationship have the strength to survive such a mighty change?

I can't, she thought. I can't do it. It would kill Father, for a start. And I'd lose all my friends. Some of them might understand – good, true friends like Val and Stella, perhaps even Felix, although he surely would not be able to approve. But I'd lose them just the same, if I had to move away. And I would have to move away. I would have to leave Burracombe.

Leaving Burracombe ... A few years ago, she had seriously considered it. Indeed, when she had first grown up it had been more or less expected of her. She would have married Henry and gone to live with him in Dorset, and nobody would have thought twice about it, least of all herself. But Henry had been killed, and her mother had been ill and then died, and she'd stayed on at Burracombe, restless but unable to decide what to do with her life. She had been on the point of leaving, to become an air hostess with one of the new airline companies, when her father had had his first heart attack, and after that she had taken on the managing of the estate, and found that this was something she could do, and do well. And, until Robert's arrival, she had believed that would now be her life.

If Robert had been older, if he had been willing to take over, she would have been set free. Scandal or not, she could have gone to David ... if only he had been free as well.

But David was not free, and the thought of what he must do to gain his freedom, even if Sybil agreed to it, was another aspect of the whole affair that revolted her soul. We can't start our lives together that way, she thought. We would be tainted for ever.

'We're here,' Russ said, leaning forward and breaking into her thoughts. 'Turn left, Dad. You can park the car over there ...' There was a slight pause as they all came out of their reveries and Joe brought the car to a halt. Then, shivering in the biting wind, they climbed out and stood in a little, undecided group before setting off towards the entrance to the hospital.

Each was wondering what lay ahead in that big, sprawling building. Hilary was thinking about Rob, and how she must proceed with him now – carefully, delicately, not to hurt him any more. And they were all thinking of Stella. Had she recovered consciousness or was she still lying there, flat and white, in the impersonal hospital bed? And of Felix, too; had he stayed by her side, sleepless, all these hours?

Dottie moved a little closer to Joe and he took her arm and held it against his side. And Maddy, quite unconsciously, felt for Russ's hand and held it tightly as they walked through the big doors.

Only Hilary walked alone.

There had been no change in Stella's condition. Felix was sitting on one of the chairs in the corridor outside the ward, almost as if he hadn't moved all night. He looked grey and exhausted, and Dottie went to him with a little cry of concern.

'Felix, you'm worn out. Haven't you had any sleep at all?'

'I don't know,' he said, rubbing a weary hand over his face. 'I might have dozed off a bit once or twice ... I'm not really sure.'

'I don't suppose you've had anything to eat either,' she said, taking the check tablecloth off her basket. 'I brought you a few egg sandwiches and some cake. I know 'tis a funny sort of breakfast, but it's better than nothing. And there's a Thermos of tea as well.'

'Dottie, you're a marvel,' he said gratefully, taking a sandwich. 'I didn't think I could eat a thing, but I have to admit I'm hungry.'

'Has there been any news?' Maddy asked anxiously, and he shook his head.

'The doctor came to see her about half an hour ago and he says there's been no change. The good news is that she hasn't got any worse, of course, but the longer she stays unconscious ...' He couldn't finish, and laid down his sandwich. The others looked uneasily at each other, and Dottie put her arm around his shoulders.

'There, there, my dear, try not to fret. Her'll wake up soon and wonder what all the fuss is about, and once they can see just what the damage is they can start putting it right. Wonderful things they can do, these days. Now, eat your sandwiches and you'll feel better. You got to keep your own strength up, you know.'

He nodded and began to eat again, mechanically, as if he hardly knew what he was doing. Hilary sat down at his other side.

'Stella's strong, you know, and she wants to get better. Even if she's unconscious, she still wants it, deep down. She'll pull through.' She knew she was probably talking nonsense. How could she know anything of the sort? And Stella wasn't strong enough, nobody was strong enough, to overcome the terrible damage that might have been done to her body. A broken spine ... possible brain damage ... and the possibility of remaining unconscious for days, maybe even weeks or months ... Nobody could know, until she woke up.

If she ever woke up.

Maddy evidently had the same thoughts and she turned on Hilary, her voice trembling as she almost shouted at her.

'You don't know any of that, Hilary! You're just saying it to make Felix feel better, but it doesn't make any of us feel better. How can it? The only thing that will make us feel better is Stella waking up and telling us she's all right. And it's not going to happen—' Her voice broke completely and she began to cry. 'It's just not going to happen ...'

Russ moved quickly towards her and took her in his arms, stroking her hair with one hand. He said nothing for several minutes, just gentled her until her tears began to subside and she leaned against him, her face buried in his chest. Then he said quietly, 'Let's go outside, sweetheart. You'll feel better in the fresh air.' And she went with him as obediently as a small child, leaning against him as she might lean against a rock in rough sea.

Joe sat down beside Dottie, who was still cradling Felix against her. He took her hand and held it between his big, warm palms. At his touch, she turned her head and they smiled at each other.

Hilary noticed the smile and felt a pang of surprise, for it was the smile of a lover, the smile that she might have shared with David. The surprise turned to a swift stab of loneliness and she felt an ache for his presence beside her, as Joe was beside Dottie and Russ had been beside Maddy.

I'm imagining it, she thought. People naturally comfort each other at times like this. It means nothing. Maddy is still grieving over Sammy, and Joe and Dottie are in their sixties. Joe and Russ are kind men, and they're American – they're always more ready to show emotion, and more ready to offer their warmth to others, even people they don't know very well. That's all it is.

A door opened and they all looked up quickly, half eager, half afraid, but the nurse who came out didn't even look their way. She hurried off down the passageways and disappeared through another door. They all sagged and looked at each other again.

'If only someone would come and tell us what's going on,' Hilary said.

'Nothing's going on,' Felix said drearily. 'They're just waiting, like the rest of us. We could wait here for months, and still nothing would be going on.'

They were silent, realising the truth in his words. People did stay unconscious for incredible lengths of time. Hilary shifted a little in her seat and said, 'I hope Maddy's all right.'

'Russ will look after her,' Joe said, his fingers still stroking Dottie's hand. 'He'll bring her back when she feels ready.'

'She's so fragile,' Hilary said. 'She always has been really, even when she was a little girl and Fenella used to bring her to stay with us. But these past few months ... sometimes, I've wondered whether she would ever get over Sammy.'

'She's suffered too much in too short a time,' Dottie said. 'I know 'twas back in the war when her lost her parents and brother, but that be far too much for a little girl to bear. I reckon that's why she took Sammy's accident so hard. And if she loses her sister too ...'

At that moment, Maddy herself came into view, with Russ beside her. She looked calmer and more composed, although her face was still pale and her eyes enormous. She sat down beside Hilary and touched her hand.

'I'm sorry. I shouldn't have shouted at you like that.'

'Don't be sorry. You only spoke the truth, anyway. Nobody knows what's going to happen, and it's better to face it than pretend it's all going to be all right.' Hilary's eyes went back to the door of the room where they knew Stella lay. 'We can only wait. All any of us can do is wait.'

'And pray,' Felix said, and she nodded her head slowly.

'And pray.'

Chapter Forty-One

Maddy sat close beside Russ, her hand still in his. Strength and comfort seemed to flow between them and she leaned her head on his shoulder. She knew that the gesture would not be misinterpreted. An understanding had grown between them that, for now, her dread over Stella and her need for his strength must take first place. Later, perhaps, the understanding would become something more, but for the present they were both content to be together in this quiet, almost platonic way.

Dottie was similarly aware of Joe. It was so many years since they had been young lovers, and so much water had flowed beneath their particular bridge. Deep water, some of it – his marriage to Eleanor, lives that had grown away from each other instead of together, and a second world war, which had changed everything. Yet there had been a time when she had believed her future lay with this man, grey-haired and craggy-faced now, but who had looked then so like the young Russ who sat with them. She stole a glance at the younger man, remembering how those attractive, corrugated looks, the bright blue eyes and crinkled, red-brown hair had stolen her heart. And not just his looks, either: his whole character. And his kisses.

That evening by the Burra Brook, she had lain in his arms, astounded by the passion that had swept over her like the sudden lighting of a fire. Their lovemaking had been a revelation of tenderness and delight, and afterwards they had lain for a long time, gently exploring each other's bodies in the warmth of the afterglow, until suddenly the flame blazed up again.

'Oh, Joe,' Dottie said at last, 'whatever have we done?'

'Something very nice.' He grinned. 'And don't worry, Dottie. I was careful ... And anyway, we're going to be married, aren't we?'

'Joe, I ...' It was what she had wanted, what she had waited for all this time. All through the long years of the war, when Joe had been in France facing horrors he had never spoken of, when she had dreaded every day to hear that he had been killed. So many men were killed in that terrible, cruel war, and so many more horribly wounded – you would see them in Plymouth, legless and propped on the pavements, begging for a few coins to be dropped into a cap lying on the ground in front of them, or standing with blind eyes on corners, selling matches. Men who had fought so that England would be a land fit for heroes to live in; but how were those heroes forced to live? Dottie's young eyes would fill with tears when she saw them and she would give them what few coins she had, or buy boxes of matches she didn't need, in pity for them and in gratitude that Joe was not one of them.

He'd leaned on one elbow, looking down into her face. 'You do still want us to be wed? I haven't spoiled it, have I?' His voice was anxious, and with his other hand he smoothed back her pale hair. 'I shouldn't have gone so far.'

'No, Joe, it's not that. It ... I wanted it as much as you. It was lovely ...' She turned her face against his hand and kissed his palm. 'Of course I want to marry you.'

'What is it, then?'

'America,' she whispered. ''Tis such a long way off, Joe. And my mother – her's not well. How can I go so far away? It would break her heart. Won't it break your mother's heart, Joe?'

'She won't like it much,' he acknowledged. 'But she and Father both know there's nothing for me here. Ted's working the farm and to tell the truth I've never been so took up with it as him. And what else is there for me in Burracombe?'

'There's the Barton. A maze of chaps went from there to the war and didn't come back. You'd get a job there, easy.'

'Gardening, maybe, or in the woods. I don't know that I want to spend my life doing that, Dottie. Since I've been in the Army I've picked up different sorts of skills. Engineering – there's a big future in that. But not in England – not for me. It's going to take years for this country to get back on its feet, and I reckon I've done my bit. The future for me's in America. It really is.'

'So you'll not stop and help us get back,' she said, withdrawing a little. 'You're just looking out for yourself.'

'No, not exactly. I'd be looking out for you, too.'

'That's not what I meant. Joe, if everyone thought like you and went off to America, there'd be no one left to help the country get back on its feet, and then where would we be?'

'Everyone's not going to though, are they? There's plenty staying behind.'

She was silent for a few moments. Then she said, 'And I'll be one of them, Joe. It seems like rats leaving a sinking ship to me.'

'Rats do that because they're intelligent,' he retorted. 'They know the ship's going to sink and they don't see no point in going down with it.'

'So you reckon England's sinking then, do you?'

'I never said that. It was you brought rats and sinking ships into it.'

They gazed at each other, both shaken by the sudden, acrimonious turn the conversation had taken. Dottie felt a rush of despair. Only twenty minutes ago, they had been in each other's arms, as close as a man and woman could be, and now, suddenly, they seemed as far apart as if the Atlantic already divided them. She tried to find a way back to that delicious closeness.

'Joe ... please don't let's quarrel.'

'*I* don't want to,' he said, but there was still a truculent note in his voice. 'All I wanted to do was ask you to marry me. I didn't think there was anything to quarrel about in that.'

'There's not,' she said, winding her arms about his neck. 'I do want to marry you, Joe, more than anything in the world. It's – it's the idea of going to America.'

'If you really wanted to marry me more than anything else, you'd come,' he said, and she drew back again, shocked.

'Joe!'

'What? What's the matter with that?'

'Don't my wishes come into it?' she asked. 'Don't it matter that you'm asking me to leave everything behind? The place where I grew up – my friends – my family?'

'It's a wife's place to go with her husband.' Then the truculent note left his voice and he pleaded in his turn. 'Dottie, I want what's best for *us* – you and me. It's not that I don't think as much of England, and Burracombe, as you do. I just don't see any future here. I can make a better life in America, but I want to make it for you as well. Say you'll come, Dottie. Please say you'll come.'

This time the silence continued longer. At last Dottie sat up and buttoned her blouse. Joe watched her without speaking and then she met his pleading gaze and said, 'I don't know, Joe. I'll have to think about it.'

'That means no.' He stood up and looked away from her.

'It don't!' she cried, and came up beside him. 'Joe, don't look like that. I can't decide something like this all at once. I got to think about it. There's Mother and Father—'

'It's nothing to do with them. They've had their life.'

'They still got a bit of a say—'

'You'm over twenty-one. You can do as you please.'

'It's not just that. I'm their only daughter. They depend on me.'

'Well, they shouldn't. They're not in their dotage. They can look after themselves, same as my folks can.'

'A minute ago, you said they'd had their lives,' she reminded him. 'You can't have it both ways, Joe.'

'I only want it one way.' He wheeled round and gripped her arms. 'Dottie, say you'll come with me. Please.'

His fingers dug into her flesh. She saw the urgency in his eyes, and longed to say yes. For a moment, she wavered and he saw it.

'It's a wonderful country, Dottie. There's so much opportunity there. I've been talking to other chaps, chaps who've been there – I've even met some Americans, they've told me what it's like. We could have a good life. A big house instead of a little farm cottage. A job with good prospects, a decent wage. I could make something of myself there, Dottie, and you'd be with me. We'd be together, raising our family there. Our children would have a better life.'

'Better than in Burracombe?' she asked, doubting it.

'*Everything* would be better than in Burracombe.'

She pulled her arms away, rubbing the places where his fingers had bruised her flesh.

'Seems to me you're the one who's got to do some thinking, Joe. You seem to have got your ideas all twisted up. Burracombe's a *good* place to live. It's suited me all this time and I don't see why it can't suit you. I don't want to go to America, or anywhere else.'

He stared at her. 'Not even to be with me?'

She turned away, feeling a little sick. Her heart was thudding painfully. She couldn't believe that everything had changed so much, so quickly.

'No, Joe. Not even to be with you.'

Their eyes met again, and now there was no tenderness between them, only a hard, bewildered anger. She wanted to call back all of the last hour, start again, but she knew that the conclusion would be the same and her throat ached with tears. After a minute or so, he turned away.

'That's it, then. Might as well forget it.'

For a second, her heart leaped as she thought that he meant America. But he walked away, his shoulders stiff with hurt anger, and she knew that the tenderness and passion of their lovemaking would not be repeated.

The door opened again and one of the doctors came out. It was a different doctor from the one they had seen last night and they watched him anxiously as he came towards them. His face was thoughtful, as if he was making up his mind what to say. Felix rose to his feet.

The doctor looked at him. 'You're Miss Simmons' fiancé?'

'Yes. And this is her sister. How – how is she?'

'There's very little change, I'm afraid.' His eyes moved from Felix to Maddy, who was now standing beside him. 'We've done some tests on Miss Simmons, and we think that the next few hours may be crucial. If you would like to sit with her for a while ... We find it helps sometimes for patients in this condition to have someone they love close by. Talking helps, too.'

'Talking?' Maddy said in surprise. 'But what should we talk about?'

'Anything at all. Reminiscences, perhaps. What's happening at home. But keep it light, pleasant talk – nothing that might agitate her mind if she does hear you.'

'Do you really think she might?' Felix asked, and the doctor pursed his lips and shook his head slightly.

'Who can say? But we believe that hearing is the last thing to go.' He saw their expressions and added hastily, 'Not that we believe Miss

Simmons to be at that stage. But she may well be able to hear and register, at some deep level, and it can do no harm. It might help you, too.'

They nodded and Felix turned to the others. The doctor looked apologetic. 'We can only allow the two of you, I'm afraid.'

'It's all right,' Hilary said. 'I should be taking Rob home anyway. Robert Napier,' she said to the doctor. 'Or Robert Aucoin – I'm not sure which name was used when he came in. He was staying in overnight for observation.'

'Ah yes. The French boy. Yes, he can be discharged. He's through there.' He indicated the door at the end of the corridor. 'He's ready now, I believe – you can take him at once.'

Rob was sitting on a bed, looking disconsolate and rather dishevelled but otherwise unscathed. He gave a nervous smile as Hilary approached, and she spoke cheerfully.

'Hello, Rob. You look as if you're all in one piece so we'll go back home now, if you're ready. I've brought you some clean clothes to change into – I thought the ones you were wearing yesterday might be in a bit of a state.'

'I got muddy,' he said, accepting the bundle she gave him. 'And my jacket's torn. These aren't school clothes, are they?'

'No, they're just ordinary things – grey shorts and a shirt and a thick jumper, and one of my scarves. They'll be enough to go home in and then we'll have to sort out some new winter things for you, since you only had summer ones with you before you went to school. Pull the curtains round your bed and change, and we'll go straight away.'

He pulled the curtains but lingered, his eyes anxious. 'Miss Simmons ... ?' He seemed unable to frame the words and Hilary guessed what he was trying to ask.

'Stella's about the same,' she said, hoping that she was right. Like Felix and Maddy, she hadn't missed the implication of the doctor's words about hearing. 'The others are with her now. They don't need me any more, and they'll let us know the minute there's any news.'

He nodded and went behind the curtains. A few minutes later he emerged, looking more presentable, and they left the ward. Hilary went to Dottie and the two Tozer men and told them quickly what she was going to do, and then put her hand on Rob's shoulder and led him away. She could feel the guilt in the stiffness of his shoulders, and knew that to face up to what he might think were accusing eyes would be too much for him just now.

'They don't blame you, you know,' she said gently. 'It's the sort of accident that could have happened to anyone.'

'They wouldn't have been there if it hadn't been for me,' he said drearily. 'I've been nothing but trouble ever since I came here.'

Hilary stopped abruptly. 'Who's said that to you? Who have you heard talking?'

'I heard it in the shop one day,' he said. 'The lady with red hair – she said it, after I fell down the mine that day with Micky and Henry. And now they'll all say it.'

Ivy Sweet, Hilary thought grimly. The baker's wife. She always did have a sharp, spiteful tongue on her.

'Well, you're to take no notice of that lady,' she told Rob forcefully. 'She doesn't know a thing about you. And you haven't been any trouble at all. You're a member of our family, and we've been pleased to have you.'

To her utter astonishment, she realised that the words she had intended simply as a comfort were actually true. The strange situation that had presented itself with Rob's arrival, the difficulties of the inheritance and her father's strong emotions, even the trouble that Marianne had caused, had none of them been Rob's doing. He had been brought to England, presented to his newly found family and his life ordered for him, without any volition on his part. And through it all, he had remained acquiescent to the point of being enigmatic, until in the end he had been pushed too far and had rebelled. And who could blame him for that?

More than anything, the turmoil seemed to have bound him more closely to Burracombe and the Barton itself and she realised that he had indeed become one of the family. She looked at him and laid one hand on his shoulder.

'I mean it, Rob,' she said. 'You haven't been any trouble at all.'

'Is my grandfather very angry with me?' he asked as they drew near to Burracombe.

Although the sun was higher in the sky now, there was little warmth in its beam, and the puddles at the sides of the roads still glittered with a thin layer of ice. While in the shade of the narrow lanes, frost glistened on the bare twigs and branches of the trees arching overhead. It's beginning to look really Christmassy, Hilary thought, and sighed. What sort of Christmas would it be in Burracombe, with Stella hovering between life and death, and this fresh anxiety over Rob?

'He was worried,' she answered. 'And we do try not to worry him, if we can help it. You must try to remember that, Rob. But he's not angry – not now.'

'He was at first, then?'

'Yes,' she said, 'he was at first.'

They were silent for a few minutes, then he said, in a small voice, 'What is going to happen to me, *Tante* Hilary?'

Once again, her heart smote her. The question might have meant, what was going to happen to him now, today, in the coming days and weeks. But somehow she felt it meant more than that. Rob was looking into a future in which the rug he had become so accustomed to, the life he had believed certain, had been pulled roughly from beneath his feet. He was asking what was going to happen to him in the next few years; in the whole of his life.

Hilary drew the car to a halt. They were only a few minutes from the Barton's gates but she felt that her young nephew needed more than a brief reply to his heartfelt question. He needed reassurance on a deeper level, and he needed it before he went through those gates to the house he had been told would be his one day, to face the grandfather he had upset and worried, and made angry, even ill. He needed to have his badly battered confidence restored, as far as she was able to do it.

'Rob,' she said, turning to him. 'Nobody can know what's going to happen to another person. We don't even know what's going to happen to ourselves.' She thought fleetingly of David and her heart twisted. 'It's like ...' She tried to think of an illustration he would understand. 'It's like going along a road we've never been along before, a road that hasn't been put on the map because it's never existed until now. Nobody can tell us what lies round the next corner. We have to find out for ourselves.' She wondered if this were too profound for him, if the idea of such a lonely journey might frighten him even more, and said quickly, 'It can be great fun, exploring our own personal road, but sometimes it can be a bit frightening. And that's the same for all of us. But sometimes our roads run very close to someone else's, close enough to stretch out our hands and help each other. And your road runs very close to all your family's roads. Those in France and those here. You run very close to my road, and to Stephen's. But you run closest of all to your grandfather's, and that's why he has tried to do so much to help you. He thinks now that perhaps he tried too hard.'

She stopped and held her breath, wondering if he could assimilate all this, and how he would react, not even sure that she had explained the thoughts that were in her mind. And what of her own road? she wondered. How close was it to David's, and would the two paths ever join and become one?

There was a long pause and then he nodded slowly. He turned his head and his dark blue eyes, so like Baden's, met hers, and then he smiled.

It was the most open and confident smile she had ever seen on his face and she felt tears start to her eyes as she gazed back at him. She wondered what reply was formulating in his mind, but all he said was, 'Let's go on now, *Tante* Hilary. I want to see my grandfather.'

Chapter Forty-Two

'She looks so tiny in that bed,' Maddy whispered, her voice full of tears. 'Oh, Felix, why did this have to happen?'

'Who knows?' he murmured, thinking that he ought to be offering comfort but unable to find any words. He thought of all the times he had offered comfort to the relatives of sick or dying people, and felt a deep self-disgust at the platitudes he had spoken. For that's all they were – platitudes. *At least he's not suffering any more … She had a good life … It's God's will … She's out of her pain … You're not really parted; you'll meet again in Heaven …* He'd believed them then, as he uttered them, but did he believe them now? He couldn't be sure. And he wondered what all those people had thought as he spoke the words that were used so often they'd become clichés. Were they angry with him, that he couldn't understand their grief? Were they simply being polite as they listened, when in truth they wanted to turn away and be allowed to feel their anguish without being told that it wasn't really necessary?

If someone said those things to me now, I think I would want to hit them, he thought as he stood beside Maddy, looking down at the white, still face of the woman he loved, the woman who had been planning so joyously to walk up the aisle and become his wife. How many people have wanted to hit me, for saying those things to them?

He wondered if he was losing his faith. Surely, if it meant anything at all, he ought to be able to draw strength from it now. But when he searched his mind and heart for something to hold on to, it was like groping in a dark tunnel for something he could no longer find. He felt very cold, and very small, as if his former confident self were a figure silhouetted against the light at the end of that tunnel, a figure seen at the wrong end of a telescope, very far away and impossible to reach.

'I don't know why it had to happen,' he answered Maddy miserably. 'I don't think I know anything any more.'

He felt her hand curl into his and gripped it tightly. Without looking at each other, their eyes fixed on the still, pale face before them, they moved nearer and sat down on the two chairs that had been placed beside the bed. Felix, close to Stella, laid his free hand over hers, and together he and Maddy formed a chain, their thoughts focused entirely on transmitting strength from their own hearts and bodies to hers.

'Stella, darling,' whispered Felix, remembering the doctor's suggestion that they talk to her. 'Stella, can you hear me? It's Felix. And Maddy's here too. We want you to get better. Everyone in Burracombe wants you to get better. Sweetheart, can you hear me? Can you open your eyes?' He waited, but nothing happened. 'Can you squeeze my fingers, just a little bit, just so that I know you can hear me?'

The room was silent. The nurse, who came and went softly all the time, taking Stella's pulse and temperature, monitoring the drips and tubes that left and entered her body, gave them a look of compassion but said nothing. Stella lay very flat, and very still. Only the minute rise and fall of her chest gave any indication that she was still alive.

Maddy spoke next. 'Stella, it's me. Maddy. I'm here with Felix. And Dottie's here too, waiting outside the room. They'll only let in two of us at a time. And Joe Tozer's here, you remember Joe – Ted Tozer's brother from America. He and Russ are both here – they brought us here in their car. Stella, everyone sends you their love and says you're to get better and come back as soon as you can. I saw Miss Kemp just as I was leaving Dottie's this morning and she's going to ask the children to draw pictures for you. You remember the ones they drew of the wedding? She's going to give me one to bring in to you, so that you can look forward to it. And Janice is looking forward to being a bridesmaid. And so am I. And—' But here, her voice, which had been trembling more and more as she spoke, broke completely and she began to sob.

Felix gripped her hand more tightly. Glancing at the nurse for permission, he stroked Stella's brow with his other hand, smoothing back the pale gold hair, and then touched her cheek with his fingertips.

'Darling, we love you so much. Please, please try very hard to get better. Please, darling, please ...'

But still Stella gave no sign; and as the day wore on and Felix and Maddy sat beside her, whispering and talking, reminding her of times past, looking forward to the future, they were both aware of a cold, creeping touch on their hearts and a sense that, for Stella, there might be no future.

Outside, Russ had gone to escape for a few moments from the smells and stuffiness of the hospital. He stood at the door, looking up at the clear, star-spangled sky, drawing in great lungfuls of cold, fresh air, and thinking of all that had happened during this long visit. He had not expected that he and his father would be able to stay so long in a tiny English village without becoming restless, yet somehow they had been drawn into the life of their family and the community; and the people they had grown to know were almost as important as those back home in America. More important, in some cases, he thought, remembering the fear in Maddy's eyes and the strange sensation he had experienced as he drove her here from Exeter – that he wanted to stay cocooned inside the car with only the two of them, together for ever. It had shaken him more than he cared to admit, even to himself, but now, in this moment of peace, he considered it again, and knew that Maddy had, even in such a brief acquaintance, become very important indeed.

The faint sound of voices singing caught at his ear, and he turned his head, startled. The night was so quiet, out here in the winter darkness, that for a moment the voices sounded unearthly, as if they came from another realm, and he looked up involuntarily, as if expecting to see their owners high above him in the glittering sky. But the stars looked back impassively and he twisted his mouth wryly, mocking himself for such a fancy.

Carols, he thought. Christmas carols. But who ...?

And then they came into sight – a little group of nurses, wrapped in their capes, moving slowly towards the doors of the hospital. He walked swiftly towards them, catching them just as they began to go inside, and the last one turned and smiled at him.

'Hello – we didn't realise we had an audience.'

'Why were you doing it?' he asked. 'Surely there's no one out here to hear you.'

'That's what we hoped! We're just practising for Christmas Day, when we go round the wards. It's such a lovely night, we thought we'd go outside and enjoy some fresh air while we did it. Now we've got to go back to our wards.' She smiled again and disappeared along the corridor after the others, leaving Russ gazing after them.

She has no idea how magical that sounded, he thought. If I were a superstitious man, or even a bit more religious than I am, I'd think it was a message – a message that everything's going to be all right. And maybe it was ...

He shivered suddenly. It had been cold outside and even though it was warm in the corridor, he could still feel the chill of apprehension. He needed a hot drink, and he'd come to find one for his father and Dottie. He turned away from the door and went in search.

The Friends of the hospital had a tiny tea-bar, where volunteers made tea and coffee and sold biscuits. Russ drank a cup standing at the cubbyhole where the two women worked and talked to them, telling them about the accident and how he and his father, two Americans, came to be involved with the troubles of Burracombe.

'My pa's back there now, with the old lady who looked after the teacher's sister during the war,' he said. 'Can you believe, they were separated when their parents were killed and sent to different orphanages. Now, what made anyone think that was a good thing to do? Crazy! Anyway, it turned out that Stella – that's the one that's been hurt – came to lodge with the same old lady when she came to the village as a teacher, and that's how they found each other again. It's as good as a movie.' He shook his head and muttered again, 'Crazy.'

The two volunteers were used to people giving them their own – or other people's life histories. It was part of the anxiety. Some people went silent, others needed to talk and this attractive young American was obviously one of the talkers. The younger volunteer, who wasn't married, or even engaged, wondered if he had a sweetheart. She said: 'And not long before her wedding, too. It's a shame.'

'It is,' Russ said. 'A crying shame. And the sister, she's in a hell of a state. Sorry – I mean, a heck of a state.'

The younger volunteer smiled. 'That's all right. People are always a bit tense when they're in here. It's easy to let the odd word slip. So if your dad and the old lady both grew up in Burracombe, they must have known each other when they were young, I suppose.'

'That's right. Matter of fact, I've got an idea they were sweethearts for a while.'

'But nothing came of it.'

'Seems not.' He finished his coffee. 'Thanks for that. I'll take two cups of tea now, for the old people.'

The volunteer busied herself making the tea and handed the cups over. Russ paid her, gave her a smile that set her heart thudding, and picked them up from the counter.

'Thanks. See you again, maybe.'

'I hope so,' she said, and watched longingly as he walked away. The other volunteer gave her an old-fashioned look.

'Not much point setting your sights there. He's already spoken for.'

'What do you mean? You think he's got a girlfriend back in America?'

'If he has, he's forgotten her. He's got his eye on the sister – the one who wasn't hurt. You could see it in his face when he talked about her. Head over heels, he is, or I'm a Dutchman.'

The younger volunteer looked at her companion, taking in the steel-grey hair in its tight perm and the pale pink twinset embellished by a string of pearls, adorned for all the world as if she were going to a tea party with the Queen.

'No,' she said sadly, 'you're definitely not a Dutchman!'

Russ had stayed chatting to the volunteers because he sensed that his father and Dottie would rather be alone together for a while. He knew that Dottie was deeply upset over her lodger's condition, and guessed that Joe was the one who could offer most support. They had known each other as children, and as young adults; they had old times to talk over, and in some ways his father probably knew her better than anyone else.

Russ didn't guess in just how many ways Joe and Dottie had known each other, but he was right in thinking they wanted to be left alone. After he had gone, they sat quietly for a while, their hands firmly clasped, and then Joe said, 'She means a lot to you, this little lady.'

'Yes, she does.' Dottie freed her hand to find a handkerchief in her bag. She held it against her eyes for a moment, then put her hand back in his. 'She'm like a daughter to me – they both are. They're the family I never had.'

There was another short silence, then he said, 'I was surprised, when I came back in October, to find you'd never got wed. It can't have been for want of being asked – not a bright, pretty young girl like you.'

She gave a little laugh. 'You always had a silver tongue, Joe Tozer.'

'I mean it,' he persisted. 'All the young chaps were after you when we were courting. And when I went away – well, I don't mind telling you, I was pretty sure our Norman would have stepped in to take my place. I knew he was sweet on you.'

'Norman! I never gave him a thought.' She looked down at the handkerchief, held in her other hand and added, almost too quietly for him to hear, 'I never gave *no* other boy a thought. I suppose I was always hoping as you'd come back.'

'Oh, Dottie ...' he said. 'And I thought that once I'd made my choice, and gone to America, you'd finished with me for good.'

Dottie sighed. 'Shall I tell you the truth, Joe? I regretted sending you away the minute your back was turned, but I was too silly and proud to call you back and say so. I nearly ran after you that day, but my mother always told me never to run after a boy, and I took her words to heart. And that weren't the end of it, neither. The times I started out to walk up to the farm, and then turned back! I even thought of going all the way up to Liverpool to get on the ship with you.'

Joe stared at her. 'Dottie! Oh, if only you had ... And if you had walked up to the farm, chances are you'd have met me coming down to the village. What a pair of fools we've been!'

'It weren't just that,' she said. 'It was just about that time Mother was took ill with her growth. I couldn't have left her anyway. And I didn't think you'd want me – not after all that was said.'

'I wanted you all right,' he said in a low voice. 'I hardly slept right for months, for wanting you.'

'But you got married in the end,' Dottie said. 'And it was a good marriage. She was a nice little body, your Eleanor. That time you brought her over, I had to admit I liked her, even though I'd made up my mind not to. You were happy, Joe, weren't you?'

'Yes, I was. We had a good life together and we had three fine children. I wish you could meet the girls, Dottie. You'd like them, and they'd love you. In fact ...' He turned to her suddenly and, looking at him, she realised that while his rugged face had grown more craggy, more wrinkled, and his hair had turned grey, his eyes had never changed. They were still the eyes she remembered from all those years ago ... the eyes that had gazed into hers as she and Joe had lain together on the grassy bank of the Burra Brook and known that they loved each other. And the same expression was in them now – the wide, black pupils that seemed to open a window into his heart, that caught at her own heart with the knowledge of his desire.

'Dottie ...' he said, and at that moment the door to Stella's room opened, and in the same instant Russ strolled round the corner carrying two cups of tea.

Maddy came out, looking worn and so white that Dottie jumped up at once and took her in her arms. Maddy leaned against her for a moment, while the older woman patted her back and made soothing noises, and then she allowed herself to be guided to a chair. Russ took the seat on her other side and handed one of the cups to Dottie.

'This one was for Dad, but I guess your need is greater than his,' he said to Maddy, and she took it almost without noticing it, nodded a vague thank you and sat with it in a hand that trembled slightly.

Russ steadied the saucer and said, 'Drink it, Maddy. It will do you good.'

'Yes,' she said in a small distant voice, but she didn't move, and after a moment he lifted the cup to her lips.

'Come on, now. Just a sip.'

'Poor little maid,' Dottie said, on her other side. 'She looks worn right down.'

'Just a sip,' Russ said again. 'That's right. Now another.' He felt Maddy's grip on the saucer strengthen and took his hand away as she drank. She finished the tea and as he removed the cup, she turned her head and gave him a smile.

'Thank you, Russ. That was good.'

Dottie looked towards the door. 'How is the poor maid?'

Maddy's face crumpled. 'Oh, Dottie, it's awful. She's just lying there, not moving, hardly even breathing. Felix and I have been talking to her all the time but I don't think she can hear us. I'm so frightened, Dottie.' She drew in a deep, shuddering breath. 'Two more doctors came in just now and they said they want to do an operation – I don't know exactly what for – but they really want her to come round first. If she doesn't, they'll have to do it anyway but ... Oh, I don't know. I don't know what's going to happen.' Her voice broke and she burst into tears again.

Russ put his arm round her and held her strongly. Dottie, who had made an involuntary movement to take her into her own arms again, hesitated and then drew back. She turned to Joe, on her other side, and he saw her distress and held her as Russ was holding Maddy, and even in that moment, she had a sudden, unexpected sensation of familiarity, of coming home. These arms had held her long ago, in what seemed another life, and yet she knew them still and the years seemed to spin away, leaving her once more on the banks of the Burra Brook in the joy of their first and only lovemaking.

Then, as swiftly as it had come, the sensation vanished and although she still had that sense of familiarity, it was a comfortable one, comfortable and comforting, and she rested her head on Joe's shoulder, glad that he was here to give her strength; and glad, too, that Russ was here for Maddy.

The door opened again and one of the doctors came out. He glanced briefly at them and was about to continue down the corridor when Russ came to his feet.

'Can you tell us anything, sir? What's happening?'

The man turned. He looked weary, as if he had been up for too long, and he rubbed his face for a moment before replying. 'There's nothing much to tell. Until she comes round ... but we may need to operate before then. We suspect something internal ... I'm sorry, I can't tell you any more than that ...' He shook his head and walked away, leaving them looking at each other in dismay.

'It don't sound good,' Joe murmured, and Dottie sighed. Maddy gave a muffled sob and Russ sat down beside her again.

'D'you want to go back, honey?'

She shook her head. 'I can't bear seeing her like that. And I think Felix wants to be on his own with her. For a while, anyway.'

He nodded, and they sat together in a row, both men holding the hands of the women beside them, waiting; because waiting was all they could do.

Gilbert was out of bed and dressed when Hilary and Rob arrived at the Barton. He was in the morning room reading the newspaper, with the two old Labradors stretched out at his feet, in front of the fire.

'We're here, Father,' Hilary said, coming in with Rob hanging tentatively back behind her. 'How are you feeling? Did Charles say you could get up?'

'I don't have to wait for him to tell me where I can go in my own house,' he growled. 'I'm perfectly well now. Where's that young man, then?'

'Here, *Gran'père*,' Rob said in a small voice, coming forwards. He walked over to his grandfather and stood before him, meeting the old man's eyes. Gilbert regarded him sombrely and after a moment the boy spoke.

'I am sorry, *Gran'père*, for giving you so much trouble.'

'And so you should be,' Gilbert said gruffly. 'But you weren't responsible for the accident, and I understand that you were unhappy at school. I can't say we'll say no more about it, because we need to decide what to do about you next. But you needn't worry about school. Dr Latimer says you need some time off to get over it, so I've talked to the headmaster and you don't have to go back before Christmas. We'll see what's to be done after that.'

Rob's shoulders seemed to sag a little with relief. His voice shook as he whispered, '*Merci, Gran'père.*'

Hilary moved forward and laid her hand on Rob's shoulder. 'Did you have any breakfast this morning, Rob?'

'A little. Some cornflakes and some toast.'

'Then I expect you'd like some more now. I'll go and see about it. Would you like bacon and egg, and perhaps a sausage if we've got any?'

'Yes, please,' he whispered. 'And could I have a cup of coffee?'

'Of course. You stay and talk to your grandfather while I get it.' She left the room, hoping that the respite would enable the two of them to come to their former understanding. With all her father's faults, she knew he was deeply fond of the boy and she believed that Rob had grown fond of him, even though his fondness was tempered by a little fear. Perhaps now they would find a way through that remnant of fear to confidence in each other.

When the door had closed behind her, the two looked at each other again and Gilbert said, 'You'd better sit down. You look all in. Did they treat you well at the hospital?'

'Oh yes,' Rob said, doing as he was told. 'They wanted to make sure I hadn't hurt my head, but it was only a small bang.' He touched his hair gingerly. 'A lump, but nothing much.'

'Thank goodness for that. You were lucky, and so was young Felix. I gather the schoolteacher came off worst.'

'They are very worried about her. Nobody has told me much, but I know they must be.'

'Pity. But she's in the best place, and there's nothing we can do about it. What we've got to do is decide what's best for you.' The Colonel considered his grandson thoughtfully. 'What would *you* like to do, Robert?'

The question seemed to take the boy by surprise, as if he hadn't expected to be consulted about his own future, and Gilbert felt an unaccustomed twinge of guilt. They *hadn't* asked him, after all – just made the decisions over his head. That was what happened with most thirteen-year-olds, but then most of them didn't have quite such momentous changes in their lives. Perhaps it had been unfair to expect the boy to fall in with whatever had been decided for him.

Rob took a moment or two to answer, but at last he said hesitantly, 'I think that I would really like to go back to France. I miss my family. But I want to come back here to see you as well,' he added quickly, as if afraid he had given offence. 'You and *Tante* Hilary and Stephen are my family too, and this is also my home now.'

'Yes,' Gilbert said, rather gruffly. 'Yes, it is, and we are your family, and I hope you will spend a lot of your time here. But I think perhaps you're right and it would be better for you to be in France for a few more years. All the same, I would like you to have an English education as well.'

Rob's face fell. 'You mean to go to France for the holidays but go back to school here? But *Gran'père*—'

'No, I don't mean that,' Gilbert said hastily, seeing the boy's distress. 'I mean, to go back to your school in France, where you're happy, and come here for the holidays. And later, perhaps in two or three years' time, when you've taken your baccalaureate, you might return here and have a further two years in an English school. I think you would find Kelly College more amenable to you by then. The boys,' he smiled faintly, 'might not be such barbarians.'

Rob looked at him and then smiled equally faintly in return. The memory of his ordeals was obviously still painful, but he was able to distance himself from them a little.

'Yes,' he said, 'they would have grown up by then.'

'They'd have grown up sooner, if you'd given them the chance,' Gilbert told him. 'Once you've been through the initiation, you're generally all right.' But he could remember during his own schooldays, boys who had never been all right, never accepted by the others, and he knew that they were boys who were in some way 'different' from the others and who suffered a good deal. And he was not himself a barbarian; he didn't want his grandson to be one of those who suffered.

'So that's settled, then,' he said. 'Your mother and sisters are coming here for Christmas and you can go back with them and return to your old school. You'll come back here for Easter and for all your holidays, so that you can continue to get to know Burracombe and the estate, and we'll think about the rest of your education later.'

'And what might Marianne think about that?' Hilary enquired, coming in at that moment with a laden breakfast tray. 'Or don't you think she needs to be consulted?'

Her father looked at her in astonishment. 'Marianne? Why, she should be very pleased. She'll have her son back with her for part of the year and he'll be here with us for the rest. I should think it will turn out to be just what she always wanted.'

Hilary set the tray down on the table, her lips twitching. Her father would never completely change. He had given way far more than she had ever expected him to, but he was still in charge, still making the ultimate decisions and expecting everyone else to fall in with his plans. Luckily, she thought that this time his plans would indeed be to everyone's wishes – even, perhaps, those of Marianne.

And what of her own plans? she wondered. She thought of her analogy of the two roads and saw hers and David's, diverging for so long and now brought together only, it seemed, to part and travel again in irrevocably different directions.

Oh David, she thought, as the yearning for him swept over her more strongly than ever. David, my darling love, I want to be with you. I want you so much ...

Chapter Forty-Three

Felix had sat so still for so long beside Stella's bed that his body was growing stiff. He held her hand between both of his, leaning forward and murmuring gently about the things they had done together, about their plans for the future, about his love for her. He knew that Maddy had doubted if she could hear what was said, but he believed that at some very deep level Stella knew that he was there, heard his voice and was struggling, through some deep fog of confusion, to reach him.

'Darling,' he said, 'you're going to get better. You're going to be strong and well again, and I'll be beside you to help. We'll all help you. Dottie and Maddy, and all our friends – Val and Luke, Miss Kemp, Hilary, Jennifer, Travis, the Tozers – everyone will be there. And we're going to be married, remember? We're going to have a wonderful wedding, with all the bridesmaids in different colours like a rainbow. Rainbows are for joy, you know, and a promise for the future. And all our friends there to wish us well, just as you wanted it.' He remembered that in truth this wasn't at all what Stella had wanted, and went on hastily, 'Or perhaps we'll just have a simple wedding, just us and a few of our friends. We'll walk to church, across the Clam and through the meadows with the birds singing and flowers everywhere.' He remembered that the wedding had been planned for January. 'Or perhaps there'll be snow in the fields and everything will be pure white, like your dress that Dottie's been making for you. Whatever we do, and whenever it is, it will be the happiest day of our lives, and we shall live happily ever after. All you have to do is get better, and we'll all be here to help you …' The story began again, to be repeated over and over until at last his voice cracked and he whispered simply, 'Please, darling, please get better. Please …'

Outside in the corridor, Russ took the empty cups and said, 'I'll take these back to the tea-bar. Maddy, why don't you come with me? A walk'll do you good – maybe we'll slip outside for a few minutes for some fresh air.'

She glanced anxiously towards the door and Dottie said, 'You go with him, maid. Me and Joe'll still be here – we'll come and find you if anything happens.'

'All right,' Maddy said, though still with an anxious look, and she got up and followed him. 'We won't go far.'

They walked along to the tea-bar where the two volunteers were still serving, and Russ put the cups on the counter. The younger volunteer returned his smile a little wistfully and her companion said, 'I told you so. You only have to look at them ...'

Russ led her outside. Just around the corner there was a bench beside a few dusty shrubs and they sat down, breathing in the sharp, cold air. Maddy shivered and drew her coat closer around her and he said, 'We'll go in if you're too cold.'

'No. It's all right for a little while. Hospitals are so warm, aren't they, and they always smell rather horrid. Oh Russ, poor Stella. It's so sad to see her like that.'

'I know. I once visited a pal of mine who'd had an accident and he was in the same state. I remember how I felt then.'

'Did – did he get better?'

'Yes,' Russ said, although he didn't add that the pal had lost a leg. 'Yes, and he's back at work now. He's a teacher too, as it happens.'

Maddy nodded. 'Stella's giving up teaching, of course, when she and Felix get married. Women have to, you know. Oh!' Her hand flew to her mouth. 'The wedding! It's supposed to be just after Christmas. It'll have to be put off.'

'It certainly might,' he agreed. 'But we can think about that when we know more about how badly hurt she is. You know, she might not be as bad as she seems. Once she comes round, she may recover very quickly.'

'I don't think she'll be fit for a big wedding, though,' Maddy said doubtfully. 'There are so many people coming.'

There was a brief silence. Then Russ said, 'This isn't the right time to talk about it, I know, but I may not have another chance ... Maddy,

I know about your sweetheart – the boy who was killed last winter. I want to say first I'm real sorry about that. It must have hurt you a lot. I guess it still hurts you.'

Startled, she looked up at him. 'Yes. Yes, it does.'

'Well, like I say, this ain't the right time, but sometimes things have to be said anyway ... Is there anyone else, Maddy? Could there be?'

She thought of Stephen. He had told her over and over again that he loved her. He had been jealous of Sammy, but since Sammy had died he had offered her real friendship and she knew that the love was still there if she chose to accept it. He too had lost someone he'd loved deeply, and he understood her feelings, but he believed they could, when she had recovered from her sorrow, share their future.

'No,' she said, aware at last that for her Stephen could never be more than a good friend. 'No, there isn't anyone else.'

'And could there be?' he repeated. He reached for her hands and held them in his. 'I know it's not long enough for you to decide – but if there could, one day, be someone else you might love – could it be me, d'you think?'

Maddy met his eyes. In them she saw what Dottie had once seen in Joe's eyes, what she had seen again this morning before Russ had interrupted them. Her heart contracted in much the same way as Dottie's had done, and she felt the colour warm her cheeks as she said first, 'I don't know ...' And then, very softly, 'Yes ... Yes, Russ ... I think perhaps it could ...'

Joe and Dottie watched them walk away and then looked at each other.

Joe said, 'Are you thinking what I'm thinking, Dottie?'

'I reckon I am,' she answered slowly. 'There's been a change in that young maid since your boy's been here. Even though she's so upset and worried at the moment ... Is there anyone back in America, d'you know?'

Joe shook his head. 'There've been a few girls, but nothing serious. He's a good boy, Dottie. You'd need have no fears for your Maddy if they took a real fancy to each other. He'd look after her.'

Dottie sighed. 'I know, Joe. He's too much like you for me to doubt that. But I'd be sorry to see her go all that way. She's been a daughter to me ever since she were a little maid. And since Stella's been with me, I've seen more of her as a young woman than I expected to. The thought of losing both of them ...' Her voice wobbled and Joe put his arm around her.

'I can see that makes it difficult, Dottie. But nobody's saying you're going to lose either of them. Stella's going to get better – the doctors can do wonderful things now – and Maddy'd only be a hop, skip and a jump across the Pond, as they call it. There'd be nothing to stop her coming back to visit, and nothing to stop you coming over to see her – and us.' His voice deepened a little and his arm tightened. 'Dottie, I've been wanting to say this for a long time now but I've never had the chance and this ain't the right time either – but there's nothing to stop you coming over permanently. Why don't you do that, Dottie? Why don't you come back to the States with me? Why don't we pick up where we left off all those years ago?'

Dottie stared at him. 'What are you asking me, Joe?'

'Why, I'm asking you to marry me, of course! I'm not saying I made a mistake in what I did – America was the right place for me and Eleanor a good wife. I loved her and we had a good life together, and raised a fine family. But you were always there at the back of my mind, Dottie. And now we've got a second chance. I don't want to let it go by again. So will you? Will you be my wife and come and live with me in America? Please?'

There was a long silence. Dottie looked deep into his eyes and saw in them what she had seen all those years ago, what Maddy had seen in his son's. She trembled a little and looked away.

'You make me feel like a girl again,' she whispered.

'You always will be a girl to me,' he said. 'The girl I loved and left behind. What do you say, Dottie?'

'Joe, I don't know ... It's all been too long. I've lived in Burracombe all my life, apart from the time I spent in London, and I was glad to get back, I can tell you. Going to America ... I wouldn't fit in there, Joe, it would all be too different.'

'You'd fit in. The girls would make you welcome, and I've got a lovely home waiting for you. You wouldn't have to work any more, Dottie – no more serving behind the bar at the pub, no more making dresses, no more baking unless you wanted to do it. You'd be a lady of leisure.'

'But I wouldn't know what to do with meself! All those things – they're not work to me, Joe, they're my life. It's the way I live. And

Burracombe – the people in it – they're like my family. I've got roots here, Joe, and I reckon they're pretty deep – I don't know as I could tear them up and go and live in another country all by myself.'

'You wouldn't be by yourself. You'd have me.'

'Even with you, Joe.' She shook her head. 'I'm sorry. It's just too late.'

He said nothing for a moment and she could feel his disappointment and almost told him she'd changed her mind and would go with him after all. We *could* have a good life together, she thought. If only it could be here in Burracombe. But Joe would never come back. His home was over there, and although he was welcome as a visitor, he'd never settle back into the village – just as she could never settle in America.

'Don't say no straight away,' he said at last. 'Tell me you'll think about it. Will you do that for me, Dottie?'

'All right,' she said, and squeezed his hand. 'I'll think about it. And – thank you for asking me, Joe. It means a lot to me.' She laughed a little. 'A proposal at my age! I don't reckon anyone would believe it.'

Chapter Forty-Four

The little room had been silent for a long time, except for Felix's murmuring voice as he alternately talked to Stella and prayed for her. Barely twenty-four hours had passed since the accident, yet it seemed an age. Crucial hours, the doctors had told him, and as the afternoon wore on into evening their faces grew graver and his anguish deepened.

It was all turning out so differently from how it should have been. The journey to Exeter to collect Robert, anxious though they had been for the French boy's welfare, had been a time of warmth and delight in being beside each other. And the wedding in the school – could that really have been only yesterday? – had been almost as tender and as touching as he believed their own wedding would be. He thought of the children, all in their seats as if in church, watching while Shirley Culliford, arrayed in a long white dress and gauzy veil, proceeded up the aisle on the arm of Norman Tozer's youngest boy, Stanley. Behind her came the bridesmaids, Betty Culliford and Wendy Cole, with Robin Tozer and Edward Crocker following as pageboys, and the whole thing would have brought a pang to the hardest of hearts had it not been for the scowl Shirley was directing at her groom, Billy Madge, who had secreted into his pocket a strip of caps meant for a cap-gun which, Felix suspected when he discovered them just before the service started, he intended to use to tease and frighten his bride.

The caps had been confiscated and a stern rebuke delivered by both Felix and Miss Kemp before Stella had begun to play the Wedding March on the school piano, but even this diversion did not succeed in spoiling the little tableau and with every word he uttered, Felix had been thinking of his own wedding, only a few weeks' distant now.

As he pronounced the final words and told Billy he could now kiss the bride, his eye had caught Stella's and they had exchanged a look of complete understanding and love which Billy's indignation had quickly turned to laughter. And now, as he looked down at her still, pale face, they could not exchange any look at all. She was white and remote as an alabaster statue and he felt a moment of terror that she had already left him.

'Stella,' he whispered. 'Stella, darling, please wake up. Please tell me you're still there … I can't let you go yet … I can't …'

But she did not move, and his despair deepened.

Images rushed into his mind. The first time they had met, in the village street not long after they had both first arrived in Burracombe. Wasn't it when the local hunt had met, with their pink-coated riders high up on horses with coats as polished and shining as the riders' boots? The sight of her in one of the pews when he gave his first sermon as Basil Harvey's curate. He had not known then what she would mean to him, for his interest was in Hilary Napier, who had been so kind and welcoming to him – so much so that he had even asked her to marry him! He shook his head now in disbelief; Hilary was and always would be a good friend, but she had the sense then to know that they should never marry, and it wasn't long after that when he had first begun to realise that it was Stella who was stealing into his heart, Stella who would be there for ever.

There had been such happiness in their friendship, such joy as it deepened into love. She knew him so well, he thought. She understood that, flippant and even irreverent though he sometimes was, there was a profoundly serious vein of humanity within him. And of faith, too. It might have seemed that, coming from a family of churchmen, he had simply taken the easy way of following in their path, but he had not. Felix was too aware of such a danger to have made his choice lightly. He had considered other paths, but had never been able to follow them very far; he had always returned to the Church.

Stella knew all this, without being told, and while she often seemed to treat him with a tolerant affection, he knew that her love ran as deep as his own, and her faith too. Both were powerful enough to sustain them through anything that life might bring.

Anything? he thought now. Even this? Even if she were to die, here in this hospital bed, without even opening her eyes to exchange one last, loving look?

'Stella,' he whispered again, bending close. 'Listen to me, darling. You don't have to open your eyes if you don't want to, but listen. We all want you to get better. Me, Maddy, Dottie, Val and Luke, the Tozers, the Napiers, everyone. All Burracombe wants you to get better and come back to us. Miss Kemp sent a message to say that the children are thinking of you – they're making cards and pictures and paper-chains for you. They're practising your favourite carols and they're going to put on the finest Nativity play you've ever seen. There's going to be a Christmas tree in the classroom, just for you.' He was making some of this up, but he knew it would all be done just as he said. 'And Val and Luke want you to share in Christopher's first Christmas. Think of his face when he sees those shiny baubles you bought last year. Dottie's already made her cake and pudding, and the mincemeat – it's going to be a wonderful Christmas, darling, but we need you to be there. It won't mean a thing to me if you aren't there.'

He paused for breath and gazed down at her, but her face was still pale and unmoving as a porcelain figurine. He watched for a moment or two without speaking, and felt his own body grow cold. Was that a tiny, almost imperceptible change? Had a shred more of her spirit let go, like a thin, gauzy web being tugged gently by an insistent breeze? Was this was death was like – a gradual tearing away from the body until the soul was free at last to leave its earthly shackles and fly into the unknown?

No! His own soul cried out against it. It was too soon. There was too much for her here, too much loving and being loved, too much life to be lived. It could *not* be taken away from her, not now, not yet.

'Stella,' he said urgently, 'you must wake up. It's important – you can't stay asleep any longer. You have to wake up.' His voice took on a new, commanding tone, a tone born of desperation. 'Wake up, darling – please. You don't have to stay awake for long, but just come out of this dreadful sleep, if only for a moment or two. You have to show us you want to go on living. Stella, you have to show me you love me. You *have* to.'

He stopped and watched her face. His heart was beating fast. Somehow, he knew that if she were ever to stir again, this was the moment. It was as if there had been a subtle change in the room, an alteration in the atmosphere. Some presence which had been hovering like a faint, barely sensed miasma had gathered itself together, become more tangible. The nurse monitoring Stella felt it too; he saw her turn her head and look intently down into Stella's face.

For a few seconds, nobody breathed. And then Stella gave a faint moan and her eyelids flickered. She opened them slightly and Felix felt her fingers move almost imperceptibly in his grasp.

'*Stella* ...' he whispered, hardly daring to believe it was happening. 'Stella – darling ... Do it again, oh, please do it again ...'

The fingers moved again, a little more strongly, and she opened her eyes and looked straight into his. The nurse came closer, and Felix gazed into Stella's blue, bewildered eyes. Did she recognise him? Did she even see him? Was she going to be the Stella he knew and loved, or would it be as the doctors had feared, and the damage to her spine and brain too immense?

'Stella. Sweetheart. You're in hospital. There was an accident – do you remember? And do you know me? Felix? The man you're going to marry – the crazy man who's always making silly jokes but loves you more than anyone could say? Please, darling, say you know me. Say you're going to get better. Please.'

The silence seemed unbearable. Stella's eyes, resting on his, were vague and troubled. Then she gave a little sigh. Her lips moved very slightly, in the tiniest of smiles

A *smile* ...

Felix felt the tears spring hot in his eyes and dashed them away impatiently, unwilling to lose a second of that precious contact. He glanced joyously up at the nurse, and she met his look and nodded. Swiftly, she left the room and he knew she was going to call one of the doctors. He bent closer to the pillow and touched Stella's cheek with his finger.

'Darling, you're awake. You know me. You're going to be all right. You've been hurt and you're going to have to stay here for a while until they get you better, but you're going to be *all right*. I know it.' He discounted the spinal injury, the possibility of paralysis. If they happened, it would be tragic, but he would still have his Stella. They could still be together. If she had to come down the aisle in a wheel-chair – if he had to *carry* her – they could still marry. *Until death us do part*, he thought, and cocked an imaginary snook at death. Not yet, his heart said, not yet.

'Can you speak to me?' he asked. 'Can you just say my name – so that I can tell the doctors – before you go back to a proper sleep? You must be so tired, my poor darling.'

She smiled again, not her usual radiant smile, just that barely perceptible movement of the lips, but it was enough. And then, with not much more than a breath of sound, she whispered his name.

'Felix ...'

The door opened and the doctor came in, followed by the nurse. Past them, Felix caught a glimpse of Dottie's and Joe's faces, with Russ and Maddy just walking towards them. Before the door closed again, he gave them a smile that told them all they needed to know and saw the relief sweep over their faces.

'She spoke to me,' Felix said to the doctor. 'She smiled at me, and she spoke to me. She's going to be all right. I know she's going to be all right.' He drew a deep, tremulous breath and added softly, 'It's going to be a happy Christmas in Burracombe after all.'